ATTACK AND DESTROY

It was suddenly rush-hour traffic in the night sky. The gunship *Pegasus* banked to the left and dropped abruptly, narrowly missing two oncoming gunships that zoomed over the treetops without warning.

A flash lit up the jungle as Charlie fired a shoulder-launched rocket at one of the other gunships.

"Fuck! They're gonna get him!" the peter pilot screamed. A second later, the chopper exploded in mid-air. The wreckage tumbled end over end into the treetops, a series of green and orange fireballs igniting the jungle below.

"We're outa here!" the pilot clicked in, and banked the ship hard away from the rolling concussion.

Fletcher wasn't listening. His ears were filled with the thunder of the M-60 rounds he was pouring down at what he hoped was the rocket launcher. Close, but no cigar. "Tracer fire on whiskey, Fletch. Coming . . . right . . . NOW!"

"Right, gotcha. No sweat!" This time he did see the enemy position and directed a steady flow of hot red tracers into it. "You die, *Du Ma*! Do . . . you . . . fucking . . . *bic* motherfuckers!" The barrel of his hatch machine gun began to glow a dull orange in the dark.

The machine gun nest just off the riverbank went up in a blaze of exploded ammo and stick grenades.

Includes a complete GLOSSARY
of military jargon

Other books in the **CHOPPER 1** series:

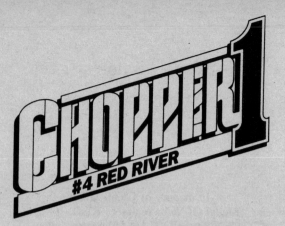

CHOPPER 1
#4 RED RIVER

Jack Hawkins

IVY BOOKS • NEW YORK

In memory of Glenn Miller,
Medal Of Valor recipient T.P.D. 1981,
who was really K.I.A. five years before
he finally pulled the pin.

Ivy Books
Published by Ballantine Books

Copyright © 1987 by Butterfield Press, Inc.

Produced by Butterfield Press, Inc.
133 Fifth Avenue
New York, New York 10003

Library of Congress Catalog Card Number: 87-90790

ISBN 0-8041-0030-6

Manufactured in the United States of America

First Edition: August 1987

AUTHOR'S NOTE

The vicious riverine battles that turned the murky water-ways a crimson red and sent an oily blanket of smoke drifting across much of South Vietnam's Mekong Delta during Indochina's 10,000-day war really occurred. The 7th Cav of the First Air Cavalry Division did indeed exist. But there is some disagreement among armchair commandos and military archivists as to whether or not there ever really was an "Echo Company" in any Army Airmobile unit.

Though Brody The Whoremonger, "Doc" Delgado, "Two-Step" Broken Arrow, and Lance "Lawless" Warlokk may remind readers and First Cav vets of soldiers they might have known in The Nam, this novel is a work of fiction. Other than well-known public and historic figures, any semblance of its characters to persons living or Killed In Action is purely coincidental.

Jack Hawkins
Manila, The Philippines
14 December 1986

"Charlie used to fear us, that first year or two. I'm telling you this because I could see the terror in his eyes—*in . . . his . . . eyes*—when I'd swoop down over the treetops and flare-in practically on top of him, mini-guns blazing . . . rocketpods belching their business. Yep, Charlie, he used to beat feet as soon as he heard the *whop-whop-whop* of our rotors approaching—'whispering death,' the Commies called it, because sometimes we could come in so low and so fast they were eatin' landing skids before they knew what hit 'em. But anymore—I'm beginning to wonder. Charlie's beginning to lose respect for the choppers. He hangs around more, eager to toy with us. Hot LZ's are becoming hairier by the mission. Now the Cong are learning new tricks. Yesterday I almost stacked it up when I nearly descended into a bunch of ten-foot-high bamboo stakes the zips had hidden in the elephant grass. Used to be combat medics had the highest mortality rate in The Nam. Now it's gunship pilots. Chopper jocks, followed by Huey doorgunners."

Warrant Officer (requesting anonymity),
upon returning from Operation Masher;
quoted in *Stars & Stripes*,
Valentine's Day, 1966

CHAPTER 1

Cho Gao, east of Mytho in the Mekong Delta

Broken Arrow was still jammin' to the rock-and-roll blaring from a transistor radio taped to the side of his helmet—that's what really blew Brody's mind. Here they were on the verge of crashing down through the treetops, into the heart of Void Vicious, and Two-Step was firing his M-60 through the helicopter's hatch nonstop. Firing nonstop, and screaming some unintelligible nonsense in time with the music.

Glowing red tracers from his machine gun shredded leaves and branches from the rain forest's triple canopy as it rose up to meet them. Brody couldn't figure out what the crazy Indian was shooting at. Maybe he just wanted to go out in a blaze of glory, the Whoremonger thought as he listened to The Animals song drift dreamlike between the harsh beating of rotors overhead.

The craft's jet turbine whined in protest, but Gabriel righted *Pegasus* finally, after what seemed like an eternity, dropping on her side toward the trees. Brody held on to the handle of his own hatch-60 as the helicopter began banking in the opposite direction. Gabriel The Gunslinger was having fun with them. Still

1

tight into her turn, *Peg* was returning to the riverbank. They weren't going to die after all. Brody began breathing again as she leveled out. The disappointment began to register in Broken Arrow's pitch-black eyes, but he kept firing. Firing and screeching out of tune. The song, appropriately enough, was "We Gotta Get Outta This Place"—the grunt's barbrawl anthem in Vietnam.

"What the hell you shootin' at, Corporal?" Zack, his light-brown skin shining with sweat, appeared in the middle of the cabin, crouched between the two doorgunners.

"I . . . I . . ." Broken Arrow released the M-60's trigger, and the abrupt lack of firepower suddenly drew him out toward the open hatch as the smoking machine gun went silent on its swivel, pink barrel dropping. Only his "monkey straps"— canvas lifelines attached on one end to the back of his web belt, and on the other to hooks in the cabin wall—prevented Broken Arrow from flying out into the void.

"'I . . . I . . .'" Sgt. Zack mimicked him, then turned his attention to the dwindling supply of metal boxes between two piles of Saigon phone books. "Save your ammo, Two-Step! We're headed back for the kill, son."

"He thought we were goin' down, Leo!" Brody said defensively as the stocky crew chief fed a fresh belt of ammo into The Whoremonger's hog.

"I know." Zack busied himself with the huge bullets, his face growing emotionless.

But Brody kept talking as their stomachs flopped with *Peg's* sudden descent again. "He thought Gabe had lost it . . . that we'd been hit and were goin' down an' dirty! He didn't wanna die in the trees without takin' out some of the Void with him before he went!"

"I know." Zack just shook his head from side to side. He fought the urge to glance back at Broken Arrow. "The Void." That's all these kid commandos talked about anymore. "Void Vicious this" and "Void Vicious

2

that." It was bad for business, paying so much respect and lip service to a stretch of jungle that didn't even have the capacity to know it was so feared and revered.

Void Vicious. Zack chuckled to himself as he thought about the rain forest below, and the power it seemed to hold over Brody's people. True, he too had experienced that strange pull that drew his attention down to the treetops each time the gunship banked above the swirl of brilliant jungle greens below. But he was sure it was only the chopper's angle.

Maybe it was just that these combat-hardened kids of his, who by law were not even old enough to drink alcohol back in The World, were so affected by killing their first man in a steaming jungle instead of some back alley that they told themselves it was all just part of the ever-present and always-changing karma of never-never land: *voodoo magic, Saigon-style.* Zack chuckled again at the thought, but what else could he come up with to explain the moods that came over every slick-sleeved newbie after surviving his first gunship mission into a hot LZ? Leo had to admit he would never forget his first few times roaring five feet above the treetops en route to a firefight call for help in the heart of the rain forest.

They left the base camps with a steep climb to gain altitude and speed when the target grid was several kilometers away. They'd swoop down to the treetops only when the pilot sensed he was getting so close the Cong would soon be able to hear his approaching rotors if he didn't. Several hundred feet above the lush jungle canopies, the soldiers looking down out the hatch first felt the trees calling to them. The sight was almost mesmerizing, hypnotic. Leo had long ago taken to busying himself with other tasks aboard the craft or he would feel it, too.

But troopers like Brody relished the view, the toes of their jungle boots an inch over the edge of the open hatch as they leaned against their swivel-mounted machine guns, feeling the warm blast of both rotorwash

3

and earthen vapors slapping them as *Peg*'s turbines whined a shrill warning overhead.

LZ takeoff was different. The rain forest seemed to awaken in all its fury, branches whipping out at the chopper, trying to pull it back down as it frantically ascended, green tracers arcing in from the ghostly shadows, silver trails billowing everywhere as hot lead zinged through the cabin, often leaving fresh, smooth holes smoking where none had been before the mission.

Zack made a conscious effort to always refer to their gunship as "it." He refused to call it *Peg*, as Brody and his young buddies did, kissing her dented, olive-drab skin as they climbed up into the hatch for an F.O.B. mission or Brass Monkey rescue or humping her bullet-riddled tailboom in mock ecstasy after returning from a hairy firefight they never thought they'd escape alive. Brody, Snakeman, Broken Arrow, and Em-Ho Lee would drag out their black-market box of booze and whip up a party in honor of their flying mare, taking time to rub their hands along her dents and creases, reassuring her, each man in turn whispering he had so many months or weeks or days remaining in The Nam and would she please keep the karma first rate until he became a single-digit midget and no longer had to fly into Void Vicious.

The Stork and The Professor had been as bad. But now Hal was K.I.A. and Shawn Missing In Action—Presumed Dead, so "it didn't much matter and meant less," as the ol' Nam slang goes.

But Zack refused to participate in such chicanery. If they wanted to paint a *Pegasus* mural on the helicopter's undersnout and call her "*Peg*," then that was fine, but he was out of it. Leo had spent enough time down on the edge of the Louisiana bayou swamps as a child to know you didn't mess with land magic or the forces of nature. The *Peg* might come "alive," if only for an instant. But that instant might just be long enough to spell doom for them all.

"We gonna get some, Whoremonger?" Two-Step was

4

yelling over Zack's shoulder to Brody.

"Roger that, brotha!" Treat flipped Chance the thumbs-up without glancing over at him. All his concentration was on the blur of turquoise green racing past beyond the front sight of his M-60. Gabriel had brought *Peg* back under control and was returning to the winding, snakelike river curling murky brown through the treetops below.

Chance Broken Arrow was known as Two-Step among the doorgunners of Echo company because, during his first Tour-365 incountry, he'd had the misfortune of tripping over a wait-a-minute vine smack dab onto a coiled and unamused bamboo krait viper. The serpent's bite is so deadly that few victims have ever been known to make it more than a couple of steps in the direction of help before succumbing to the poison and dropping on the spot. Broken Arrow managed to make it to a medic, who radioed in a Dustoff.

The med-evac chopper carried Broken Arrow to an aid station twenty klicks away, where the baby-faced corpsmen, stern-looking doctors, and army nurses all treated him with awe, marveling at his ability to survive the legendary reptile's kiss of death. Both smiling modestly and grimacing for the lone combat correspondent clicking away with his Rollicord for an *Overseas Weekly* Christmas 1964 Front-Page miracle story, Broken Arrow credited the small, brown medicine man's pouch he'd held over the wound with saving his life. Broken Arrow had put it together himself before leaving the reservation for the Army, and Vietnam. It contained all the necessary ingredients to protect him overseas and see him safely back home to the land of his ancestors: little bits of the earth and the forest, little representatives from nature. Broken Arrow had religiously worn it on a leather string around his neck since basic training.

Brody could smell that odd Delta aroma now. It was close.

The PBR gunboat had radioed for helicopter assistance only ten minutes earlier. When *Pegasus* arrived on station, the riverine patrol vessel was already half beached and tilting onto its side. Smoking heavily from several direct RPG hits, it was a total loss. The aft section was rapidly sinking. American soldiers hung over the side of the deck, most dead, the few survivors bleeding heavily from serious upper-torso wounds.

As *Pegasus* swung around for its third pass, Brody's people could see an entire platoon of black pajama-clad sappers rushing out from the treeline toward the gunboat, their fixed bayonets gleaming in the crimson shades of dusk lancing in off the western horizon of dark jungle.

"Get some, Warlokk!" Broken Arrow screamed as they watched a sleek, shark-snouted Cobra gunship swoop in beneath their own flaring craft and pound the rain forest's edge with mini-gun fire. Rockets erupted from the helicopter's ordnance pods with silver streaks of smoke and rolling concussions that rocked and bucked the troopers aboard *Pegasus* as Gabriel brought her in for a landing.

"Lima-Zulu in dirty sex!" The Gunslinger called back over his shoulder as jagged, hostile treetops suddenly rose above *Peg's* roofline on one side.

"We're landing?" one of the grunts crouching beside Brody yelled against the thump of beating rotors overhead as the blades changed pitch.

Brody was about to say something, but the craft's landing skids were already scraping bamboo, and then *Peg* was pranging across roots rising from the gnarled riverbank vegetation, and the more experienced vets were leaping out into the drifting blanket of black gunsmoke.

"Move it or lose it!" Zack was ushering the newbies out through the hatch, and then the big, black NCO was gone, too, leaving Treat Brody to lay a fanlike arc of cover fire over the assaulting cavalrymen's bobbing helmets. Every other fraction of a second, his smoking machine gun belched neonlike bolts of red tracer at flashes in the treeline a hundred feet away, then suddenly stopped, its barrel glowing.

"Well, fuck me 'til it hurts," Brody growled under his breath as he began clearing the heavy M-60 with routine hand actions. His eyes remained on the distant stretch of jungle and the movements of his buddies as half the team rushed to the beached gunboat while the others dove for cover behind logs and debris. Except for the lone rifleman harassing them within the dark treeline, they met little resistance now. Warlokk's Cobra had inflicted a heavy toll on the ambushing communists. A dozen Vietnamese lay facedown in the riverbank's foamy surf, their rifles tied to their arms by the sling and floating between raised wrists.

"Well, shit . . ." Brody went through the clear-a-jam motions, but his M-60 still refused to fire. For the first time, he glanced down and saw that the weapon was empty. So was the ammo can beside it. The *last* ammo can.

When he looked back up, he saw the woman. Clad entirely in black, she had leapt off the far side of the gunboat and was running with two other male VC away from the tree-line skirmish, down toward a curve in the riverbank.

Brody began shouting at Zack and the others, but because of their positions, they could not see the trio, and because of the chopper rotors, Treat's warning went unheeded.

Rapidly sliding his M-16 free from across his back, Brody flipped the rear sights to long-range and the fire-selector to SEMI. The rifle had two 30-round banana clips attached to it, one inserted into the magazine well and the other taped to one side of the first, open end down, for a quick switch. He took in a deep breath and brought the M-16's front sights down on a pair of shoulders. The man on the left was already a football field away. One hundred yards, and growing. Brody pulled the trigger in five times. Smoothly. The weapon bucked so softly its buttplate could have been against his nose and not broken it. Neither was his concentration broken as the sprinting VC dropped into the mud, four bullets in his lower back.

Brody moved the rifle slightly to the right, passing by the woman with long, black hair tied behind her back. The sights came to rest on a man's head, and an instant before he squeezed the trigger several more times, Brody raised the rifle a hair. The distance compensated for now, two rounds slammed into the crease between the communist's shoulderblades, and he too disappeared from the rifle's sights.

When Brody took aim at the woman, it was her face he saw. She had glanced back over her shoulder, but was looking at the Americans on the gunboat, not the Huey doorgunner standing even farther away. Without taking his eyes off her, Brody switched to AUTO—full automatic—and hurled the remaining twenty rounds down along the riverbank at the fleeing woman. She anticipated the rock-and-roll spray, though.

No novice at this kind of no-second-chance game, she was zigzagging now, and all the rounds save two smoked past her on either side harmlessly. One bullet struck her shoulder like a sledgehammer, however, knocking her forward, off her feet and to her knees, and a tracer ripped into her left side as she struggled to regain her footing.

Little control left in her movements, the woman managed somehow to rise to her feet again. She dodged to her left as Brody withdrew the magazine, twirled it around without taking his eyes off her, and slammed the fresh clip into the rifle well. He tested its seal with a palm slap and took aim again, but she was gone.

His hatch machine gun useless without ammo belts to feed it, The Whoremonger abandoned his post and gave chase. Rifle against his hip, he rushed past a bewildered Sgt. Zack and vanished into the swirling rainforest mist.

CHAPTER 2

Brody would not normally have cared. If one of three targets escaped his crosshairs, he usually would not have honored the near miss with another thought—and he certainly would never abandon his post! Jumping from his gunny slot in a combat zone while the rotorblades were still whipping at the thick and sticky Nam heat was just not done; it could get him a court martial and death sentence if he ever survived to defend himself.

But Brody was not thinking about any of that. He was not deserting under fire. And Zack would understand, after he explained all his *dinky-dau* antics later. What occupied Treat's mind that very moment was the woman. She no longer was simply target number 10,000. She was *Brody's*. His personal vendetta, his obsession. Only *he* could kill her, so he couldn't let her get away.

Brody was bathed in sweat by the time he reached the clump of bushes he'd watched her dart into. Pausing only an instant to catch his breath as he gauged her progress through the trees, he ignored the calls of warning ringing between his ears and listened to the other voices instead: *It was the only way to do it!* they declared, spurring him on into the dark, suddenly all-consuming rain forest that rose up around him. Brody would not be able to explain it for several months afterwards, but a strange force had seized him from within, guiding him through the maze of trees, after her. He caught sight of her. Only fifty feet ahead now, she had paused against a massive tamarind trunk, her blood spraying out onto its thick roots with each heartbeat.

That Brody was pursuing her must have come as a great shock, for when the branch beneath his boots snapped, she screamed with a start. She met his gaze for only an instant, then whirled off to one side. The bullet fired from his rifle slammed into her elbow, shattering bone. She was sobbing loudly now as she trampled off into the brush, disoriented with pain.

"*Dung-lai!*" Brody shouted, sending a five-round burst into the jungle growth after her. He knew full well that shock from the multiple gunshot wounds was finally setting in. It would not matter if she were drunk on adrenaline—as he was. The pain would overcome even that, now.

The woman's only response to his Halt! command was a crashing about through the reeds. Brody chased after her, firing from the hip again when he saw the outline of a pistol rising in the murky distance.

The burst of rounds sent her stumbling backwards. But he knew the string of bullets had strayed high: splinters of bamboo from the dull impacts overhead were what now sliced into the woman.

When he caught up to her, she was face down in the elephant grass at the edge of a jungle clearing, breathing in shallow gasps, the pistol on the ground several feet away, blood streaming from flesh wounds in her scalp and neck.

The woman's gunhand was twitching as Brody approached cautiously, M-16 barrel leveled at the back of her head. Her haunches were propped up slightly to one side, a few inches off the ground.

A whimper left the woman. A whimper, and then a muffled cry, a chillingly haunting sob that sent a danger tingle down through Brody's gut. Something was wrong.

He dropped to one knee, careful to keep the M-16's muzzle trained on the nape of her neck. But he knew there was no need for caution. This woman would be dead in a few minutes—the pool of blood spreading around his own jungle boots was testimony to that.

But it was the whimper that melted Treat Brody's Air Cav resolve and cunning, for it was not a woman's cry at all but that of a child. He realized, as he drew closer to her, that there was not one being dying at his feet, but two. The young mother had her two-year-old, malnourished child strapped in a black bundle to her chest.

Brody carefully took hold of the woman's shoulder and rolled her over onto her back. That was when the young girl nestled against her breasts began screaming up at him. She too had been wounded. Brody watched blood spurting like weak fountains from three holes along her stomach as he recoiled.

"You . . . die . . . *du-ma*!" The woman's eyes opened as she spoke. Black as onyx and seemingly bottomless—for he could find no emotion in them— they locked onto his, staring through him, mesmerizing the young soldier, drawing his thoughts into hers until he saw death. His own death, at her hands.

Brody rose to his feet as the woman released her child to reveal shredded breasts and a jagged gash across her belly. With her free hand, she was trying to hold her intestines in, but, forced into movement when Brody turned her over, they kept oozing out between her fingers.

He watched her child roll away into the sharp blades of elephant grass, and when his eyes darted back to hers, he finally realized what she had whispered. *You die, motherfucker!* And that was when he saw the Chicom stick grenade. She had been holding it all along, clasped against her bosom, waiting for him to turn her over.

Lower jaw slowly dropping with indecision, Brody was still thinking about what she had said, and how amazed he was that she would carry her baby into battle, subject it to such risks. He was still trying to understand how dedicated these people must be to their beliefs in order to carry their infant daughters through a free-fire zone, when the grenade exploded.

Brody was hurled back off his feet. He felt the branches of a towering mahogany tree grab onto him from behind, trying to tear him apart and crush him. A bright fog entered his head, and his coordination abandoned him. He felt the tree's roots rip up from the earth, and he was lifted off his feet and carried away by the trunk as it lumbered off through the mist, deep into the heart of Void Vicious.

The woman who had killed him, the Viet Cong mother and her screaming, gut-shot daughter, were forgotten as Sergeant Treat Brody gave in to the smothering trees, allowing them to drag him down off his feet. He closed his eyes and dropped back into the black, bottomless pit of all-consuming pain, hoping Satan was really a whore in heat.

CHAPTER 3

There was fire in hell, and the flames were yellow and red.

Brody The Whoremonger was shocked to see the fog in front of his eyes clear to a bright, white sky. Clouds and other heavenly things were white. Brody had never thought he would see the pearly gates, either. But that was surely where he must be at now, for there was no doubt in his mind that the grenade explosion had done him in. Especially when he was out in the heart of the rain forest on his own, semi-AWOL and unaccounted for, with no corpsmen to call for when the shrapnel started flying.

He could remember the scene of his demise quite clearly; was even now, once again, from a limbolike perch above the jungle canopy, watching himself chase the female guerrilla through the tangle of trees below.

He saw the tracers ricochet about in the bamboo all over again, watched the woman fall at the clearing's edge, saw the grenade go off moments after he pulled her over. He was trying to yell down through the triple canopy, trying to warn himself, screaming at Treat Brody to ignore the wounded kid and concentrate more on the bitch growling at him with her grenade. But history was ignoring him as it repeated itself over and over: his mind saw the explosion toss him backwards a dozen times, until he could taste the powder on his lips and feel the blood running down along his rib cage from the stomach wounds.

He could still hear her singsong voice mocking him, "You die, *du-ma*," though the words had changed, had become even more musical, it seemed, with a guitar somewhere in the background accenting the syllables. And then he was drifting back into the warm, soothing fog, trying to forget about the child.

"Damnit, Nurse Hieu! Turn off that radio!" A harsh, male voice pierced Brody's ears, penetrated the unending throbbing between his ears, and when his eyes opened again, he was staring up at an antiseptically white hospital room ceiling. It was an American voice. "I won't tell you again."

"If you're gonna sneak in a tune"—he heard a different voice, farther away—"at least play some soul, honey, not that gook jive."

A third voice cut in, and Brody felt his head moving slightly to hear the man better, though his eyes remained glued to the ceiling. "Leave her alone, Stubbs."

"Screw you and yo' mama, white boy!"

"You go right ahead and keep it tuned to your Viet station, Nurse Hieu," the second voice said. "I like those songs. They're sooooothing!"

The first man, sounding older than both the other Americans combined, raised his voice firmly. "No more Vietnamese station, is that clear?"

The nurse answered meekly. "Yes, Doctor. I'm sorry."

"No need to be sorry." The tone softened somewhat as Brody began counting small black dots in the ceiling. "It's just that Vietnamese music is bad for morale, and . . ."

Brody was totally ignoring their conversation now. As if for the first time, he heard something else. A different sound, yet his mind told him it had been there all along: a baby screaming in pain.

Brody's head fell to the side, and his eyes scanned the

14

row of hospital beds extending several dozen yards off into the olive-drab distance. Dark green, lightweight army blankets covered three-quarters of each of the mostly empty racks. Even with his vision still slightly blurred, he could tell the sheets were folded under the thin mattresses tightly enough to "bounce a dime."

His eyes crossed as he attempted to focus on the bed nearest his own, and the pain struck him hard and suddenly, like a jackhammer to the back of the head.

He felt himself drifting again, back toward the edge of the pit. But the infant's screams remained his bond to this white cloud he was floating in.

His eyes opened again, and he found that his head was turned the other way, that a short, dark-skinned woman with almond eyes and billowing black hair piled up into a nurse's cap was holding his chin and peering deep into his eyes with a needlelike beam of light. Then she turned away from him and adjusted the dial on an I.V. tube. The side of his face dropped slowly against the cool pillow again, and he was looking out across the other half of the ward.

In his peripheral vision were black and brown and yellow and white bodies in various poses of recuperation: two legs in casts raised here, a GI with his chest heavily bandaged and arms missing over there. But his eyes locked onto the bed nearest him—a gurney, really, on wheels, just sharing his space temporarily.

It was the woman.

Her left arm seemed to reach out stiffly from under the sheet, dangling down over the edge of the gurney, trying to point at him to accuse. Streaks of dried blood were caked along the wrist, and along the elbow, where he had shot her. A sliver of ivory-white bone protruded several inches from a long tear in her bicep.

"No," Brody heard himself whisper as the infant's screams became a picture of that nowhere clearing in the middle of the rain forest, and he realized he had, in a matter of tension-laced seconds, snatched this child's mother away from her.

15

You have never lived until you have almost died. He heard the other voices too, like a legion of dead warriors' ghosts haunting him. *For those who fight for it, life has a flavor the protected will never know.*

"How are we doing, son?" Solid sounds were intruding on his thoughts, and he tried to shake the doctor's words from his head.

There is no hunting like the hunting of men. The doctor suddenly became Ernest Hemingway with pipe and safari pith helmet. *And those who have hunted armed men long enough, and liked it, never care for anything else thereafter.*

The doctor was examining his dogtags. "Brody, Treat," he read the inscription off dryly. "A sergeant now, eh, son?" He slapped Brody lightly on the side of the shoulder. "Last time you were in here, you were a Spec4 or a corporal or something."

"Somethin'," The Whoremonger muttered.

"Busted from corporal to PFC, then promoted back to Echo-4 with a specialist's patch instead of chevrons." Nurse Hieu spoke with a slight hint of distaste, as if the two of them had met somewhere before. But when Brody fought the pain and glanced up behind him, he found she was simply reading his 201 file. He had never seen her before in his life. "Quite a colorful character, for a doorgunner." Her fluency seemed to be impressing the other patients around them but Brody simply closed his eyes, exhausted. He wondered briefly how they had obtained his personnel jacket so quickly.

"This is, what, wound numba five, or six, Sgt. Whoremonger?" The doctor laughed softly.

Treat fought the pain in his gut and forced his eyes open again. "That you, Doc—Doc Szell?"

"The one and only, super trooper. The usual rule around here is, two Purple Hearts and it's back to The World."

"That's what I've heard." Brody still could not focus on the man's face, but he recognized the voice now: the same army doctor who'd stitched him up last time

16

Charlie was lucky enough to draw blood.

"But you stay in The Nam, collecting glory medals, right?" Major Szell spoke with a mixture of sarcasm and sadness.

"Everybody's gotta have a hobby, Doc." Brody sighed heavily, and the doctor held his wrist, checking his pulse.

"But I thought yours was conquering snatch in the far corners of the Orient," Szell challenged with a sly grin. Nurse Hieu cocked an eyebrow at the stock six-footer but remained silent as the child covered in bloody bandages behind her filled the room with unending wails.

"You've got me confused with Nelson, sir." Brody spoke slowly, as if he was tiring of the word game. "The procurer of pubic-hair samples."

"Ahhh, yes."

A voice from the far side of the ward yelled out suddenly, "Somebody shut that goddamned kid up! On top o' ninety-five stitches, the little bitch ain't helpin' matters any!" But he was ignored for the most part.

"She gut-shot, Private Warner." Nurse Hieu finally spoke up when no one else did. "Gut-shot is most painful, you know."

"Well, she shouldn't even fucking be here, if you'll excuse my French. She's a goo—she's indigenous personnel, ma'am! She should be in an Arvin hospital, or *Cong-Hoa*, not here with—"

"As soon as she's stabilized, Private Warner," the major said, his tone laced with irritation. "Then she'll be transferred."

"How bad am I, Doc?" Brody's hand shot up, and he latched onto Major Szell's elbow. "How bad is my belly?"

"Not bad, Sergeant," Szell said as he checked the stomach dressings. "Not bad at all."

"No deserve Purple Heart." Nurse Hieu switched to her pidgin-English and stress syndome psychology. "No even deserve our attention."

17

Brody ignored her. All he could see was the little girl rolling away from the protective embrace of her mother on the edge of that dark rain-forest clearing. "How long before I can get up?" How long since it had happened, he was wondering.

Szell chuckled with disbelief. "A couple of weeks, at the least," he said.

"You have suffered several minute abdominal punctures," Nurse Hieu translated in a businesslike manner, avoiding Brody's eyes as she consulted his chart. "From the stick grenade. But we do not anticipate any infection setting in."

"Well, that's mighty generous of you." Treat frowned as a corpse was wheeled through his fragmented field of vision.

"So long you refrain from your usual games and follow all the recovery rules regarding stomach wounds. No horseplay."

"Roger wilco, honey. I'm not exactly in the mood for any grab-ass right now, believe me."

"Then we're going to get along just fine." Lifting her chin slightly in the air, she whirled around and quickly exited the ward.

Brody listened to the click-clack of her heels fade into the distance. "The girl," he asked Major Szell. "Is she going to make it?"

"She was D.O.A.," he replied matter-of-factly. "Never had a chance. You stitched her pretty good, sergeant." He was sounding almost jealous now, more like a military officer than a MACV surgeon. "A real diagonal jobber: hipbone to clavicle, right between the boobs." He made a slashing, invisible Z in the air with the edge of his hand.

"I meant the other one. The baby-san."

"Oh, her. Hard to tell, son. Three rifle rounds in the gut can ruin a kid's whole day, you know."

"Spare me the Marine humor, sir," Treat said without emotion.

Szell saw that there must have been something differ-

18

ent about this firefight, and his voice immediately grew somber. Glancing at his Rolex, he said, "It's fourteen hundred hours now. At the rate she's been hanging on, I'd give her another eight, maybe twelve hours. Until midnight tonight, perhaps."

"Fourteen hundred hours?" That was two in the afternoon, civilian time. Brody tried to sit up, but pain lancing through his system froze his upper torso halfway off the bed, and Szell gently eased him back down.

"Mellow out, son. The war'll still be waiting for you when you leave here. There's no rush. You go gettin' mighty on me right now and try anything stupid, you'll be right back in here with even more painful complications. I guarantee it!"

"But fourteen hundred hours?" Brody couldn't believe what he was hearing. It had been dusk when *Pegasus* and her crew answered the gunboat's call for help on the Mekong. "You mean I've been out for close to eighteen hours?" He thought about the little girl he'd shot, and how she was still screaming, and how bewildered and confused and terrified she must feel. Didn't they believe in administering painkiller to the locals around here?

Nurse Hieu was back beside his bed. His eyes were tightly closed, but he could tell by her little laugh. "Eighteen hours?" she sounded amused. "Not quite. Sorry 'bout that, but you've been unconscious for three days, big boy."

CHAPTER 4

The next morning, Major Szell told Brody that the woman who tried to kill him with the grenade had clung to life for over seventy-two hours, despite her wounds. Throughout the ordeal, she had kept her face turned to one side. Toward Brody's bed, staring at him in unmoving silence, almost as if she was savoring his suffering, waiting for him to awake so she could taunt or confront him. Finally the trauma overcame her. The shock that had set in some three days earlier took control of the woman, and clawing at the air that separated their beds as she tried vainly to reach him, she finally succumbed to her injuries only a few moments before Brody himself awoke.

The little girl would make it, Szell told him, *if* she could just survive the next few days. The constant screaming was a good sign, he maintained. She was not crying from pain so much, it was more in bewildered terror.

"I want her, Doc." Brody struggled to rise again. The tearing sensation along his insides did not seem as harsh as before, and the major did not attempt to restrain him.

Szell appeared to read the buck sergeant's mind. "Impossible," he said immediately.

"You have to listen to me, Doc," he persisted. But the major waved him silent.

"It's natural to feel what you're feeling, son," he said. "You're not the first trooper to share a med-evac slick with a wounded orphan and—"

"But I'm responsible for—"

"Nonsense. This The Nam, Treat, a bona-fucking-fide combat zone, okay? You *bic*? Waifs and war are mutually—"

"Listen, sir,—"

"No, *you* listen up, slick." A hint of irritation mixed with impatience colored the army doctor's tone. "I'm the cluck in charge here, and what I say happens to carry some weight in these o.d. green corridors."

"Spare me the hand-job, Major." Brody turned his head to one side and slowly closed his eyes. The twitching two-year-old remained in the middle of his mind, crystal clear. "After she leaves here, how long before she—"

"Well, there's no telling about something like that, actually. She's shot up bad enough to hang around for several months if we weren't hurting for racks, but that's not what I'm talking about. Soon as some I.G with scrambled eggs drippin' off his cunt cap struts through here lookin' to soil his white gloves with dust from lockertops, you can bet your whanger this major is going to have to explain why the kid wasn't transferred north to Saigon or booted back to the boonies long ago."

"You just rattled off bookoo b.s., Doc, without ever coming close to answering my question. Now if you'd just—"

"Well, Sgt. Brody!" A dainty little angel of mercy, clad in white, fluttered up to the edge of Treat's bed from his blind side. He recognized Nurse Hieu's voice immediately. "I'm so glad to see you awoke on your own this morning without us having to poke and prod, the way we have to with *some* of the tenants around here." Her sour tone rose somewhat near the statement's end and she glanced over at a frowning GI propped up against several pillows in a bunk across the aisle.

"Your comment doesn't even deserve a retort," Pvt. Warner replied dryly as he turned to stare out a nearby window. "This gunny's short—so short, in fact, he don't even need to listen to nurses of the indigenous persuasion. I can't even read Arvin collar rank, and I don't know anyone that does, so—"

"I do not happen to be a member of the South Vietnamese army, Private Warner, and—" Nurse Hieu was preparing to tear into the American soldier when the ward's double doors swung inward, admitting a group of ragged, red-eyed warriors. The infantrymen were escorting a tall, stocky Caucasian clad in a gold robe, and Nurse Hieu rushed over to confront them.

"Well, what in hell's name do we have here?" Major Szell laid his clipboard down on the foot of Brody's bed and folded his arms across his chest in anticipation.

The American wearing the gold robe and Ho Chi Minh sandals was one of the tallest men Szell had ever seen. His hair was jet black—so black, in fact, the major almost suspected it might be dyed—and combed straight back. He had a somewhat prominent chin, but in a noble sort of vein, not one that would detract from his appearance, which, Nurse Hieu was quick to observe, bordered on the handsome. His shoulders were broad, and his waist trim. Szell did not think the man was a bodybuilder, but the robe or cape or whatever it was made it hard to tell. He did carry himself quite confidently, though; that was definite, the medical officer decided.

When the visitor glanced over in Brody's direction, it was with a mere preoccupied glaze in his dark, colorless eyes. He didn't really seem to see any of them clustered around the wounded cavalryman. Szell and The Whoremonger both noticed that his mustache, which drooped down to the lower edges of his chin on either side, Fu Manchu style, was as black as his hair.

Sinister looking, Brody decided as he watched the grim-faced group escort the caped Westerner past. Brody wished he could sit up and cradle an M-16 in his arms. These dudes were nothing but bad news; he could taste it on his blood-chapped lips. And he knew them all.

A half dozen privates, in their late teens at most, surrounded the robed soldier as the entourage glided soundlessly toward PFC Warner's bed. Rifles suspended below shoulder slings rode against their hips, horizontal to the mirrorlike hospital tiles. Warner had taken to reading a comic book rather than argue with Nurse Hieu, and had failed to notice the group entering the ward. When he felt hushed movement approaching, he glanced up. Brody watched his eyes grow wide. Instant recognition creased his surprised features, and he attempted to sit up, ignoring the massive bandages wrapped around his chest and upper arms.

"Be still," the man inside the robe said, raising a hand, knuckles up and fingers extended, as his teen-aged bodyguards parted on either side of him. His tone carried a pleasant, almost soothing tone to it.

"Master Le Loi!" Warner was still trying to respond to the appearance of someone he obviously respected and held in high esteem.

Brody glanced up at Szell to gauge his expression and, as he had expected, the major was not very pleased with the show intruding into his wing of the aid station. Three of the armed riflemen at the caped man's flank whirled around as the doctor approached to protest this obviously unauthorized visit. The menacing glare in their eyes effectively muted Szell's intentions and cooled his anger: the good doctor was a lover at heart, not a brawler.

"The Master desired to stop by here and check on your progress personally," a soldier nearest the robed man told Warner.

Brody winced at the strangeness of what was transpiring before him: this group was acting like some sort

23

of weird cult, and the more he shook the numbing haze from his head, the more he began to remember.

Brock. The sergeant from Fourth Platoon: Echo Company's very own enigma of the supernatural.

Sgt. Brock had been halfway through his third year in The Nam when he finally snapped a tripwire and kissed Lady Death on the lips. It had been in this very province, too, and Doc Delgado, who had helped work on the mutilated NCO, still told stories about the strange vibes that possessed him for weeks after he had joined the other crew members donating blood to save the man.

A weird, unearthly voice had seemed to take control of Sgt. Brock as they brought him back from the edge of Death's bottomless pit. The surgeons at the aid station claimed it was just a manifestation of Brock's already twisted sense of humor and entertainment, but his closest buddies, the men in his squad, were convinced he had returned from never-never land a 500-year-old royal reincarnate. And not just any recycled spirit, but one of the most revered warriors in Vietnamese legend: Le Loi, who, as a guerrilla leader during the first quarter of the fifteenth century, defeated the Chinese in the year 1418, creating the longest dynasty in the history of Vietnam, some 400 years.

Sgt. Brock's voice changed when he went into his Le Loi routine, Brody learned one moonless evening in the mist-enshrouded Ia Drang Valley. The NCO's followers had invited him over to their bunker for a "session," and The Whoremonger left laughing but not unimpressed. Brock had put on quite a show. Recalling battle after battle in vivid detail as he gestured with those massive arms and stared off into the blue clouds of cigarette smoke, he was an impressive sight, even to combat-hardened Brody, a devout cynic. But Treat just couldn't accept the claim that a long-dead Vietnamese national hero had chosen to return spiritually in the form of a "long-nosed, round-eyed foreigner."

Brody still refused to believe. The jungle was all that

mattered, in his book. Void Vicious, and the rain forest firefights, and the power of *Pegasus*. They meant the world to Treat Brody, in fact. They were his religion, his motivation for remaining a member of the Green Machine; he had nothing else in this life. Nothing else that mattered.

Brody's people left Brock and his fourth platoon to their own devices. So long as they pulled their weight during the missions, there'd be no complaints from The Whoremonger. He couldn't help but think, though, how strange it was that "Master Le Loi" Brock never went into his "trances" during an operation into the bush. He always waited until the crews were back safely in the rear before pulling out his golden cape and assuming his ancient identity. So convenient. Brody smiled at the thought, but he had to admit the hairs stood up along the back of his neck that night in the bunker.

"And how does the sunrise find you, Follower Warner?" Brody and Doc Szell strained to catch the conversation between the tall man in the golden cape and the bedridden PFC.

"Well, Master Le Loi, the sunrise finds me well!"

"The Master was wondering when you would be returning to the unit." A short, stocky corporal beside Brock spoke, and Brody got the feeling he would be doing all the talking from here on out.

"They tell me I'm going to be here for quite some time." Warner appeared distraught. "At least for another—"

The corporal raised a hand, cutting Warner off. "Master Le Loi requires your services as soon as possible," he explained cryptically. "You proved yourself well on the field of battle; that is why Master Le Loi is here. The Master recognizes your skill and courage under fire. He wants you back with us, with the legion, as soon as possible."

"I will heal quickly." Warner spoke in an icy monotone now as he stared into Brock's eyes, unblinking. Sgt. Brock must have sent for a hypnotize-your-friends packet from one of those mail order companies advertising in the *Overseas Weekly*.

Brody wanted to chuckle aloud, but the troopers accompanying Brock were a grizzled team, not to be messed with right now. Brody knew they had just returned from extended duty in the Bong Son, where Fourth Platoon had taken heavy casualties. That these six had survived was probably being attributed to "Le Loi" Brock's good graces and influence with the powers-that-be.

Brody was not in the mood or physical condition to challenge them with his skepticism. The conversation at Warner's bedside was taking on a dreamlike quality anyway, the words reaching his ears becoming a jumble of faraway, unintelligible sounds.

When he turned away from the spectacle, he found another visitor had slipped unnoticed into the ward and was standing beside his own rack.

"Will he survive?"

Brody recognized Lt. Vance's voice as the question was posed to Doc Szell. There was a slight pause, as Brody imagined the major forcing his attention from the group across the aisle to the newcomer standing beside him.

"Oh, he'll make it all right." The doctor sighed as he focused on the subdued black bar and Infantry emblem on Vance's collar. "Just a couple of puncture wounds where the sun don't shine. Young Sgt. Brody's got a ticket home out of all this; I'm just trying to convince him to accept it."

"You want to stay on in The Nam, do you?" Vance stared down at him, and Treat forced a slight nod. Better to humor these two and get it over with as quickly as possible so he could resume his nap. "Well, it won't be with the rank and privilege of a noncommissioned officer anymore, my friend."

Szell cocked an eyebrow at the twenty-three-year-old. "And what exactly is *that* supposed to mean, Lieutenant?" The major spoke in a tone that told Vance he'd better have a good reason for trying to upset one of his patients, or *he* might just be facing a reduction in rank as well.

"Sgt. Brody left his post during an engagement with the enemy," Vance responded dryly, reading from a freshly printed set of orders bearing a bright red line across The Whoremonger's Christian name. "He abandoned his hatch machine gun and raced off into the jungle without notifying—"

"I was chasing down three sappers," Treat cut in with a dry, rasping voice. "Zack knew what I was doing! I wasn't deserting, if that's what you're getting at. Did Leo file the paper on this?" he asked in disbelief.

"*I* had to," Vance admitted softly.

The lieutenant had been there, Brody remembered clearly now—in the thick of it. Once, he had even disappeared beyond the drifting blanket of oily gunsmoke, and Brody had feared he'd bought the farm. "You know what went down on that riverbank too, Jake."

"Yes, and that's why I've put you in for another Silver Star, Brody. But I must also account to the Brass for your injuries. I have to explain why you lost half your hide three hundred yards away from *Pegasus* instead of right there in the gunship hatch."

"I got the bitch, though, didn't I, sir?" Brody grinned and gazed up at the ceiling. Being busted was no big thing; he'd been down that road before. In the Nam, it didn't mean nothin'. He hadn't really enjoyed his recent promotion to E-5 anyway: three chevrons on your sleeve could do an awful lot to alienate you from your buddies and to kill close friendships that had been forged under fire. He didn't fancy being a leader, anyway. His place was in the chopper hatch, behind a Hog-60. The men in his squad knew they could count on him when things got down and dirty, and that was all that mattered, not three lousy stripes. Zack usually called the shots when they went into the Void anyway.

"Ain't that the shits," Major Szell muttered, turning

away from Vance. "Get busted and put in for some silver on the same day."

"I don't relish any of this," Vance was still staring down at Brody, but he spoke to Szell.

The ranking officer was watching Sgt. Brock's entourage across the aisle. Two of the enlisted men were lifting the edge of the imposing NCO's gold cape out of a trail of fresh blood that ran the entire length of the ward. "*That's* who you should shift your attention to." Szell motioned in the direction of Brock. "The soldier thinks he's a ghost from the land of long-ju-ju or something!"

Vance remained defensive. "Brock and his people pull their weight. So long as they don't go driftin' off in the gunsmoke during a firefight, the Colonel told us platoon leaders to lay off 'em."

"Well, they're all buckin' for a psyche confinement, if you ask me." Szell stalked away.

"Sorry, Brody, but . . ." Vance leaned down close to the side of Treat's face, whispering, when a sudden commotion at the corridor entrance caught everyone's attention.

Two MPs were chasing a heavily bandaged Vietnamese through the swinging access doors into the ward. The MPs were not your usual clean-cut, khakied static post sentries that manned the hospital's perimeter. These two sported open flak jackets and paint-blackened faces. Both had jagged tears along the thigh pockets of their jungle fatigues, where dried blood—their own, it appeared—was caked along the openings, as if they'd met up with a Cong boobytrap out in the middle of the sticks somewhere. And recently.

The Vietnamese wore black calico trousers resembling pajamas, and no top. His chest and one entire arm were wrapped in crimson-soaked bandages. His eyes were wildly darting about as he frantically sought an escape route, in contrast to the military policemen's, grim and businesslike, despite expressions that announced they'd recently been to hell and back. Alert

28

Team members, Brody decided in an instant. *Reactionary* Force. He could tell by the graffiti on their steel pots.

Brody was not immediately alarmed by the foot chase. The first thought that entered his mind was that the Vietnamese was an Arvin who'd just been brought in from a rain-forest battlefield somewhere and was trying to escape his mental demons. He brandished no firearms, and didn't appear to be wired for satchel charges. Surely the medics would have detected any explosives while wrapping half his torso up like an Egyptian mummy.

"Sapper!" One of the MPs was yelling, however, as the trio raced past the foot of Brody's bed. "Everybody on the floor!"

"Under your racks!" the second MP was directing as his left hand jerked the slide back on the .45 automatic in his right. "Sapper!"

Apparently the Viet had been innovative—maybe some C-4 sewn into the crotch of his pants for the ultimate, orgasmic suicide attack, Treat decided. The three were nearly out the door now.

In the same instant in which Brody decided moving under his rack would be more painful and probably unnecessary than it was worth, the explosion blew his entire bunk over on its side. The rolling blast snatched away his hearing, but the sapper's upper torso flip-flopped out the door while his severed legs blew back onto the bloodied and shrapnel-riddled patients.

Blackness drowned out everything else as Treat Brody spasmed in pain, then collapsed.

CHAPTER 5

"Toss some o' that stateside solvent over here, Nasty Nel!"

Pvt. Nelson, who had been scrubbing the barrel of his M-16 hard for the last thirty minutes and trying to mind his own business, ignored Corky Cordova and continued working on his weapon.

"Hey, what's your problem, fuckwad?" Cordova elbowed Fletcher as he continued speaking to Nelson. "Finally lose your cherry to some local lady of questionable virtue?"

Both Nelson and Fletcher glanced up for the first time at that remark, and then Corky remembered Nelson's legendary collection of female pubic-hair samples. "Oh, that's right," he recalled finally. "Disregard my last, over."

"What is your problem, though?" Fletcher nudged Nelson with his knee as he snatched the newby's "gift from the U.S.A." from a considerate uncle back in The World.

Nelson stared at a large brown, short-haired mongrel slowly walking toward their bunker from the distant tree line. "Here comes trouble." Em-Ho Lee grinned as the mutt stumbled over a set of mortar fins protruding from the red clay. "Looks like one of the Lurps been feeding him acid again." Nelson glanced over at Lee as the Japanese-American snickered. Lee had been reading a thick hardcover book while the others cleaned their rifles around a solvent trough. The book was a Nicholas Uhernik classic: *Saigon Alley: A Study of the People of the Night.* Lee started to set it down upon the dog's approach, losing his place, then changed his mind and slipped a thumb between some pages while still watching Choi-oi. Em-Ho, which was not Japanese at all, but boot-camp lingo for Early Morning Hard-On, stood up and started over toward Echo Company's mascot after slipping the book under his arm.

"What's the fucking problem, Big N?" Snakeman persisted.

"Nothin' that means shit." The eighteen-year-old buck private ignored the solvent greasing his fingers and ran them through his shaggy blond hair, forcing beads of sweat to ooze down over his temples. "Nothin' at all."

"'Nothin' that means shit,'" Fletcher advised Cordova sarcastically, mimicking Nelson. "Nothin' at all."

Nelson started to stand up, but Snakeman latched onto his elbow. "Sit the fuck down, slick. Mellow out."

"Snakeman's just havin' a little fun" Corky added.

"Aw, what the flyin' fuck do you two skates know about it anyway?" Nelson stared at the disassembled parts of his rifle lying on a straw Vietnamese sleeping mat as he resumed his seat. "You've both been fuckin' off in Singapore or somewheres for the last two or three—"

"Bangkok," Snakeman Fletcher corrected him, glancing over at Corky with a satisfied wink.

"While I been gettin' my ass run ragged by Jake The Jackass the entire time you was away. It just ain't fair, man. I didn't do nothin'."

Fletcher's smile faded. "Lt. Vance been on your case, Nel?" he asked seriously.

31

"Somethin' like that." Nelson stared at the glassy-eyed mongrel stumbling toward them. Choi-oi reeked of an unidentified alcoholic beverage. "Not that you two would give a damn! Not that you two could care less about a newby no-account's troubles and—"

"Why would Vance be fuckin' with Nelson?" Cordova asked no one in particular as he began slamming rifle parts back together. Corky still considered the FNG a pogue who didn't deserve to socialize with the vets yet. He just didn't have his time in, pubic-hair collection be damned.

Before Nelson could explain, Choi-oi, who had frozen in his best bird-dog imitation as a huge orange dragonfly hovered over the gathering of doorgunners, suddenly pounced. The slightly intoxicated and thoroughly undocumented mutt leapt at the dragonfly, missed, and cannonballed, as only a canine can, right into the tub of rusty, disgusting cleaning solvent.

The entire squad got splashed—everyone except Em-Ho Lee and his treasured tome. The Snakeman immediately commenced cursing, grabbed Corky's M-16, and searched frantically for an ammo magazine as Choi-oi, sensing trouble and bad feelings over the near miss, struggled to climb out of the filthy vat.

"Mother*fucker*!" Fletcher cried as Cordova jerked the weapon back and The Snakeman rose to find his crotch soaked. Two housegirls, carrying handwashed laundry past the soldiers, giggled at Fletcher's predicament, mistaking the cause for something else.

"Poor Choi-oi!" Lee reached over and helped the whimpering dog out of the trough. Tongue hanging out, Choi-oi's eyes bulged as they remained locked on Snakeman over a brown shoulder. "He just hasn't been the same since Brody went TDY on us to a hospital." But Fletcher was not laughing.

"I'm gonna KILL that worthless little . . ."

It continued that way for several hours, as the tropical Asian sun, Indian-red and swollen, edged closer toward the horizon: the men of Echo Company trying to clean their weapons in preparation for Operation Coronado, and Choi-oi returning again and again to make a nuisance of himself. Fletcher never did shoot the mutt, though Choi-oi had been wounded in action on numerous occasions in the past.

It was Em-Ho Lee who finally suggested they blow away the dragonfly, and after Snakeman killed it with a smoke grenade, Choi-oi began chasing swamp butterflies in and out of the tents and bunkers, which got the housegirls to giggling again. Nelson thought it might be because the young women just wanted something to giggle about and break the ice with these "big beautiful foreigners" and that they couldn't care less about Choi-oi's antics. Snakeman argued they just wanted to nab the mutt so they could apply make-up to the animal as a gag. Vietnamese women had an odd sense of humor, he maintained. Cordova insisted the ladies of the Mekong Delta didn't have cosmetics to waste on an ugly mongrel like Choi-oi, and that they only wanted to nab him for supper.

Housegirls were a new and mystifying extravagance the men of Echo Company were unaccustomed to. A battalion of the First Air cavalry division had arrived in the Delta recently to assist the American riverine forces with patrolling the maze of waterways, both natural and manmade, that plagued anti-communist fighters in the fertile rice-growing region southwest of Saigon. From its source in Tibet, the Mekong River meanders through several countries in Southeast Asia, finally reaching the South China Sea 12,000 miles later, in South Vietnam. The Delta itself encompasses some 25,000 miles of difficult and treacherous terrain that rarely rises in excess of ten feet above sea level.

The provincial capital was Mytho, a town of some 40,000, and it was at an abandoned compound between Mytho and Cho Gao, a smaller ville toward the east on Highway 24, that Col. "Bull" Buchanan set up his base camp.

The compound was one mile square in size, most of it

old C-130 runway tarmac, and encircled in sagging coils of concertina wire atop a chainlink fence. Double-decker conex guard towers adorned each perimeter corner, with two-man defensive positions placed behind dug-in sandbags every fifty yards or so.

A sprawling Vietnamese housing project nearly a kilometer away was the only civilian enclave nearby, and across the roadway from the camp's main entrance, an ARVN compound, home for a South Vietnamese Ranger Battalion, blocked the western horizon and turned the nightly dusk an eerie crimson with a wall of smoke from its countless cooking fires.

The housegirls had been living in a rocket-damaged villa in the center of camp when the 7th of the First arrived to "clean house," and rather than run them out, Bull Buchanan, called Neil Nazi behind his back, opted to hire them to take care of the laundry, housework, and certain other chores conveniently available. Half of the women seemed to be war widows, but the others were camp followers who had no one left to follow when the former tenants were shipped north to reinforce the farce of a DMZ. There was a sprinkling of children and younger, innocent-looking women among the hard-core honeys. Though Bull knew he might be risking trouble with his cherry-boy FNGs, keeping the skirts around seemed the lesser of two evils. It increased morale to see a shapely young thing slinking about now and then, and freed his troops from washing their own uniforms and policing up the place, so they could concentrate more on keeping their weapons ready and their birds airmobile.

There was no telling how long Operation Coronado might last—it could be three weeks, or three years. The canal Cong were getting out of hand, and as soon as the Cavalry reinforcements helped the gunboat detachments even the odds, Buchanan could forsake the land of soggy crotch rot and take his troopers back into the choking red dust of the Central Highlands or wherever they felt more at home.

"You never did tell me, Nasty Nel"—Fletcher located Nelson near a triangle of unoccupied bunkers, fifty yards from where Cordova and Lee were giving Choi-oi a doggy bubble bath—"just what exactly is Vance's problem?"

"Don't worry about it, Snakeman." Nelson was slapping his rifle's handguards and sling back in place. "I never should have mentioned anything. Just forget I—"

"Look." Fletcher kicked him lightly with the toe of his jungle boot. "That's fine. You don't wanna talk about it, fucking fine. But I don't have much more patience than anyone else in this unit, and I don't like bein' knee-jerked about the lifers. You're not fucking paranoid, are ya, Nasty Nel?"

"It's my collection," Nelson said softly.

"What?" Snakeman dropped into a squat in front of the private. "Your snatchbox?"

"Yah. The lieutenant's got a hard-on for me 'cause everyone in Echo brags to the other companies about my samples of papa-hotel." "Papa-hotel" was military phonetic for pubic hair. "The lieutenant says he finds the whole matter embarrassing, and that if it keeps up, he's gonna have me transferred to an armor unit."

"Tanks?"

"Right. Where Charlie lobs RPG's at ya, and you're twice-fried meat even before ya know what hit ya."

"Well, that sucks the big one, kid." Snakeman glanced up at a gaggle of Hueys descending from the dark storm clouds to the north.

"Most definitely." Nelson stared at the hollowed-out python head hanging over Fletcher's canteen, stretched-apart jaws facing forward. It belonged to Brody The Whoremonger, but Treat had surrendered it to Snakeman for safekeeping when the medics were carrying him to the Dustoff the week before. "But I know that ain't really the reason."

"Huh?" Fletcher had been watching the two dozen olive-drab gunships float in over the concertina for flaring landings in the middle of the camp. A muffled

35

blast from the other side of the compound reached them, and Elliott's ears perked slightly. But there had been no distinctive mortar *whump!* preceding the explo-sion, and when no secondary reports or enemy-attack sirens went off, the tension drained from the lines beneath his eyes.

"The real reason he's constantly on my case like stink on shit is because o' somethin' else, I'm tellin' ya."

"Oh, you're tellin' me, are ya?" Fletcher wasn't really listening to Nelson anymore. He was getting powerful-bad vibes from somewhere, and he stood to get his edge back. Something dirty was going down, but he couldn't place the exact direction the gut feeling was coming from. And then, quickly as it had hit him, the gnawing along his spine was gone, and his eyes darted up just as a helicopter glided past, barely fifty feet off the ground.

Three soldiers from Charlie company were sitting in the open hatch, their legs dangling over the side. Recognizing him, two men flipped Snakeman the thumbs-up, but the trooper in the middle responded with an obscene gesture, benign of malice and an acknowledging wad of spit. Batted down by the intense rotorwash, the streak of saliva vanished before it struck the ground. Before Fletcher could react with more than a frown, the gunship was gone.

Its flapping rotors still beating rhythmically in their ears, both Echo company soldiers turned as they sensed something approaching closer to the earth: an army jeep appeared between two Quonset huts. Fletcher recognized the driver—a Headquarters Company clerk-n-jerk E-5—but the other four men clinging to the vehicle's folded roof bars were definitely fresh meat. He could see it in the metallic green shade of their new jungle fatigues and the red dots on their pale forearms. The newbies couldn't be more than a couple days off the troop transport. How they rated assignment to Operation Coronado before a bodycount demanded replacements was a mystery only Puzzle Palace, down in Saigon, could answer.

"Yo' mama, Snakeoil!" The clerk-n-jerk imitated Leo Zack as he roared by, his grin ear-to-ear and both hands off the steering wheel, waving.

"Yah, and up yours!" Fletcher's fist came up. Sgt. Zack was the only man who could get away with calling him Snakeoil. He'd make a point of paying Specialist 5th Class Farney a personal visit after he straightened Nasty Nel out.

Nelson observed the blank, bewildered expressions on the three enlisted men's faces before the rolling cloud of dust hid the jeep's departure. "They sure look terrified, don't they?"

"Like you were your first week in-country?" Fletcher challenged him.

"Hell no, Snakeman!" Nelson seemed to be regaining some of his old spirit. "I was born for this kinda blowjob. The Nam's got me by the balls, and won't let go, bro! I'm bein' nurtured for something humongous, my man. I'm being taunted and teased in Vietnamese and—"

"Save the jive for somebody who gives a shit, okay?" Fletcher said, staring into the swirl of dust hiding the clerk's jeep, and seeing the mosquito-marked faces of the nervous newbies.

Seeing their faces, and seeing himself. How long ago had it been since he arrived in South Vietnam? Going on two years now? *Over* two years now?

As if he'd been using binoculars, Fletcher's mind's eye had zoomed in on their faces, noticing the red dots left by the mosquitoes on every patch of exposed flesh, and in their recent lesson he saw a reflection from his own past. Saw himself that first night in The Nam, herded into a crowded processing barracks, yet all alone with his thoughts. Alone with his thoughts and fears, yet too exhausted from the 15-day boat ride "across the pond" to worry much about dying already.

Sleep was paramount among his first goals of the

dreaded Tour-365, and no one had warned him about the marauding insects who hovered just outside the grenade screens, waiting for lights-out. He awoke the next morning to find his eyelids swollen shut from the countless bites, and red dots covering his exposed arms and neck. Fletcher had slept with his trousers and boots on, that evening.

A half dozen sets of jungle boot soles striking the earth in some semblance of orderly fashion reached Fletcher's ears, and the whisper of a back-in-boot-camp cadence coaxed him out of the daydream.

Sgt. Zack was leading a squad of troopers along the perimeter, relieving the bunker guards with a night shift. "The Lieutenant wants to see you two back at the CP," Leo muttered as the squad passed by grimly, well aware he was the bearer of bad tidings and not enjoying such duty in the least.

"Lt. Vance?" Nelson sought to clarify, hoping there might be some mistake, some confusion. Maybe some other Lou wanting an audience with him. Fletcher just shook his head from side to side slowly, saddened that the members of Echo in general and Nasty Nel in particular were being forced to grasp at straws in such a fashion lately.

"You know any *other* lieutenant'd be roustin' you two this time o' day?"

"Gottsa t'be a shit detail, white boy," a short, black trooper said, flashing a set of ivory-white teeth in Nelson's direction.

"Spread your legs, grab your ankles, an' bow to Buddha," the "brother" beside him added, "then kiss your ass goodbye, honky!"

The taunt brought raucous laughter from the others in the marching formation, both black and white. Snake-man frowned and turned away, in the direction of the Command Post, but Nelson didn't seem disturbed.

Roustin' you two, Zack had said. That was it, Nelson decided. The key words: you two. Him and The Snake-man. And Elliott had just returned from R and R. They

38

hadn't had time to get in any trouble together—nothing Nel could remember, anyway.

Maybe it was just another shit detail; emptying the crappers or something equally degrading. But at least he wouldn't be alone with the officer, face to face and pushed to the point of insubordination, or worse: assault and battery. In the Nam, that could mean not only the stripes he didn't have, but a noose in Nha Trang or a firing squad at LBJ.

When they arrived at the CP, Vance seemed preoccupied with a sheath of papers in his hand. He barely glanced over at Nelson.

Two of the newbies they'd seen cruise past in the clerk's jeep were standing at the position of parade rest in front of the lieutenant. "Take these two men," he told Fletcher, ignoring Nasty Nel, "and walk 'em through the static posts and LPs. I don't want 'em goin' out on the ships until they know the camp inside and out. Is that clear?"

"Clear as a Saigon whore's see-thru blouse, sir," Snakeman replied dryly, glancing off at another gaggle of slicks passing by. An unamused Lt. Vance looked up briefly from the handful of permanent-assignment orders.

Vance's eyes shifted to Nelson's face, then back again to Fletcher's as he paused, digesting the comment. "Good," he said finally, blank-faced. "See to it they're acting like vets in record time, Fletch. I'm counting on you."

Vance turned and walked off without giving Fletcher a chance at some off-color, witty retort. "Okay." Snakeman shook his head again, this time in surprise. "Might as well get the show on the road."

"Before it gets so dark we stumble over the tripwires," Nelson added.

The twilight was turning a deep purple. The men paused a moment, watching a Phantom jet's glowing afterburners rise into the violet haze miles off, then Fletcher clicked his heels together smartly and muttered, "Clusterfuck, about *face*!"

"Hey, d'you guys hear about the abortion over at the aid station?" A stocky, shirtless GI with skin the color of copper, wearing cut-off camou shorts and Ho Chi Minh sandals was jogging past. He slowed as he came abreast of Snakeman, but continued running in place.

"Greetings, Two-Step! And negatron on your last. Fill us in." Fletcher's premonition was taking form finally.

"Lawless is a father," Nelson joked half-heartedly.

"Naw. Serious shit." Chance Broken Arrow's face was a granite-hard, emotionless mask. "Sapper blew up half the trauma ward. Kissed his balls goodbye, and took two MPs with him. Real mess, from what I hear."

"Brody!" Fletcher reached out and grabbed the Comanche by his upper arms. "What about Brody?"

Two-Step made no attempt to break free. "Treat's tough. He can handle whatever Charlie throws at him."

"But you don't *know*?" Snakeman's eyes grew wide. "You don't *know* one way or the other?"

"Holy shit," Nelson muttered at the news.

"Tried to check out the situation, Snake, but they got the place sealed off while they search the prisoners in the E. R."

"Never should med-evac Cong suspects into an American hospital in the first place." Nelson spat. He followed the newbies' eyes as they watched the red dust rise in small puffs where spittle struck the ground. "Should shoot 'em right on the spot, back in the Void." He locked eyes with the closest recruit. "Back in Void Vicious."

"Well, let's get over there right now and check on The Whoremonger, for crissake!" Fletcher whirled around, only to find that Lt. Vance hadn't left the area after all.

"Proceed with your instructions," he told Elliott coldly.

A distance of twenty feet separated officer and enlisted man, reminding Nelson of the hilltop duels he had read about as a schoolboy. The good lieutenant would do well not to turn his back on *this* group, however, he thought.

"I'd like to jog with Two-Step here over to the aid station, sir, and check on my buddy, Sgt. Bro—"

"*Corporal* Brody is K.I.A., Fletcher." Vance's eyes had grown red as the sunset. "I just came from over there. Brody and a couple others. Never knew what hit 'em. Now get on with your duties as they've been assigned. You can attend the memorial services at dawn when they chopper the chaplain in from Mytho."

"But—"

"Get . . . on . . . with . . . your . . . duties." Vance rested a palm on the exposed butt of his holstered .45.

Grinding his teeth, Elliott Fletcher complied. But Vance had crossed the line. He'd crossed that thin line officers seldom returned to, and it was time. Time for Snakeman to nominate the lieutenant for induction into the fraternity of the frag.

CHAPTER 6

Nelson hadn't been in The Nam long enough to earn his Combat Infantryman's Badge yet, but as he and Snakeman Fletcher walked the two newbies through the LPs, he felt proud as a double-vet. Nelson "knew his shit," as the GI jargon goes. He loved his low-paying job as a grunt, and he enjoyed duty in South Vietnam. Adding to his confidence was the fact that he had quickly learned all there was to know about the compound outside Cho Gao. Familiarity bred confidence and job satisfaction, Nelson felt. He was a very happy buck private.

One of the few luxuries enjoyed by infantrymen in the boonies was watching the newbies sweat over the unfamiliar surroundings in which the vet felt so at home. It wasn't a luxury one indulged in for long: the faster you trained a pogue to adapt, the better your own chances of survival in the long run became.

But Nelson was truly enjoying this half hour of harassment and mindfuck he had allotted himself. "And this LP is Bravo-two-niner." He spoke quickly, nodding to the two PFCs unrolling their poncho liners against the threat of coming rain. The PFCs ignored Nelson's gesture, busying themselves with their preparations.

One man frowned for Fletcher's benefit. "You've got claymores set up there, there, and there." Nelson pointed at bushes in the distance. "Any movement in the free-fire zone not preceded by a radio authent' or password requires immediate response: you grab that claymore clacker and squeeze three times. Got that? Three quick times! Four, if'n ya need to. Squeeze it hard, like a whore's tit, until the damn thing blows."

Fletcher was ignoring Nelson's antics for the most part. The Snakeman was still upset that Lt. Vance had not allowed him to check on his best friend, Treat Brody. He stared off into the growing night, watching the ghostlike shadows dance below flares drifting beyond the barbed perimeter. For nearly fifteen minutes, Fletcher daydreamed about rolling a fragmentation grenade into the lieutenant's tent, only to realize the officer had been right. Brody had *bookoo* friends. Half the men in Echo Company considered him their "best." What should Vance do: allow the whole damned night shift to ignore their duties and tromp on over to the aid station with flowers? The Whoremonger was dead. Nothing was going to bring him back. Nothing.

You got just what you deserved, schmuck, Snakeman mentally reprimanded himself. Getting friendly with someone after all the double-vets his first week in-country had warned him against it. "Stay cool," they had warned. "Don't form any friendships; just be friendly and get along, so help will be there when you need it. But don't make any friends. It'll be all that much easier to accept death and loss when it strikes. And it will.

Fletcher wanted to drop a tear or two into the rice paddies of the Mekong Delta in honor of Brody The Whoremonger, but try as he would, they would not come.

Sgt. Zack found them near the farthest LP outpost an

hour later as he was making his 2100 rounds. "D'ya scrotebags get the word?" he asked in the usual monotone, his face a mask devoid of expression.

"The word?" Fletcher sounded drained of his usual limitless energy.

"About Trick-or-Treat."

"Brody?" Snakeman's eyes lit up.

"Yep. The skate ain't chasin' whores in hell after all. Just heard over the commo he's in ICU with some kind of nasty concussion, but he'll make it."

"But I thought . . ." Fletcher was nose-to-nose with Zack now.

"Yeah, me too. Vance told me Major Szell's rippin' some corpsman a new asshole for taggin' Whorehumper's toe and droppin' a sheet on his face without checkin' closer, but the medic claims our man Brody was cold meat, no doubt in his mind."

"Fuck."

"Yah. Typical meatlocker malfucktion. If he wasn't in the Green Machine, I'd tell him to sue." Leo laughed and started to walk away, continuing his rounds, but Fletcher grabbed him by the wrist.

"You gotta let me beat feet over there to see him, Leo. Just for a minute. Nobody'll even know, and—"

Zack laughed again, louder this time. "No way, Jose. It'd mean my stripes. That kid Vance is on the rag about somethin'. I don't know exactly what, but I don't wanna be in the crosshairs of a first-louie who's huntin' for bear. Do you, Snakeoil?"

Fletcher swallowed hard. It was a dry swallow, and it hurt. "Well, fuck me 'til it hurts." He gave his best Whoremonger impression, eliciting another chuckle from Leo the Lionhearted. "Don't this suck the big one."

"Life's a bitch, and then you fry." Zack started to turn away again, only to drop into a squat as all five of them were suddenly bathed in bright headlights.

The stocky sergeant's M-16 came up. "Douse them fucking headlights, Farney!" he yelled.

The company clerk frowned at his tactical blunder, extinguishing the bright yellow lights as soon as he realized he was illuminating an irresistible target for every Cong sniper within rifle range. But no tracers flew in over the wire this time.

"What the fuck you doin' cruisin' the perimeter with your lights on, anyway?" Nelson tore into the paper-shuffler, who outranked him by four stripes.

"I'm nightblind." Farney frowned but did not seem otherwise upset or repentant. "That's why I'm a clerk-'n-jerk an' not a grunt-'n-bear it. Anyway, the colonel wanted me to assign you guys a detail!"

Both Fletcher and Nelson groaned in unison.

Farney motioned behind him, and for the first time they all noticed two women sitting in the rear of the jeep.

Vietnamese women. Relatively *cute* Vietnamese women, Nelson observed. Snakeman eyed them suspiciously, but even with their lower faces wrapped in white cloth to protect them from the dust, Nelson recognized one of them as the housegirl who'd giggled almost seductively at him earlier.

Nasty Nel grinned mischievously.

Fletcher eyeballed the shovels Farney's passengers were carrying. "Bravo-two-one on the east perimeter reports a hole under the wire," the clerk advised Zack. "The bull wants a couple of your men detailed to escort these two lovelies over to the breach and keep an eye on them while they fill it up, then escort 'em back over to their quarters ASAP."

"Lucky youz." Zack waved a meaty forefinger at Nelson in mock warning. "But no goofin' off." His expression turned deadly serious as he glanced at his watch. "I'll be back around 2200 hours, and everyone better have their jockstraps and dixie cups in place. Is that clear?"

Fletcher slowly shook his head from side to side. "These are just cherrygirls anyway, Leo, with twats too tight to tickle. Give us some credit, will ya?"

While Zack was trying to determine how serious Fletcher was, the scramble siren atop Buchanan's CP began blaring in its irritating hi-lo manner. The peculiar pitch told the men standing in front of Zack that a Brass Monkey call was going out.

"Out!" Leo motioned the two Viet maidens from the vehicle. "You too, Farney!" he told the clerk.

"But I'm signed on to this jeep and—"

"You're now unsigned, specialist!" Zack turned to face Fletcher as he pulled Farney out and slid behind the steering wheel. "Come on, Snakeoil! I'll need you aboard *Peg*."

A Brass Monkey was a call for immediate assistance from the nearest American unit by a U.S. force or forces under attack and threat of decimation. It was an urgent plea for help that necessitated a seven-gunship response, minimum; more, if the post under siege could provide details as to the enemy's strength and the choppers were available.

"You can walk back to the CP," Zack told Farney as the Snake flew into the jeep's back seat. "And you!" Leo pointed at Nelson. "Take these two boots"—he gestured toward the new men—"and escort the work detail over to that hole in the wire!" Knowing he didn't need to wait for an acknowledgment, Zack was off in a cloud of smoke and swirling dust before Nelson could say anything.

He watched the jeep's dim red taillights fade in the murky distance, a twinge of jealousy coursing through him as he envisioned Snakeman behind his M-60, bringing smoke down on Charlie from the open gunship hatch.

Nelson turned to face the newbies. They both glanced away as he appraised their uniforms and build critically, helmets to jungle boots. Nelson was upset: he was missing out on the action, and stuck with a couple of pogues who didn't know their elbows from assholes. But, he decided reluctantly, Fletcher deserved the mission. Seven flesh wounds a couple months earlier had

46

demanded a touch-up in Tokyo, but to everyone's shock, Snakeman returned—after a little intoxication-and-intercourse in Bangkok, Thailand. You just couldn't keep a good grunt stateside, Nelson mused.

Movement to his side caught Nasty Nel's attention, and he glanced at the two women in long, unflattering, throat-to-ankle sarongs and tiretread sandals. The slender girl—the one who had caught his attention again by shifting her hips and her attitude while waiting impatiently for him to get this show on the road—winked at Nelson from within her mysterious cloth veil again.

Perhaps tonight would not be a total loss after all.

Nelson grinned, and he could tell by the movement of her high cheekbones behind the sheer cloth that she was smiling.

CHAPTER 7

Snakeman slapped a fresh belt of seven-point-six-two in the hog's mouth and slammed the lid shut, making sure the latch was in place. They were racing only a few meters above the treetops at over a hundred miles an hour, and Fletcher leaned into the heavy machine gun's buttplate, feeling good. He was back in his favorite slot, watching the Void's blur work its magic on the twinks crouched behind him nervously waiting to jump from the cabin when Gabriel set her down. There was no place else Snakeman would rather be, except perhaps between the amber thighs of a sleek and finely toned maiden from the Imperial City of Hue—their skills on blue satin and Thai silk were legendary; but even that might rate a close second place. Elliott Fletcher had never known a life with such satisfaction. And soon, he would be proving himself again, killing Cong in the heart of the rain forest, earning his flak jacket's Hog Heaven patch, and hoping for a chance at joining the Dirty Thirty—the hand-to-hand combat fraternity of which Brody The Whoremonger was the only surviving member. That he knew about.

"Como test, you assholes."

Chopperjock Cliff Gabriel clicked into the ship's intercom as he brought *Pegasus* down even closer to the jungle's gnarled triple canopy. Now and then the craft's landing skids would clip a branch or two, eliciting a charged chuckle and grin from Fletcher, a death's-head grin that sent shivers through the pogues preparing to jump out onto the LZ rising rapidly to greet them with jagged bamboo poles and hidden boobytraps. Boobytraps that were partial to the private parts.

"I hear ya lima-charlie, Gunslinger, hotel-mike?" Sgt. Zack plugged in and responded as he readied his M-16: Loud and Clear, How Me? Leo, his usually shaved crown sporting an afternoon shadow, was on the rebound himself, pampering a fresh thigh scar, souvenir of Ia Drang Valley. He too had refused DEROS back to The World.

" 'Bout time someone back there answered me," Gabriel replied angrily. "I been fuckin' talkin' to myself for the last two minutes: Lima Zulu in dirty-sex, ladies."

"Still a hot one?" Lt. Vance had clicked in too.

"Rodg your last, Lou," the warrant officer responded dryly, a few seconds after a glowing green tracer from the ground punched up through the cockpit floor, missing Gabe's left knee by inches.

"Hey *HEY*!" Zack shook his fist for Snakeman's benefit. Leo was nearly drunk on adrenaline now. He'd just swiped an entire crate of the new thirty-round banana clips from one of the crew chiefs in Alpha company, and was smiling like an army brat who'd bagged Santa Claus and stolen all his toys the moment the fat man came near the Christmas tree.

"Arghhh!" Broken Arrow, his crossbow slung upside-down over the back of his flak jacket, an M-79 thumper cradled across his forearms, crouched beside Zack, grunting like an ape preparing to tear the bars from his cage. Two-Step beat his chest with one hand and rose as treetops outside the hatch disappeared from view above the glittering whir of rotorblades.

Fletcher began yelling too, trying to help Two-Step psyche up the three new men waiting anxiously between

Vance and the other hatch gunny. Blood trickled from one of the twink's lower lip—he was not even aware he'd bitten through it. Fletch began his morbid Eenie-meenie-miney-moe in an attempt to guess which one wouldn't come back.

Pegasus was still ten feet off the ground when the shower of green-and-white tracers flew into the port hatch, opposite Snakeman. "Bank!" Zack was yelling, when he meant Turn!, but he wasn't even plugged in, and it didn't matter anyway: Gabriel sensed trouble and fanned to the left, nose cannon exploding over and over, each discharge jarring the ship slightly.

"Let's go! Let's go!" Zack was trying to usher the newby nearest the hatch out into the Void, but he wouldn't move forward. "I said, LET'S GO!" Zack grabbed him under the arms, finally realizing that the man was dead—a round through his heart.

Dead in The Nam with less than a week under his belt. K.I.A. in the murky Mekong River Delta.

The lieutenant had been hit, too. Fletcher saw the blood spray from his elbow when he was whirled around, back into the remaining two FNGs. But Vance was still on his feet, stumbling over the dead trooper, trying to jump down into the madly swaying elephant grass below the skids.

Snakeman had flipped two latches and was removing the big M-60 from its swivel mount, carrying it to the other hatch. The hog on that side was silent, its doorgunner missing his lower jaw, right arm, and a heartbeat.

The Snake nearly slid out onto the skids, so slick was the cabin floor with the dead gunny's blood. "MOTH-ERFUCKERS!" Fletcher was screaming at the top of his lungs as he rammed the MG's lifeline clip onto a steel rod running across the top of the hatch and began firing nonstop at the flashes in the treeline twenty yards distant. He didn't bother with his own monkeystraps. Snakeman had the feeling Gabe wouldn't be lifting *Peg* out of this one, that they'd finally dug their own grave near Cho Gao, and damned if he'd die in a scorching

50

ball of flames. Fletcher would fire into the muzzle flashes until he smelled the fuel leaking, and then he'd jump after Vance and the others, charge into the thrashing branches and . . . .

The helicopter's blades overhead changed pitch, beating furiously at the sticky air that plastered Elliott's hair against his forehead and flak vest to his back. The gunship was suddenly rising out of the tempest, nose dipping.

"Ho Chi Minh sucks donkey dick!" Fletch screamed as he leaned into the smoking, kicking, bucking M-60, aiming the barrel nearly straight down as Gabe rose rapidly above the treetops. Bewildered, Elliott glanced around as he continued firing. When had everyone jumped off?

They were all gone: Zack, Vance, the two surviving newbies. Between his boots, empty brass was piling up on the mutilated face of the dead gunny. The gold cartridges clinked about beneath his feet as Gabriel banked sharply, pulling away from the other chopper that had landed and ascended at the same time as *Peg*, only a few meters to her right.

"Fuck!" Snakeman yelled, releasing the M-60's pistolgrip handle and grabbing a huge protruding screweye as *Pegasus* rolled nearly onto its side. The momentum kept him in place even without the monkey straps holding him aboard, but his feet were slipping toward the open hatch. The Void knew, too. Fingers of wind whipped at his unbloused trousers, trying to snatch him back, pull him down into the angry, green hell. But then Gabriel was leveling the ship out and returning to the LZ, swinging around in a wide arc to provide cover fire for the remaining five Hueys attempting to land where *Peg* had disgorged her cargo.

"Get your shit together, Snakeskin!" Gunslinger's peter pilot had been monitoring Fletcher's troubles from the corner of his eye. "We're goin' back down for seconds."

"Don' worry about me, Mister!" He'd regained his

footing and was trying to drag a fresh ammo box of MG belts out from under one of the corpses. "Just point the port hatch toward Charlie, 'cause that's where the ol' Snake's gonna be bringin' smoke down on—"

A jarring explosion rocked *Pegasus* as she flew over the LZ. Fletcher nearly flew out the hatch again. And would have, had he not been lucky enough to clip his lifeline on another screw-eye as he was hurled across the cabin.

He stared down through the billowing black smoke to see one of the two choppers still on the ground lying on its side, bright orange and green balls of flame rising from its tailboom. Soldiers were climbing from the crumpled hatch, rolling to the ground, many without their weapons, and sprinting for the second ship, their bodies bent over and heads low.

"Sweet Jesus!" Fletcher watched a trooper, who'd been thrown from the helicopter when the first rocket-propelled grenade struck the fuel cell, hustle from beneath the melting tailboom, only to be engulfed in flames when his kerosene-soaked uniform ignited.

Putting the man out of his misery raced through Elliott's thoughts, but then Gabriel was banking sharply again, making room for the other prowling gunships, and brilliant stars in the sky close enough to touch filled the nearest hatch.

"What ya waitin' for, Snakeman?" Gabe The Gunslinger called back over his shoulder. "An open invitation?"

The mild sarcasm, meant to taunt and not be taken seriously, angered Fletcher anyway. "Shit!" he yelled over the roar of unceasing rotorwash. "You guys keep rockin' the boat, man!" The Snakeman took his job seriously, and it wasn't often one of the chopperjocks made him look bad.

"Hold onto your gonads, gunny," Gabriel said over the intercom in a monotone. "Here's your chance to prove you've still got what it takes!"

The last ship on the ground rose through smoke from

the exploding craft, and the clearing was finally open season.

"Cavalry on the whiskey!" the peter pilot clicked in. "The rest of it's a free-fire zone, Snakeman. Strut your stuff, fella!"

"Which way's whiskey?" Fletcher called out frantically; he'd lost his bearings on that last pass.

Gabriel was circling over the clearing in a tight, counterclockwise circle now, and Elliott finally had a clear shot of the entire area. He could still see the man on fire stumbling about, flames several feet high rising from his hair and shoulders, but the rest of the Americans had melted into the brush.

"Fuck!" He slapped the huge machine gun's hatch out of frustration. "*Mother*fuck!"

Then three or four black pajama-clad guerrillas rushed from the treeline and began bayoneting the burning cavalryman.

Fletcher, using his left hand to hold down the kicking barrel, directed a steady stream of hot lead down onto the Viet Cong. Every fifth round a brilliant red tracer, the bullets slammed into the communists' backs, knocking them all forward, off their feet. The walking corpse, smoke rising from his mortal burns, blood pouring from the blade wounds in his neck and belly, staggered off into the trees and collapsed.

Flames soon licked at the leaves and branches around the dead American, and more smoke blanketed the clearing as several low-lying bushes caught fire. The taller trees of the rain forest, however, were too moist this day to burn.

"That's four." The peter pilot was counting Fletcher's hits. "Time for some more!"

"Only four?" The Snakeman's evil grin finally returned, but in reply, Gabriel descended suddenly, swift and violently, and Elliott was forced to his knees in a painful squat.

"Say again?" The Gunslinger's smile could be felt in the ragged intercom static.

"Fucking chopperjocks," Fletcher muttered to himself. He'd pop a round or two into the cockpit if he didn't need some idiot to fly this damn whirlybird to his targets of opportunity.

"Wonder what the hell we were sent out here to save, anyway?" Gabriel's co-pilot scanned the clearing below as they took turns with the other gunships strafing the clearing's edge. "Haven't seen sign one of any GIs since we got here."

"Beats me, bumblebee." Gabe hovered off to one side, between two massive oaks and slightly behind a treeline of thick, golden bamboo.

"Ours is not to wonder why," Snakeman clicked in during a pause in the shooting.

"Ours is but to fuck or fry." The peter pilot sounded drunk on more than adrenaline.

"Or something like that."

"H-Hey, *right*!" Gabriel responded with a burst of minigun fire that tore several bamboo saplings in half.

"Shooting at anything in particular?" Fletcher watched birds three and four zip past, and knew it would soon be *Peg*'s turn to make another pass while the other glowing hatch hogs cooled down.

"There was a monkey climbin' up that one in the middle," the peter pilot advised him coldly.

"Oh."

"SHEE-*it*!" Gabriel flooded the turbine with power as several AK rounds stitched across the Plexiglass windshield, shattering much of it.

Pegasus rose into the night sky like a black cat whose tail has been stepped on. Fletcher fired madly at the source of enemy rounds, green tracers flowing from the top of a palm tree every couple seconds. The sniper fell from his perch, and Gabriel, using his lips, imitated the passing of gas as the last lone tracer arced up into the heavens. "Lucky shot," he mumbled into the mike.

An instant later, more automatic rifle slugs were coming from the same tree, however, and Gabe banked around swiftly and pounced from behind, decimating the tree trunk with mini-gun fire, 6,000 rounds per minute. *Peg*'s snout glowed for less than thirty seconds, then Gabriel took evasive action and banked in the opposite direction as the last of the palm fronds fluttered to earth.

"I think you showed him a thing or two thousand, Cliff baby."

"With you on that, clit-breath."

"Wait a minute!" Fletcher interrupted the pilots' mutual appreciation seminar.

"Wait a *what*?" Gabe The Gunslinger was running low on fuel and enthusiasm.

"Make another pass," Fletcher yelled into his headset.

"What? *Where*?" Irritation colored Gabriel's tone now, but he ascended slightly and began circling around. Snakeman rarely told him how to fly his ship unless there was a good reason for it.

"There!" he clicked in again. "Right there!" Fletch pointed straight down into a thicket of mahogany trees.

"I see it," Gabe muttered without emotion.

"There it is!" Fletcher began stomping his boots on the cabin floor as he swung the M-60 back and forth, looking for Cong to smoke.

"I said I fucking see it, Snake; mellow out. Not much we can do—"

"Pilot's dead," the warrant officer seated beside Gabriel observed.

"Yep. Get the mark!"

It was a small, black Loach, lying nose up halfway through the top layer of jungle canopy.

As *Pegasus* flew over, the multi-layered ceiling of trees shook violently and with a screeching cry, the helicopter slipped through its tangled floral net, only to be caught again by the middle layer of vines and branches.

The pilot side of the Loach's cockpit was smashed beyond recognition. The passenger's side door was wide open and smeared with blood.

"Air America?" the peter pilot asked Gabriel as they circled back three more times, waiting for more information from the C&C chopper hovering a mile above the battlefield.

"Probably," Gabe replied to his reference to the CIA's unofficial airlines.

He kept *Pegasus* far enough above the downed craft so that her rotorwash didn't cause the Loach to plummet any farther toward earth. The Agency might want to recover it, though Gabe was convinced the bird would never fly again. Right now, it was suspended about fifty feet above the ground, vines clinging to its warped and collapsed tailboom, an offshoot of the river directly under the precariously hanging craft. "Think it's gonna get dunked?"

"Yep."

"Hey!" Snakeman Fletcher was yelling in their ears again. "Did you guys see that?" Elliott was leaning out his hatch again, straining to spot something near the Loach.

"See what?" Gabriel was losing patience with his favorite doorgunner. He was losing patience with Snakeman, and the war, and the bodycount, and everything else associated with Indochina.

"Down there!" Fletcher pointed. "On that big branch running through the Loach's underbelly. Holding on or something. Looked like white meat!"

"White what?" Gabriel said as his co-pilot became suddenly busy with the radio.

"Snakeman's right." The warrant officer beside Gabriel sighed as another string of tracers zinged up toward them and *Pegasus* banked hard to the right, descending into a dark valley. "Better take us back around. Just got the poop direct from Disneyland East. There *was* white meat aboard that Loach. One of the dancers recruited by MACV to entertain the troops, amigo. The Brass Monkey was from the pilot flying her down from Saigon into the Delta. Was headed for a USO show in Mytho."

"A round-eye?"

"Aussie."

"Same-same."

"Fuck."

"You wish."

CHAPTER 8

That 1966 happened to be the Year of the Horse in the Chinese and Vietnamese lunar calendar was not at all lost on Corporal Treat Brody, for, as a cavalryman, horses had always played an important symbolic role in his military career. The First Air Cav Division combat patch on his right shoulder bore the likeness of a horse's head, and his favorite gunship was adorned with a winged Pegasus for good luck.

Now, Sgt. Brock was several rows of chairs in front of him, standing alone, arms beneath the golden robe raised horizontal with the rest of his body, head leaning back. The soldiers seated in front of Brock had locked hands with the men on either side of them, and their heads were bowed forward as an odd chanting tone filled the room.

There was an almost electric charge to the sound emanating from Brock's close-knit group of followers, and though Brody did not immediately join in, he believed.

The chaplain, knowing little about troopers from the airmobile ranks—his experience was mostly in dealing with rear-echelon support personnel assigned to units Mytho—had enthusiastically granted Brock's people use of the nondenominational chapel at the tall, imposing NCO's first request. The chaplain wasn't quite sure what it was all about, but these men all looked like respectable Christians, and the chapel had been so empty these last several months— ever since he had arrived in the Delta to replace the priest who'd been shot between the eyes by a VC sniper during church services a half year ago, in fact.

Treat Brody was not sure why the ghost of the great and legendary Vietnamese warrior Le Loi had chosen to visit the Americans, using Sgt. Brock as a medium. Brody was not fooled by cheap theatrics, which was what he considered Brock's flowing cape and facial expressions. He did not think Brock was anything more than a tall, powerful man who happened to be in the right place at the right time when an ancient warrior decided to return from the dead. But he did believe the unquiet spirit of Le Loi happened to choose the American sergeant, a mere mortal, to speak through, to make contact with this new contingent of soldiers fighting for his beloved land, Annam. That, Treat Brody could believe in. That, he needed to believe in. Finally, there was a reason for all the anguish and the suffering. It was destiny.

Brody had read about similar manifestations before. Some had been proven to be cruel hoaxes, where naive followers had surrendered their trust and their life savings. Others were simple cases of desperate people putting their faith in a madman with a split personality, who truly believed he was a voice for lost souls from the other world, needing to be heard by friends and loved ones one last time.

Brody did not feel Sgt. Brock fell into either one of these categories. Before the sapper attack at the hospital, he'd always dismissed Brock as just an attention-seeking over-the-hill jock draftee who got his jollies from leading his flock. Now, Brody was not so sure.

He did not know if he'd actually died while at the aid station. Nurse Hieu told him later that the plastic explosives blast had struck him with such force as to

59

possibly cause a traumatic condition of paralysis resembling cardiac arrest. Mere concussions usually did not have such severe results. All he knew was that he was down for the count until Brock pulled him out of it.

The ward had become a zoo after the sapper pulled the wire triggering his C-4 charge. Blood was everywhere, and a corpsman had checked Brody for vital signs, found none, ordered him wheeled out of the way, and rushed to the next victim.

When she burst through the double doors leading into the morgue, Nurse Hieu saw one of Sgt. Brock's men pounding on Brody's chest. And then Treat was suddenly sitting up, white as a ghost. It was as if he'd returned from the dead right in front of her.

Brody spent several hours thinking about what Nurse Hieu had said. But as the seconds ticked away, he found he was remembering less and less about his time "under the white sheet."

There was no doubt in his mind he'd experienced something unearthly. His bunk had been too close to the blast for him to have survived. If they'd wheeled him to the morgue, he must have been dead. Brody even had a faint memory of bright lights and voices. And then there was Sgt. Brock.

Brody was a reader. He read everything he could get his hands on: newspapers, newsmagazines, gossip rags, pulp paperbacks, and the classics. As a field soldier, there were many opportunities to break out the books, too. He considered himself somewhat learned, despite the lack of a college degree. Brody had read about patients who the doctors "temporarily lost" while on the operating table, only to be "brought back again." Some of them remembered nothing. Some had incredible stories to tell about the spirit world and a bright light they perceived to be the Supreme Being, the Creator. He wondered if he might not have gone through a similar experience.

The human brain was notorious for taking information received by the senses under inclement conditions and distorting it. Perhaps that was what had happened to him: In shock and gravely injured, he'd retreated into himself, surrendering to death, giving in to the irresistible invitation to be free once and for all of the problems that had plagued his life. Only to have one of Brock's goons bring him back.

That would explain some of it. But what about the feelings Brody felt for Sgt. Brock and his followers now? It was as if they were all blood brothers; as if, like Brock himself once said, they were a legion of one yet many "through Le Loi."

In Le Loi, Brody found both security and purpose. A reason for remaining in The Nam. He finally had something he could relate to: a legendary warrior who manifested himself through an American soldier who, in Brody's opinion, was no less courageous or cunning. There were weirder things he'd seen in the heart of the rain forest, stranger events transpiring in jungle darkness, miles from civilizations where meeker men than he gathered for protection from the beast.

Was the apparition calling itself Le Loi so much harder to accept?

Brody had tried to believe in a god. He investigated the teachings of Buddha, and delved in the occult, even lived with a "white witch" who taught him the only power on earth was the planet itself. Natural forces.

He tried desperately to find something to believe in, something to sustain him in Vietnam, something to help explain why he survived when others didn't.

Once he had thought he'd found the answer. It was while circling a particularly violent LZ in the middle of a notorious stretch of woods. The helicopter, descending rapidly as it looked for a fight, rolled onto its side through a sharp turn, and Brody nearly fell out the open hatch. Only his lifeline canvas ropes running from clamps in the chopper's wall to his web belt had saved him. The gunship's screaming rotors had clipped a dozen treetops, sending leaves and twigs and branches flying into the cabin. Brody and the other doorgunner just grinned and endured it; they knew Krutch The Stork was just toying with them. But the trees had bled all over Treat Brody that afternoon. Fresh sap splattered the cabin.

Krutch had brought *Peg* up above the treetops successfully, however, and Brody survived to challenge the Void another day. But it was after that LZ landing and the ensuing firefight, while they were returning to camp, when Brody was most moved by what he saw below: The trees seemed to be waving to him. Mesmerizing, hypnotizing him. The whore in the Void was trying to seduce Brody and left him feeling weird.

For weeks he refused to board *Pegasus* and return to the Void. It was not until he hiked into the jungle on foot, on his own, that he came to an understanding with the evil of that place, and was able to strap on his pistol belt and gunny's vest again. Surviving the Void became his religion; returning to her, over and over again, his addiction.

It was a never-ending dilemma. If the game ever played itself out, he knew he would die.

When he eventually reached Dirty Thirty status—successfully having engaged thirty of the enemy in hand-to-hand combat and survived the encounters—Brody's feelings changed. He knew he had won, and the power of the rain forest had lost its mystique.

Life in The Nam became insipid. Returning to The World would be worse, though. It would be suicide.

Brock gave him new hope. Le Loi, or whoever or whatever it was, existed. Whether he was truly a ghost, or just the embodiment of all the dreams and despair of 30 million dead Vietnamese, Brody didn't care anymore. He would follow the two of them until they proved unworthy of his attentions.

"Three wounds." Major Szell was standing beside him in the chapel.

"Yes, three," Brody whispered back as Brock and his followers continued their chanting.

"Two's the magic number, three's a charm. When are you going back?"

"I'm not." Brody stared straight ahead and locked eyes with Le Loi's spirit.

"Why did I have the feeling you'd tell me that?" Szell laughed without making either of them feel silly.

"I just extended for another six months."

"Yes, so Nurse Hieu's told me." Major Szell glanced up at the man in the gold robe and frowned. "Is it infatuation, Corporal Brody, or simply desperation?" The doctor sounded very sad now.

Brody felt him staring down at the back of his head. "Does it matter? I'm happy now. I'm still confused, and haven't completely figured it out yet, but I'm happy. I'm at peace with myself, and that's all that really matters, isn't it, Major?"

"Instead of extending another six months in uniform, you could have gotten completely out of the Green Machine, become a no-account civilian, and devoted all your time to worshiping this clown. You could make big bucks and give it all away."

Brody's confident smile faded. He was being singled out, only to be cast away with the fanatics, labeled a religious zealot now. "We don't worship Sgt. Brock, sir," he said patiently. "Le Loi, a long-dead warrior, is speaking to us, his fellow soldiers, through—"

Szell cleared his throat quietly. "You don't really believe that shit, do you, Corporal?"

"Everyone needs something, sir."

Szell paused a moment, then said, "Yes, I guess they do, Corporal Brody. I guess they do."

"Do you think I've gone insane, Major?" The question was barely audible above the unnerving hum in the room.

"No, son." The doctor sat down beside him. "I think you've been through a very traumatic experience, and you made the mistake of canceling your therapy sessions. Nurse Hieu says she misses you, believe it or not."

"Oh?" The grin returned to Brody's face, but he was not really interested.

"Yes. If I was, in fact, a few years younger myself," he smoothed back his receding grey hairline, removed his eyeglasses, and placed them in a shirt pocket, "I might consider tapping into that."

"Major?" Brody said, distracted by the chanting.

"Nurse Hieu. Some of the corpsmen tell me she's unusual for a Vietnamese woman: has got the hots for foreigners. 'Course, I'm sure she's just looking for a meal ticket out of this quagmire, but maybe that's all you really need to get you back on track."

"A hot and horny hole, sir?"

"Or a Numba One blowjob." Szell nudged him with an elbow. "You ever really looked at her close—Nurse Hieu, that is? Not much of a bottom, but what a mouth. And two knockers to rub your balls raw while she smokes your *ceegar*."

Brody just sighed and stood up. "Excuse me, sir," he said, feeling both annoyed and flushed, as if his father had just approached him about the birds and the bees. He walked to the altar without looking back at the major, and joined the others who were listening to Le Loi recount a particularly bloody battle his men had fought and won in the year 1413.

CHAPTER 9

"Orson's my name, orgasm's my game." The taller of the newbies reached out to shake Nelson's hand as the two Vietnamese women under his watchful eye began filling the hole beneath the perimeter fenceline. Orson spoke to Nelson, but his comment was obviously directed at the young, shapely girls.

Nasty Nel smiled. He liked this trooper's approach. "Wish *I* could think of introductions like that." He shook the private's hand, deciding to spring his pubic-hair collection on them later. Orson was taller than his partner and a bit stockier, with a black crewcut and a nose that had been flattened in more than a couple of fistfights, but definitely several years younger than the slender PFC with curly red hair and wire-rim glasses.

Nelson reached for the PFC's hand.

"Graham," the twenty-five-year-old said without conviction.

"First or last?" Nelson's smile remained intact.

"Does it matter?" Graham glanced away.

Nelson's smile faded. "Nope, I guess it really don't."

"How long you been in-country?" Orson asked.

"A few months," Nelson replied uneasily, shifting his

stance as if trying to watch the women closer.

"More than six months, or less?" Graham asked.

"Does it matter?" Nelson mimicked him, and Graham laughed loudly.

"Shit," he said. "You're just as much a Fucking New Guy as we are."

"Not quite, slick." Nelson wiped his lips with the back of his hand, mind drifting back to the dozen firefights he'd already survived.

Graham remained contentious. "My ass."

"At least he's not a draftee like you, huh, Nelson?" Orson folded his arms across his chest proudly. "Are ya, boy? I can tell. You're Regular Army, just like me."

"Volunteered for this shit, I must admit."

"Ha! I knew it." Orson slapped his knee.

"I think I'm gonna be sick." Graham turned away in mock revulsion.

"What about you?" Nelson asked, ignoring the older soldier.

"Hell, yes, brother. Dropped outta high school to enlist. Got a draft number of three-sixty-four and fucking proud of it, too!"

"What?" Graham whirled around.

"You heard me, numb-nuts."

"Three hundred and sixty-fucking-*four*?" Graham made as if to pull out his hair.

"Roger-dodger. Couldn't wait to get over here and chalk up a couple binks for the bodycount."

"That's 'dinks,'" Nelson corrected him softly.

"Whatever. Anything to spite the old lady. Really pissed her off, in fact; she still hasn't gotten over it." Orson began laughing as he moved closer to the women shoveling soft dirt into the fenceline hole.

"Your mother?" Nelson asked, thinking back for the first time in months about the stepparent who'd seduced him when he was but a boy.

"Yep. She's one of them anti-war nuts. Just got arrested last week for chaining herself to a recruiting office door and throwing red paint on the GIs inside."

66

"The drill sergeants?"

"Naw, the enlistees!"

"Bummer."

"Yeah. So I went down, called her from a pay phone after she got out of the slammer, and told her I was signing up too and was she gonna come down and throw red paint on me?"

"And what happened?"

"She came down and threw red paint all over me."

"Oh."

"And then she went to jail again. It was great!" Orson erupted into more laughter, reached down, and pinched one of the Vietnamese women on the bottom as she bent over to shovel some dirt.

Letting out a sharp, high-pitched shriek, the tiny bundle of sensuous curves whirled around and tried to hit him in the chest, but Nelson blocked the blur of a shovel.

"Whoa, lassy!" He grinned, glancing at the other, more peaceful woman, the one who had giggled at him earlier. "Meet Orson here. He didn't mean nothin' by it."

"Orson's my name, orgasm's my game!" He held out a hand, the girl with the sparkle in her eyes rattled off a ten-word sentence in rapid-fire Vietnamese to her friend, and the woman who'd been pinched promptly spat into Orson's soft palm.

"You think we don't know word 'orgasm'?" She bared her teeth. They were straight, white teeth, and Nelson felt himself growing hard.

"Well, if you don't, I was hopin' to explai—"

The woman raised her shovel again, and the slightest hint of a smile crept into her features as Orson backed away, hands raised in surrender.

"Okay, okay." Nelson's palms came up, too. "He's sorry." The encounter grew silent as seven gunships passed overhead with a roar of rotors and screaming whine of turbines.

"Okay." The offended woman's shovel jabbed dirt

again. "He sorry."

"Bookoo sorry." Orson had already picked up on some of the local lingo, but his hand came out again as soon as the girl glanced away. Nelson playfully batted it down.

"Oops." Orson grabbed his own wrist and wrestled with it for a second, as if it were a separate entity and he was unable to control its desires.

"So whatever happened with your old lady?" Nelson noticed a pile of torn sandbags beside a clump of bushes and sat down on them. "I mean, did she ever get out? Did she ever write to you in Basic or AIT?"

"Ha!" Orson laughed again. "The bitch disowned me."

Graham shook his head from side to side slowly. "You refer to your own mother as a bitch?"

Orson was not intimidated. "It's what she is: a commie-sympathizing whore," he amended his evaluation of her slightly.

Graham's eyebrows rose as he digested the harsh words. "Did you ever think that maybe it's just her way of trying to prevent her son from going off to war in a stinking country like this?"

"Shit! My old lady kept a poster of Ho Chi Minh on her bedroom wall, pal. My old lady is a card-carrying member of the Socialist Party. My old lady sent a box of dog shit to the Marines when they landed in Danang. My old lady loves Traitor Jane like a sister, for Christ's sake!"

The woman with the shovel glared up at Graham. "Vietnam no stink."

"Okay. Forget it!" He turned and stalked off toward the tree line.

"I wouldn't stray too far, Graham-cracker," Nelson warned. "There's claymores out there. And that's just what Charlie planted. We've got our own boobytraps out there somewhere, too."

"Zero-twenty-three." The draftee was muttering as he paced back and forth along the fenceline. "A draft number of twenty-fucking-three, and Uncle Sammy zapped me. Now I'm stuck with these two aspiring lifers, and—"

"So what does your old man think about your mom's antics?" Nelson asked Orson.

"My father? Shit, like I said, bro: she's a whore. Been screwin' every swingin' liberal dick to come along since I was old enough to remember. The old man finally got wise and blazed a trail—here to the Far East, in fact. Last I heard, he was shackin' up with some Filipina cutie on Mindanao, livin' in a bungalow on stilts at the edge of some picture-postcard lagoon."

"Born of a whore." Graham had returned, but he was still talking to himself.

Orson ignored the taunt and its implications. He chose to fuel his smile instead. "I do write her, though. Nearly every week. Pen my correspondence as if we were the best of buddies, you know, telling her everything: my most personal feelings, my triumphs and tribulations, my failures and fuck-ups—the whole crock o' shit. I'm sure it really pisses her off. Least I hope it does."

"You really crack me up, Orson," Nelson said. "You know that? I think we're gonna get along just fine."

Slinging his rifle, Nasty Nel succumbed to a sudden idea, and, stepping down into the sapper hole, gently relieved the woman with the sparkling eyes of her shovel. She hadn't been using it anyway—just leaning against the handle and watching her friend do all the work, mainly—but it was obvious in her surprised expression she appreciated the gesture. "Allow me, ma'am," Nelson said.

"Well, thank you, sir," she replied, and all three Americans glanced her direction at the accent: had she really used a Southern twang?

Nelson laughed suddenly. The joke was on them.

She must have worked around Americans before, he decided, wondering how long it would be before he got into her pantaloons.

"My name is Nasty," he told her later, after the sapper hole had been filled and Farney had signed out another jeep and come looking for them. Farney took Orson and Graham back to the sea of green tents that was the 7th Cav's new home, and Nelson walked the two women back to the ramshackle villa in the center of camp where the civilians had been allowed to stay.

"Nasty?" She cocked an eyebrow at him but did not wink, as he'd hoped she would.

The younger girl had pinched his cheek and warned him in pidgin English to behave, before she disappeared behind the dwelling's doors alone twenty yards away. Now, Nelson wondered if the woman standing in the palmtree shadows with him knew what "nasty" really meant.

"Do you know why?"

"Do I know why what?" A puzzled look creased her nose—a nose that was lowlander flat yet flaring in a sexual way that kept him excited. Her hand came up to brush a speck of floating ash from the Arvin curfew fires that had landed on his cheek.

"Do you know why I ask you to stay with me awhile tonight? To talk and . . . just be together."

"I think I know," she said softly, glancing away shyly, as if to watch the flares floating on the horizon, and Nelson found himself comfortable with this woman. He did not have to speak pidgin English with her. She was nearly fluent and, he guessed, more educated in the ways of the world than she let on. "But it is not my place to say. You are man, I am woman." She giggled softly, but it was more a shy, ladylike titter than the sound a schoolgirl might be expected to make. "Why don't you tell me?"

He reached for her tiny hand. It was cool to the touch, and she slid out of his grip, choosing to fold her arms under a swell of modest breasts. "I'm not really sure. I am lonely because of the job I have here. I only see soldiers, all day, all night. But I am not that kind of person. I need to talk. With a woman, from time to time."

70

"You need an all-nighter from time to time," she corrected him. The sly, knowing grin crept in again as she stepped back a pace, pretending to survey his looks and intentions again in a new moonlight.

At least she hadn't said You need a quickie, Nelson decided, or You need a sucky-fucky five-dollar blow job. "All-nighter" was not much better, granted, but at least the words coming from her lips did not seem so vulgar.

He rested his own hands on his hips in mock challenge. "Let's start with your name."

"Anna." She tilted her head to one side to gauge his reaction.

"Anna?" Nelson's own features contorted in thought, and he rubbed at the whiskers along his chin in feigned confusion.

"You think it is not a good Vietnamese name?" she teased.

"It is American," he said bluntly, voice lacking the admiration she had expected to hear.

"Maybe it is Chinese." She drew closer, sensing she was losing his interest.

"No." Nelson's eyes dropped to the earth, and he shook his head slowly, looking disappointed. "It is—"

"I worked for the Americans before," she finally admitted, turning her back to him as if revealing she'd had a child out of wedlock. In Vietnam, an Americanized name was nearly as bad to some people.

"Oh, I see."

"Sec'tary," she added quickly, as if that would grant her some degree of respectability.

"Ah, of course. That's why you speak English so well."

"You think I speak well?" She moved a bit closer. A flare popped overhead, drifting away quickly with the warm, humid breeze, and when it broke free of its parachute, plummeting to earth, he realized she'd draped a hand over his wrist.

"At least you don't cuss." He smiled, watching the

71

jagged silver trail of smoke left by the flare against the night sky.

"Well, *shoot!*" She hissed in surprise as another flare popped directly above them once more. Again, the breeze caught the silk umbrella over the flare, whisking it away before they were illuminated.

"'Shoot' is not a cuss word," he said in jest, feeling again the coolness of her hands. They were actually ice cold, and he thought about what Brody The Whoremonger, an avowed expert in such matters, had once told him: Cold flesh is good, he'd said. Means they're clean. Watch out for skin that's hot to the touch: means they're claptraps, sure as shit. Well, other in-the-know types, such as Snakeman Fletcher and Two-Step the Comanche, might argue that point, but it was a warning that had stayed with Nelson these last couple months. Anna's hands were like ice.

"*Choi-oi!*" she gasped as still another flare rocketed up from the guard tower a hundred yards away. "Damn *cao bois!*"

"Now, 'damn' *is* a cuss word, but I'll pretend I never heard it." He glanced over at the bored teenaged tower guards playing with their army-issue bottlerockets.

"Do you like Anna?" She moved so close their chests were touching now, and she gazed up into his eyes.

You're spoiling it, he said to himself, disappointed that she was suddenly coming on to him so fast. Or was it really a come-on? "Your hands are cold," he found himself saying. "Very cold."

Anna's smile disappeared. "I am sorry." Her face dropped. "Cold woman not good for American man, no?"

"That's not what I meant at all." His fingers went to the bottom of her chin, lifting it.

"I understand." She started to back away, but he held her against him and started to remove the veil from around the lower half of her face.

"No." She grabbed his wrist, but the clasp was already free, the cloth falling away.

"Anna," he said softly. Then sadly, as the veil dropped to reveal a long, razor-thin scar along the bottom edge of her chin. It was about three inches long, but barely noticeable in the crescent moon's silver glow.

"I go now." She tried to pull away again, but Nelson was holding onto her firmly, prepared for her move to flee.

"Why?" he asked with genuine disappointment in his tone, and she picked up on this, looking back up into his eyes again, worry creasing her high cheekbones.

"You are not offended?" She tried to bring the veil back up, but he was holding both her wrists against the small of her back as he pulled her closer.

"By what?" He stared into her eyes, not at the scar, but in his mind he saw her running from the Cong as a child, or maybe a teenaged girl, her shredded clothes falling from her as women-hungry guerrillas chased her down, slashing her with a bayonet or machete.

Anna freed one of her hands and ran a fingertip along the scar. "By this," she said matter-of-factly.

Nelson swallowed, but he did not think she noticed— she was too busy fighting back tears. "It makes you look worldly," he said quickly, without pausing, feeling suddenly stupid.

" 'Worldly' make Anna sound like tramp," she challenged him, feigned fire in her dark, sloe eyes.

"That's not what I meant at all," he said, and shook his head defensively.

Anna frowned skeptically. He brought his cheek close to hers and ran his lips against her ear. Anna's entire body seemed to contract and twist slightly at the intimate caress, and Nelson whispered, "American men . . . soldiers, we like our women tough looking, but not too tough." His hand dropped, moving along the firm swell of her haunches.

"Vietnamese women," she cooed hesitantly, "we don't own leather."

Her words conjured up images of an expensive prostitute wearing slick black and snapping a whip at some john chained to a brass bed. "What I meant was, when I saw your face, I was not upset."

"You were not offended?" The brilliant stars overhead reflected in her jet-black eyes when she looked up into his again.

"No, not offended. When I saw your face, I saw a woman with a rifle . . . a freedom fighter, living in the rain forest . . . hard as nails and tough as a tigress, yet soft to her man . . . soft *for* him, when he needed her most . . . when the homeland no longer came first. The two of them together in their thatched hut deep in the heart of the jungle, lying side by side, sharing each other's dreams."

When he had finished, Anna cocked her head slightly for his benefit, grinned impishly as if unsure about the speech, then said, "I think you the most *dinky-dau* American I ever listen to!"

They both laughed.

Movement behind Nelson startled Anna, and her lips drew back as a huge shadow fell across them both. Nelson whirled around, his pistol already out of its holster, but metal scraped against metal, and a black man twenty years his senior and a hundred pounds heavier casually knocked the barrel to the side, using an M-16's muzzle. "Well, excuse the fuck outta me!" the giant silhouette lowered his own weapon.

"Sgt. Zack!" Nelson holstered his automatic.

"Where'd *you* get a .45?" the NCO asked. But he appeared more curious about the woman as he rose up onto the tiptoes of his unauthorized jump boots, peering over Nelson's shoulders.

"Lawless got it for me on the black market his last trip to Saigon, Sarge," he explained.

"Hhmph." The NCO seemed upset this mere enlisted man was carrying a weapon normally reserved for officers or MPs. "What's with the bitch?"

And then another flare popped overhead, and Nelson noticed for the first time that he was not speaking to Zack at all, but another crew chief—one of the much-disliked, brown-nosers from Headquarters Company who'd been banned from flying slicks because of his weight and reduced to shuffling transfer orders and busy work rosters. "You're not Sgt. Zack," he said stupidly.

"No shit, Sherlock," came the gruff reply. "Never said I was." The man smelled of days in the boonies. "Now answer my question: What's with the cunt?"

"She's not a cunt." The words slipped from him before he could keep silent.

"Spare me the heroics, kid. A hole is a hole." He tried to move Nelson aside for a better look, but the grunt stood his ground.

"Don't push me, Sarge!" The private snapped.

"Don't 'push' you? Hey, kid, I'll fucking *kill* you for talkin' to me like that. Now—"

"What's the problem?" Two First Division MPs appeared behind the NCO. Cradling M-16s in their arms, they wore bored expressions that said they'd seen it all before.

Nelson was both relieved and tense. He *was* in a restricted area. "This guy is tryin' to—" he started to say, but the sergeant turned around, blocking the shafts of moonlight and his words.

"What problem?" He grinned at the no-nonsense military policemen. "There's no problem here."

Both MPs were slender, but they stood over six feet— one was taller than the NCO—and they had that look in their eyes, that fearless look, that impatient and wary, tired and weary look that warned the NCO they'd spent time in the sticks, too, and worse: battled the drunk-on-adrenaline grunts that floated out through the bamboo from steaming battlefield victories, eager to fight the despised REMFs—Rear Echelon MotherFuckers. Only it didn't quite work that way in the Green Machine. And they were NCOs, buck sergeants on roving patrol, prowling for problems, bored with the routine of garrison duty in Cho Gao yet unwilling or uneager to soil their uniforms or scuff their boots over a no-show

75

idiot's antics and bravado.

"There's no problem," the black sergeant repeated.

"Then I do believe it's time you take a hike, sergeant." One of the MPs stepped forward, slung his rifle over a shoulder, and folded his arms across his chest.

It was obviously meant to be a silent challenge, and though he was impressed, Nelson wasn't sure these guys—even two of them together—could take him.

"This area is off limits to unauthorized personnel," the second MP said, raising his voice for the hesitant NCO's benefit.

The first MP repeated, "I think it's time for you to take a hike."

The black NCO glanced back at Nelson, ignoring the woman now, then shook his head violently and stalked off into the night, muttering, "Mo'fucking REMFs!"

After he was gone, Nelson wrapped an arm around Anna's shoulder, pulling her close. "Thanks," he said quietly as one of the sergeants shined a flashlight briefly in their faces.

Dousing the light, the MP did not return the grin. "I take it you're authorized personnel," he grumbled skeptically, a set of handcuffs already sparkling in his palm. He swung them around and around in mild anticipation, waiting for the right answer.

"Actually, Sarge"—he swallowed hard again, and Anna, hearing his anxiety, squeezed his hand for support—"I was assigned to escort a work party out to the fenceline to fill in a sapper hole, and—"

"We know," the MP swinging the handcuffs interrupted him. "We were the ones that called the breach in. That was hours ago, friend."

"He good man." Anna suddenly spoke up, patting Nelson's stomach affectionately. "No try nothing."

Both sergeants immediately broke into smiles. Nelson was quick to add, "I was just escorting her to her hooch over there, Sarge. Really."

"But you just stopped under the palm trees here to hold hands *tee-tee*, eh, kid?" The MP replaced the handcuffs in their black leather case on his web belt.

"Come on." The other MP's grin grew as he motioned his partner to leave the two alone. "The kid's already deeper in trouble than he knows." Turning to Nelson, he added, "Good luck, son; you're gonna need it!"

Leveling an accusing finger at the private, the other NCO sad, "Better behave, boy. 'No try nothing.'"

After they left, Nelson rushed her over to the large villa where the Vietnamese civilians lived. He had abandoned all thoughts of trying to spend the night with her.

Anna held onto his arm after he opened the huge double doors leading into a courtyard, then made as if to leave hastily. "Please," she whispered, the look in her eyes a desperate plea for him to remain a moment more. "I'm sorry if I cause you trouble, Nasty."

She spoke the nickname seriously, forgetting the humor in it. "Yeah . . . Nasty trouble indeed, if I hang around. You don't mess with the MPs in Nam, honey. If Treat Brody my buddy taught me one thing, it's you don't accept an MP's first warning lightly, 'cause the second one's liable to be nightstick splinters in your head, and a one-way ticket to the monkey house."

"Monkey house?" She was still gripping his hand like a steel vise.

"It's a long story, Anna." He lifted her hand to his and, trying to slow his breathing, gently kissed her knuckles.

Concern about the military police drained away in an instant. Suddenly, he saw the look deep in her eyes, then tears appearing along the edge of one eye.

The tears were streaming down her cheeks now, collecting along the bottom of her chin, along the scar, before they dropped onto his wrist. Like lonely raindrops falling from a roof's edge, down onto an uncaring street.

"Do you want to see me more?" she asked softly, tracing hearts on one side of his face with her finger-

77

nail, as she stared up into his eyes.

"I want to see more of you," he found himself saying. He gently pushed her back through the doorway where they had been standing. "Tonight." He glanced over her shoulder, into the dark and peaceful courtyard.

An old French fountain rose gracefully in the middle, but there was no running water, only a squalid pool filled with leaves, beneath a naked marble maiden. Vines covered the four walls enclosing the courtyard, and what appeared to be a garden decorated one corner with cucumbers and bright flowers. A dim, yellow lantern burned in the lone window along the opposite wall, and silver shafts of moonlight lanced down from above, throwing a dreamy and romantic glow across everything. A door beside the lantern led into the living quarters surrounding the courtyard. Nelson stared at it. "Tonight," he repeated, and lowered his face against hers to nibble at an ear.

But Anna stood her ground. Gently, she pushed him away, then backed into the courtyard and hid behind the partially closed doors. Her face peeked out, barely visible, and she said, "It would not be respect'ble for me to let you in." She smiled, nodding as if helpless to invite him further.

"You . . . teased." Nelson's expression soured, and he glanced at his watch.

"If you truly like Anna," she whispered, glancing around to make sure there was no one within the courtyard, "you will come back."

Nelson smiled again, returning to her until they were separated by only the doors' inner edges. "To court you in the courtyard?" Now *he* was taunting.

"Yes." She sighed, relieved his reply had not been an angry one, powered by his disappointment.

"Very well. I will come back. Tomorrow afternoon." He moved even closer, until they rubbed noses briefly, in the traditional Vietnamese fashion. "Plan for a picnic."

"A picnic?" Her eyes lit up, and he saw the reflection

of a falling star in their depths.

"Yes, down by the river. I'll borrow a jeep. You pack the food."

"Yes! I will." She beamed eagerly.

"Vietnamese style."

"I cannot cook hamburger and hotdog." she laughed in her high, singsong voice, and Nelson felt a warmth course through his veins.

"May I have a goodnight kiss?" The request announced he was leaving.

Anna flung the doors open and wrapped her arms around his neck, but she did not kiss him. Not immediately. She hugged Nelson as he had never been held before, and finally, after several seconds, she pulled the side of her face from against his chest and looked up into his eyes.

"I want to share your dreams," she said softly, whispering into his ear as she rose up on tiptoe. "I want to hold you tonight, hold you to my breast, and never fall asleep for fear I will lose the precious feeling. I want to hold you tightly, and if I fall asleep inside your arms, I want to join you in your dreams."

And then she pulled him inside, and quietly closed the courtyard doors.

CHAPTER 10

Using hand signals and the slightest movement of three fingers on his right hand, Zack directed Lee, Cordova, and Two-Step past him and, fanning out ahead, into three separate furrows through the bamboo. Sgt. Leo Zack wasn't quite sure how the furrows got in the tall wall of green and gold, but he damned well wasn't going to use the main trail.

Time was of the essence, however, and after two more troopers rushed by, swift, silent, and deadly, and a half dozen gunships roared past a break in the thick jungle canopy overhead, Zack checked his compass one last time, motioned the rest of the cavalrymen to maintain their positions along the riverbank, then disappeared through the trees after First Squad.

The Brass Monkey rescue attempt had been a romeo-foxtrot: a no-show, to say the least. They'd found nothing in the rain forest clearing except an incensed platoon of NVA with no sense of humor.

After fighting their way out of the encounter—and losing a chopper and seven men in the process—they regrouped on the west side of the smoke-enveloped clearing, preparing to evade a larger and hostile enemy force prior to Chinook extraction somewhere down the river, only to have Gabriel The Gunslinger radio them that the source of the help call had been located. It was a downed Loach helicopter, carrying a blonde USO entertainer, lodged in the middle layer of jungle canopy immediately east of the initial LZ. The pilot was confirmed K.I.A. visually by Gunslinger, and Zack was radioed the coordinates and advised to give it his best shot. The Loach was hanging precariously over a swift-running branch of the Mekong River, well known for its communist barge and sampan traffic.

Zack approached a break in the bamboo before he noticed the team had taken cover. He almost tripped over Lee, so well was the short, compact trooper camouflaged.

Leo ducked behind some bamboo saplings just as a file of Vietnamese, wearing pith helmets, jogged past beyond the break in cover up ahead.

Cordova watched the dim AK-47 silhouettes pass by in the green mist, then began writing on a small notepad he silently withdrew from a thigh pocket of his jungle fatigues. The notepad had olive-drab pages. He wrote in black ink, slipped the page from its subdued iron holder, and handed it to the sergeant.

Zack read quickly.

> In the canopy fifty meters beyond
> the break in bamboo: Loach at 11
> o'clock. Charlie trying to get
> to it too.

Zack removed a small metal packet from his flak jacket pocket. It looked like an o.d. green cigarette case, but opened up into an army-issue set of folding binoculars. He scanned the canopy, spotted the dangling Loach, sighed at the impossibility of reaching it from the ground, started to lower the field glasses, then did a quick double take.

"Sweet Jesus," he muttered under his breath.

The men closest to him turned: it was unheard of for Leo The Lionhearted to break rules of silence in the sticks. Zack made a gesture universally known to represent the vivacious and seductive curves of an exceptionally well endowed member of the opposite sex.

Broken Arrow motioned for the binoculars, but Zack already had the lens back up against his bulging eyeballs.

He scanned the huge branch fifty feet off the ground until he found the mangled helicopter again, then worked his way to the left until he spotted the white woman.

She couldn't be more than twenty-five years old, he decided. She had a Las Vegas showgirl figure, accentuated by the tears in her tight-fitting safari suit. One pantsleg had been ripped away midway up the thigh, and all the buttons along the front of the khakied shirt were missing. She had the blouse tucked in, with the bottom pulled together inside the snakeskin belt, but there was no hiding her breasts, bouncing about and struggling to push free each time she slipped while trying to maintain her footing on the rain-slicked branch. At least there was no blood in evidence, Zack was happy to see.

The woman was trying to make her way back and forth along the branch ahead of a long bamboo pole two Vietnamese on the ground were trying to prod her off with. The pole was long, buoyant, and hard to control. The guerrillas were not having much success. She was easily staying ahead of them, and simply kicking the pole away whenever it swayed toward her.

Zack watched one of the Hueys hover briefly over the break in the canopy through which the Loach had plunged. Concentrated ground fire from several different locations along the riverbank flew up in response, but the pilot had anticipated the green tracers and banked off a moment after he appeared. A sleek, shark-snouted Cobra darted overhead an instant later, nose low, tailboom up, and fired several rockets down into the communists' ranks.

82

A grenade exploded on the ground, and Zack's people all flattened prone in the rotting jungle floor as shrapnel peppered their positions.

"No way." Two-Step was beside him now, whispering. Zack had to read his lips because the rolling concussion had left them all with a ringing sensation in their ears. "No way can we get to her. We're outnumbered ten to one. She ain't worth it, honcho-san, just ain't fucking worth it."

"Thing I can't understand," Zack replied matter-of-factly, "is why they don't just shoot her lily-white ass! They obviously don't care if she dies, judging by the way they keep tryin' to knock her off her perch."

"A fall from that height would definitely be morgue city," Two-Step agreed.

"*Christ*!"

Someone stepped on Zack's ankle, and he spun around, preparing to backhand whichever newby had been stupid enough to—

A startled North Vietnamese soldier towered over the cavalrymen lying against snake-infested logs.

"*HOLY SHIT*!" Lee sprang up, forgetting to pull his rifle from the pile of leaves he'd dropped it into during the grenade explosion.

Despite the pain in his ankle, Zack shot forth too. As Lee went for the throat, trying to strangle the NVA private, Leo The Lionhearted slashed with his commando knife, ripping the man's belly open.

Blood gushed forth as M-16s behind him erupted on either side, blasting away on rock-and-roll. Red glowing tracers raced past Zack wildly. He watched Em-Ho Lee stumble off into the bamboo, yelling war cries at the top of his lungs and still trying to strangle the already dead Vietnamese, quite unaware the man's insides were plopping out onto the ground everywhere they danced. Zack watched Em-Ho disappear through the murky haze and sea of saplings, then he charged the first enemy soldier to appear where they'd been laying dog.

Bullets from Cordova's and Two-Step's M-16s punched several mean-looking faces back out of his reach, but Zack finally latched onto a North Vietnamese. He ripped the teenager's Adam's apple out with the crimson-coated blade, threw him aside, grabbed another, jabbed, slashed, and punched, then reached for a third. A rifle butt suddenly connected with the side of his head.

Stunned, Zack staggered a moment, then regained his footing in time to watch Lee rush past again. Zack dropped to his knees as a burst of green tracers tore into a tamarind tree where his upper torso had been only an eyeblink earlier.

Fanning from left to right with his rifle on full AUTO, Corky Cordova took out the six NVA who'd fired at the big crew chief, sidestepped a bayonet-thrusting twenty-year-old from Tonkin, shot the man in the back of the head as an afterthought, then kicked another charging Regular in the groin and slammed a knee into his nose on the way down.

Cordova felt his knee drive cartilage up through the skull into brain matter. The Vietnamese was dead before he collapsed onto his back in the leech-infested leaves.

A virtual hornet's nest of hot, stinging lead flew back and forth from both sides for nearly a full minute. And then, except for a few sporadic shots nearby, it was suddenly quiet.

Zack heard ammo magazines being switched all around as he slammed a fresh thirty-round clip into his own rifle. Everyone ducked when a U.S. gunship passed so low over the treetops that severed branches showered down on the soldiers. Then the nonstop firing resumed with a vengeance that made Zack, for the first time since arriving, wish he'd never herd of Vietnam.

Miraculously, none in his squad were hit, except for the routine splinters of hot, ricocheting lead in thighs and elbows.

"One left!" Lee was running down between them in a

84

crouch. "There's only one of the motherfuckers left, and I know *RIGHT* where he is!" He began firing four- and five-round bursts from the hip.

"Em-Ho!" Cordova and Two-Step both called out at the same time.

"Cover 'im!" Zack yelled, directing his own aim at the clump of logs where he'd spotted the only move- ment during the last few gulps of hot, sticky jungle air. Licoricelike gunsmoke lining his lungs as his chest heaved, the crew chief rose to one knee for a better look when a lone, wild round struck him over the right breast.

"Leo!" Cordova watched him fall back out of sight like a limp rag doll.

Lt. Jake Vance waved his contingent of gunship troopers up to the riverbank, motioning every two or three helmets for everyone to stay low. He wasn't sure what Sgt. Zack had run into a hundred meters to the northeast, but the flak was sure flying. Every now and then a chunk of shrapnel or stray round from the pitched battle would sail over to Vance's position.

He had lost two men already, the first to a wild ricochet from Zack's firefight, and the second from loss of blood when he stumbled into a punji pit and two of the urine-soaked stakes pierced his aorta.

It had been agreed upon via radio communications on the way into the LZ: Vance would take two chopper- loads of troopers into the whiskey (west), Zack would take another two toward the November (north), and an Alpha Company captain would take the rest in a direc- tion due south (sierra). The captain was one of the first men killed in the exploding gunship, which rolled over onto its side and burst into flames, and Vance wasn't sure where the other two cabinloads of legs were.

Now, Zack wasn't answering his prick-25, and the only thing left to do was move toward the Loach's position along the riverbank, exactly as the Vietnamese had done—and right on their heels.

"Lieutenant!" One of the enlisted men whispered harshly, and when Vance turned to motion for silence, he heard the straining, smoke-belching motor and saw the communist gunboat racing toward them on the water.

"Everyone down!" he ordered, not convinced they'd been seen yet. But the American-made PBR's deckgun popped a circle of silver smoke, and before the discharge even reached them, the shell slammed into the riverbank below.

They were standing on a low cliff, twenty or twenty-five feet above the riverbank at the highest point, with gullys running up it that could be scaled by any commando in top shape. One of Vance's men crawled over for a look. "Kiss your asses goodbye!" he heard a cocky buck sergeant announce as the thump of two more discharges reached them," 'cause the next one's gonna be right on tar—"

An ear-splitting screech ripped through the air currents buffeting the cliff's face, and the Americans watched, slack-jawed, as a LAW projectile rose from the riverbank below and, trailing a bright plume of smoke, rocketed across the rapids toward the captured vessel. The Light Anti-tank Weapon struck the gunboat head-on at about the same time Vance's men proned out for cover again.

Two shells from the PBR's deckgun slammed down amidst the cavalrymen, right on target, but one was a dud. And the second came down directly on top of a treetop, shattering the trunk fifty feet up but doing little harm to the grunts hugging the ground.

Vance, as if doing an exhaustive one hundredth push-up, slowly forced his upper torso up out of the rotten leaves and decaying animal matter, just in time to see several seriously wounded Vietnamese tumble off the crippled gunboat as it sputtered around in a tight circle on its side, sinking swiftly.

"Fucking A!" One of the new arrivals rose to his knees and threw up a fist as the vessel's nose suddenly flipped into the air. Its engine flooded, the craft went under completely, leaving behind an oil slick and a layer of blood.

Vance watched giant bubbles rush to the surface, with little sign of abating. He slowly shook his head, wondering what had happened to her American crew, and wishing he'd gotten the bow ID numbers before she capsized.

The newby who threw up his fist in one final salute uttered an unintelligible exclamation and suddenly dropped back into the dust. He was urgently waving the lieutenant over to the cliff's edge.

Muttering irritably under his breath, Vance slid a fresh ammo clip into his rifle, recalling enviously how Zack had flashed his recently bartered and chromed thirty-round magazines at him back at camp but never offered to share any. He glanced around at the treelines, trying to resurrect the survival instincts from a nauseous gut, then sprinted over to the private's position.

The moment he plopped down beside the man, several black hoods suddenly rose from the cliff's edge. Vance's brain automatically counted over five before his motor command overruled a moment of hesitation and brought up the M-16 barrel.

By then it was too late.

CHAPTER 11

Brock stared down at his followers. His eyes roamed the room until they came to rest on the new one. The former NCO. Corporal Treat Brody.

Brock wasn't quite sure what to think about the young man. He was quiet, showing little of the enthusiasm displayed by the others. Which meant absolutely nothing. The silent types often made the best representatives, and were usually the bravest warriors, with the least bravado. Yet, there had been that period of time early on when he'd suspected Treat Brody might even be a plant. A spy. An agent of sorts, sent into the ranks to disrupt the group and gather intelligence about Brock's true goals at the same time. But if there had been misgivings early on, Le Loi had set his mind to rest. The important thing was to help the men survive their trips into Void Vicious, to give them something to have faith in, and to instill a comradery and brotherhood where there had been none before. That was how warriors endured. That was how they came back from the rain forests with their sanity and their faith and their priorities intact.

Sgt. Brock looked down at Treat Brody, who stared back without either skepticism or contempt in his eyes. Only a yearning to understand. And make contact.

Brock was not sure any of his followers had actually seen Le Loi as he, Brock, was able to see him, for the manifestations were purely spiritual, always in Brock's mind. It was as if Brock was on mind-altering narcotics during the sessions. Or how he envisioned such "trips" must be, for Sgt. Brock had never even smoked a single marijuana cigarette despite the easy availability of high-grade Buddha sticks and Thai hash in The Nam.

True, he felt his own voice change when Le Loi took over. The men always claimed afterward that when Le Loi spoke, Brock's voice became gruff and much deeper.

Brock raised his arms, feeling the power grow stronger in the pit of his chest. He leaned his head back, closed his eyes, and saw Le Loi. He was just as the ancient Vietnamese war hero looked in the drawings at the Saigon library, except that now the spirit's likeness was not bright oils on velvet but brilliant and shifting outlines of electricity floating in front of his mind's eye. Outlines that were a man's face, and, strangely enough, as warm and human and lifelike as if Brock were looking into a mirror.

Le Loi spoke to him. "Your company is in the bush now, pursuing the enemy along the Mekong, outside Cho Gao, and attempting to help a woman in trouble."

Treat Brody listened to Sgt. Brock speak as Le Loi. He was always amazed at how eerie the tall NCO's voice became, and how frightened yet safe and protected Brody himself felt when the room seemed to fill with a certain power. Was it something Brock projected mentally? Was it simply a subtle form of mass hypnosis? If Brock was a fake, then he was a very good actor.

Treat Brody always wanted to leave shortly after the sessions began. Something deep inside warned him he was wasting his time and making a fool of himself. Someone, somewhere was surely watching the group. It would all eventually end up in his 201 file; of that, he was certain. But every time he attempted to leave, he felt the desire drain from him. There was nothing waiting for him outside. Nothing except uncertainty and loneliness and guilt. Guilt over the ghosts, and the memory of the women he had killed in the name of God and country, duty and honor, liberation and lust. So he sat, remaining where he was, grateful there was something to occupy his time, something to hope for, and to wonder about.

For there was certainly nothing waiting for him outside, except the faces. Accusing, deformed, and mutilated faces that no longer waited for dark to pop out and startle him. He was tired of confronting the ghosts.

Le Loi spoke through Brock to Brody and the others.

"You are members of the combat support platoon and have yet to be called in to supplement the forces currently engaging the enemy.

"That, however, has now changed. You are to gather up all your weapons and supplies and leave for the battle at once. A woman with white hair is about to be captured by the northerners. You will not let this happen. You might not think a force so small as yours can possibly make a difference, but it will.

"Now proceed to the helipad. *Pegasus* will be waiting for you there."

"Zack!"

"Corpsman up!" One of the newbies yelled for a medic the instant he witnessed the NVA bullet slam Leo The Lionhearted back down into the earth. "Corpsman UP!"

"Mellow out, kid." Zack amazed them all by slowly, painfully, rolling over onto his side. The air had been knocked out of him, but the bullet had failed to penetrate his flak vest. Using shaking fingers, Zack dug the misshapen AK slug from the shredded top layers of fiberglass, and held it up for all to see. "Leo The Lionhearted limps into luck once again."

90

Doc Delgado slid up to him on bruised knees, batting the hand down. "Jesus, Zack!" His teeth flashed in anger. "Wanna catch *another* round, you shit-for-brains gorilla?"

As if in a daze, Zack tried to hold the bullet up again, his soft grin a mirror of his present attitude. "Must I remind you who's the lowly buck sergeant, doc?" He tapped Delgado on the chest as the medic furiously ripped Zack's flak vest apart down the middle and pulled his o.d. green T-shirt up.

Delgado knocked the fist down again.

"And who's the ranking—"

"You know where you can shove your six stripes, Leo," Doc Delgado interrupted. Another string of rounds peppered their position with dirt clods and splinters of hot lead.

"Holy buffalo balls!" The twink who'd called for a corpsman dropped back on his haunches and stared with wide eyes as Delgado succeeded in rolling Zack's sweat-slick T-shirt up over his shoulders. A bruise was spreading across the big NCO's entire chest. Beads of perspiration rolled from his shaved bald crown down onto it.

"You'll be all right," Delgado said quickly, noticing Zack's sudden concern at the newby's shocked look. "No penetration, but you're gonna have one helluva nasty bruise to write home about! Can you hang in there, or you want me to radio for a Dust—"

Zack's good arm flew up, and his fingers latched onto the front of Delgado's own flak jacket. "You better not phone for no fucking Dustoff!" he growled, obviously offended. " 'Course I can make it rest o' the way. Just point ol' Leo in the right direction and hand me my rifle, chump. Just gotta get my wind back, that's all."

Cordova and Broken Arrow had low-crawled over to their position. "What's the hold-up?" Two-Step spoke first, the expression on Zack's face immediately speaking the word *heartattack* to him. He'd seen the look before.

"You okay, Sarge?" Corky grabbed Zack's wrist.

Doc Delgado knocked Cordova's hand away impatiently. "Come on!" The medic drew his .45 pistol and waved it in the direction of the enemy positions. "Let's get this clusterfuck on the trail!"

As if sliding into home plate, Em-Ho Lee slammed into Zack suddenly, knocking the sergeant over again with a low groan. "What's the hold-up?" His concern was an imitation of Two-Step's, but the look in his eyes was more wild.

"Jesus, Em-Ho!" Delgado shook his head as he and Cordova reached down to check on Zack.

"Leo just got zapped!" Broken Arrow explained, and the gung-ho glaze in Lee's eyes was replaced with a surge of anxiety.

He reached down to grasp Zack's shoulder too, but the NCO responded to all the attention with a coarse chuckle. "Fuckin' Early Mornin' Hard-On." He sat up as another shower of lead rained across their position. Everyone else flattened against the ground, but Zack remained sitting up, shaking his head again as puffs of dust rose all around him. "Gonna get you reassigned to the Z if it's the last thing I do." He laughed. "Always attackin' ol' Leo on his blind side. Typical Nip strategy."

"So sorry, Sarge." Lee started to rise, but another flurry of discharges kept his face in the twigs, spider eggs, and shedded snakeskin.

A rifle round struck the tree rising beside Zack, and a large chunk of bark bounced off his right cheek. That seemed to knock the last of the stars from his head. His ears suddenly perking at the sporadic discharges all around, Leo glanced from side to side, realizing he was in the middle of a vicious firefight. He proned out between Delgado and Cordova, gasping for air.

"Welcome back to the war," Corky muttered as rounds zinged in all around, covering them with a fine coating of jungle decay.

"One o' you clowns shoulda bopped me up side the

head," Zack complained.

"Lee tried," Two-Step commented from beneath his steel pot, without elaborating.

"What's the situation?" Zack's head rose up slightly from cover behind several logs, as if he were still trying to get his bearings.

"Your guess is as good as mine." Delgado motioned toward the river swirling snakelike beyond a break in the dense treeline. "Charlie's tryin' to sweep reinforcements in to the crash site. I think they were caught off guard by Vance's party, and the way we appeared out of nowhere on their flank. But we're still outnumbered."

"No doubt about that." Cordova's helmet clinked against Broken Arrow's.

"The dinks want that white bitch worse than we do." Delgado slammed his face into the dirt as a monstrous shadow obscured the flares drifting overhead. Something huge and dark and ominous suddenly roared past, a few yards over their position. Then the discharge of dual hatch guns and the beating of rotorblades told him the choppers had returned for another pass.

White bitch. . . . The two words helped Zack remember. Up in the trees. She was up on a branch somewhere, her clothes torn, trying to stay one step ahead of dinks on the ground, who were trying to knock her off her perch with a long bamboo pole.

An unearthly screeching from high in the jungle canopy up ahead reached their ears. The Loach was slipping down through the tangle of branches and vines another couple of feet, and its fuselage was protesting with an ear-splitting, ghoulish scream of metal being torn and ripped.

"When was the last contact with Lou?" Zack asked Delgado as he prepared to move.

"Zero-five ago, Leo." But Doc was shaking his head in resignation. "Prick-25 took a couple rounds since then."

"Inoperable?"

"Worse." Delgado motioned toward a couple of

trunks several meters away, where two corporals were treating the radio man. "Zapped the battery. Kid's got acid all over his ass. Wish we could get him out."

"We will." Zack sucked in a deep breath, feeling alive again, feeling in control. "But first we assault that treeline, clean out the zips—"

"I think there's only one of 'em left." Cordova had come up for air too.

"Right." Zack pointed at a muzzle flash, and they all ducked, an instant after the round had already split a bamboo sapling inches above their helmets. "We mop up that last motherfucker, then beat feet right through there"—he pointed at the trail the enemy troops had used—"until we can link up with Vance's crew." The threat of left-behind boobytraps did not concern him right now; it was all part of the game, risks of the hunt.

"Then we rescue the round-eye cunt." Lee put in his two cents' worth as if jungle interest had dropped a grand into his account.

Zack worked on priorities. "First we blow the Loach."

Sgt. Delgado agreed with him. "Who knows what the spooks were carrying besides the blonde."

Zack nodded. "Then, we rescue the broad."

"If we survive tryin' to link up with Vance's people." Broken Arrow's unenthusiastic comment was a mild protest, submitted for the record.

One of the other corporals, a lanky, unshaven black, agreed with Two-Step. "Ain't worth it, Sarge. We're fucking outnumbered a million to one, man! I got a LAW in tow, bro." He patted the Light Anti-tank Weapon secured across the top of his rucksack. He pointed up at the dangling Loach, barely visible several hundred yards away. "Let me blast the fucker outta the jungle, then we can boogie back to the extraction point."

"And what about the cunt?" Zack said flatly.

"Screw the white cunt, blood! She knew the risks comin' here to The Nam, man!"

94

"Comin' to The Nam to entertain Americans, dude!" Cordova argued mildly, shocked at his own outburst as Broken Arrow elbowed him.

Zack locked eyes with Corky briefly, as if the private had made his point for him, then nodded with satisfaction and slipped his last grenade from an ash-blackened web belt.

"Soon as the show's over, we move!" he told them all. He pulled the safety pin from the M-33 and drew his arm back. "Then you turks guide on ol' Leo, y'hear?"

Without allowing time for discussion, Zack heaved the grenade at the lone NVA rifleman hiding in the treeline.

CHAPTER 12

Lt. Jake Vance was flooded with relief when the men in black failed to cancel his ticket after scaling the cliff's face and charging into his position brandishing exotic, sterile weapons. His confusion was only partially placated when one of the Occidentals plopped down beside him and said, "Agency, Lou! Apologies for crashin' your party."

"Agency?" was all Vance could mumble back.

"Rodg. C.I.A."

"I know that." Vance sounded miffed over the translation. "Why the hell are spooks getting involved in—"

The man laid his German-made MP40 submachine gun across one wrist, and the cool barrel's edge touched Vance's own hand. "You got no need to know that!" The agent waved a finger at him in gentle, almost comical reprimand as rounds ricocheted about their position like angry hornets.

"It's the broad, right?" One of the new men had low-crawled up between them. "She's C.I.A. too, right? The best-lookin', most-stacked spook on the face of the earth. If I'm a-lyin', then I'm a-dyin'."

"Get back over there and man that position, or you'll be a-dyin' all right!" Vance snapped. Frowning first, for the agent's benefit, the PFC rolled away, slammed against a ledge protruding from the hedgerows, and began firing with a vengeance at the enemy positions.

Five more Caucasians clad in black calico, all carrying weapons of East-Bloc manufacture, were bursting up over the cliff wall as Vance's men laid down showers of cover fire for them. All of the agents crawled in behind the spook conferring with Vance, quietly waiting for further directives.

Vance noticed that the closest agent's gun arm was bathed in blood. "Superficial, Lou!" the man whispered in response to Vance's look of concern.

"What about it?" Vance asked the apparent leader of the jungle ghouls.

"What about what?" Eyes cold as frost stared back at Vance, unblinking from behind the mask.

"The broad. Is she—"

"We've orders to secure the ship," came the dry reply.

"Vance's right eyebrow rose slightly. "The Loach?"

"Right." Bullets tore several branches from overhanging trees above their position.

One of the men clad in black brushed dirt and dead insect matter out of his eyes. "I don't think this is the right place for a chat, Lou," he said.

Vance remained semi-defiant, feeling a sudden power from the troops at his disposal and a prejudice bred into him at West Point against the C.I.A. coursing through his veins. "It is if you want our help." He flexed his muscle.

"Meaning?"

"Meaning I don't wanna commit all these cherries to some spook cause that ain't worth dyin' over! My boys aren't going to eat shit and die just to appease some glory-hungry armchair commando back in The World, unless it's righteous."

Another string of bullets sprayed their position, and one of Vance's men spotted an enemy mortar team moving into place from the rear ranks. "Tubes in the trees!" he warned the lieutenant.

"We've orders to secure the Loach," an agent several feet away revealed quietly. Apparently the man closest to Vance was not the team leader after all.

"Just the chopper?" Vance lifted his M-16 above the mound of earth protecting them and fired off half a magazine without aiming. He used one hand, pistol-fashion. The rest of the men in his unit fired into the trees on semi-automatic, trying to keep the enemy mortar crew pinned down. The mortar crew had Vance worried: There was no need for them to move up. They could just as easily decimate his people from several hundred yards away. They were up to something else.

"Right. It was a courier ship, from Saigon to Mytho. Carried some important information that Uncle Sammy would hate to have fall into Charlie's hands. The woman was just along for the ride. She's genuine USO material. The Cong can have her. Or you can fucking have her, Lou! I don't give a rat's ass. Just deliver us a secured grid, so we can search the helicopter in peace."

"The pilot's dead," Vance told him.

"Don't mean didley."

"Then we're not talking human courier."

"Your routine messenger packet, Lou." The chief agent moved as if to signal the chat was over and it was time to resume the fight before Charlie terminated them all. He rose to one knee and began saturating the treeline with his submachine gun.

The spook beside him rose too, imitating his boss's bravery. Two AK rounds ripped his face open, forehead to chin. Vance's lower jaw dropped. Not a sound from the man—no scream, no grunt, not even a grizzly thump from the wasp-like bullets. He simply plopped forward into the muck as a string of tracers floated through the space he'd just been occupying. Forward. No catapulting backward, like in all the war movies Vance had grown up on. The lieutenant shook his head, upset at his own ridiculous thoughts. He'd been in The Nam long enough to know better.

A gunship dropped from the dark skies to hover over

the river, directing its hatch gun at the source of the green tracers. The chopper was blacked out, and the only way Vance and the others knew it was even there was from the lancelike bursts of crimson tracers coming from the din of beating rotorblades. He listened for a moment to the dull, almost sluggish rumble of M-60 discharges and the fifty-foot blades slapping at the Mekong's hot, sticky air, before reacting.

This was one of those nights old Asian hands often talked about, where there was very little twilight between dusk and sudden darkness across the land. Vance had to think. Should he pop more flares, risking the possibility of wind changes and illuminating his own men, or should he lead his troops into pitch-black battle?

Vance chose the night cover, hoping to guide on the NVA's muzzle flashes and tracer glow. Instinct told him to dig in and wait it out, wait for sunrise; they would be inviting suicide to charge a numerically superior force in the dark on Charlie's own territory. He gritted his teeth with determination. They must want this one bad, to send in a combined VC and NVA force.

But now a second and a third gunship had dropped from the clouds. Cruising back and forth along the riverbank, they showered the treeline with belt after belt of MG ammo. And now and then he spotted Warlokk's Cobra darting about, going to work on the Vietnamese with its mini-guns.

When a particularly concentrated salvo of air-to-ground seven-point-sixty-two lit up the jungle's edge, bright as high noon, he motioned his men forward toward a fortlike pile of blackened logs. Three red arcs of tracer fire had just dipped down into the enemy positions from a hilltop to the east. That had to be Zack's team, finally working their way toward the downed Loach!

Vance had no idea how many Cong lay between him and his objective, but hopefully Zack's people could cut through the enemy ranks, using a pincerlike maneuver that would rely on Vance's troopers as a buffer on the west. He just wasn't sure who would be waiting farther to the east to help Leo's men on that side. As far as he knew, there were no friendlies out there.

Chrissy LaVey was pretty upset about the whole thing. Especially the manner in which the situation had deteriorated so rapidly after their small black helicopter was forced down in the middle of the Mekong Delta due to mechanical problems. She could take the cruel jokes of fate and destiny. And death was not something new to her after two years as an entertainer in Saigon, where open-air cafe and cinema bombings had introduced her to ripped-away faces and severed body parts long ago. So the jagged tree limb shooting up through the floor of the craft, forcing half the pilot's spine through the top of his head, had not really shocked her; she was simply glad to avoid a majority of the blood spray.

Chrissy was losing patience with her rescuers, the Americans who had arrived with considerable fanfare in the form of heavy automatic weapons fire and a half dozen or so Huey and Cobra gunships. They were making a real show of everything, but here she was, still high up in the treetops, an hour after dark, and with more than a couple of overzealous guerrillas trying to jab her with a long bamboo stick.

A hot lead splinter or two had even found its way into her shapely bottom, and Chrissy was afraid the next shock-induced slip might be straight off the slimy, snake-infested branch and into the river below.

"Ouch!" She squealed softly as the bamboo pole rose up through the dark, bouncing off her shin again. Whenever she heard one of the guerrillas cry out in pain, she would clap defiantly, taunting them from her treetop perch.

LaVey had accepted the temporary posting to the

USO Club in Mytho for two reasons: the pay was fifty dollars over what she was making in Sin City, and she needed to get away from one of the MACV officers, who had a wife in every port but still couldn't keep his hands off of her. Maybe a few weeks TDY to the Delta would give the Colonel someone new to pursue.

She didn't know the chopper pilot. She had been scheduled to ride south in one of the large, troop-ferrying, twin-rotored Chinooks, but the night before had been rather trying, to say the least, and she wasn't in the mood for the gawking stares or cherry-boy conversation.

On the way to the airport, her escort to Tan Son Nhut drove through a pile of nails some VC sympathizer no doubt had dropped in the middle of busy Cong Ly Boulevarde as his or her contribution to the war effort, and while thumbing a ride to the helipad, she was picked up by a second jeep with a Vietnamese driver and American passenger. The American wore civilian clothes—a TV safari suit, not unlike her own, though less expensive, she noted—but Chrissy knew immediately he was no journalist. The jeep was painted blue, which was supposed to tell the Arvins and communists alike that it was a Department of Agriculture vehicle, but anyone possessing the slightest of street smarts knew it was an Agency jeep, which were often black, because the Ag people drove anything *but* mere government-issued wheels.

When the jeep pulled up to a heavily guarded strip of tarmac, and he sauntered over to the small, black two-seater sitting patiently beneath a concrete open-ended hangar, she knew it would be better not to ask too many questions.

The ride south had been a quiet, uneventful one. The pilot glanced over to appraise her firm curves now and then from behind mirrored sunglasses. Chrissy thought about touring a new town.

And then the hydraulics went out.

The rest was a matter of record, and she was afraid

she too might become just another tidbit of forgotten history, if the First Air Cav didn't get off its buff and rescue her *rikky-tik*!

There had been times, back in Saigon, where she had carried a small, snub-nosed Smith & Wesson .38—during the shake-down days when local flesh kingpins were fighting over territory, and white women were a much sought-after and valuable commodity. White women in Indochina were still rare, but they were losing some of their allure and mystery in the eyes of the Oriental men. It was just as easy for a Chrissy LaVey to end up floating face down in the Saigon River as Nguyen Thi Plain Jane. She wished she had her trusty two-inch revolver with her now; at least she could take out a couple of the vermin on the way down.

That was the way LaVey thought. Not really about revenge, or survival. She was a realist, and the odds were looking more and more against her as the minutes flew past in the form of mesmerizing tracer glow. Her only concern right now was about going to her watery grave below with a few hole-in-head insurgents in tow. She mentally laughed at the no-win situation. Time to convert some commies to Christ. She could not see how the Americans could possibly save her.

And then the thought struck her: it had been a spook Loach! That was the real reason behind the alert force response. MACV would surely not send this many men and helicopters out after dark just to rescue *her*! It had to be something about the chopper itself that was valuable. Or perhaps the pilot. Thinking back now, as sizzling slugs of chemical-coated tracers ricocheted off tree trunks all around her and gunsmoke lined her throat like the aftertaste of black licorice, Chrissy realized it was doubtful anyone even knew she'd been aboard. She had hitched the ride at the last minute, after all. And she couldn't remember the pilot ever advising the tower he'd brought a passenger aboard. Though after the rotors kicked in and they ascended out over the jungle west of Tan Son Nhut, he had spent a few seconds mumbling something into his headset. Maybe he had mentioned that an Aussie blonde USO singer-dancer was aboard for the ride.

The ten-inch-thick branch she was on began to vibrate. The soles of her bare feet trying to clutch and curl against the rough bark, Chrissy reached out and latched onto nearby vines for support as the branch began shaking violently. And then the screeching tore at her ears again. The Loach was slipping farther down through the canopy, down to the next and final layer.

She glanced down at the rough waters swirling half a football field below her bare feet. Then her eyes darted down the limb to the helicopter.

The Loach!

She would have to make her way back to the craft and search it as best she could in the darkness. She had to find whatever it was that made this mission so important. The only problem would be her weight. At five feet seven, Chrissy still managed to keep her figure under a voluptuous hundred and fifteen pounds, but that would probably be all the Loach needed to plummet the rest of the way down to the river below.

It was her only hope, and she knew it. She had to get whatever the Agency had been sending south. It might be her only bargaining chip—regardless of which side won the pitched battle raging below.

Damn! Another sliver of hot lead struck her shapely behind, nearly sending Chrissy out into space. *If this keeps up, I'll only have a couple of things of interest left to share with my GI audiences.* She grimaced, moving back down the shaking limb like a confident tightrope walker.

The Loach had slipped about twelve more feet down through the tangled network of vines and branches, but Chrissy was confident she could still get to it. The vines were dry this close to the main trunk, dry and flaky. They made excellent handholds.

Pausing to tighten what remained of her garments, she surveyed the firefight raging below. From her

103

vantage point along the forest's edge she could see the American gunships swooping in over the river, pausing a moment or two to fire off hundreds of rounds in an eye's blink, then darting away, to be replaced by other Hueys in the fleet. Below, two separate groups of uniformed Americans were slowly moving closer to the crash site. And, just before the final rays of dusk died along the smoke-lined horizon, Chrissy had seen two black rubber motorized rafts cruising up one of the river's heavily wooded side tributaries. They appeared to be headed for the cliffs along the riverbank, and had not been noticed by the Vietnamese in the sampans along the main waterway.

Chrissy quickly made her way down to the helicopter. The vines were easy to grab on to, and the profusion of knobs and bumps along the main tree truck made for excellent footholds. She even tied one vine around her waist and one to her left wrist in case she lost her grip. That way, she wouldn't plunge all the way to the ground, but could scurry back up into the canopy before the gooks with the pole were even aware she had slipped and fallen.

During its last descent down through the canopy, the Loach had remained nose up, but shifted slightly so that the undamaged door was solidly against the tree trunk. By tracer light and flares drifting over the river, she could see there were not packages or briefcases in open view within the cockpit. There had to be secret hiding places for confidential messages, especially in a combat zone. If she tried to slip into the cockpit, the movement itself, regardless of the addition of her weight, would no doubt send the chopper the rest of the way to the jungle floor. A bounce on the trip down could easily send it into the swiftly moving river.

Another flare drifting past revealed that an entire section of windshield in the bug-eyed, bubble-faced craft's snout was missing. Perhaps she could reach in and fumble about the wreckage without disturbing the ship's precarious perch.

104

Glancing down at a crescendo of shouts at the edge of the communists' positions, Chrissy realized she would have to work fast. Several sampans loaded with Cong reinforcements were pulling up along the riverbanks.

Her face etched with determination, she reached into the mangled Loach cockpit and began sifting through the debris as best she could.

When the scrawny yellow hand latched onto her wrist from within the chopper, she screamed.

CHAPTER 13

Anna brushed the long shaggy locks of hair from Nelson's eyes after he rolled off her onto his side. He shifted his weight to a bent elbow, his right ear resting in the palm of his hand. Their eyes locked, and Anna asked, "Does the Army not reprimand you for such long hair?" Blond hair normally did not excite her—she left such games to younger, thrill-seeking city girls not inhibited by culture shock. But Nelson's was unruly, defying his every attempt to control it, and that intrigued her.

"It's only long in front." He smiled slyly. "I can easily comb it back, over the top. Nobody says much, anyway. This *is* The Nam, you know."

"*Viet* Nam." She rubbed the edge of her forefinger against his nose in mock reprimand.

"Yes," he whispered into her ear as their cheeks rubbed slowly. "Vee*yet*-Nam."

Nelson was laughing to himself: four hours on the floor atop this sweet young thing's sleeping mat, and we've still got our clothes on. Is Nasty Nel losing his tender touch?

"You are the first man ever to come in here," she whispered, as a rat scurried across the top of the dwelling's tin roof. "I hope I am not making a mistake."

Nelson made a show of checking his wristwatch. "All this time kissing your neck, and I still haven't tried anything." He chuckled lightly. "Isn't that proof of my being a gentlemen, Anna?" He ignored the sound of a cockroach falling off the far wall on the other side of the one-room cubicle.

She nodded, unable to keep the smile inside. "Yes. I suppose it is." Anna had not noticed the pest, so mesmerized was she by this man, this Nelson. She felt at ease beside him.

Nelson ran his fingers under her chin, bringing her lips to his again. She wrapped her arms around his neck and, as he pulled her on top of him, slowly pushed her tongue into his mouth.

They began kissing harder and breathing as if the air had been sucked from the room.

Before, he had felt no desire to rush things. She had brought companionship back into his life. That was enough. Until now.

Nelson was the kind of soldier who could go two, maybe three months on his own, isolated and alone, consuming himself with duty, fulfilling the long hours with meaningless busywork, patient shifts on post, scanning the perimeter from dusk to dawn with a starlite scope for Charlie. But then it would strike: that need for feminine companionship—not someone to talk to, so much, but simply a female, with long hair and soft lips and jutting breasts and hips that molded perfectly against his own when the lights were turned down low and they wrapped their arms together.

Fulfilling the simple need had been enough. Until now. He felt himself heating up inside, growing restless as they explored each other's mouths. His hand slipped between them, cupping her breast gently, and when she did not protest, his fingers inched downward, until they'd moved inside the folds of her sarong and were slipping beneath the loose waistband of her undergarments.

Her pelvis shifted suddenly when he probed the warm, moist spot where her thighs came together, and Anna ended the kiss, drawing her face back several inches from his. He continued to massage her there, and beneath the dim lantern hanging in a corner, an evil grin crept across his features.

"Please stop," she said softly, staring through him, the plea in her eyes ignored because Nelson was becoming mesmerized himself by their reflection of lantern glowing in the dark.

"Pardon?" It was not really a question. There was no surprise in his tone, though he gave accent to the words as if perplexed. His fingers kept working slowly, gently, when she made no physical move to protest further.

"I do not want it to be like this." She grew cold, breaking eye contact.

The tear edging down her cheek stopped Nelson cold. He froze, slowly withdrawing his hand. "You do not want it to be like this?" he asked tenderly, lifting her chin again. But she refused to look into his eyes.

"No."

"Then how do you want it to be, Anna?" His hand dropped away, but he quickly brought it around to fall on her back, in the hollow between her shoulderblades. Nelson began massaging the tightness from the back of her neck, moving slowly upward until he was at the base of her skull.

Anna sighed, allowing her face to drop forward as he rubbed harder, nearly putting her to sleep in those few weary breaths. Her shoulders began to sag as well, and she shook the fog from her head, trying to concentrate.

"Then how do you want it to—" he started to repeat as they rolled onto their sides again, facing each other.

"I don't want it to be on our first night," she whispered, clearly embarrassed now.

Breaking eye contact again, Anna glanced over at the wall. A tight smile creasing her features, her eyes wandered until she spotted two small lizards hanging upside down in a corner of the ceiling, tangled together in sexual intercourse yet unmoving as they seemed to gaze back down at her. "I want us to be friends first." She chose her words carefully. "I want you to come back to this place again and again. I want you to sleep with me many nights without making love to me." She kissed his lips softly, then pulled away to examine his expression. "I want the 'first time' to be special," she whispered, trying to read his thoughts.

His reply nearly brought out the tears again. "*Our* first time? Or *the* first time, Anna."

Anna collapsed onto her back and sighed heavily. Startled by the sudden movement, one of the lizards on the ceiling tried to scurry away, forgetting perhaps it was stuck to the other, and both silver reptiles dropped onto a hotplate, leaped down to the floor, and scampered across the teakwood planks in opposite directions.

"How old do you think I am, Nelson?" Anna's hands rose above her face, as if she was inspecting her wrists silently, then the right one slowly dropped across his chest.

Nelson didn't reply.

"You do not understand my English?" she snapped, aware he was stalling.

"Of course. But, I don't care, I think you're—"

"Do not sweet-talk me, Nelson." She punched him lightly in the side, but Nelson barely noticed it. "All men stare at woman for first time and wonder how old she is, how many babies she—"

"I think you're wrong, Anna," Nelson said, staring at the ceiling. "Most men look at a woman the first time and wonder whether or not her tits will sag when the bra comes off."

Anna was taken aback by his frankness. "Oh," she said without further argument.

"Of course, after four hours in the dark with you, I can tell that would not be a problem." He fought back the smile trying to creep across his lips.

"Thank you, Nelson," She sounded more somber than serious. "I was about to get up on my knees and pull the sarong over my head to prove they are still—"

"Other men, of course, wonder about other things," he interrupted her, unwilling to giving her the satisfaction of even a few sarcastic words.

"Such as?" Anna was almost afraid to ask, but the curiosity was more than she could bear.

"Well, other men, especially here in the Orient, wonder if they have any . . . any . . ."

Anna laughed loudly, clutching her flat belly for his benefit. "You mean, do they have women's hair."

"Yes." Nelson sucked on his lower lip silently, thinking about the pubic-hair collection lying back in his rucksack and hoping the thoughts would control his emotions.

"Anything else?" She took gentle hold of the flesh along the inside of his waistband, preparing to twist, and Nelson found himself flashing back to other girls, back stateside. Why did women the world over enjoy pulling on his love-handles?

"Well, then there's a few others who are really turned off by mothers."

"Mothers?"

"You know, the ones who already had a kid or two on the side, and have stretch marks across the belly to prove it. That's a definite turn-off for lots of—"

"I assure you I am childless," she whispered confidently, sounding not the least bit offended.

"Anyway," Nelson did not want to exaggerate, so he picked a number he thought would be safe. "I would think that you are around nineteen," he said carefully, preparing to block another elbow.

"Nineteen?"

Nelson was not sure if she was upset or delighted. He swallowed hard, then said, "Okay, seventeen going on eighteen."

Anna laughed again. She took his chin this time, pulling Nelson's attention from the ceiling to her face.

110

He thought she would still be laughing, but her expression had turned serious. "I am twenty-nine," she said, the gleam in her eyes smothered now, as if she sought compassion instead of laughter.

Nelson swallowed again. "Twenty-nine?" he asked, wanting to glance away, wanting to search for the lizards again. *Twenty-nine*? She looked like a teenager. He told himself he should be pleased at her youthful good looks despite having spent her life in a war zone. But twenty-nine? That made her eleven years older than he was.

"Twenty-nine," she affirmed.

"Well." He stammered and kicked himself mentally for it. "Well, there's certainly nothing wrong with that." He got it out, feeling his lips clamp shut. He felt suddenly as if he was lying beside one of his high school teachers again, and then a chill went through him. He saw his stepmother's face in the darkness, and Nelson shuddered, remembering with crystal clarity the afternoon he came home from school and found her in her usual place on the living room couch, glass in hand, clad in something sheer and lacy, always allowing him that certain flash of inner thigh, only to have him bolt into the hallway and up the stairwell, into his room. Until that one day she needed help with something, and he got close enough to the sofa for her to latch onto him in her drunken flurry of limbs, pulling him down . . .

Nelson shuddered again, realizing that Anna had climbed back on top of him. Her sarong was off. She had slipped it up over her head as he stared through his flashback at the ceiling, never even noticing, and now, her elbows locked, her palms rested against the sleeping mat on either side of his face. The erect tips of her breasts brushed against his lips as she rubbed her groin over his, moving back and forth, up and down, side to side. . . .

"I have changed my mind," she announced, sensing she was losing him.

"Changed . . ." Nelson's eyes blinked rapidly for a moment before focusing on hers again.

"Anna gives herself to you tonight, Nelson." She began removing the GI belt holding his trousers in place.

He found himself working the trousers down around his hips. She was helping him almost hectically now, and then he found himself totally unclothed, her warm body rubbing against his.

"First time?" He repeated her words, but with some skepticism in his tone, wondering why he could not control his feelings, get his thoughts in order.

When Anna realized she was doing all the work, that he was not responding, was not excited, she froze up, collapsing across his chest. Fighting back the tears, she said, "I never make love to man before."

That plucked Nelson from the fog.

"I wait," Anna revealed slowly, taking him into her confidence. "I wait long time, thinking Vietnamese man want me someday. But . . ."

Anna sat up again and ran her fingertip along the long, razor-thin scar. "Why should Vietnamese man marry woman with mark on face?" She posed the question hypothetically, asking it of herself as much as Nelson. "When he can have young girl with no mark?"

"You are beautiful, Anna. "The mark is hardly noticeable. And didn't I tell you, it made you look more desirable than other women."

"Thank you, Nelson. Thank you for kind words. You are nice man," she said, kissing the tip of his nose lightly. "But nebbah mind. No longer matters. I give up hope. You are next best thing to Mekong marriage: tonight Anna gives herself to Nelson."

He noticed the ample swell of breasts jutting down in front of his face for the first time, and felt himself growing instantly hard.

"We should wait," he said finally, realizing he wanted her. But it was not fair to Anna, Nelson decided. She was granting him first-man status. Despite his reputation, that meant something to the American soldier.

"I do not want to wait any longer." She flattened his lips with her own, becoming overaggressive in her attempts to seduce him now.

Grasping her shoulders gently, he forced her face away. "As you said," he reminded her in a manner that got her attention without worrying her, "tonight is special."

"No."

"We should wait." He seemed to be insisting, yet he could not convince himself either. "Until we have spent more nights together. Until we have spent days down on the riverbank, sharing picnic lunches."

"No."

"I want to wait, Anna."

"No. I can tell. You will never come back. Tonight Anna gives herself to Nelson. I will try . . . I will try my hardest to enchant you, my lover. Then you will return to me. It is the only way."

Nelson was at a loss for words. But he remembered something Treat Brody told him once. Something about Vietnamese women and how, when they got to really trusting you, and becoming your friend as well as lover, there was a little thing they did to display their feelings. Brody told him they would wrap their tiny forefinger around yours, locking both together so that it was very difficult to pull apart, unless you really wanted to.

Nelson took Anna's forefinger in the Vietnamese manner, locking it with his. "This week I become your best friend," he whispered, kissing her gently, the whole time thinking how, when he got back to the unit, he'd tell Brody how his little tidbit of advice had gotten him out of another tight spot. "Next week I become your lover." Proud of himself and his restraint in the face of gifts difficult to resist, Nelson smiled.

"I no believe." She gently took hold of him between the legs, forcing it up into the warm folds of her own flesh. The sudden heat made him swell, losing nearly

113

all self-control. Anna was still atop him, balancing herself clumsily now as they shifted about, beginning to move against each other, and he plunged up into her, eliciting a startled gasp.

Nelson had never experienced such bodily delight. She was firm and smooth everywhere he touched. Eager to please, yet impatient with him as the moments of ecstasy passed and she loosened, wanting to experiment further. The woman leaning over him was a finely toned tigress, a tightly wound woman, her mystery finally unraveling. Anna seemed both shocked and relieved at the sensations consuming her. "Tonight . . . Anna . . . place Nelson . . . under her spell." Her breathing became irregular as he toyed with her, and she struggled to compensate, trying to lead him in further, but slower than he wanted to go.

"No." He suddenly took control, rolling her onto her back. "Tonight Nelson put a love curse on Anna!" Out of habit, feeling back in The World on a white sand beach in Oahu, making love beneath an orange crescent moon, he forced her legs farther apart with his knees, preparing to force himself on her with powerful thrusts, hoping to hear her gasp some more.

And then he remembered. He remembered where he was, and he fought back the urge to dominate her.

Nelson remembered who he was with, and what, after all these years, she was finally surrendering, and he became gentle again, withdrawing slowly so they would have more time to tease and explore.

Anna wrapped her arms around his neck, holding him down close to her, fearing, perhaps, she had displeased him, and he was trying to leave before they had finished. But the manner in which Nelson kissed her, moving his lips to her chest, then back up to her trembling mouth, seemed to reassure the woman, and she finally began to relax.

And then he made her feel what love is really all about.

114

CHAPTER 14

Snakeman Fletcher was nervous in the service.

Gabriel The Gunslinger had gone all-out back at the LZ, swooping in repeatedly like a bat out of hell so Elliott cold fire up the bad guys. But Gabe, in his zeal, had overdone it, and they'd had to return to the Cho Gao field for fuel and ammo resupply.

It was supposed to be a quick trip: prang up to the fuel bladders, commandeer some ammoboxes, then beat blades back to the battle. They had not expected to see Sgt. Brock and Brody The Whoremonger waiting alongside half a dozen other wild-eyed troopers, eager for action.

Gabriel unenthusiastically invited the entire clan aboard for the ride, opting for less fuel so he could deliver more bodies to the firefight. Prior to lifting off, Snakeman overheard him muttering something to his peter pilot about "giving free rides to rain-forest ghosts."

There was none of the usual grunting during the flight into Void Vicious either, Fletcher noted. The men were not trying to psych each other up for battle. There was no apelike pounding of chests, no stomping of jungle boots, no growls inviting hot lead to chew on, no mock prayers for hand-to-hand combat and initiation into hell's elite, the Dirty Thirty fraternity.

These men needed no encouragement, no pep talk. They were not worried about their fate. The cold look of determination and confidence in their eyes told Fletcher they were hoping to meet Lady Death face to face and kiss the bad bitch on the lips. It was mindfuck to the max, Snakeman decided. And it sent a chill down his spine.

"Lima-Zulu in dirty sex," Gabriel called back over a shoulder, announcing their descent toward the LZ. "And it's gonna be a hot one, ladies."

Fletcher, the knuckles of both hands turning white as he gripped the hatch-60, glanced around, taking in the emotionless hard-core faces one last time before *Pegasus* dropped into the storm. That's an understatement, he decided, wondering if it was really a ghostly aura he was floating over Brock's close-cropped head or just part of the blue halo from outside the hatch from the rotorblades twirling beneath the orange crescent moon.

Private 2nd-Class Shannon Orson was having trouble completing the letter. Dull, rolling explosions from the firefight raging less than five miles away carried to the tent he was sharing with PFC Graham, repeatedly breaking his concentration.

When a particularly harsh series of secondary blasts rumbled across the land, he slammed down his pen.

Graham glanced up from his tattered copy of the *Overseas Weekly*. "What?" he asked, eyes rising as if the look on Orson's face accused him of thinking too loud while the other soldier was trying to write.

"We shouldn't be here," Orson grumbled in sync with muffled explosions in the distance.

"Huh?" Graham tore the black-and-white pin-up from the tabloid and licked the shapely model's paper crotch.

"I said we shouldn't be here."

116

"No shit." Graham laid back on his air mattress and draped the pin-up across his face. "I should be in New York City or Miami—wherever the model who posed for this spread lives. I should be lying in her waterbed, overlooking the Big Apple skyline, or Palm Beach, or the Golden Gate Bridge. And she'd be sitting on my face." He rattled the double-page poster for Orson's benefit. "Just like this."

"That's not what I'm talkin' about."

"Sure it is, Shannon."

Orson glared. "Don't call me that. I told you never to call me that. Orson's the name, orgasm's my game."

"Right. So you've said." Still lying beneath the pin-up, Graham pushed his luck. "So where the hell did your mama-san come up with a name like Shannon, anyway? Little ahead of its time, isn't it?"

Orson's expression shifted from irritated to thoughtful, though he was definitely experiencing no surge of fond memories for the woman who brought him into The World. "Like I told ya, Graham-Cracker: my old lady was one o' them beatnik types tryin' to corner the headjob market with off-the-wall first names for their kids. Couldn't stick with John or Joe. Had to come up with crap like Olive or Zachary."

"Or Shannon."

"Right." Orson sighed in resignation. "You know, typical flower-child mentality: let's give the kid a light-hearted, peace-in-the-valley name to hang over him the rest of his life. Never mind if the kids in school razz him for twelve years straight and he ends up going to therapy because of it all."

"Flower children don't plan that far into the future."

"No shit."

"Shannon." Graham repeated the name, laughing lightly.

Orson chuckled along. "Yeah. It's supposed to mean 'small and wise' in Gaelic."

"You're Irish?"

Orson burst into more laughter. "Hardly," he said.

117

"Well, maybe it means something else in another language."

"Naw." Orson seemed to contemplate Graham's remark for a moment, then he said, "The old lady was a clown, like I've told ya a hundred times already. A prevert too, if you want my opinion."

"She probably stared at your ding-dong the day you came into the world and said, 'Ahhh, so small.' Then papa-san chimes in with 'But wise, honey-buns.' And that was how you came to be Shannon Q. Orson The Martian."

"What?" Orson did not seem particularly upset that Graham was insulting his father too. He was just glad they were talking again after the tense silence that followed the confrontation with Nelson out on the perimeter earlier. "Where'd you get the Q, anyway?"

"Well, it only seems fitting that someone named Shannon O'Bannion D'Orson The Third would also have a middle initial of Q, don't you think?"

"Q?"

"For Quincy."

"Oh. Of course." Orson frowned, and resumed scribbling something on an Air Force blue tablet decorated with military murals in the lower left corner.

"What ya composin' over there, anyway, Orgasm?" Graham sat up again and began carefully folding the newspaper pin-up.

"Oh, just writing one of my three daily status reports back to—"

"Mama-san in Minnesota."

"Right. But make that Berkeley. Berkeley, California."

"Should have known."

"Rodg. Wanna hear it?" A sly smile crept into Orson's blank expression.

"Might as well. Nothin' else to do around here except listen to the circle-jerk goin' on in the tent next door." Halfway into folding the pin-up, he changed his mind and laid it flat on the dirt floor beside his air mattress.

118

"Okay, here goes." Orson raised the tissue-thin sheet of paper over his head, shook nonexistent dust from it, then was about to begin when the tent flaps flew back, and a tall master sergeant poked his head into their dubious domain.

"What's cookin', Sarge?" Graham held up his short-timer's calendar for the NCO's appraisal.

"Put your puds back in your pants, grab your gear, and report to the POL point!" the lanky Latino replied.

"What's up?" Graham carefully folded the pin-up poster away and tucked it into his rucksack.

"Some more gunboat girlies ran into trouble coupla klicks away. Cap'n wants reinforcements rounded up so we can supplement the—"

Graham, who had stood with an excited sparkle in his eyes, frowned, shook his head in dismissal, and sat back down on his air mattress. "Naw, Sarge." He almost chuckled. "Me and Orgasm over there already tried to volunteer our services, but they told us there weren't any more helicopters goin' out to the—"

"Just get your ass in gear, newby!" The sergeant was in no mood for debates. "Report over to the POL point in zero-five or less!"

"Okay!" Graham was still trying to act nonchalant.

"And don't forget your weapons and as many bandoliers as you can haul!" the sergeant added, then disappeared into the darkness.

"Roger, wilco, over and out," Graham said sarcastically as soon as the man was out of earshot.

"What the heck is a POL point?" Orson asked the ranking private as he tightened the straps on his ruck.

"Fuck if I know, doofus."

Orson wadded up the letter to his mother and threw it at Graham, then proceeded to lace his jungle boots.

Chrissy LaVey pulled as hard as she could without losing her balance on the trembling branch. Back-to-

119

back explosions on the ground were causing the huge tree to sway from side to side now. She pulled as hard as she could, but the yellow-faced man grimacing behind the Loach's mangled windowframe held on to her wrist and began yelling. It was a scare tactic, she was sure—he could not possibly have expected her to understand such a rapid torrent of Vietnamese threats and profanity. So she tried jerking her arm away again. That's when the small helicopter began to scream in protest as it shifted within the tangle of vines and branches, sounding like it was finally ready to plummet to earth once and for all. So convincing was all the racket, in fact, that the communist inside the cockpit began yelling excitedly himself. Chrissy was not sure if there were others inside, but they were probably nearby, and she began using her feet.

She kicked viciously with her bruised and scraped bare feet, connecting with the Vietnamese soldier's jaw, and he finally released her.

She scampered back several yards, away from the groaning craft, and waited for it to work its way down through the canopy. But after sliding a couple of excruciatingly slow inches, the Loach stopped, held up by the network of vines and limbs. If there really was a secret packet hidden aboard somewhere, Charlie could have it, she decided. Recovering a courier packet wasn't worth losing a drop of blood over. She was a B-grade entertainer and the first to admit it, not a Mati Hari.

More Vietnamese suddenly appeared on the other side of the Loach. A gasp escaped her when three youthful faces poked out around the crumpled fuselage and their bulging eyes locked onto her with devouring, lustful leers that told the woman she would never make it to a POW camp alive. The insurgents were naked, except for a conglomeration of ropes tied around their limbs and upper torso. They were greased down from shoulders to toes, and had been hoisted into the jungle canopy by an intricate pulley system carried into place above the Loach by a single climber while Chrissy was busy fending off the pole swingers on the ground. With the pulley in place, a half dozen scavengers had relayed each other up to her perch, intent on cleaning out the chopper even as the battle raged on below.

"Oh, shit!" Chrissy's world slipped out from under her suddenly. She felt herself flying away from the branch, trying to grasp at elusive vines and handholds. The Vietnamese on the ground had finally managed to strike her with the bamboo pole, knocking her off the branch, while her concentration was focused on the Loach scavengers.

In the darkness, she reached out for anything to grab on to. But the pole, striking her in the lower back, had knocked her several feet out from the tree, and it was as if she was tumbling head over heels into a vast, bottomless pit.

Her ears heard the river's rapids rising to meet her, but in her head, Chrissy LaVey heard a familiar voice laughing, "Good morning, Vietnam!" It was the American armed forces radio disk jockey in Saigon, a nameless, faceless man who nevertheless was invited into her room at the Caravelle every morning. She couldn't imagine why, at this final climax in her life, the words came to her.

Chrissy was confident she would be a mangled pulp of shredded flesh and broken bones in another heartbeat. But then the river's roar filled her ears again, the darkness became a sort of luminescent silver, and she was slapped about by swirling currents as she struck the Mekong tributary feet first and plunged several yards beneath its surface.

Swim! her instinct commanded as the warm water tore into her nostrils. *Swim away from them! Escape!* but her reflexes were still stunned by the high fall. Her limbs were not responding to her will to survive. And then she felt the net envelop her like a giant, soggy spider's web. The air exploded from her lungs.

She was sure she'd drown before her captors could

ever drag her back to the surface.

"Did you see that?" Cordova whispered to Broken arrow as Zack's team moved closer and closer to Lt. Vance's position.

"They got her," Two-Step affirmed quietly.

"Life sucks and then you die," muttered Leo The Lionhearted. His expression reminded them their first priority was blowing the Loach and any sensitive documents or equipment it might carry.

"Right." Em-Ho Lee nodded in resignation as he concentrated on the blur of a trail winding through the dark reeds and elephant grass before them. But Lee's narrowed eyes belied what they were all thinking: the team should be rushing over to help her right now, their chances of survival be damned!

That was when the five sampan-loads of Viet Cong ambushed them from the left.

"What was that!"

"Claymore."

"*Christ*!"

"Yeah. Double bummer. I'd hate to be down there on the receiving end."

"Really! It was one of ours, wasn't it?"

"Hard to tell. I caught some green tracers out the corner of my eye before we banked. They were coming from the same direction."

"Charlie?"

"Rodg."

"Triple bummer."

Snakeman Fletcher listened to Gabriel conversing with his co-pilot as *Pegasus* circled around for another pass over the battle. He didn't bother clicking in. It would do no good to report that he'd seen Zack's shaved crown reflect moonlight right after the claymore anti-personnel mine was detonated. Leo had been on the receiving end of 600 angry ball bearings ripping toward him and his men through the bamboo. There was nothing that could be done for them now. Nobody could have survived that. All they could hope to do was set down along the riverbank somewhere and release Sgt. Brock's team in time to help Vance's people.

"That's the spot." Gabriel found a narrow stretch of terrain outside the free fire zone. "Right where the river bends."

"Rodg," his peter pilot acknowledged, as the roaring rotors overhead changed pitch and *Pegasus* dropped down through an abrupt break in the trees. "Right on the mud."

"Un-ass!" Sgt. Brock yelled over the turbine's piercing whine, but his men, led by Treat Brody, were already climbing down on the skids and leaping into the sharp reeds despite the heavy sixty-pound rucks on their backs.

Fletcher leaned into his hatch-60, weaving side to side silently, eyes bulging as he scanned the tree line. But no muzzle flashes greeted them, and he would not fire first, marking their position. Gabriel had picked a good spot to set down, but it would be only a matter of seconds before the communists swarmed toward the sound of descending rotors.

He thought he spotted pith helmets bobbing up and down, through a break in the bamboo several meters away from the riverbank, but just as he was about to pull the M-60's trigger, *Peg*'s tailboom rose and, with a gut-flopping suddenness, the gunship leaped up over the trees and rose into the thick, oppressive night sky, leaving the LZ behind.

"I don't envy 'em *this* one," Gabriel clicked in, referring to Brock's seemingly hopeless mission of linking up with the encircled cavalrymen on the ground.

"It's definitely a rat-fuck," the warrant officer seated

beside him agreed.

"To the umpteenth degree."

"Rodg."

No shit, Sherlock. Snakeman sneered at their seeming indifference. He read it in their tone, not the content of words exchanged over the intercom. *Why aren't we banking around tighter? We should already be back over the battle! I got belts to unload, gentlemen!* Fletcher was bouncing about on the heels of his jungle boots, eager to taste gunsmoke on the air again. *The Snakeman's cruisin' for a bombastic bruisin,' so let's shit into the fan or get off the friggin' pot!*

It was suddenly rush-hour traffic in the night sky. *Pegasus* darted to the left and dropped abruptly, narrowly missing two oncoming gunships that burst forth over the treetops without warning on either side

Gabriel was cursing into his headset mike, but Fletcher didn't bother listening in. His ears filled with the roar of M-60 rounds pouring down into the Void as he spotted a burst of green enemy tracers and zeroed-in on their estimated point of origin. "You die, *Du Ma!*" he yelled until his throat ached, well aware it was doubtful anyone on the ground could even hear him. "Tonight you fry for sure, you *bic*? Do you fucking *bic*, motherfuckers?" The barrel of his hatch machine gun began to glow a dull orange in the dark.

A flash bright as the sunrise lit up a long stretch of the jungle as one of the Vietnamese fired a shoulder-launched rocket a hundred yards to the port. The three men aboard *Pegasus* gasped into their microphones as the projectile zigzagged madly after one of the other gunships.

"Xin Loi and sorry 'bout that" the peter pilot muttered without further emotion.

"No way," Gabriel disagreed, as if it would help the Huey escape. But an eyeblink later, the rocket slammed into the craft's tailboom.

"Jesus." Fletcher bit into his lower lip as the helicopter exploded in midair. He watched the wreckage tumble end over end down through the treetops, a series of billowing green and orange fireballs that set a snakelike stretch of the jungle canopy aflame.

"Snakeman!"

Fletcher vaguely heard the gunslinger calling back to him over the intercom at the same moment he realized himself what he was doing: as they banked away from the rolling concussion, his finger was still on the trigger. Red tracers arced out harmlessly into space, across the river, as *Pegasus* circled around.

"Shit, Elliott! Conserve ammo, goddamnit!" Gabriel jumped on him verbally.

Fletcher knew he deserved it, and he knew The Gunslinger was really upset whenever he used Snakeman's first name like that. It didn't happen often.

Gabriel's attention quickly returned to his flying, however, and he began conversing with the other pilots, trying to avoid any midair collisions as the five craft swooped in and out of the area using every off-the-wall angle imaginable in an attempt to avoid and evade ground fire.

"They're gonna get him! They're gonna get him! THEYREGONNAGETHIM!" The peter pilot's concern became one long, drawn-out multisyllabled word as he and Gabriel watched a string of green tracers arc up toward the chopper ahead, overcorrect, then fall back slowly until both ship and bullets came together in a sudden flash of rapidly expanding silver.

"Fuck," Gabriel muttered into his mike as black smoke billowed out behind the stricken ship, obscuring his own vision. Except for blue and gold flames crackling along the bird's undercarriage far up ahead, the sky went black again.

"Goddamnit!" His co-pilot's tonal inflection told Fletcher he was beginning to dwell on self-survival and the dwindling odds of returning from this romeo-foxtrot.

"He's not goin' down an' dirty," Gabe announced as the bird banked sharply to the right, out of *Pegasus*'s way, limped over some treetops, and began gaining altitude again despite the obvious damage. The radio net resumed its nonstop cacophony of garbled chatter as the other pilots advised the AC in the crippled Huey what type of damage they could observe in the dark.

"Think he'll make it back?"

"Nope. But he'll make it out of the kill zone."

"That's all that matters."

"Rodg your last, brother. Three down and four to go."

"You're counting the first ship back at the initial LZ. That's not fair."

"Who's playing fair?"

Snakeman shook his head as he listened in to the anonymous, nonsensical exchanges taking place on the net. He was half out the hatch, hanging by his monkey straps as he scanned the free fire zone below, seeking green tracerflash. He wanted to draw enemy blood so bad now he could almost taste it, could smell it on the muggy, rain forest air. The rotors overhead tried to bat it back down, tried to push the Void away. But The Snake could still smell Cong blood, and he wanted the river to run red with it.

Something caused him to glance back over his shoulder, but there was nothing there except dead space between his position and the opposite, open, unmanned hatch. His eyes drifted to the stack of ammo boxes latched to one wall of the ship. Several thousand rounds, minimum. More than he could possibly unload before Gabe had to return for fuel. And that motivated Fletch to let go. To abandon his usual ammunition conservation practices.

He leaned into the M-60 and fired long, sustained bursts down into the trees, confident he knew where the friendly forces were and could avoid them. He unloaded on everything else, well aware only one in a hundred rounds was striking flesh, if that many. But he kept firing, long after the barrel began glowing again, and it felt good. His weekly communion with the Void;

126

his guarantee of everlasting life and jungle justice.

Someone on the ground popped an illumination flare, and as the silk parachute drifted toward *Pegasus*, Snakeman reached out, feeling suddenly godlike, trying to grab it. But the rotor downblast knocked it away long before it was within reach.

Fletcher leaned farther out the hatch as they swooped low between the treetops. He leaned out as far as he could, forgetting his hog for the moment, desperation in his moist eyes as he watched the flare wobble back and forth uncertainly in the powerful rotorwash. Would the 'chute collapse? Would Snakeman's giant firefly die on the sticky, fetid breeze?

"Well, aw*RIGHT*!" he chanted, both fists raised as the parachute recovered, billowing out again to drift gracefully down toward the treetops.

He lost sight of it as Gabriel circled around and the fire raging in the distance destroyed what little remained of his purple vision.

Opening his right eye—his guneye—which he'd kept closed out of habit the moment he first saw the flare rising up through the jungle clearing, Fletcher caught sight of a group Americans on the ground. He'd lost his bearings due to The Gunslinger's evasive flying maneuvers; all he could tell was that they were heading toward the river. But he couldn't see them well enough to recognize faces or unit characteristics. And the location of the other team they were to link up with was unknown.

"Gabe," he clicked in, but *Peg*'s pilot had already spotted them.

"Rodg, Snake. We got 'em."

"Can't be sure if there's other friendlies, though," the peter pilot cautioned, "or where."

"Switching over." Gabriel announced he would try to contact someone on the ground, but there was no response to his repeated attempts. "The usual clusterfuck," he muttered, bringing his ship around for another low pass. "Keep your eyes glued, Snakeman.

We're goin' down on this bad bitch, and I don't wanna catch nothin, you rodg?"

"Rodg, Gunslinger," Fletcher muttered under his breath without clicking in. "Just do it, dude. Spare me the bullshit."

He got his wish in spades.

Gabriel turned *Pegasus* onto her side as he negotiated a narrow break in the canopy, and before Fletcher recovered, they were over the firefight. He could practically reach down and grab a pith helmet if he wanted to.

"On the whiskey," the peter pilot was advising.

"I see 'em," Gabriel acknowledged. Then his tone changed. "You see 'em back there, Snake?" Meaning, *If so, then why the hell aren't you shooting?*

"No sweat." Fletcher began firing just to be firing, but he hadn't seen a damn thing. He was careful to direct the bursts out over the river, and Gabriel was too busy flying to notice where the tracers, behind his line of sight, were going.

"Brock's people are moving into position," he heard the peter pilot saying.

"Yeah," Gabriel replied dryly, "but into position where? And to help who?"

"Your guess is as good as mine, honcho-san."

"That's what I thought."

Fletcher strained to see Sgt. Brock's group, hoping he'd see his best buddy, Treat Brody. But just as he spotted the centipedelike glow of luminous helmet tape bobbing up and down through a jungle trail near the river's edge, Gabe was banking again, and he lost them.

"Tracer fire below ya, Snakeman. Right . . . NOW!" Gabriel clicked in.

"I see it." Fletcher resumed firing straight down, though he'd missed the burst of glowing green in his zeal to find The Whoremonger.

"Not there." Gabriel was bringing the ship around in a tight circle now, and Fletcher felt the Void grabbing at him. Trying to snatch him from the hatch, drag him down into the top tangle of angry canopy. "There!"

"Right. Gotcha, Gabe—no sweat!" This time he did see the enemy position and he directed a sustained flow of red, lancelike lead down into it.

"Bingo." The peter pilot cheered without genuine enthusiasm as one of the rounds hit the machine-gun nest's ammo supply, and a bright fireball rose from the jungle floor.

"Not bad, Snakeman," Gabriel chided. "A hundred rounds for one MG nest. Big fucking deal."

Fletcher was no longer listening. Out the corner of his eye as they zoomed away he'd caught the sight of Cong being blown from the fortified position as their stick grenades or satchels or whatever exploded. It was the sight Snakeman both lived for and dreaded. The scene replayed itself over and over in his head for days afterward. Days and nights. The only difference was that, at night, Charlie didn't die like he was supposed to. Whether missing a head, or both arms, or his entire belly, Charlie always came looking for the Snake. And always found him.

"Fuck this shit." The peter pilot's words reached his ears as Fletcher sought more targets of opportunity.

"They just keep on comin', don't they?" Gabriel was referring to another half dozen sampan-loads of Cong reinforcements pulling up to the riverbank on the edge of the battlefield.

"I tell ya, I just don't know if—"

"Did you hear that?" the AC's co-pilot cut him off.

Fletcher's ears perked, too. He'd also heard the muffled cry for help over the radio net. Somewhere on the ground. It was a voice he didn't recognize. A kid's. One of the twink's.

"Sharkskinner, this is—"

Intense static flooded the net, covering the soldier's call sign.

"We need a Dustoff. Request a Dustoff, do you copy? We've got—" More static. "—and the medic's guts are hangin' out all over the—"

The mournful hum of static became even more powerful, and as *Pegasus* rose above the treetops again, banking hard to the right, they lost the transmission altogether.

A vision of Doc Delgado's face filled Fletcher's mind, and he prayed to Buddha and the forces of the rain forest and any other god that might be listening to spare his favorite corpsman. He hadn't seen Delgado with Zack's team earlier and the man was not part of Brock's contingent, but he wasn't sure who Lt. Vance had on his battered and undermanned squad. "Doc don't deserve this crap," he head himself saying as *Peg* descended again.

A lone green tracer spiraled wildly in through the hatch, bouncing off the rim of his headset, and Fletcher dropped to one knee, stunned and shaken. Stunned, shaken, and mad.

"You okay, Fletch?" the peter pilot called back, but Snakeman didn't bother answering. Rushing back to his feet, he leaned out the hatch, attempting to spray the area.

Pegasus rose up and banked too quickly, however, and most of his own tracers flew out over the river again. "Take us back!" he yelled into the mike. "Take us back to that exact same spot, Gabe! Those fucks got me, man! They got me right in the head! Take us back around, the same spot! *The same goddamned spot*! I'm bringin' smoke down on those sonso'bitches, you hear me? Bookoo smoke!"

Signs of genuine concern crackled in Gabriel's tone as he clicked in. "The head?" he asked. "How bad, Snake?"

"You want us to beat blades back to camp?" The peter pilot glanced over a shoulder as he spoke into his own mike. "We can have the medics standing by and—"

"Disregard my last!" Fletcher shouted into his own headset. "My error. It was just a helmet hit!" he yelled, even though the impact had left a deep bruise

130

where the bullet ricocheted, and the impact caused his chin strap to gouge a chunk of flesh out of his cheek. "Just take this crate back over that exact spot!"

"Your request is my command," Gabriel muttered with a grim smile.

"Run that by me again?" The co-pilot was not laughing, but his eyes seemed to twinkle.

"Nebbah mind." The Gunslinger shook his head from side to side slowly. "Don' mean nothin' no how."

Snakeman tensed as they circled around and began dropping. Treetops rose up on either side, and he felt the hairs rise on his arms and neck "This is it, you bastards." He leaned into the M-60, preparing to unload on the enemy. "You're sure to go to heaven, 'cause you've spent your time in hell!"

"Comin' up on 'em, Snakeman," Gabriel warned. "Right where those two long logs part, sorta like a fallen V. That's where the tracers came from."

"Goin' down on the beaver," Snakeman heard the peter pilot join in. "Make her happy, Elliott, 'cause the bad bitch is in a mean mood tonight!"

CHAPTER 15

"Tell me about the mark."

Anna tensed, but Nelson anticipated her uneasiness, and his lips dropped again to the breast over her racing heart.

She sighed as his mouth went to work gently, taking her into him as he had been consumed earlier. Anna never imagined it would be this way, lovemaking. The sensations still wracked her body, curling her toes, and now he was going at it again, fingers massaging. Probing. Entering her again. Exciting her, making her want to wrap her legs around him for the fifth time in half as many hours.

He had made love to her four times already that night. Four times. Anna stared at the lizard clinging once more to the ceiling overhead as his tongue forced her nipples taut and erect.

In her mind, she saw the women of the compound, long before their men had been sent away, when she was younger. She saw the women gathered around their laundry trough, and she heard their voices, their laughter as they taunted each other about the soldiers in their lives.

"He can only do it once," she heard one of the mama-sans in her memory complaining. "Once, and then he's done for the whole week. He collapses on my chest, snoring in my ear."

"That's better than nothing," the woman beside her commented.

"Oh?"

"My man expresses interest only once, maybe twice a month."

"That's why she buys so many cucumbers at market," a middle-aged woman across the washing trough accused, and the others giggled.

"My man," one of the newlyweds in the group boasted, "makes love to me twice a night, *every* night!"

The assemblage of women erupted into a chorus of skeptical guffaws. "If I'm lying, I'm dying!" the newlywed protested in GI jargon. Her singsong voice remained musical in its tone, but the laughter only increased.

Twice a night, every night. Anna thought back to that day at the washing trough several years ago. She could still hear the newlywed's voice as if it were only yesterday. The woman had sounded so proud, basking in the obvious envy of the others. She had not been fooled by their taunts and teasing. They believed her, remembering, perhaps, their own first weeks after the wedding.

Anna sighed. Nelson was trying to work her thighs apart with his knee again. Gently, slowly, preparing her for round five. She was eager to comply, but she found herself whispering, "Do you never tire, Nelson?"

His lips were working along her flat stomach now, and she found herself wishing his mouth would drop between her legs again. Now that had shocked her to Bien Hoa and back! She had never imagined that a man's tongue could bring such pleasure. Though she had tried to pull his face back up to her, out of the shadows below her waist, he resisted, and she found that her mild, mock protests soon dissolved as the clouds possessed her, lifting Anna up off the modest sleeping mat, up out of her ramshackle home, high into the heavens.

"Do I ever tire?" Nelson repeated her question with an evil grin. He sighed with satisfaction, laying the side of his face against the smooth curve of her lower abdomen. "Not tonight. Not with you."

"This will make five times we have made love," she whispered, wondering if the women sleeping on the other side of the walls could hear, and if they would be gossiping about the sounds tomorrow, when they gathered around the washing trough. She would have to listen carefully as she approached. If they suddenly went silent upon her arrival, then she would know. And she would smile proudly, though there would be those few who would disapprove of her sleeping with a foreigner. Most of them would only be jealous, though, she knew. The older mama-sans would remain silent, no doubt, uncommitted. And she would know they sided with her. Most of them. Then again, maybe she would not trek down to the washing trough at all tomorrow. Perhaps she would disappear for a few days and nights. The way the newlyweds always did. If she could persuade Nelson to remain with her. But she knew he would have to go in the pre-dawn darkness. Soldiers always left their homes before the sun broke free of the eastern horizon, and her man would be no different.

Nelson made as if to roll away from her, and for a moment, Anna feared he would be leaving already. But then she realized he was only toying with her, and before she really knew what was happening, he was between her legs again, tongue buried in her mouth, and her thighs rose up against his hips, ankles locking over his back as her haunches pressed against the floor firmly, making the teakwood planks creak and sigh along.

When they were through, Anna lay with her knees bent and her toes curled against the soles of her feet and the side of her face against the cool wooden floor, lips slightly parted and eyes tightly shut. He asked her to tell him about the scar.

"What?" Her lips curled back from her teeth, animallike. She tried to open her eyes, tried to flatten the soles of her feet against the teakwood planks, but the sensations were still swirling about inside her, still devouring her. She was possessed with love, still consumed with desire for him, yet she no longer had any control over her body. Could not even bring herself to reach out to him once more.

"What?" she sighed again, finally opening her eyes. The first thing she saw was the lizard, still clinging upside-down to a corner of the ceiling, still watching them closely.

"Tell me about the mark."

"No," she replied softly, unperturbed. "Not tonight. Later. Tomorrow, maybe; next week."

Nelson rolled close to her. He ran the edge of his finger along the scar, and the aroma rising from his hand wrinkled her nose and pulled a deep laugh from the pit of her belly. She tried to roll away from him, thinking how odd it was that the fragrance of their mixed juices both aroused and repelled her. She tried to roll away, onto her other side, but he reached out and grasped her shoulder firmly. "Ready for Numba Six?" His eyes gleamed mischievously, and she feigned intense fear.

"No!" she replied in mock terror. "Not again!"

Anna reached down between their sweat-slick bodies and took hold of him. "*Choi-oi!*" her voice rose several octaves with the last syllable. "Still?"

Nelson rolled his head from side to side proudly, imitating Jackie Gleason. "It never goes down," he said.

Shifting his hips against hers, Nelson jabbed Anna with it playfully. "Now, talk! Or else."

"Or else what?" She grabbed and twisted slightly.

Her man of the world did not even flinch. It seemed he no longer had any feelings below the waist. But

Nelson wanted Anna to remember tonight. If he never repeated this performance again, he was going to make sure she never forgot what she'd learned and felt and experienced tonight.

"Or else I lock it up in an iron jockstrap, and you don't get to play with it again for one year."

"Not until we speak of love?" Her expression turned serious as she gazed up at him with sad eyes, but Nelson knew she was still teasing.

"Right. One year. Three hundred and sixty-five long, lonely nights without Little Joe to go riding the range with again."

"But I would still be able to hold you?" she reluctantly released him.

"Yes. And I would be able to do anything I wanted to do with *your* body." He smiled almost demonically. For some reason, Sgt. Brock's face flashed in front of his eyes, but he shook the vision away, and added, "For example . . ." and began licking the inner slopes of her breasts until Anna's head fell back. The flesh along her throat tightened, and when Nelson resumed massaging certain parts of her body again, she sighed.

"This . . . does . . . not . . . seem . . . fair." Her entire frame shuddered as his fingers went to work, expertly finding the most sensitive spots.

"It's not supposed to be fair."

She was twisting side to side now, like a snake trying to make its way across a sand dune while a little, mischievous boy held onto the tip of its tail, and Nelson did not think she even heard a word he had said.

"Okay." She shuddered again as the tingling sensations reached still anther climax. "I . . . will . . . talk."

With the edge of his foot, Nelson rubbed the soles of her own. They were not rough, sandpapery, like other Vietnamese women he'd already known during his brief stint in-country, but soft, smooth as silk. Anna was a city girl. Or had been. "Your toes have curled up on you." He tried to pry them open with his own, but she

136

seemed frozen. Her knees bent as she began curling into the fetal position, chest thrust out, breasts jutting proudly, belly sucked in until he could see the outline of her ribcage.

"I cannot help it." The sigh, this time, left her not unlike a child's happy tune. "I never feel this way before."

"That's good," he whispered close to her ear, glancing at the sleeping mat as she raised her thighs off the ground slightly. But he could see no blood. Wasn't there supposed to be blood? he asked himself, mildly surprised yet uncaring. If even just a smear, as evidence? Maybe women Anna's age didn't leave proof of their previous "untainted" virtue. He shrugged off the thought, and pulled her close.

Anna laid her face against his chest, listened to his heart beating slowly for a few moments, then began to talk about the mark.

"It was with a tiger," she said. The long-buried memories flooded back to scream in her head, memories that gnawed at her each time she looked in a mirror but had failed to surface clearly until tonight.

"A tiger?" Nelson drew his face back as if to gauge her expression, her truthfulness, but Anna was staring up at the ceiling. Two more lizards had joined the first.

"Yes. You did not know Vietnam has tigers?" Her words shifted into that peculiar, childlike voice she often used when posing questions or revealing surprise.

"Well, yes, but . . ."

"We have elephants, too. And buffalo. Water buffalo, and big, long python snakes, and—"

"Yes, yes, I know. Please continue." He reached down behind her and gently pinched the curve of her buttocks, but Anna didn't seem to notice.

"I was in a jungle clearing, all alone, deep in the heart of the rain forest," she said, trying to envision the scene she was making up for him as she went along. But all she could see was the gang of Vietnamese bandits chasing her along the Saigon docks nearly fifteen years ago.

"Sounds spooky." Nelson wrapped his arms around her, soaking up her body heat as he rested his nose and lips against the top of her head.

"It was. I was with my girlfriends. We had just gotten out of school for the day, and decided to take a shortcut through the forest."

This is beginning to sound like the fairy tale mama-sans back in The World told misbehaving American children, Nelson decided. The one where the big bad wolf suckers the cherry girl into grandmother's house, then rips her tits off.

Anna shifted her head against his chest, and some of her long jet-black hair fanned across his cheek. He breathed in her fragrance as the radiant, silky strands covered one of his closed eyes, and Nelson wondered how long he could hide in this little cubicle of theirs. How long could he stay with her, if he really wanted to? Nestled in a villa located smack-dab in the middle of one of the U.S. Army's most fearsome fighting units, would they ever think to search for him here? Surely they'd assume he fled to Saigon, or deserted to Danang. They'd never consider the possibility that he was living right under their noses.

But Nelson knew he loved the service more than any woman. It would never be worth going AWOL for love. He just hoped he felt the same way after spending the entire night with Anna.

Would he feel differently about her after the harsh rays of a tropical sun woke them in the morning? When he saw her in the dawn's early light, would he still be mesmerized by her beauty?

But of course he would, Nelson realized. Anna had been gorgeous out on the perimeter, when he first laid eyes on her, and she had worn no makeup then. She would not change in the morning; she would still be as striking as ever. That was the one thing he could give these Annamese maidens credit for: they didn't need cosmetics, and they didn't need nylons. And that was proof positive in Nasty Nel's guide to Girls of the

Orient. They didn't peel and scrub their good looks off before climbing into the rack with you.

Nelson felt himself drifting from her as an intense desire for sleep suddenly settled over him. He could still hear her voice, though, faintly, as if in an echo chamber. He saw himself walking beside her, through the rain forest clearing, as the tiger stalked them from beyond the bamboo. He knew he was dreaming—or half-dreaming, for he was still conscious of lying beside her—of listening to Anna's story.

"We wanted to take a shortcut through the woods, but dusk passed more quickly than we expected, and darkness fell across the land before we got halfway through the long stretch of trees between our village and the next one over.

"My girlfriend, Cuc, grabbed my arm without warning, pulling me into shadows as a tiger with brown and orange stripes rushed past, chasing a wild boar," Anna said, trying to envision the huge cat but seeing only the group of four men chasing her through the maze of back alleys that ran uphill from the Saigon docks. All waving machetes. She watched them surrounding the younger Anna, forcing her to run into a fenced lot, and finally, an abandoned warehouse.

"We thought we were safe, Cuc and I, but then, just as we ventured out into the clearing, trying to get back our bearings, a second tiger leaped from the shadows. It struck me in the shoulder, knocking me aside. The only injury I received was this single mark on my face," she claimed. Memories of the men catching her in a corner and throwing her down onto the ground flooded back to haunt her.

"The tiger, all he did was scratch my face with his claws. He wanted Cuc. I don't know why, but he held little interest in me. Perhaps it was because Cuc was younger. Ahhh, my precious girlfriend." Anna sighed as she opened her eyes, stared at the ceiling above—and still saw the men ripping her clothes away, threatening her with the long blade if she did not open her mouth.

"Poor little Cuc. The tiger jumped on Cuc, knocking the wind from her lungs. And then, while I watched, it ate her."

Nelson's eyes opened as explosions in the distance roused him, and he remembered instantly where he was. The fog lifted from before his eyes, and he concentrated on Anna's story, remembering clearly every word she had spoken about Cuc and the tiger and the jungle clearing thus far. But he knew. Anna was lying. Or, at the least, hiding from the truth.

The mark on her face was not from a tiger's claw. Tigers ripped and slashed and gouged. They did not leave clean, razor thin cuts. The scar on Anna's chin had been inflicted with a sharp knife.

But if she did not want to tell him the whole story, that was okay, too, Nelson decided. After all, this was only their first night together. Later, after a few weeks had passed, he would bring up the mark again. Maybe he would get her good and drunk first. Maybe then Anna would open up to him.

Anna's lips pursed, as if she wanted to say more, to reveal the truth to her man. But she said nothing. She stared up at the ceiling, suddenly mute, the lower lip starting to tremble slightly. She could still see the *cao boi*. In her tortured mind, the younger Anna was still on the ground, pinned down by four men, one holding onto each limb as she kicked and tried to strike back. The younger Anna was still refusing to open her mouth for the fifth *cao boi* unzipping his trousers.

One of the hoodlums was running the knife against the bridge of her nose now, threatening, in Chinese, to cut it off. Anna didn't understand Chinese, but she knew what he was going to do, how he planned to carve her up with the switchblade.

When the warehouse doors burst open and two *canh-sats*—Vietnamese policemen—rushed in with revolvers drawn, the man with the knife slashed her chin before fleeing with the others. He slashed hard and deep, but she considered herself lucky. Anna knew he had been

140

aiming for her eyes, trying to slash across her eyeballs. So she would not be able to point him out, later, in court.

Typical *cao boi* manner of thinking.

The officers shot four of the hoods, killing three. But they missed the man with the switchblade. He escaped, and the other *cao boi*, whose spine stopped three bullets that rainy monsoon night, was crippled, and could still be found pushing himself around in a toy wagon, down in the Tu Do redlight district, begging from the American GIs.

Rain began falling lightly on the roof of Anna's tiny, one-woman cubicle.

They listened to the growing clamor of drops striking hot tin. Strong sheets of rain lashed across the tiny camp nestled between Cho Gao and Mytho in the Mekong River Delta, and they held each other tightly as their minds wandered to different places.

Nelson was listening to the thunder rumble across the land. No matter how tightly he closed his eyes, lightning crackling directly overhead seemed able to reach the very center of his mind, his conscience. He listened to the thunder mingling with explosions in the distance and he felt guilt at being warm and secure and sexually satisfied beside one of the most beautiful women in Vietnam while his friends in Echo Company low-crawled through the muck and mud, perhaps only a few thousand meters away, dodging hot lead, and sometimes stopping it with their flesh, as the battle raged in glowing shades of green and red tracer light.

Anna saw a little girl kneeling in a rain forest clearing, all alone, crying over the mutilated carcass of Cuc, her dead girlfriend. Tears began sliding down her cheeks as she realized how foolish it all really was, making up the story about Cuc and the tiger and the rain forest clearing.

Anna wondered if she was finally losing her mind. Perhaps she had already lost it. But the fact that she could still clearly remember the incident in the Saigon docks warehouse proved she was still sane. That she could still compose a harmless story about a tiger and two schoolgirls meant her sense of humor was still intact.

Wiping her tears away, she glanced over to see if Nelson noticed she was crying, if he was appraising her behavior critically, in muted silence. What could he possibly think of her now? He would be able to sense they were not tears of happiness. But would he care?

When Anna looked up into his face, she realized he was asleep. Was he dreaming? she wondered. And would the dreams be about her?

Both disappointed and relieved, Anna resisted the urge to cuddle him again, to hold him tight. Slowly and quietly, she rolled away, turning her back to him. Anna wanted to cry some more, to let the tears flow freely, now that she was no longer alone in the night. This time she would cry because she was happy.

But the tears had stopped. Her eyes were already dry, and hard as she tried, she could not lure the emotion from her heart again.

CHAPTER 16

Zack's men watched the blond-haired woman plunge feet first into the murky Mekong. Vance's people saw her get flung from the tree limb, too. But there was little they could do for her; their first priority was blowing the Loach, and they'd be lucky if they could accomplish that much. Right now, both teams were fighting for their lives, just trying to survive.

That the VC picked that particular time to land another half dozen sampans full of comrades didn't help matters any. What did help was a lucky lob by Corky Cordova, whose fragmentation grenade landed in the midst of the guerrillas as they began assembling in ankle-deep water along the riverbank. One of their claymores—captured, no doubt, from U.S. forces weeks or months earlier—exploded, taking several Cong out of commission. Flying shrapnel hit some of Zack's troops, too, and one of his two medics died slowly in Delgado's arms, from ruptured stomach and sucking chest wounds.

"Well, awright!" Two-Step had slapped Cordova on the back as shattered AK's and shredded tire-tread sandals flew through the air. "That's a half dozen for the body count, troop! Not bad, for a southpaw!"

"Ain't a southpaw!" Cordova and Broken Arrow both

rolled for cover against the same cluster of water-logged trunks. "But my right arm's all screwed up, brother. Think I caught some shrapnel back there."

"Let me look at it." Broken Arrow saw the crimson-soaked spot along his armpit immediately and, setting his grenade launcher down carefully on the soft ground, started to rip the seam of Cordova's fatigue shirt.

"Hey!" Corky protested. "These is the only threads the Cork's got left, dude! Go easy, will ya?"

"I just wanna make sure the Cork don' bleed to death on us, dude." Broken Arrow elected not to rip the shirt open after all. By the light of a flare passing low overhead, he made the decision then and there not to call for Delgado, the medic. Slapping Cordova on the flak jacket, he said, "No sweat. Just a couple puncture wounds. In the muscle. Gonna hurt like a raw ding-dong come morning, sunshine."

"Wish I could complain about a raw ding-dong, you fuckwad." Cordova checked his rifle magazine, then slammed the clip's bottom with the palm of his hand to make sure it was still seated securely in the M-16's feeder well.

"Just glad it's you and not me." Broken Arrow started to rise, but Cordova grabbed his arm.

"I was just wonderin,' " he began sarcastically, and Two-Step jerked his arm away.

But the Indian was grinning again. "You was won-derin' what?"

"You gonna fire that fuckin' thing," Corky motioned toward the M-79 thumper, "or just stroke it all night?"

Broken Arrow laughed and started to move off into thicker elephant grass. "Where the hell you been, skate?" he asked, dropping the weapon against his crotch. It normally looked like a swollen sawed-off shotgun, but now it appeared to be a ghastly erection, throbbing in the flickering flarelight. "Me and m' blooper been blowin' away Charlie Congs all night, brothaaaa!" And then he was gone, another shadow in

144

the reeds. Sporadic discharges rattled from the riverbank, fifty yards away, and three green tracers sizzled
through the black space Broken Arrow had just tra-
versed.

Cordova squinted, scouring the treeline for movement. "Two-Step! Two-Step, where the hell you goin',
boy?" He sounded suddenly worried. "Don't leave the
Cork out here by his lonesome, goddamnit!" When
they'd rolled for cover, away from the others and
against the logs, the rest of the squad had moved on
toward Vance's last known location. And Cordova was
no longer sure just exactly where that was.

Broken Arrow still had not replied. Cordova listened
to something rustling in the treeline where he'd last
seen the Comanche, but then he heard the thumper's
distinctive discharge quite a distance away, and guerrillas screaming down along the riverbank after the grenade exploded, and he knew the rustling wasn't coming
from Broken Arrow. The rustling of leaves was only a
dozen feet beyond the bamboo.

Cordova glanced around, already drenched in sweat
in the short amount of time his friend had been gone.
There was no sign of the others, either. Zack had led
them down one of the other trails; they'd be circling
around, trying to link up with Vance's people for a
counterassault. Leo would not have bothered worrying
about whether or not Corky kept up. Cordova was one
of his seasoned vets. The newbies were his current
concern.

Cordova's mood shifted from worry to anger. Anger
at himself for having let the situation get away from
him. This was the jungle. You didn't fool around in the
rain forest. Yet, those mere thirty seconds had cost him
the edge. He was lost in the middle of a firefight. Fear
tainted his anger now. Noises were coming from the
opposite tree line, too. Were they Americans? He'd
seen one of the Hueys set down along the riverbank,
surely unloading more troops. But when he rolled for
cover with Two-Step, he'd lost his bearings. He lis-

tened for the river, and glanced up, searching for the dangling Loach.

When he got hold of Broken Arrow, he was going to personally wring the crazy Indian's neck for getting him into this mess and—

Cordova froze. He suddenly felt like an unwilling participant in some childhood nightmare. The trees were beginning to move. Cordova held in his breath as he watched branches and then whole sections of elephant grass shift and part as several dozen pith helmets emerged from the grainy darkness.

Another flare passed overhead, and he sank deeper into cover as the pith helmets froze in place. Were they really there? he wondered. Or was it just his imagination?

A gust of breeze ushered the flare past the treetops, and in the flickering yellow light he watched the pith helmets start moving again. Toward him. Several dozen of them. Viet Cong on the prowl.

Something sparkled in their midst, and then the sparkles began multiplying in the intense darkness.

When the Vietnamese communists were only twenty feet away, he realized they were fixed bayonets, reflecting the moonlight.

Orson and Graham stared at each other with that typically terrified newby expression intact as the deuce-and-a-half roared down the narrow, winding dirt road. They were speeding to their doom, Graham was quite confident. The explosions and small arms fire were no longer distant, but just around the corner, it seemed, growing louder and louder with each breath he took.

A short, stocky buck sergeant stood up in the back of the troop transport. He was a black NCO, with close-cropped hair, a long, drooping mustache, and scars crisscrossing his forehead.

146

"Okay!" the sergeant yelled, waving his M-16 over his head to get their attention. "If you haven't already, then lock and load, mates, 'cause this is it! Echo Company's reporting heavy contact just around the bend. And we're the only help left in Cho Gao—me and ten motherfucking cherries!"

He closed his eyes tightly and lowered his head in a swinging expression of resignation as if to ask his Lord what he had done recently to deserve this. "When the truck starts to stop, you don't dick around! I'll give you the command, then we bail out two at a time—straight out the tail gate, understand? No John Wayne heroics. Two at a time, and split apart when you hit the ground. Roll opposite each other, toward whatever cover's available!"

The black NCO scanned ten sets of bulging white eyes. As an afterthought, he added, "And don' go divin' in no roadside ditches less'n you're pos'tive ain't no damn punji stakes waitin' for yo ass!" His lips puckered skeptically, and he shook his head again. "Got that?" he asked, but there was no time for responses. The truck was not slowing, it was skidding. Skidding sideways, the front windshield shattered and the driver dead. Tracers were spiraling through the cab of the truck, trying to bite men scrambling for the tail gate in the back. "MOVE IT!" the buck sergeant was screaming. He and Graham and Orson did not waste time waiting for the men to jump off. The trio vaulted over the truck's wooden side railings.

"Fuck this shit," Graham muttered after they'd tumbled and rolled to an unceremonious halt in the roadside gully. Sharpened slivers of yellow bamboo rose up on either side of them. The odor of stale urine was heavy on the air.

"Damnit." The NCO ground his teeth as they watched the disabled truck, its gears in neutral, engine racing, and front tires hissing with puncture wounds, begin rolling backward toward them.

"We gotta move!" Graham yelled. The truck would

roll right back onto them any second, and it was gaining speed.

"Fuck it!" The sergeant frantically kicked some of the punji sticks away and pushed the two newbies aside as the vehicle dropped backward into the deep gully with a muffled scraping of iron against cracking bamboo and unyielding earth. Graham and Orson watched the truck's front end rise up diagonally into the night air and stay there, driver hanging halfway out the open leftside door. "Now you two pogues stay right here!" the NCO hissed, eyes glaring. "Use the truck as cover. But don't move from this spot! I'll be right—"

"What if—"

"Cram your what-if's where the sun don't shine, sonny!" The sergeant grabbed the front of Graham's shirt for emphasis. "I'll be right fucking back!" He could barely be heard above the loud hissing of the front tires, still spinning a few feet over their heads.

Orson glanced directly up the road. Green spurts of MG tracer flew out at them from a clump of logs. It was a Cong machine-gun nest, or possibly just one man placed there with an RPD to slow down any American reinforcements. Either way, it was obvious the black NCO intended to take it out by himself.

Orson scanned the dark roadway behind them. He could see none of the other eight men who had accompanied them from the base camp. Probably just hugging dirt a few meters away, he decided. Just like us. Waiting for someone to tell them what the hell to do. "I'll cover you!" Orson volunteered.

Ignoring him, the sergeant reached up and stabbed his forefinger into the driver's neck, searching for a pulse. Shaking his head from side to side, he pulled the man's body out of the cab just as a burst of rounds put several holes in the door. The sideview mirror exploded, showering them all with more glass as the corpse flopped onto the ground between Orson and Graham.

Orson stared at the dead GI. His face was a pulpy,

crimson mess. Unrecognizable. The top part of the back of his head was missing where one of the bullets had exited. Orson did not want to stay in the dark ditch with the mutilated man. "I'll cover you!" he repeated, much louder than the first time.

The NCO almost laughed. "You stay right here!" He pointed a finger directly in Orson's face, reminding the private of the Uncle Sam Wants You poster that had greeted him at the recruiting center seventeen weeks earlier. "I'm gonna have enough troubles without havin' to babysit a green cherry!" And then he was off, zigzagging from tree to tree along one side of the roadway, firing short bursts from his M-16.

"Green cherry?" Orson turned to face Graham. "What the flyin' fuck is a green cherry?"

"We're green cherries, dipshit." Graham was keeping his face close to the earth. "Just do what the lifer says, and maybe we'll make it out of this."

"Bullshit!" Orson rose up on one knee in time to see a single green flash spit from the enemy position. The tracer missed but another bullet struck the NCO in the chest as he got to within a dozen meters of the MG nest.

"Don't do nothin' stupid!" Graham had watched the sergeant go down too. He grabbed Orson's wrist, but the private jerked his arm away.

"I'm not!" Orson jumped up and began firing over the fallen NCO's head. "I'm doin' my duty, asshole!" And then he was gone.

Graham watched him fire several more shots with the rifle butt against his shoulder as he awkwardly crossed the roadway. None of the rounds seemed to come even close, but the enemy position did not respond. Graham shook his head from side to side in resignation. "Asshole," he muttered under his breath. "The dumbfuck has the gall to call me an asshole." He watched Orson somersault down into the ditch on the other side of the road.

Graham stared back over a shoulder. There was still no sign of the other eight men who'd shared the truck

149

ride in with them. "You guys okay back there?" he yelled, expecting to receive no reply whatsoever.

"Yeah, we're okay, and we're gonna stay okay!" a defiant voice yelled back.

"Notify us when it's all over!" another voice called to Graham.

He could imagine them all clustered together at the bottom of the ravine, back to back, ready to die with their rifles blazing, but not about to assault any enemy positions without a bonafide NCO to lead them.

"God damnit." Graham could see Orson low-crawling toward the black sergeant, M-16 draped over his wrists and held in place with the sling—just like the confidence courses back in Basic, where they'd have to scurry under barbed wire, live ammo firing over their heads. That had been a joke. This was suddenly dead serious. "Man, if this don't suck the big one, I don't know what does." But he knew he couldn't just let Orson face the enemy machine gunners alone. He stared at the NCO. The sergeant had rolled onto his back and was breathing heavily as small puffs of dust rose up all around him. Hopefully he'd just gotten the wind knocked from his lungs. Hopefully his flak vest had done its job.

"Wait up, you cocksucker!" Graham yelled at Orson as he rose up out of the ditch. But his words were drowned out by the heavy MG down the road suddenly blasting away again. The enemy had anticipated movement near the disabled truck, and were just waiting for the next hero to emerge. Rounds ripped into the dirt all around Graham, and a splinter of lead lanced into one of his testicles. *"Damn!"* he screamed, grabbing his crotch as he ran, and instantly releasing it—touching the wound hurt even more!

Orson was firing at the enemy position again and the MG shut down just long enough for Graham to make it halfway to the sergeant.

When he looked up again, Orson was scrambling on all fours right up to the fallen NCO. Rolling onto his

150

own back as a burst of tracers passed inches above his face, Graham ejected his half-spent magazine and slammed a fresh twenty-round clip into place, switched his selector to AUTO, and unloaded the full twenty on rock-and-roll as he rushed, in a low crouch, toward the two soldiers.

A ten-round burst stitched across the roadway in front of him, throwing dirt into his face and against his chest, and several splinters of lead struck his thighs. But the machine gunner abruptly pulled back on his weapon, and several tracers arced up into the heavens.

He'd hit the man!

Graham had been planning to dive beside Orson and the wounded NCO. Instead, he rushed past, glancing down just long enough to see the gaping belly wound and nearly severed wrist hanging in the dust.

Graham began yelling at the top of his lungs as he charged the machine-gun nest. He was screaming at himself, more than anything, angry that he was reacting this way. He should be back with the other eight men, supervising the dug-in circle-jerk, not playing battle-field hero. But here he was, rushing an enemy position, just like John Wayne.

And then he was flying through the air, landing boots first on the two dead North Vietnamese soldiers, twisting his ankle slightly on the unmanned machine gun.

One of the NVA was staring up at Graham with lifeless, unblinking, almost defiant eyes, and the American was suddenly insulted. Suddenly insulted and never so offended before. Were they mocking him and Orson and the dying NCO, even in death? Was this "struggle for reunification" of theirs so damned sacred that no foreigners regardless of their good intentions could ever make a difference, even if they sacrificed their blood to keep South Vietnam free? Graham the pacifist, Graham the anti-war draftee suddenly found himself bringing his riflebutt back.

He slammed it down into the dead man's face. Over and over and over, trying to close those eyes forever.

151

He was still crushing the soldier's skull into chunks of mushy bone when Orson appeared beside him.

"The sarge is dead," he announced, glancing around wildly as they stood in the open. But there appeared to be no other enemy troops nearby; the big firefight was raging two or three hundred yards beyond a bend in the road.

"I said the sergeant is dead!" Orson finally realized what Graham was doing, and reached out to grab the swinging rifle. "Okay, Graham-Cracker!" He wanted to laugh, but couldn't. "The lousy fuckwad's dead. Jesus, cut the slope some slack, man!"

A wild, animal-like look in his eyes, Graham slowly turned to face Orson. He was trembling violently. Streaks of blood covered his face and arms.

Orson forced a chuckle finally when the PFC stared down at his crimson-laced M-16 as if it were a severed body part. His hands shook, as if he wanted to throw the weapon far away but found it too sticky to release. "Boy, you were really gettin' your jollies off over that, eh, Graham-Cracker?" Orson slapped him on the back heartily. "Come on, bud. Let's trot back on down the road and blow away all them chickenshits hidin' in the ditch for desertin' under fire!" he joked.

Graham was still horrified by what he'd done. He stared down at the mangled face of the dead man, at his rifle, then back at the bloodied faceless pulp again.

Slowly, he locked eyes with Orson. "If you ever tell anyone about this," his voice was low and threatening. "I will rip out your lungs."

Orson's smile faded. He stared into Graham's eyes, wondering if he was talking about the way he killed the Vietnamese, or the fact he'd had been so enthusiastic about it.

Treat Brody became immediately suspicious.

He was only two men behind Brock, rushing down

152

the dark jungle trail toward Zack's besieged position, when the tall sergeant began giving directives in Le Loi's imposing, authoritative voice. Treat Brody still felt that odd tingle that filled him, body and soul, whenever Sgt. Brock took on the ancient warrior's spirit, but tonight was different: Brock had never pulled the rain forest ghost routine when they were actually out on a mission, actually in danger. And this time, the NCO had assumed Le Loi's identity without going through the trancelike state first. That immediately placed Brody on guard.

Could it be no mental preparation was needed out here in the heart of the jungle? Could it be this was Le Loi's old stomping grounds, and his personality shot forth instantly, like the bullets they were hearing zing about in the near distance?

A voice in Brody's head repeated his thoughts as he followed the bobbing, luminous strip of tape on the man moving in front of him down the dark trail. Could it be that Sgt. Brock was really crazy? Or could it be they were all being had? But what did Brock have to gain if he was just putting on an act? He didn't seem to be on an ego trip—far from it. The man was modest as the Madonna. And Brody had never been approached about donations of any sort, which, he'd read, was the mark of a true con artist.

Brody did not want to dwell on this. Any moment now, they would be engaging the enemy. He needed his head clear. He needed to concentrate on survival, not Brock.

But that gut instinct kept nagging at him. He felt the same uneasiness that overtook him whenever he walked through the carnies section at festivals and county fairs back in The World. That I'm-gonna-get-ripped-off feeling. But he always tossed his dimes onto the glass plates anyway, and one time he even won a giant, stuffed panda for Skulljob Jody. One time.

Screw it, he decided. This was no time to waste mental energy on Brock's antics. He needed to concentrate all his faculties on the unknowns that lay ahead. The nauseating stench of imminent hostile encounter was on the air. It was only a matter of seconds now. He could feel danger rustling the leaves.

Brody fell back silently, away from the imposing figure of Sgt. Brock mumbling directives in Le Loi's accent. He edged out of the formation so expertly that the men behind him never even noticed. He watched the first few rush through the murky darkness of the rain forest to catch up with the soldier that had been between him and Brock.

Treat Brody would take up the tail, far from Brock's influence, where he could control his own actions, be his own man again.

Following Brock into battle had been a test of his faith in Le Loi, and Void Vicious was laughing in his face.

CHAPTER 17

Zack counted two gunships in the night sky. Only two. The rest were either down 'n dirty, or had beat blades back to camp with too many bulletholes in their fuselage to stay airmobile.

When this was over, he made a mental note, Zack would make a point of putting Broken Arrow in for at least a Bronze Star for Valor: For the last fifteen minutes, he'd heard roughly two dozen blooper rounds sail out into the enemy positions. He recognized Two-Step's M-79 instantly, and it seemed a majority of the grenades were scoring high on the NVA body count. Their resistance had dwindled down to two pockets of combined VC and North Vietnamese, and his people had been able to link up with Vance's squad with few casualties. Only two men missed the headcount: Broken Arrow and Cordova. Broken Arrow was accounted for, and Zack wasn't going to worry about the other grunt. Corky could take care of himself.

"Whatta ya think, Sarge?"

Zack's eyebrows rose. Lt. Vance was actually asking his opinion. Perhaps it was because he feared for his ass, Leo decided.

"I say we hang tight right here, sir," he responded dryly, "until we can get some gunships down from

155

Saigon, or a couple PBR boats over from Mytho. Then we can wipe the slate—

"To do that, you need commo," Vance argued. "And both the radios are out."

"Warlokk and Gabriel know what the situation is." Zack searched the night sky for any sign of *Pegasus* or Lawless's Cobra. "I'm sure they radioed for support long ago. It's only a matter of time. Thanks to Two-Step, we've got Charlie right where we want him."

"I just hope Corporal Broken Arrow's supply of grenades holds out," Vance said.

"No sweat." One of the men behind Zack chuckled as another blooper discharge reached their ears. After several more Viet Cong screamed their lives up at the uncaring stars, he continued with, "Two-Step always carries his weight in M-79 rounds. That's why no one wants to hump near 'im. One hot-to-trot tracer between the shoulderblades, and everybody within a hundred meters becomes instant ash."

Vance did not immediately reply, but sucked his lips in in thought.

"Don't worry, Lieutenant." Zack spotted movement in the distant tree line and brought the rifle's rear sight to his gun eye. A single discharge ripped at their ears, and the sound of a body crumpling against the earth drifted across the clearing. Lowering his rifle slowly, Zack continued as if there'd been no interruption. "Two-Step wouldn't be firing so many rounds if he was runnin' low."

Lt. Vance snickered, shaking his head from side to side. He'd been worried about this, about finding himself dug in beside Sgt. Zack. The NCO would take over, naturally, the whole time talking as if he, Lt. Vance, were really in charge. But every man worth his salt would know Leo would lead the charge when the time came. This both sickened Vance and relieved him. Zack could be the leader. Vance just didn't care about appearances anymore. All he wanted was to survive his tour in-country.

"So what's the plan?" the private asked suddenly. It was so dark each man could barely see the outline of the others' faces, but it was obvious he was speaking out of courtesy, to the lieutenant.

Yeah, Vance's mind said to Zack. *What's the plan, Sarge?*

After pausing a moment, Leo said, "I think we oughta wait one, sir. Until I figure out where the hell that chopperload of grunts are—the ones that un-assed down on the riverbank 'bout five ago."

"You think Charlie saw 'em?" Vance asked.

"I'm sure the commies saw the bird land, but beyond that, your guess is as good as mine."

"I bet they're preparing for the worst."

"Right. Now if I can just figure out who's leadin' 'em, then I can get some kinda idea what strategy he's gonna use and—"

"Them spooks are going to throw a real stick in your spokes, Sarge." The private referred to the Agency commandos, who'd split from the uniformed troops almost immediately after scaling the cliff wall..

"Naw, they won't be a problem," Zack countered. "All they're interested in is the Loach, and I know right where they're at." He pointed at a depression in the earth between two huge trees rising up toward the few stars visible above.

"They don't give a shit about us," the private protested softly.

"It's not their job to give a shit about us," Zack whispered, feeling through his rucksack to determine how many extra ammo clips he had left. The two three-mag pouches on his web belt were empty. "If they have to help us cancel some Cong tickets in order to accomplish their mission, they'll do it. Otherwise . . ."

"Don't hold our breath," said Vance.

"Right."

Clouds black as the darkness enveloping them were rolling swiftly across the heavens above, and soon heavy sheets of rain were lashing the entire area again.

"Shit," grumbled the private. "What else could go wrong?"

A sudden downblast of air overhead answered the grunt. Because of the storm's winds, *Pegasus*'s whopping rotors were not heard until the craft was hovering directly over Zack's group.

On board, Snakeman Fletcher unloaded down into the enemy's positions with his usual unrestrained ferocity. The tracers roaring through the treetops became a single, lancelike bolt of light, glowing shifting shades of crimson in the rain. The chemical coating on the 7.62s were actually orange, but something about the composition of heat waves blanketing The Nam often made them appear to give off a bloodred sizzle instead.

Zack watched the first green tracer reply from fifty yards away, then he unloaded on the bright muzzleflash with ten rounds of his own.

Fletcher had spotted the discharging AK-47 also, and he adjusted his aim until the enemy position was a smoldering pit filled with blood-soaked bodies.

"Well *AWRIGHT*, Snakeman!" The private beside Vance raised a fist in the dark. *"Get some!"*

The rest of the men huddled behind Zack and the lieutenant were not so enthusiastic. *Pegasus* was hovering directly over them. They could not believe Gabriel was being so bold. Already, they'd watched nearly half a dozen gunships get knocked from the skies by groundfire. And those birds had been moving. It was even easier to down a stationary craft.

Didn't The Gunslinger know they were taking cover directly below? If *Peg* dropped in a ball of flames, they would all be consumed too.

When green enemy tracers began smoking up at the helicopter from two other points in the tree line, the entire group of soldiers responded with rifle on full auto. The clatter of AKs went silent, and *Pegasus* darted off into the dark.

Vance, Zack, and the others listened to her rotors fade in the distance, then grow stronger again. "Mister

158

Gabriel's circling around for another pass," the private decided.

Zack nodded at the warrant officer's display of courage, but he would not be able to continue buzzing the enemy positions much longer. The rain was increasing, and choppers didn't operate well under inclement weather conditions.

Warrant Officer Warlokk's sleek, shark-snouted Cobra swooped down between the trees without warning, causing the entire platoon of men to flatten out in the mud. The two-man gunship unleashed a trio of projectiles from its rocketpods, then vanished just as abruptly as it had appeared.

"What the hell was *that*?" Vance listened to the private gasp in feigned surprise. Every soldier there knew exactly what *that* had been.

Vance wanted to stuff the trooper's mouth with a knuckle sandwich, but restrained himself. "I say we rush the tree line, Leo." He whispered so that only Zack heard his words. "Rush the tree line, kick ass and take names!"

"Rush 'em?" Zack was momentarily taken aback. It was the first time Lt. Vance had ever used his first name.

"Right. Rush the bastards. This waitin' around, by-the-book bullshit is a crock. Let's get it over with!"

Zack did not immediately respond. He swallowed hard, glad the sound his throat made was covered by the rush of raindrops against the branches along the jungle canopy's edge. The young lieutenant was beginning to act a little strange. Was he seeking glory, or just going through that disenchanted stage every officer Zack had ever worked with endured when the stresses of combat started to fray nerves.

Zack did not immediately respond, because you just did not rush what appeared to be a fortified enemy position in total darkness during a monsoon downpour. Lt. Vance was feeling the stress, he decided.

Zack just hoped the young officer's burnout didn't get them all blown away.

Corky Cordova swallowed hard. Despite the thunder crackling overhead and the rain pouring into his hiding place now, he was convinced the Cong heard his Adam's apple scraping against a dry throat.

Several had moved past slowly on either side of his clump of chin-high reeds, missing him in the pitch-black darkness. *Thank you, Brody*! His thoughts screamed as he recalled Treat telling him he shouldn't wear aftershave lotion into the boonies. The Cong can smell it a mile away, Brody had said. And though Corky had protested silently at first, he finally relented under pressure from Two-Step and Snakeman, who both sided with The Whoremonger. Now, as the stench of *nuoc-mam* fish sauce wrinkled his nose, he was glad he had.

Half the enemy platoon had now passed on either side of him. There were five, maybe six shadows left to go, but a terrible fear had seized Cordova. He was sure the last man in the formation would spot him.

Corky kept the muzzle of his M-16 snugly beneath his lower jaw. Pointed directly into his brain. There was no way he could take them all out; he knew he didn't have enough ammunition remaining in his magazine. And he sure as hell wasn't about to be taken prisoner. Cordova had been in the bush long enough to know what Charlie did with Americans. And it was worse with First Air Cavalrymen. Charlie soaked their gonads in lighter fluid, then used their crotch as a lantern on the Ho Chi Minh trail until they died from shock or loss of blood.

And then a ray of hope entered Corky Cordova's miserably dark and wet world. It appeared as if the entire formation of Vietnamese was going to sweep past him without—

But a bright, drawn-out lightning bolt spider-webbed across the sky, illuminating his face, and he locked eyes with the last enemy soldier bringing up the tail of the patrol.

Cordova allowed only a heartbeat to lapse before he sprang. Thunder beat at the earth like a million war drums when he clamped his fingers across the Vietnamese's throat. Startled into inaction, the NVA was no green recruit, however. He wore rank equivalent to a corporal, and fought back. But Cordova outweighed him by a good fifty pounds, and kept him flat in the elephant grass as he squeezed harder and harder, trying to crush the man's windpipe so he could not scream, alerting the others.

Even then, Cordova had visions of the rest of the North Vietnamese feeling the commotion behind them, whirling around to confront him. Even then, he had visions of a half dozen NVA regulars fighting over the chance to run their bayonets through his back as he strangled their comrade in muted hand-to-hand combat.

But then the soldier beneath him stopped kicking. The fingernails that had dug into Cordova's wrists relaxed, and he felt the stinging sensation in the cuts for the first time as rain water and his own sweat mixed with the tiny rivulets of blood trickling down his arms onto the communist's throat.

The man was no longer breathing. Cordova stared down into his eyes, not caring to search for anything dramatic—no big answer to the great riddle of life and death in the jungles of Void Vicious. He already knew all he wanted to about that. Corky just wanted to make sure the NVA wasn't faking, that he wouldn't sit up and start screaming the minute Cordova went back to search for his rifle.

There was only one way to make sure.

He brought the palm of his hand back and took in a deep breath as more lightning crackled overhead. He slammed the palm's edge against the man's face, shoving the splinterlike bones within his nasal cavity up into his brain.

161

Swift, silent, and deadly.

Cordova found himself wishing he had some First Cav Ace-of-Spades playing cards left to stick between the soldier's lips after he finished the job, but he'd already used an entire deck up.

Someone grabbed his arm from behind, just as he had flattened the Vietnamese's nose. Cordova whirled around, to realize his worst fears had come true.

CHAPTER 18

A single bullet fired from Sgt. Brock's rifle knocked the NVA back away from Cordova before Treat Brody, who was flying through the air, made it halfway to the Vietnamese. Brody crashed into a tree instead, and rolled to the side, dazed and shaken. Cordova dove on top of him as a hail of bullets decimated the enemy soldiers. All but one were cut down by Brock's people firing their M-16s on automatic, and the lone survivor threw down his weapon and began yelling, *Chieu Hoi*! *Chieu Hoi*! which was Vietnamese for "open-arms," an amnesty cry often given by enemy troops who were backed into the corner.

Under President Diem's 1963 decree, any communists wishing to change sides during battle needed only to cry out the proclamation to be ensured peaceful transfer to a re-education facility and possible induction into the ARVN Armed Forces as a Kit Carson scout—one who would work with the South Vietnamese military henceforth, guiding them through enemy territory as a sort of combat zone guide.

"*Chieu-Hoi*, my ass!" Sgt. Brock was commanding in Le Loi's electricity-laced voice. "Finish him!" Brock stood on a knoll behind his men, right arm raised menacingly as he pointed at the NVA soldier. All he needed to complete the show was his golden cape, but tonight the NCO wore olive drab like everybody else.

"No!" Treat Brody knocked an eager corporal aside as he rushed the enemy troop, pistol drawn. "Take him prisoner!" He gave the directive, only to find himself rushing over to the North Vietnamese. No one moved to cover him.

To show the collection of hostile, grim-faced Americans he wasn't getting soft-hearted, Brody's knee came up, and the NVA went down face first, groaning and clutching his groin. "He might be able to provide some intel!" Treat tried to reason with them as he hurriedly tied a strip of cloth around the prisoner's eyes. He forced the man's arms behind his back roughly and began wrapping twine around his wrists.

Several of the Americans glanced back over a shoulder at Sgt. Brock, but the towering NCO did not seem upset in the least. Glancing about as if surveying the situation, he motioned toward the bodies of the dead NVA. "Check 'em out," he ordered. "Collect the hardware. And be careful."

In his zeal to comply, a young, baby-faced PFC rushed over to the nearest body and turned it over. A ChiCom stick grenade the Vietnamese had been clutching to his disemboweled stomach as his final defiant act in the face of death immediately detonated.

Blinded, with his right arm hanging in shreds, the youth picked himself up out of the elephant grass and stumbled back toward the knoll Sgt. Brock had been standing atop. Everyone else had proned out against the earth, fearing additional boobytraps, but except for the rumbling thunder overhead, the small clearing was silent again.

Treat Brody stared at the critically injured American from his position of cover beside Cordova. Sgt. Brock, hands on his hips during the explosion, was shaking his head from side to side now as he started down toward the dying trooper. Brody spotted a trickle of blood coming from a small wound directly above Brock's left knee. "Well, the ghost bleeds," Treat muttered under his breath.

"Huh?" Cordova nudged him.

"Nothing," Brody said. "So are you the last one left from Zack's team?" He decided to let Brock, who was comforting the wounded PFC now in his old down-to-earth voice, handle the casualty.

Cordova met Treat's concerned look with relief of his own. "Naw! Naw, man! Just got separated. We just got separated, tha's all."

"Which way did they go?"

"Who?"

Brody grabbed Cordova's shoulders. He'd seen the wild, thousand-yard stare coming on before. "Don't go gettin' shell-shocked on me, douche-bag!" he snapped. "Zack! Zack and the others. Which way?"

Cordova suddenly seemed in control again. Anger flooded his features. "Fuck, Brody! I don't know, man! This was a rat-fuck mission from the start! I lost my bearings!" His voice started to rise. "We got mother-fucking separated, man! We got—"

"Okay, okay." Brody motioned him into silence. The others—the outsiders on Brock's squad—might over-hear them. Sporadic discharges had been coming from only one direction since the stick grenade went off. Brody recognized both M-16s and M-60s, as well as AKs and a couple Soviet SKSs. "I think I know where the block party moved to."

Zack was confident they had the enemy force whittled down to just two positions. One was along the river-bank, where what remained of the bullet-riddled sampans were moored. The other was a trench beside the tree supporting the crashed helicopter.

The Vietnamese along the riverbank were pinned down on two sides. Lt. Vance had taken his men upstream fifty meters to make sure the communists could not circle around and attempt an ambush on the Americans. The C.I.A. commandos would fire into the enemy position anytime the communists tried to move south toward the precariously suspended Loach. Their only avenue of escape was back into the river on the few boats that remained seaworthy, and they weren't about to try that, with *Pegasus* and Warlokk's Cobra prowling back and forth above the winding, snakelike Mekong tributary ready to pounce without warning. On the riverbank, they had a series of deep ravines to take cover in. In the water, they were sitting ducks of the twice-fried Peking persuasion. No way.

"Is it a woman?" Zack asked Doc Delgado.

"These days, ya can't tell anymore, Leo."

"Ain't that the truth."

"The Saigon *cao bois* got such long hair, I wouldn't even wager *your* paycheck on—"

"Yeah, it's a broad." The PFC between them was using Zack's folding binoculars. "Her face is charcoaled out real good, but there's no hidin' the chest, bossman. 'Bout a thirty-six, I'd say, maybe little more."

Delgado exhaled loudly. "Not on a Vietnamese chick, brother."

"Okay, so she's exceptionally well endowed for a zip." The PFC sighed. "Whatta ya want *me* to do about it, Sarge? Frisk her for falsies?"

"If you can get close enough." Delgado sounded serious.

The Private First Class glanced back at him, they exchanged sarcastic smirks, and when the younger soldier placed his eyes against the fieldglasses again, the woman in black was gone.

"Shit," he muttered.

"What?" one of the soldiers nearby asked, but Doc Delgado already sensed the female cadre member had disappeared.

"You think they might have a tunnel right there?" he asked.

"No way, Sarge." The PFC sounded confident. "No such luck."

Zack agreed.

"Right." Delgado nodded, deciding not to pursue his often-voiced theory that the whole goddamned country was one giant underground tunnel system. "Okay." He turned back to the PFC. "Did it appear she was in charge?"

"In charge, Sarge?"

"Leadin' the group o' dinks." The medic was quickly losing patience. "Did it look like she was leadin' 'em, or what?"

"Yeah. Yeah, possible, Sarge," the PFC said, eyes still against the binoculars lens. "I saw her waving her arms around, but nobody was payin' much attention to her—'least it didn't seem like they were."

"Hopefully, this is turnin' into as much a rat-fuck for them as it is for us." Zack rubbed the barrel of his M-16 as he turned to face Delgado again. "Let's do it."

"Yep," the senior corpsman agreed. "Might as well."

They listened to another *thump!* in the distance, as Broken Arrow kept Asian heads down along the riverbank. One grenade overflew its target and detonated a few feet into the river, sending a geyser of water back over the proned-out communists.

"Ha! That Two-Step." One of the men slid a banana clip home noisily as the team got ready to assault the enemy positions.

"Can't be on target 100 percent of the time." Doc Delgado was not defending him, though. As he spoke, two more grenades exploded in the middle of the swiftly flowing tributary.

"*Ha!* He's aimin' for the river, dudes!" The anonymous trooper laughed. "As usual, Charlie's all wet, and we've got Broken Arrow to thank."

"Okay!" Zack hissed. "As of right now, we're observing strict rules of silence, got that? Sgt. Delgado's gonna take you, you, and you three." He pointed to five of the men nearest the medic. "You guys'll come with me!" His meaty arm swept out to encompass the squad nearest him—men he knew at least by face if not name.

"And I've got the rest." Lt. Vance sighed, looking like a dejected team captain who got the worst picks before a gym class basketball game.

"Shirts, or skins?" Zack laughed quietly, but no one seemed to get the black humor, and his expression soured. "Okay," he continued, "with your permission, sir," he glanced at Vance, "I'll take my troops around that end of the tree line." He motioned to the dense patch of flora located directly between the Loach and the sampans on the riverbank. "Delgado's people can swing around to the right. But move in no closer than that ridge up there, so we don't subject ourselves to a direct crossfire."

"Sounds good to me." Vance smiled slightly. Sgt. Zack was placing his team in the greatest danger. The only spot left was the hollow where they now lay. It was also the safest place right now. Someone would have to lay down cover fire from this position, while the other two teams moved out. And Vance's group was the only one left.

The lieutenant was in no mood to argue over Zack's strategy. He just wanted to get the show on the road. "Okay. Let's do it."

But before any of the cavalrymen could move, tongues of flame from several submachine guns arced out from the C.I.A. commandos' position near the canopy's edge.

"God damnit!" Zack hissed. The Agency squad was assaulting the area beneath the suspended Loach on their own.

"Let's go!" Vance waved his team toward the other group of communists along the riverbank. Delgado's troopers followed. Zack's plan evaporated with the jungle mist.

"DAMNIT!" Leo The Lionhearted roared. He felt like he was suddenly being benched from a game he'd spent months preparing to play. And he knew he had no

168

other choice; that crafty, conniving Vance had pulled a fast one on him, and rank had its privileges. There was nothing he could do now except remain in place, providing cover fire. "Okay, zap the riverbank!" he directed, sending a short burst—three tracers, or fifteen rounds' worth—toward the sampans, to get the enlisted men started. Then he switched targets, and began firing single shots at the shadows darting around beneath the Loach. It would still be a few seconds before the Agency commandos overran the area, and he'd try popping caps on a few black pajamas while he could.

The river snaking through this stretch of terrain along the edge of the rain forest was not the mighty, slow-moving Mekong itself, which ran deep and murky about a thousand meters to the southwest, but one of many thousand offshooting tributaries that made up the Delta region. The Loach helicopter was dangling between two giant trees along the canopy's edge directly over a portion of the river, which ran through the jungle for several kilometers, then dropped down through a stepping-stone network of lush rice paddies and into the South China Sea. A jagged strip of clearing ran down the gently sloping hill from Zack's position to the low cliff overlooking the riverbank, where the clearing expanded to an area about half the size of a baseball diamond, filled with man-high reeds sharp as razors.

It was down into this wind-swept sea of green elephant grass that Lt. Vance was now leading his dedicated troopers, all of whom, it appeared to Zack, were firing their M-16s from the hip.

"Fucking Junior John Waynes," he sighed, ejecting a spent clip and sliding a fresh magazine home in the blink of an eye.

"Okay, let's beat feet!" Leo ordered, as soon as it became evident that laying down further cover fire would put both the C.I.A. commandos and his own cavalrymen at risk. The Americans were all in hand-to-hand range now.

When Zack's people reached the riverbank, Vance stood proudly at the heads of about ten dead communists. They were lined up in the moist mixture of sand and mud, waves lapping at their ankles, heads misshapen and faces missing in most cases.

Two cavalrymen were filling a sampan with bulletholes, but there was no other activity. Vance was standing over the kills, his rifle draped over a forearm at a cocky angle. When Zack slid to a face-to-face stop in front of the lieutenant, Vance's head seemed to wobble back and forth slightly atop his shoulders.

"Looks like we're a little late for the party," Leo remarked, glancing down at the bodies. Downriver, sporadic rifle and pistol fire announced the Agency commandos were still engaging the communists. "I don't suppose you saved anything of intel or propaganda value in the boats."

"Wasn't no intelligence party, Sarge," one of the NCOs spoke up behind Vance. "Just Cong reinforcements. They musta beat feet down here *rikky-tik*. Commandeered some villagers' sampans, or something. These things are hollowed-out cheap-Charlie models, for sure."

"Then why are ya sinkin' 'em?" Zack asked, as Warlokk's Cobra chased *Pegasus* overhead. Swooping low along the edge of the tree line and only a few yards above the soldiers' heads, their sudden downblast of rotorwash sent nearly every man there into a crouch.

"Fuckin' sky-jockey wingnuts," Vance muttered, slinging his rifle.

"Wha'?" A PFC directed his question at Sgt. Zack.

"I said, then why did you go and sink the goddamned boats? How do you expect to win Victor-November 'hearts and minds' if you go around destroyin' all their property?"

"Well, we . . . uh, didn't know that the—"

"Bullshit." Zack turned his back on them and started off in the direction the gunships had taken. "You just told me they were commandeered from the villagers, slick," he muttered.

"Well, fuck me 'til it hurts." The PFC turned defiant, imitating his hero, Brody The Whoremonger.

"Who gives a shit about 'hearts and minds'?" The man next to him spat on one of the corpses. "I just wanna get laid."

Grinning, his partner began rolling Cong bodies over onto their backs until a set of full breasts pressing against a black blouse came into view. The soldiers watched them jiggle from side to side slightly after the body came to a rest, then settle back placid and listless against the woman's ribcage. "There ya go, sport. I'll bet she even accepts credit cards."

Some of the other men began laughing. But the soldier who had voiced his desire for female companionship turned away, disgusted, and started off after Zack.

"Turn her back over and leave 'er alone," he heard Lt. Vance order without emotion.

CHAPTER 19

When Zack arrived beneath the creaking, groaning Loach, he found the leader of the C.I.A. commandos supervising his men as they pulled body after body from beneath a pile of telephone-pole-sized logs.

The shooting was all over. He counted the same number of spooks standing now as when they'd first appeared in the river aboard their black rubber raft.

"What's the story?" Zack kept his rifle at the ready. It appeared an old logging wharf had once stood here. Several dozen rotting logs were latched together at the cliff's edge, jutting out over the river, and the cavern the commandos were pulling bodies from looked dark and dangerous.

"Not to worry." The Agency man noted the look of concern and wariness in Leo's features. He patted his black web belt, and Zack spotted the color-coded grenade canisters.

Gas.

Zack glanced at the bodies again. Only a few displayed bullet wounds. He wasn't sure if the Cong had been knocked out with some spooky-tunes formula or killed outright with poisonous gas. And he didn't want to ask.

"That's the last of 'em!" A stocky American sporting

a dark, tropical tan and sun-bleached flattop threw the limp body of a teenaged boy out of the passageway leading beneath the pierlike structure.

"Any tits on the team?" Zack motioned toward the pile of corpses with the muzzle of his rifle.

"Tits?" A tight grin cracked the Agency man's grim expression.

"Cunts. Any women in the group?"

The blond with the deep tan began shaking his head in the negative when a green tracer flew between Zack and the pile of bodies, striking him in the forehead.

Leo watched the bullet slam the spook back down into the dark cavern beneath the pier, and then he hit the dirt like everyone else.

"Sniper!" someone called directly behind him as soldiers began bumping into each other as they low-crawled to and fro, seeking cover.

Zack rolled, unslinging his rifle as he thudded against a tree trunk already filled with flattened slugs of rifle lead. *I knew Charlie was still out there somewhere, waiting. Watching and waiting*, he said to himself. "Keep your heads down!" he yelled at two men who were trying to pinpoint the enemy rifleman.

But the spook team had been so nonchalant about the whole thing. The entire operation was turning into a C.I.A. affair, what with the downed Loach, and their carelessness had rubbed off on Leo. "Damn," he muttered under his breath as the woman slid down the vines dangling beneath the helicopter.

"Get that bitch!" he yelled. But his words were covered by the sudden roar from an outboard motor directly beneath them, under the pier. "*Get that bitch!*" Zack screamed again, rising to his feet as fast as he could, yet feeling far too sluggish, limbs refusing to respond. The world was starting to turn around him, was starting to spin.

And then everything became crystal clear again, and he was rushing after her, firing from the hip and screaming like a banshee as he chased her across the clearing, over the pile of bodies, and toward the passageway leading under the pier and down along the cliff to the riverbank.

She had either lost or abandoned her weapon, probably to facilitate the climb up the tree vines to the chopper, and back down to the ground again. She was now carrying a small cardboard tube.

Zack instantly recognized it as the same kind of container the Department of Defense shipped its satellite photos in. He poured on the speed, hoping his recent regimen of daily PT would head off any protests from his wildly pumping heart. For all he knew, the drop tube contained nothing but the daily series of routine weather snapshots from space—bluetint prints MACV regularly posted right in the main corridors of Puzzle Palace for anyone, including the Vietnamese janitors, to see. He doubted the woman in black knew what was inside the container either, but was just seeking to retrieve whatever could be salvaged from the craft. Even the Cong knew black Loachs were usually Agency ships and that anything on board could win them recognition and perhaps even promotion from their cell cadre.

Out the corner of his eye, he saw *Pegasus* hovering overhead, off to one side, then setting down in the dark clearing, rotors kicking up a storm of dust and twigs. And then Zack was sliding face first toward the passageway entrance, trying to grab one of the woman's ankles as she slithered down under the pier.

But he wasn't fast enough.

Rolling like a professional gymnast, the long-haired, lithe-figured guerrilla tumbled out into space, arched her slender body into a graceful dive, and entered the water only a few feet beside the waiting, motorized sampan. Barely a splash was made, but Zack erupted like an atom bomb.

"GABRIEL!" he exploded, waving his arms at the chopper pilot aboard *Pegasus*. "Keep them rotors turnin'!" He didn't bother climbing down after the woman; the sampan was already pulling away as two Viet Cong helped her and the drop tube up over the side of the boat.

"Gonna get two fucking birds with one stone!" Zack was muttering to himself under his breath as he sprinted toward the Huey gunship.

Also aboard the sampan was the blond entertainer Chrissy LaVey, lying inside a fishing net, unconscious.

The C.I.A. team leader and two of his men climbed aboard *Pegasus* after Zack.

"Destination, ladies?" Snakeman Fletcher produced a toothy grin. "Sorry I can't offer ya no coffee or tea, only—"

"Can it, Snakeoil!" Zack leaned between the two pilots, ignoring the doorgunner now as he told Gabriel, "Downriver, Mister! Take this crate downriver. Got a sampan headed eastbound, with a hostage onboard and a Queen Cong to boot!"

"What?" Gabe The Gunslinger's tone was a protesting one, but he was already pulling pitch. With a jerk, a shuddering wobble, then sudden weightlessness, *Peg* ascended, nearly clipping some treetops as she banked low over the river.

"There they are!" The Agency men pointed out the side hatch for Fletcher's benefit. But when Elliott acknowledged with an eager grin and took aim with his hog-60, the spook knocked the barrel skyward. "Spare the barrel or spoil the pussy, gunny!" he warned.

"There's pussy down there?" Fletcher flipped the black visor up from in front of his face and made a show of peering down through the darkness.

"Theirs and ours!" the spook yelled into his ear.

"Well, fancy that." Fletcher nevertheless kept both hands on the M-60. He knew Gabriel would soon bathe the area below with a powerful spotlight. The Cong would undoubtedly try to knock it out, and all the ground fire might not just come from the sampan.

When the silver beam finally lanced down through the swirling river mists, they found that the sampan was zigzagging from bank to bank. "They think we're gonna zap 'em!" Zack tugged at an ear. It was something he often did when the tension reached a breaking point.

Fletcher overhead him. "We oughta zap 'em!" he said. "One burst, Leo! Just one righteous burst, and I could cut that sampan in two!" They could see the blonde was still unconscious near the front portion of the boat, while the female guerrilla and her two friends crouched near the motor in the rear.

Zack could see what he was talking about. A clean burst from the hatch machine gun just might rip the boat in two, but even if Snakeman was that good—and Zack doubted he was—while the rear half of the vessel, aided by the motor's momentum, went under immediately, the front part would sink almost as swiftly.

"Long before we could flare in for a rescue, anyway," Zack answered his own thoughts with a harsh whisper.

"What?" one of the agents hissed above the roar of rotors overhead. The anger shone through in his eyes: he didn't like foul-ups, and this had been a major disaster. Zack read it in the man's face. Maybe the drop tube had contained much more than satellite weather photos after all.

"Nothin'," Leo shook his head as a burst of green tracer flew up from the rear of the boat. Under normal chase circumstances the bullets would probably not have come close to hitting the chopper, but because the sampan was zigzagging back and forth and Gabriel was not attempting to match the maneuver, two lucky rounds from the thirty-bullet burst struck the helicopter.

"Christ!" the C.I.A. team leader yelled as the searchlight in *Pegasus*'s snout exploded with a loud pop that could be heard even back in the cabin. The river below was drenched in complete darkness again, except

176

for a green tracer or two flying up wildly from the sampan every few seconds.

The second bullet had struck something vital in the gunship's undercarriage and ricocheted along one of the landing skids until it came to rest in a fuel cell. The men all tensed as they listened to the warning alarms screaming at the two pilots in the cockpit.

"Are we goin' down an' dirty?" Fletcher called forward.

Neither Gabriel nor his peter pilot replied verbally, but the Gunslinger nodded in the negative a couple of terse times.

Fletcher noticed that they were still flying above and slightly behind the sampan. The riverine pursuit had not been terminated. "Aw, fuck."

Zack's eyes narrowed with challenge. "Eat it like a man, Snakeskin."

Finally, after Gabriel had muted as many of the alarms and warning signals as he could, he called back over his shoulder, "We're not gonna ditch her, but we gotta call off the game for tonight. *Peg*'s losing power *rikky-tik*. Got a chip indicator goin' bananas in one of the fuel cells. We were low on fuel to begin with."

"Any way you can stay on 'em just a few more minutes?" Zack asked. "Five or six more klicks and we'll be below Tang Hoa! The Game Wardens've always got a coupla PBRs cruisin' the Cua Tieu channel there." His reference to "game wardens" was the code name given some American river patrol operations in the Mekong Delta.

"I'm tryin' to raise the gunboats now," Gabe's co-pilot responded dryly. A few seconds later, he produced the thumbs-up without looking back. The radio conversation had been covered by *Peg*'s roaring rotors, but it was obvious the warrant officer had made contact with one of the PBRs.

"Any way we can stay with 'em until a game warden arrives on-station?" Zack was referring to the sampan. "I'd sure hate to lose these pricks."

"Yeah!" The agent sounded in total agreement as he crowded the cockpit. "You know the second we pull off, they're going to ditch down some side canal or something. Maybe even turn around and head back up river just to throw us a curve!"

Gabriel was shaking his head in the negative again. "Wish I could, gentlemen."

"One PBR!" the peter pilot announced dramatically as a vessel came into view downriver. "Hold the *nuoc-mam* sauce."

The twenty-eight-foot-long MK-II *Swift* was traveling at about twenty-five knots. Its dual search beacons swept across the river's surface, bank to bank, back and forth. One of the spotlights quickly bathed the sampan in blinding silver, and when two more powerful PBRs appeared even farther downriver, behind the first, the wooden sampan left the center of the waterway and began heading for the bank. The two VC in black garb had their arms raised in the air, while the woman controlled the motor's stick.

"Hey *hey*!" Snakeman released the M-60's handle, allowing the barrel to rise. "Score one for the brown-water navy!"

Zack responded with an unenthusiastic clap, and one of the C.I.A. agents whistled with relief to his partner as Gabriel banked hard to the right, taking them out over the South China sea, then back toward Cho Gao.

CHAPTER 20

When the door came crashing in on its hinges, Nelson fumbled for his weapon.

He thought for sure he had to be dreaming. He was lying on a teakwood floor, not packed earth, yet the roar of descending gunship rotors was still heavy in his ears. A black giant of a man was trying to grab him, and when Nelson reached for his M-16, he came up with a shapely, smooth-skinned leg.

Anna screamed, and Nelson knew it was no nightmare. This was real, and he still couldn't find his weapon.

The rain had stopped, if only temporarily. Heat lightning continued to crackle through the window, and by its ghostly, surreal light, he could see that the huge black man lifting him up over his head now was the intoxicated NCO he'd had the run-in with earlier.

Anna charged as Nelson was carried toward the window. Obviously on his way out through the bamboo shutters, Nelson wagered what his chances were of penetrating the multiple layers of steel chicken wire that acted as a bug screen on the outside. Anna was stark naked when she charged, swinging a rice cooker by the cord, but she was not about to act modest at a time like this. The woman was well aware that if

Nelson was thrown out into the night, she would be left alone with an animal three times her size—and with only one thing on his mind.

Anna swung as hard as she could. She swung so hard, in fact, that she missed the black NCO completely. The momentum of the flying pot pulled her off balance, and she slammed sideways into the shattered door. A splinter lanced into her calf, and she screamed as Nelson's head was rammed against the chicken wire the first time.

Anna screamed in fright and pain and fear for her man. And then she got to her feet again and took another swing at the big sergeant.

This time, the rice cooker hit him squarely on the back of the head. But it didn't seem to do much damage. Unable to force Nelson out the window on the first lunge, the huge sergeant threw the dazed and bloodied private onto the floor and began chasing Anna around the room.

Despite the three-inch splinter sticking out of her calf, Anna easily dodged the lumbering, out-of-breath NCO's every attempt to capture her. When he paused to catch his breath, he did it in front of the doorway so she could not dart past him.

When the pursuit around the tiny cubicle resumed, Nelson was on his feet again, and he caught the taller man with a swinging elbow to the temple.

Stumbling toward the door, the NCO threw a thick-fingered hand out against the frame to brace himself, and Nelson and Anna both hurled their bodies at him.

They succeeded in forcing him outside, into the courtyard, and, like children taunting a water buffalo with whips made from thatched elephant grass, guided him through the villa's swinging front doors.

Where Nelson jumped on his back.

Letting out a loud bellow, the NCO began staggering backward in a tight circle as he tried to reach behind his head and pull Nelson free. Nelson was striking the sergeant's ears with the palms of his hands as hard as he could, hoping the action would at least stun his opponent. It was not having any effect, however, and noticing this, Anna rushed back inside, past several women who had clustered around the courtyard entrance in their nightgowns.

"You should call the Colonel!" one of the women shouted in rapid-fire Vietnamese.

"Yes! Call Col. Buchanan!" another urged her.

"Call the MPs!" a third tenant of the villa yelled above the grunting of the two Americans.

"No! Don't call the MPs!" Anna pleaded, tears in her eyes as she realized for the first time that she was naked in front of her friends.

She fumbled with the lantern, got it going, and found Nelson's rifle beneath the sleeping mat. Anna picked it up, draped a sarong around herself, and ran back outside.

Nelson was sparring with the big brute. At least he was still on his feet, Anna observed.

He threw a roundhouse punch, connecting squarely with the sergeant's jaw. Though the bigger man staggered backward for a moment, teetering as if ready to collapse, he quickly regained his composure. Rubbing the sweat from his eyes, he slapped his own cheeks viciously, and charged after Nelson again, roaring like an enraged bear.

The cavalryman easily evaded the black giant, who might have been quite menacing and agile in his younger days. Now, he was just a drunk, old, out-of-shape NCO.

Nelson made his mistake when he landed a lucky kick to the midsection, his assailant doubled over in pain, and the women clustering in the doorway let out a boisterous cheer. The cheer went to Nelson's head, and instead of remaining cold and calculating, he began to dance circles around the other soldier.

Nelson was quickly becoming overconfident, almost invigorated by the feminine signs of support and encouragement from the sidelines. He took his eyes off the NCO more and more to survey the pretty Oriental faces just rousted from their sleep by his nighttime activities. That was when the NCO decided to dart left when it appeared he was about to stumble to the right. And he caught Nelson around the waist.

Both men rolled across the ground. Nelson was trying to smash the NCO's nose with the edge of his hand, hammerlike; the sergeant was trying to squeeze the life from the younger soldier.

They rolled past the growing crowd of women, straight into some sagging strands of concertina wire.

The sergeant took most of the razor-sharp barbs across his lower back. Nelson lost a strip of flesh from his earlobe, but used the opportunity to knee his opponent in the groin.

The NCO buckled in pain, catching another barb in the nose, which rekindled his anger. Just as Nelson was about to get away, the man grabbed him, twisting an arm back.

They rolled away from the concertina, coming to rest directly in front of the women from the villa. The sergeant, on top, clasped both massive hands together and began slamming them down, trying to hit Nelson's face.

"Ooooh!" Anna cried as blood sprayed from the side of Nelson's face each time he was hit.

The cavalryman attempted to block the assault with his wrists and forearms, but most blows were connecting, and soon his face was covered with his own blood.

"Stop it!" Anna screamed. But her words had no effect on the giant beating her man. "I said stop it!" And when the shadow from the M-16 barrel fell across Nelson's face, the NCO sitting across his chest looked up for the first time.

His lower jaw sagging, saliva bubbling over swollen lips, eyes bulging, and chest heaving, the sergeant, his clasped fists still raised over his head, focused on the rifle muzzle, shifted his gaze to Anna's tear-streaked eyes, then back to the muzzle. It didn't look like he cared about Anna anymore. It didn't look like he cared about anything. "Go ahead," he sighed. "You might as well pull the trigger, bitch. I jus' don't care anymore!" And he brought the fists down again.

Anna took careful aim on the back of the man's head and started to squeeze the trigger, but she hesitated. Tears filled her eyes, and she wiped them away, glanced over at her friends, seeking guidance.

"Do it, Anna!" several of the women encouraged her in English. If Nelson was her man, then damn the consequences.

Anna was dwarfed by the weapon, even though M-16s were small in comparison to earlier American service rifles. She shifted her shoulders and rubbed her cheek against the warm, black plastic stock. She lined the front sight up with the rear one, going out of focus as perspiration and salt clouded her eyes. She tensed from head to toe, then slowly squeezed the trigger.

Nothing happened.

Anna squeezed the trigger a second time as far as she could bring it in. Still nothing.

"Anna! Shoot him!" The women were growing restless. Nelson was now obviously losing the fight, and it looked as if the black man wanted not just to win, but to end this contest with his opponent's death.

Anna jerked the trigger in a third time, and there was still no discharge. Sobbing, she dropped to her knees. I can not make it work!" she cried, fumbling with the breech.

Two women rushed up to assist her with the weapon, just as Nelson kneed the NCO in the scrotum again. Yelling in pain, he dropped over onto his side.

Nelson got in several good slugs to the side of the face, but they were having no apparent results. The NCO slowly got up, and pinned the cavalryman to the ground again.

"Safety! Safety!" a widow in her late twenties said, perhaps remembering something about her dead husband's army days spent cleaning rifles and pistols. She joined the others and ran her fingers along the nomenclature on one side of the M-16. "There!" she screamed suddenly, overjoyed. "See! The safety! It is on safety! It must be on AUTO!"

"Switch it to AUTO!" the woman on Anna's other side demanded.

The safety disengaged, and Anna ran up behind the man and took aim again. She spread her feet apart in a no-nonsense stance, raised her right elbow, placed the riflebutt against her tiny shoulder, and quickly squeezed the trigger.

Again, nothing. Not even a click.

Anna screamed at the top of her lungs, dropped the rifle in the mud, and picked it up again, this time by the barrel. She swung the M-16 with all her might, just as the two fighters rolled to one side. The wild swing missed its target, and the momentum spun her around on her bare heels. She slipped and plopped face first into a mud puddle.

Her female coalition of weapons experts rushed up, ignoring Anna, and retrieved the M-16. They examined the trigger for defects and played with the rate-of-fire selector, while Nelson lost more and more blood.

None of the ladies knew anything about a charging handle, or that an M-16 will not fire until the charging handle is jerked back, allowing the bolt to slam a live round into the rifle's chamber.

Anna struggled to stand up, wiping the tears and mud from her eyes, only to have a second black giant rush past, knocking her back down into the puddle.

This was another NCO, the ladies crowding around observed, only his head was shaved bald and his massive frame looked a bit more solid and firm.

He dove toward the two combatants while still ten feet away, striking the man on top with a grueling body block to the side.

The sergeant who had been beating Nelson shot down into the mud, too, just as another sheet of hard-driven rain swept across the compound.

"Zack!" Nelson recognized the crew chief's gleaming crown instantly. "Sgt. Zack! Am I glad to see you, sir!" Lightning flashbulbed overhead to accent his relieved grin as both cavalrymen slugged each other on the bicep in greeting.

"I'm no 'sir,' son." Leo The Lionhearted laughed as his fellow NCO slowly got to his feet. "I work for a living!" And the adrenaline still rushing through his veins from the firefight along the riverbank, Zack delivered a crushing ju-jit-su chop to the throat as the NCO rushed past, going after Nelson again.

Stunned, the overweight sergeant still managed to reach Nelson. He bowled the private over, but suddenly dropped back to his knees and, in true martial-artist form, appearing to ignore the aggressor now, Zack swung his boot around so swiftly most of the women watching missed the blinding-fast move. The right heel connected with the NCO's temple, and he went down hard, face first into a puddle.

Anna rushed over and started kicking him about the shoulders and head. None of her girlfriends attempted to restrain her.

Sgt. Zack dropped to one knee beside Nelson. He grabbed the waistband of the private's shorts and pulled his midsection up slightly out of the muck and mud. "You okay, kid?" he asked, his smile growing ear to ear as huge raindrops beat down on them. "Just get the wind knocked outta ya, or is it somethin' serious—somethin' ol' Leo's gonna break paper on?"

"J-Just lost my wind, Sarge." Nelson tried to sit up but couldn't. He felt along his nose, wondering if it was broken, then realized the bolts of pain were really coming from his cheeks. He groaned loudly, more from relief than agony. And then he remembered Anna.

"Anna!" he called out to her, sitting up easily now. "Anna, are you okay, baby?"

Zack rose to his feet, and pulled Nelson up with him. "I think you and I both need a shower." He laughed, examining the front of his shirt. Somehow he had torn it completely down the middle.

"Mind if Anna joins us?" Nelson forced the question out between loose front teeth.

Zack laughed again, much louder this time. "I don't if you don't, slick!" He slapped Nelson on the back as they started away from the villa and toward the portable shower stalls rising in the misty distance beyond one row of tents.

As they passed by the unconscious NCO, Zack leaned down and scooped up Anna, whose feet were still flying as she tried to get in one last good kick. "Bite down on this." He forced a leather belt keeper between her lips and plucked the splinter hanging from her calf before she could scream or protest. "Feisty little lady." He glanced over at Nelson. "You better get a dressing on that before it gets infected."

After they had gotten about a dozen feet, Zack suddenly halted. He set Anna down and glanced back at the battered sergeant.

"What is it, Sarge?" Nelson asked. The rain was falling more intensely now, and the mud was quick disappearing from their clothes. "If we don't boogie on over to the shower stalls, ain't gonna be nothin' left to clean off. Now what kinda fun would that be?"

"Naw. You two go on over without me." Zack had never really intended to shower with them anyway.

He could not take his eyes off the black man lying face down in the mud puddle. The adrenaline high was wearing off, and he was coming back down to earth and reality and consequence, and it dawned on him.

Zack began running back to the unmoving NCO. Nelson was right on his heels.

They dropped to their knees on either side of the career soldier, and Leo turned him over.

His eyes were wide open, and Zack nearly sprang back at the startling sight. Nelson placed his middle finger against the big sergeant's throat for a few seconds, then he dropped the side of his face down, resting an ear against the sergeant's nose.

Taking a moment to think how he should put it, Nelson finally rose up. He locked eyes with Zack and said simply, "He's bought the farm, Leo."

The dead man's body seemed to shudder violently, and this time Zack did spring back onto his haunches before they both realized Anna had kicked her would-be rapist in the side of the head again.

"I hope the no-good sumbitch rots in hellfire!" she snapped, folding her dainty arms across the outline of taut nipples poking through a rain-soaked sarong. "I hope he rots in hell forever!"

CHAPTER 21

It took Gabriel and his co-pilot less than thirty minutes to patch up *Pegasus*. After the fuel cell was repaired, the tanks topped off, and MG ammo replenished, they were ready to rock and roll some more.

The Agency men had disappeared. Fletcher was not sure, but he thought he saw them hop aboard John Graves' blue jeep and burn rubber down through the compound's main gate, headed for Highway 24. Zack had never returned, either. He said he was just going to trot on over to S-2 for the latest on the PBR assist, and that he would be right back. But the Snakeman could not concern himself with the minor irregularities of lifers who outranked him and were probably even then, at that very moment, dipping their wicks in more than they could handle. They had commies to kill, and Fletch didn't have time to pussyfoot around with malingerers and skates, regardless of the number of stripes on their sleeves.

"We'eze *off* to waste the wizard!" he screamed above the slap of rainslick rotors as Gabriel fired up *Peg*'s turbines. Nelson, several hundred yards away, watched the ship lifting up over the tent tops, Snakeman's clenched fist still raised in silent salute to Void Vicious and what she held for him tonight.

A tight grin formed on Nelson's features, then quickly faded as the thump of chopper blades also died away. Nelson watched *Pegasus* vanish in the swirling blue mist, wishing desperately that he was aboard her, answering the call to action and adventure with Snakeman and The Gunslinger and all the others.

Sighing, he shook his head in resignation, then started over toward the tree line, where Sgt. Zack was busy with an entrenching tool.

As *Pegasus* circled around over the compound, Fletcher peered down out of the hatch, trying to get a better look at the two men gathered in the middle of a long line of palm trees. He thought he recognized one, maybe both, and then he noticed a Vietnamese woman with a fine figure appeared to be keeping them company.

An evil grin crept across Snakeman's face. *What was that Nasty Nel up to*? he wondered. He'd also been wondering where the crafty cavalryman had been keeping himself lately.

Pegasus made one final flyby of the compound as Gabriel checked out all her equipment, and Fletcher unfastened his monkey straps and scurried over to the opposite hatch for a better look. Was that Leo The Lionhearted down there with him?

Snakeman rubbed his chin thoughtfully as Gabe, satisfied with *Peg*'s performance, took her out toward the coastline.

It appeared to Elliott Fletcher that Sgt. Zack was digging a grave.

Fletcher noticed that two field radios were strapped tightly to the support bar running the length of *Peg*'s cabin. Obviously destined for the teams whose RTOs had been killed. Fletch was silently thankful he knew neither soldier.

After running a maintenance check on his hatch-60, he fed a fresh belt of ammo into the heavy machine gun, gently snapped the cover shut, rubbed it thoughtfully, like a lover's inner thigh, then settled back to watch the nighttime panorama stretch out for as far as the eye could. Not much, really, with this rain and pitch-black blanket smothering the land. But here and there he could see campfires and village lanterns as they flew past small Vietnamese communities at treetop level. Silver smoke rose from the fires, giving off a warm glow.

He strained to see faces in the huts, longhouses, and thatched dwellings, but it was too late at night. The doors were all securely barred against the darkness and the Cong.

Fletcher settled back on his pile of Saigon phone books, watching solitary stars appear in rare breaks in the cloud cover now and then. He clicked in, and mused about Zack and what the bald-headed NCO could possibly be doing at three o'clock in the morning in the middle of a cluster of palm trees, with Nelson and a Vietnamese woman. A kinky threesome, perhaps? Naw; Fletch shook his head at the thought. Zack was too dedicated to the crew. He would have made it back to the helipad long before *Pegasus* lifted off had something important not come to his attention.

He listened to Gabe exchanging chatter with his peter pilot. "Which ones you wanna pick up first?"

"That Brock gives me the creeps," the co-pilot admitted openly. "Let's opt for Vance's team."

"You're sure we can't get that med-evac down from Mytho, right?"

"I already told ya, Gunslinger. There ain't no damn W.I.A.s down there to chopper out. Only body bags."

"Yeah, but we could use it to extract Brock's people."

"Whatever. You can give Mytho another try, honcho-san, but if I were you—"

"You ain't The Gunslinger, slick!" Gabriel's voice raised several octaves in mock pride. "Never were, and never will be! But you're right about one thing, bossman, you're the peter pilot. *I'm* flyin' this grunts so lovingly refer to as *Pegasus*. You may call to Mytho."

Before Gabe's co-pilot could switch frequency, however, they received a message from PBR Control via the CP commo bunker at Cho Gao. "This is Python-Lead," he said into the mike sarcastically, meaning there was no one *to* lead.

Buchanan's XO came on the air. "Reference the sampan your crew was chasing earlier. Be advised the gunboats lost it six klicks east of initial intercept, how copy, over."

Simultaneous groans left the two warrant officers manning the cockpit. After a slight, calculated pause, Gabriel replied, "Lima Charlie, Six-Echo. I knew from the start it was gonna be a romeo-foxtrot. Thanks for the bravo-november. Python Lead out."

Snakeman Fletcher slowly shook his head from side to side. He had really wanted to get a look at the blond dancer's rainsoaked chest up close.

Nelson awoke with a start.

He almost jumped up. He seemed to be lying on the floor, and something was moving across his chest. Something *black*. He tried to glance down without moving his face.

And then the fragrance of Anna's radiant hair registered as her body shifted against his, her face sliding slowly across his chest as she dreamed. They were on the floor. On her thin sleeping mat.

Heat lightning still crackled against the black of night, but it was a distant flicker beyond the dented window screen. The storm was moving on, and light sheets of rain whipped across the tin roof overhead.

Nelson slowly moved his arm out from beneath Anna, just far enough so that he could lift his wrist

191

lightly. The luminous hands on his watch read four o'clock.

That was all? Barely an hour had passed since he and Zack had buried the dead NCO's body.

Anna shifted in his arms again, restless. How could she even sleep, after the events of the last few hours, he wondered. Nelson listened carefully to her breathing. It was labored, not smooth and regular. She was either struggling through that half-sleep stage, or was still wide awake, just trying to get comfortable.

He decided against whispering her name, though he wanted desperately to talk right then. More than anything, he needed words. Reassuring words. White lies. Anything.

He stared up at the ceiling, letting the side of his face drop against the one satin pillow Anna owned. He searched for the mating lizards, but they were gone. Zack's face came to him, and he tried to shake the vision free, but he couldn't forget the look in Zack's eyes when he realized he'd killed a fellow American with his bare hands.

Nelson closed his eyes tightly, trying to squeeze out Zack's face, only to have a whole collage of flashbacks swirl through his head: making love with Anna, arguing with the black NCO beforehand, making love to Anna, watching Sgt. Zack kill the drunk lifer after Anna failed to shoot the man with his M-16. And making love to Anna only a half hour ago, after they'd leaned the door back in place against its torn hinges, sealing out the storm and the curious faces.

As he stared up at the ceiling, he worried about Sgt. Zack. The man had been devastated by what he'd done. And Nelson couldn't understand that. Anna certainly had not been affected. They had to restrain her from kicking holes in the corpse's bloodied head. And Nelson himself considered the entire matter a simple case of self-defense. What was the big deal? Zack had wasted countless Cong, hadn't he? Death was death, wasn't it?

192

In Nelson's book, this was a righteous killing. He was still bewildered by Zack's actions following the man's death. Why, for instance, had they gone to all the trouble of burying the man in the rain? Col. Buchanan, and even CID, would surely have understood, once all the facts were presented in Zack's defense. Once all the witnesses came forth, and all their statements were taken. He and Anna would make sure the ladies of the villa talked. There would be no typical South Vietnamese silence over this incident.

Zack had always known what was best in the past, though, and Nelson never protested. Strange, as he thought back on it now, but it had actually seemed the proper thing to do, burying that blood-caked, mud-splattered corpse in the rain, palm trees rising up almost hauntingly on all sides and thunder and lightning crackling overhead.

He would never forget what Zack had said after they dug a shallow grave in the mud. Nelson had asked if maybe they should say a prayer or something before dropping him down into the earth, and Zack just cleared his throat skeptically, pushed the private aside, picked the corpse up, and tossed it into the grave. The body landed face down, and Nelson asked if maybe they should at least turn him over, regardless of the asshole he might have been while alive. Zack was already kicking mud onto the body.

"Shee-it," Zack had muttered. "Leave him like he is: butt up. Now the Viets can kiss his ass forever."

"I'm sure that's the way he would have wanted it," Nelson agreed somberly, never noticing the sarcastic glare Zack cast in his direction before picking up the small folding GI shovel.

That was what puzzled Nelson: Zack had killed the man with his bare hands, yet, instead of just carrying his body over to one of the jeeps, taking it off-post, and dumping it into the river, he went—they went to all the trouble of burying the man, in the middle of a monsoon downpour.

193

The compound First Cavalry Division honchos had picked to house their men and choppers stretched approximately a mile square, midway between the provincial capital of Mytho and Cho Gao, a smaller village to the east. Double-decker metal conex containers, some topped with sandbags or coils of concertina, served as guard towers in each of the four corners. A chainlink fenceline surrounded the compound, and between each tower were foxholes, trenches, and sandbagged static posts, all manned by heavily armed troopers.

Approximately a hundred meters in front of each corner tower, located outside the defensive wire, was an LP, or listening post. These were designed to serve as an early warning system in the event of a surprise enemy sapper attack or recon patrols moving through the area. Because of all the activity along the riverbank several hundred meters away, most of the soldiers on guard duty were wide awake and alert, facing the mesmerizing darkness with rifles in hand.

Sgt. Leo Zack sat alone atop one of the perimeter towers, watching flares float along the Mekong a thousand meters away. He sat on the edge of the double-conex structure, unbloused boots dangling over the edge, his flak jacket off, M-16 rifle balanced across his thighs, daring Charlie to take a bead on his shaved-smooth crown and blow him away. But Charlie must have been busy elsewhere. Zack glanced at his watch. Quarter after four. He'd been sitting there out in the open nearly a half hour now, and not a single cap had been busted on his account.

Zack saw the fight again and again. He watched himself slam into the black sergeant, knock the NCO off a dazed and bloody Nelson; saw himself kick the man, and deliver the fatal blow to the temple.

Private Nelson had tried to console him afterward, while they were dragging the body over between the trees. "You didn't kill the asshole, Sarge!" the kid had exclaimed. "He drowned, man! Face down in the pool of mud, the motherfucker drowned, that's all! Ain't no different than a drunk GI drownin' in his own vomit, which happens an average o' once a night in the glorious Green Machine. You know that. We can beat this rap, Sarge, we can beat it!" But Zack knew.

The professional soldier knew what it took to kill another man in hand-to-hand combat. And he was well aware that the blow he had delivered to the black NCO's temple was double what was necessary to instantly cancel the average brawler's ticket.

But that was not the clincher.

After they rolled the dead man out of the mud puddle, onto his back, Zack had recognized him.

Franklin Parker.

They had crossed paths twice before. The first time was in Korea, over fifteen years earlier. Both buck sergeants, they shared a foxhole on the outskirts of Seoul. While Zack was unconscious from wounds received during the vicious fighting between joint U.S.-South Korean forces and the invading Chinese, Parker radioed in an artillery bombardment near an American compound. But he gave the wrong coordinates. Ten U.S. personnel were killed when cannon fire decimated the camp, and Parker blamed the mishap on Zack, who he believed would soon die from his wounds anyway.

Zack himself was not really sure if he had called for arty or not. But he had survived his wounds, and later, with the confusion accompanying the attack on Seoul, no great judicial fanfare followed the terrible tragedy. Zack was busted back to Private E-1 and reassigned to another unit after six months in an army hospital. He never saw Parker in Korea again. No apologies, no explanations. Nothing.

The second time they crossed paths, Zack was in a boxing ring, four years later. It was the 1955 Army-Marine championships, and Leo was representing the Green Machine. Unfortunately, his fifth and final opponent died in the ring from a first-round knockout he never got up from. Parker had been Zack's fourth opponent, just prior to the fatal match—a contest which Parker lost—and the man later testified that Zack was using illegal thumb punches and unsportsmanlike tactics in their match. Leo couldn't understand why the man was out to get him.

The judges apparently didn't believe Parker's claims anyway, for he had gone down in the initial thirty seconds of the first round from a solid, textbook punch to the mouth. Parker had a glass jaw, and problems accepting defeat in a fair contest. That an autopsy showed the man in the fifth fight died from complications sustained in an earlier bout and aggravated by this latest knockdown, weakened Parker's claims further.

Over the years, he had won his rank back, and his respect. A certain notoriety followed Leo wherever he went. The lifers always saw to it that the younger troops knew about the Black Buddha's rather illustrious past and reputation.

And Zack was confident there was a file two or three inches thick on him in at least a half dozen CID offices around the world. Not that he wasn't a law-abiding soldier. He felt that he was more than responsible. He was a leader, and you could not lead unless your men respected you. And they didn't respect you if you were a no-account, low-life, crime-committin' bum. Those were Leo Zack's words, verbatim.

The two cavalrymen were monitoring Zack's odd behavior from their LP post. They had watched the tall sergeant pull up in his blacked-out jeep a half hour earlier and relieve the guards at the corner tower, telling them to go ahead and take the vehicle back to the mess tent for a coffee break. As would be expected, the two corporals who pulled the cooler tower duty were late in getting back.

"Whatta ya think the old fart is up to?" one LP grunt asked the other.

"I don't know, but I'll tell ya one thing: he's gonna get his pecker shot off by some passing VC patrol if he don't get behind that pile o' sandbags."

196

"You think so?"

"I know so, brother."

His partner chuckled. It was an evil little chuckle. "Well, watch this." He brought his M-16 up, ejected the ammo magazine, and pulled a personalized, purchased-in-Pleiku-City clip from his rucksack. The thirty-round banana mag had a strip of green tape around it. It was the clip he saved for special occasions.

"What the hell you gonna do?" His partner swallowed hard, well aware what was about to happen. The private crouched beside him was going to use Leo Zack for target practice. He grabbed the PFC's arm. "Don' go wastin' the Black Buddha, man! The Black Buddha is one of our lucky charms. He never did wrong by you, and—"

"Don' fuckin' get your hemorrhoids in an uproar, Homar!" The Private First Class jerked his arm back, inserted the magazine filled with thirty green tracers into the well of his M-16, and, as quietly as he could, pulled back on the charging handle. The VC preferred green tracers.

"But—"

The bolt slamming forward echoed along the perimeter, so he fired quickly. In three long bursts of ten rounds apiece. Aiming at the bottom of the conex. He watched the flowing green tracers ricochet through the thin metal walls and arc up harmlessly into the night sky.

Leo Zack nearly flipped head over heels off the tower roof in his eagerness to drop back to earth. By the time he low-crawled to cover and chambered a round into his own rifle, the "enemy" fire had stopped.

Tensed for action, ready to face death and take some Cong with him on the way down, Zack's eyes darted back and forth along the perimeter. But there was no movement. No black pajama-clad sappers rushing up to the concertina in droves, flinging satchel charges and pole-vaulting over the wire with bangalor torpedoes.

All he could hear was a peculiar trickle of suppressed

laughter coming from one of the LPs. He realized then why things did not feel right: the tracers had been green, but the discharges sounded more like an M-16 than any AK-47 he had ever heard.

Sunlight blinded Nelson.

Shafts of harsh sunlight, lancing into the dark room, struck him full in the face.

"Damn," Nelson muttered, rising up on his elbows. "A dream." But the pain!

He glanced around, noticed Anna beside him. She was sitting up, clutching a sheet to her chin, staring wide-eyed at the tall shape blocking the doorway and obstructing the brunt of sunlight.

Nelson rubbed at his lower jaw. It was still there, but hurt like hell. Against his hip lay the door to Anna's cubicle. It must have bounced off his face on the way down.

"All I did was knock," the big man in the doorway said innocently, "and the whole damn thing caved in. You gotta invest in better real estate, kid!"

It was the Company clerk, Farney.

"You asshole," Nasty Nel muttered, still rubbing his jaw.

"Sorry 'bout that." It didn't matter to the specialist that he outranked Nelson by more than a couple of grades yet was still the target of disrespectful language.

Nelson glanced over at Anna. The outline of her nipples was plainly evident against the thin white sheet. He wrapped an arm around her, pulling her close, and she hid her face against his chest.

"To what do we owe the honor?" he asked the clerk.

"Damn." The soldier checked his wristwatch. "Took me long enough to find ya. This was the last place on earth I'd ever think to look." He snickered. "But I guess they don't call you Nasty Nel for nothin', eh, troop?"

198

"And fuck you and the horse ya rode in on," Nelson replied with little enthusiasm.

The clerk invited himself in, and the sunlight became even more intense. Nelson closed his eyes tightly, and shielded his face with an open hand. "So what exactly can I do for ya?" He suddenly remembered about the fight, and Zack, and the dead man, and he swallowed hard.

"Ooooooh-*wee*." The clerk dropped to one knee and examined Nelson's face in the dusty rays of sunlight. "Did ya get the license plate number of the big-rig that ran over you?"

Nelson brushed his hand away, using the moment to set the wheels in his head turning. "Un-assed off one o' the gunships last night, straight into a punji pit," was the answer that automatically came out.

"Punji pit? Ooooooh-*wee*. Lordy-Lordy, trooper! You're lucky you didn't lose the family jewels over a mistake like that."

"It was dark," Nelson replied dryly.

Standing up again, the clerk nodded in the affirmative.

"Yeah, tell me about it." He plopped a wad of bubblegum into his mouth, worked it around for a few seconds, then said, "Anyway, just makin' the rounds to count heads and inform everyone we're on red alert."

"Red alert?" Nelson swallowed again. Visions of the rain forest ghost passed through the dust particles floating in the shafts of sunlight. At least last night's violent storm was over, he observed.

"Yep. Rainwater washed away bookoo dirt last night, troop. Uncovered a goddamned shallow grave."

"A shallow grave?" Nelson spoke convincingly, as if it was all news to him. Beneath the white sheet, Anna's fingers clutched his.

"Yep." The clerk started to leave. "A freshly dug shallow grave. One o' the lifers from Headquarters Company bought the farm. Neil Nazi thinks one of the housegirls did it." He glanced back at Anna with mock suspicion on his way through the doorway.

"Housegirls?" Nelson started to get up. "No way."

"Yep. The Colonel thinks one of 'em is coldblooded Cong to the core."

CHAPTER 22

Brody The Whoremonger held onto the sides of the sampan as Sgt. Brock swerved from one side of the narrow tributary to the other. Their boat had a small motor attached to the rear, as did the craft they were chasing, the sampan that had eluded the PBRs an hour earlier. Brock was zigzagging without apparent motive, but Treat knew he was just trying to avoid the high waves left in the other sampan's wake. It was the only way they might hope to catch up, and besides, if they struck one of the crests at this speed, their frail craft would probably disintegrate. It was built to ferry ammo and blackmarket supplies from communist cellblocks to VC field units, not play cat and mouse on an offshoot of the mighty Mekong.

Sampans were the main reason elements of the First Air Cavalry were sent down to the Delta from South Vietnam's Central Highlands in the first place. Charlie was increasing his use of them to transport weapons from one jungle base camp to the next, bypassing roadways on land whenever possible, and thereby ARVN patrols as well.

The VC had become increasingly brazen as of late, shooting back when confronted by American and South Vietnamese PBR gunboats, and even going so far as to tie up riverine patrol efforts by sending out diversionary sampans first, to keep the gunboat crews busy with boarding inspections while the craft laden with armament cruised past unhindered, their black pajama-clad occupants smiling and waving at the overworked crews. Chases were becoming more commonplace, with the enemy suddenly darting down narrow vine- and root-enshrouded tributaries the larger PBR boats could not negotiate.

Back at the Loach crashsite, Brody decided, Sgt. Brock had given a performance worthy of a Silver Star Medal. The Whoremonger had hung back, initially, observing his methods of leadership, but when Brock led the charge toward the heavily defended Cong position, Brody followed. They didn't cease firing until over a thousand rounds had decimated the communist emplacement, and Brody himself had slammed a half dozen clips into his M-16. When the gunsmoke cleared, they counted thirteen enemy dead. Only one American bought the farm, Warner. The soldier who never should have accompanied them into the sticks in the first place. Warner, who had gone AWOL from the aid station, so he could join Sgt. Brock, and Le Loi, in glorious battle.

When it became apparent Brock's people were no longer crucial to securing the area, he had them scour the riverbank downstream from the crash site, until they located several VC sampans hidden within crevices along the bank, underneath natural flora and improvised camouflage.

Brock himself sunk several of the boats, then assigned three men each to the three remaining craft. He, Brody, and the corporal, who always seemed to remain nearest Brock, took the lead sampan, planning to paddle upstream and mount a surprise assault on the VC entrenched near the other cluster of enemy boats.

That was when the sampan carrying the buxomy blonde raced past. With Brody manning the "bow gun"—an M-16 balanced between his knees—Sgt.

202

Brock operated the motor and rudder.

The two sampans carrying the remainder of his squad were directed by Brock to carry out their plan of assaulting the position upstream without him. And then he was off, a fine spray of mist in the air behind him as his sampan sped after the craft piloted by the female insurgent.

They made slow, steady progress gaining on the Cong sampan, until Brock nearly hit a floating log in the dark. The swerving detour cost them several precious seconds, and nearly left them beached.

When they finally caught up to within fifty yards again, *Pegasus* or one of the other gunships appeared overhead, and Brock pulled back, giving the Huey room until he could see what course of action the helicopter's pilot would take.

A few shots were fired up at the ship, but its doorgunner did not respond. And then they came within sight of the river's mouth, several gunboat spotlights appeared up ahead, and the helicopter banked away.

The woman piloting the Cong sampan was smart, Brody observed. She allowed the lead gunboat to bathe her own vessel with silver beams of light, making it appear the riverine task force had her trapped, and waited until the Huey banked away and left the area before she swerved between two of the gunboats and darted down a tributary too narrow for the PBRs to maneuver in.

Brody believed that he and Brock remained on her tail, twenty or thirty yards behind, speeding through the rain-drenched moonless night quite some time before the woman even realized another sampan was chasing her. Teeth loosened by their bow crashing through the other sampan's wake as it bounced against the river rapids, the three Americans ducked low as a burst of shells suddenly roared back at them.

A moment of intense darkness swept back in as Brock slowed down. The tributary was narrowing even further until they could reach out on either side and touch the ferns and vines overflowing the backs. And then suddenly the night erupted with dual blasts of automatic weapons fire. Long, thirty-round bursts, only fifty or sixty yards ahead, that forced Brock to ram their sampan ashore. There was just no way they could remain in pursuit without risking annihilation.

After the echo of discharges died down, Brock, Brody and the other soldier listened intently for the rattle of an outboard motor fading in the distance. There was only an eerie silence as gibbons raced through the nearby treetops, away from all the noisy racket.

Allowing a few minutes for his eyes to readjust to the dark after the blinding muzzle flashes, Brody scanned the almost pitch-black waterway up ahead. Using techniques taught him at boot camp, he felt confident he'd be able to spot the woman's sampan if it was still floating upstream from them, even if she'd pulled off to the bank, as Sgt. Brock had. It would appear as a hazy outline, trying to trick his purple vision. But it would be there, and he would know how to distinguish it from the other phantom shadows merging into a shifting blur in the darkness.

But the waterway was clear.

Lt. Vance kept his M-16 balanced across his thighs at the ready while Doc Delgado bandaged his elbow. The lieutenant's eyes remained narrowed suspiciously as they scanned the tree line. He still couldn't believe that it was over, that all the shooting had stopped. For a while there it had almost seemed worse than the clusterfuck at Plei Me's Green Beret outpost a couple months before. Close, but no cigar—and in The Nam, there were no second place winners. This was the land of sin and sorrows, and Void Vicious played no favorites. She was a vengeful bitch, and typically Vietnamese. Vance had learned quick: women in this country had an unnerving quirk. They quickly forgave, but they never forgot. And in the Void, one grave mistake and that twenty-thousand-dollar GI insurance check was on its way to your next-of-kin.

Funny, Jacob Vance decided, how all these weird thoughts were racing through his head as he waited for the medic to patch up his elbow. He didn't like it.

How was he supposed to run a platoon—and a hot-dog gunship team, at that—when his mind was preoccupied by a newby's fear of the jungle. It was bad enough that Treat Brody ran around with his lucky-charm amulets dangling from his dogtag chain, and Snakeman Fletcher wanted to fuck his hog-60 every time he got drunk. Now this Sgt. Brock character was running around the rear echelon wearing a gold cape, pretending to be a reincarnated spirit, and the Colonel was ignoring the whole affair. Almost condoning it. It seemed Buchanan was spending more and more time airborne, high in his C&C Loach, hovering over the battlefields in his own little world, unapproachable, delegating his authority to the captains and lieutenants below him.

Initially, his first few weeks in-country, Vance had restlessly awaited his own command duties out in the boonies. The Colonel couldn't give him enough search-and-destroy missions to run. But now Vance was hardened and cynical and burned out, and the most important thing on his mind was getting out alive. He didn't care about medals anymore, and the thought of extending in order to make his personnel packet shine repulsed him. He preferred the possibility of sustaining that precious million-dollar wound. Nothing messy, thank you. Nothing that would snatch away a limb. Just a tiny bit of shrapnel or a splinter of lead. One more injury to make two Purple Hearts, and he'd *walk* to Bien Hoa for that freedom bird back to The World.

After Zack helped Vance wipe out the final pocket of resistance near the downed Loach, they swept the area, expecting to find the bodies of Brock's men littering the riverbank downstream near where *Pegasus* had dropped them off. Instead, they found enough Cong corpses to fill a mass grave. But no sign of the illustrious "Le Loi" or his glassy-eyed followers.

Delgado had told him about the female VC escaping with the Aussie entertainer and the Loach's courier pouch, and about the C.I.A. commandos giving chase in their sputtering rubber raft. Perhaps Brock and his crew had commandeered a sampan or two and joined the riverine chase too.

There were so many possibilities. "And quite frankly, I don't give a *dinky-dau* damn," Vance muttered under his breath as Doc Delgado put the finishing touches on his elbow bandage.

The medic glanced up warily. "Pardon me, sir?"

"Nothin', Doc." The lieutenant waved his concern away. "Just blowin' off steam."

"Right." Delgado stood and left to check on the other casualties that hadn't already been med-evaced out with the first rays of dawn.

Vance glanced at his watch. Zero six hundred. It was still early. There would be some time before Buchanan asked for a head count. Vance would give Brock and Brody and the others twelve hours before placing their names on the M.I.A. roster and filing an official report with the C.O., though he would notify Buchanan of the situation verbally as soon as someone choppered in a Prick-25 that worked worth a damn.

Private Nelson's face flashed in front of his mind's eye for some reason, but vanished just as quickly. Perplexed, Vance wondered why he would think of the kid just then. A tired chuckle escaped him as he shifted about on the tree trunk, massaging his calves. Poor Nelson. Probably thinks I'm harassing him, Vance thought to himself. Well, I guess I was. Sort of.

Nelson's pubic-hair collection, and the manner in which the young soldier flaunted it every time a newby twink arrived at the unit, irritated Vance. What was worse, the kid bragged about losing his virginity to an oversexed stepmother. Which was no capital offense, except that Vance himself had had a similar experience during his own youth. Though it had not been a pleasant one, as Nelson always proclaimed. And it had involved the lieutenant's natural mother. Not some "play" mom, as Nelson referred to his.

She was an alcoholic, and his father, a career military man, was away, serving overseas in the Korean War. It had not been simple seduction, either, as Nelson claimed was the circumstance in his case. The unkempt woman waiting in the hallway for him, when he came home from school one afternoon, gave him a black eye and bloody lip during the fracas that led to her bedroom. There, she had to overpower him before he would submit. It had been incest, pure and simple. The kind that doesn't make it into the psychology annals.

"What is this?" Anna asked.

She had been helping Nelson gather his equipment together when the object wrapped in waterproofing plastic rolled from his rucksack.

Nelson's eyes went wild. "Oh, nothing." He raced across the room, reaching for the article, but Anna, grinning and suddenly feeling mischievous, whirled around until her back was to him.

She held the item up to her eyes and giggled. "It is eggbox, no?"

"Yes. I mean, no." Nelson reached over her shoulder, trying to snatch the package away, but Anna darted, birdlike, out of his reach.

"Yes, I think so it is!" She fumbled with the wrapping. "I never know GI before who carr' eggs with him except in C-rations. May I have one?" Her eyes grew large and sad as she rubbed her flat stomach and kept a safe distance from him. Every time he advanced closer, she backed away. "Special treat for Anna, okay?"

"No, no." Nelson suddenly erupted into uneasy

laughter at his unforeseen predicament. If only the guys could see him now. "They're old as a Buddhist temple, Anna. Make you bookoo sick." He reached a hand out, palm up. "Now hand it over."

"Oh, no, no." She imitated him, body bowing sensuously as she remained just out of reach. "Nelson is being bookoo selfish! He is saving for his other girlfriends, no?" she accused.

"No, no." He waved her suspicions aside, smile growing ear to ear.

"Yes, yes." She waved a forefinger at him accusingly. "Anna bets they are Saigon city girls, too, huh? Nelson save nice, fresh duck eggs for Cholon bargirl with soft feet, no?"

"You have soft feet, too, Anna. Besides, I haven't even gotten the chance to check out Saigon yet, and probably never will."

She finally succeeded in slipping a fingernail under the edge of tape sealing the package, and ripped it back noisily. "Just one, lover!" Her eyes pleaded, and Nelson was no longer sure if she really longed for the egg or was just teasing him.

He lunged for her. Anna slipped away at the last instant, and Nelson leaped, sudden lust coursing through his loins again as he watched her bare chest jiggle about with each evasive movement.

They fell onto the thin, uncushioned sleeping mat, Nelson groaned with the impact, and Anna let out a little surprised cry as the egg carton rolled across the teakwood floor, spilling out its multi-colored vials. "No eggs!" she exclaimed, holding her hands over her mouth.

Glancing over at Nelson as they both rose to their haunches in an Indian-style position of crossed and tangled legs, she leaned over and snatched up one of the vials as it rolled toward them.

She stared into the vial, glanced over at Nelson again, gauging his expression before she really realized what she was looking at, then stared into the little plastic container again. Anna's nose wrinkled slightly, and her lips pursed in bewildered revulsion. "They are hair," she said flatly.

"No. Wires, Anna. Small wire for electronics purposes: fixing damaged radios, fuses in jeeps. You know, military stuff. Complicated, boring—nothing to concern your little ol' self with." He reached for the vial, but she moved her hand away. "My secondary MOS is electronics."

"No." She shook her head with considerable certainty while concentrating on the vial's bright red contents. "Is hair. Fo' sure."

Nelson's head rolled back and forth on his shoulders slightly, and he sighed. "Okay," he admitted, forcing his face to flush. "Yes, it's hair, Anna. You caught me with my pants down."

"What?" Anna glanced down at his crotch, then back at the bright red strands, her expression softening into innocence and curiosity.

"I might as well tell you." He swept his thick blond hair back, trying to feign a receding hairline. It was impossible, he knew, but maybe Anna would buy it. "They're from a mail order company."

"The hair?" she asked. "The hair in the little plastic bottles?" Anna stared past the vial in her hand, down at the others still rolling back and forth across the teakwood planks.

"Yes. They're samples from a company that sells toupees."

"Toupee?" Anna looked puzzled.

"Yes," Nelson helped her. "I've been losing large amounts of my hair since coming to your country," he lied. "Something about the water or climate or latitudal longitude or something. And I'm really a vain person deep down inside. Just couldn't accept the thought that I might return to The World bald when my Nam tour's over, so I decided to check into toupees. The company's got a branch in Taiwan. I can stop there on my way back."

Anna's eyes were narrowing suspiciously as they searched his for even the smallest sign of truth. "I no believe," she whispered, her expression announcing she was beginning to realize she'd surrendered her virtue to a pervert.

Nelson shrugged his shoulders innocently. "Some guys save up so they can have a shiny new Corvette waitin' for 'em in their driveway when they get home. I'm investin' in a full head o' hair, tha's all, honey-san."

Pushing her full, cherry-blossom lips out skeptically, she blew air in his face. "Anna no believe," she said firmly. Placing the vial in front of her eyes again, she patted her own crotch and added, "This is hair from a woman's pussy, Nelson." Her hand swept out to encompass the other vials rolling about the room. "Bookoo women." She tossed the vial a few inches into the air for him to catch it. "You have weird hobby, lover-man."

He tried to wave her worries aside. "No."

"Yes." Anna's smile returned and, exerting little effort as her firm, finely toned thighs pushed her body to its feet, she promptly untied the sarong wrapped around her waist and allowed it to drop into a fluffy pile around her ankles. "Maybe you want sample from Anna's pussy, too?"

Nelson laughed uneasily. "Oh, no, that won't be necessary." He rose to his feet and began gathering up the vials.

Anna skipped over to the kitchen table, rummaged through a small shoebox filled with needles and spools of thread, and came up with a pair of scissors. "How much you want Anna to cut?" She spread her legs in a businesslike stance and roughly grasped a midnight-blue wisp of strands along the mound's bottom, where her muscular swells of thigh came together.

Nelson shook his head with a that-won't-be-necessary, anxiety-laced grin.

"Maybe you would prefer Anna shave away all, so

Nelson can have smooth and bald, like *moi* girls in big city—like his head someday be!"

Laughing, he rushed across the room, snatched the scissors away, and lifted her sarong off the floor. He handed it to her. "And put a blouse on, while you're at it." His tone remained loving. "Looking at those nipples beckoning to me all morning makes for a perpetual hard-on, and ol' Nasty Nel's balls are already draggin', honey-san."

"Okay!" She sighed as if the last throes of an orgasm were sending tingling sensations down her long, slender thighs, curling her toes. "Anna save pretty beaver for Nelson."

PFC Nelson whirled around, shocked at her choice of words. "Where the heck did you learn a word like that?" he asked. But the defiant smirk told him more than he wanted to know. "Your mother should wash your mouth out with soap, young lady."

Anna's confident grin faded, and her eyes dropped to the smooth, polished teakwood planks beneath her narrow feet. "Mother dead, Nelson," she revealed softly, glancing up now at a faded and cracked photograph hanging on the wall beside a small brass statue of Buddha. "Father dead, too. Nobody left for Anna. Anna all alone." It had been an act, at first, a skit designed to elicit compassion from her man. But genuine tears began sliding down her cheeks as she remembered the old days, the childhood years between wars, before her family died in the rocket attacks. "Nobody left in Anna's life except Nelson. Tha's all. Just Nelson and Anna now."

He rushed over to her as Anna dropped into a squat to retrieve her sarong. She held it to her breasts as he grasped her shoulders gently, taking Anna into his arms when she stood again. He kissed her on the forehead, knowing this was no time for a passionate French-tongue session, not with memories of the old Parisian-Viet Minh conflict swirling about in her head. Anna buried her face in his chest and began sobbing as the

211

memories flooded back now. He wanted to know what she was thinking about, but dared not ask. He wanted to tell her he loved her, but recalled what he himself had said about waiting a year, and thought better of it. Nelson simply held her tight, waiting the emotions out, being her man, for the moment. Being there.

"I'm okay, Nelson," she finally whispered, wiping the last of the tears away. "I'm sorry. I don't know why I cry like that."

"It's okay, babes." He massaged her shoulders for a few seconds. "That's what Big N's here for."

"Sometimes I just have to."

"I understand." He watched her glide gracefully over to the bureau mirror, pick up a tissue, and proceed to wipe her face and quietly blow her nose. "No sweat."

"Bookoo sweat," she said, eyes shifting until she was staring at him through the mirror. "Anna no want Nelson to think she big cry-baby."

He wasn't sure why, but it aroused him when she switched to pidgin-English like that. Nelson wanted to pull her from the dresser, lay her down on the sleeping mat, and fuck her silly. But time was tight, and he decided to change the subject to get his mind off his pecker.

"I want you to remember what Farney said."

"Farney?" She slowly turned to face him.

"Fatso."

"Oh. Big man, wake us up."

"Right. He mentioned that my . . . my boss—"

"Your commanding officer." Anna tilted her head to one side, producing her most innocent expression.

"Uh, not quite. Anyway, I guess the Colonel suspects the women of the villa here might have somehow been involved in that incident last night, and—"

"I will talk to them," Anna said somberly, smile warping into a deep frown.

"The QCs might come around asking questions." Nelson referred to the Vietnamese military police.

"No problem. Anna talk to everyone. Make sure they

212

keep silent."

"You know no one who might decide to turn us in?"

"Anna friends with everyone villa. They all like big sister, little sister. No problem, Nelson. Forget it. Anna handle. You go to work."

"Anna's sure?" he asked, shaking his head after catching himself.

"I'm sure." Her smile slowly returned. "Now go."

"Well . . . okay." He hesitated, finding it hard to leave such a beautiful, scantily clad specimen of womanhood. He pursed his lips and shook his head in admiration, then turned to leave before he was unable to further restrain himself.

"Oh, and Nelson?" she asked as he started out the door.

He turned and locked eyes with her. "Yes, gorgeous?"

As if testing his resolve, she lifted her sarong for a brief moment, giving the grunt a flash of what awaited him tonight. "Don't forget to come back to Anna."

Nelson smiled lasciviously and blew her a kiss. "Oh, I won't, dearest woman of my dreams. Believe me, I won't."

Anna flew across the room and, throwing her arms around his neck, pulled herself up and kissed him fiercely.

A few minutes later, the sarong still piled around her ankles on the floor, Anna finally released him. Smiling and unable to lower his eyebrows, Nelson sat on the only chair in the tiny room—a rattan stool in front of Anna's cardboard bureau—and pulled his jungle boots on, then walked out the door without lacing them up, trying to whistle through his grin.

CHAPTER 23

Doc Delgado patted Vance on the knee after putting the final touches on the uncomfortable elbow bandage. "You're all set, Lieutenant."

"Thanks, Nelson," Vance muttered under his breath, obviously preoccupied with other thoughts. He turned to watch several haggard-looking soldiers emerge from the woods down a narrow trail that ran parallel to the dirt road.

"Huh?" Delgado cocked an eyebrow at the lieutenant, both taken aback and annoyed.

Vance cleared his throat upon realizing the error, and shook his shoulders as if to clear the fog from the unattached head floating above them. "I'm sorry, Sergeant," he said. "I was thinking about someone else. No offense."

The usual cautious smile returned to Delgado's face. He shrugged and turned to walk toward the newcomers. "Sure. Okay, no sweat, sir."

Orson and Graham led the squad of eight men. They all had that classic thousand-yard stare. Except for Graham, who just looked angry at recent events, and Orson, of course, whose lower jaw hung open slightly, while his head bobbed about, barely blinking eyes taking in all the sights as if he was touring the War Room at Puzzle Palace for the first time and in complete awe of what he saw.

"Everyone hunky-dory?" Delgado, the buck sergeant, whipped an informal, half-salute on Orson, the private with no time in grade.

Graham answered for him. "The squad leader and truckdriver are K.I.A. 'Bout a mile or so back."

"Graham here *kaka-dau'd* a whole fucking battalion of Cong!" one of the soldiers standing at the rear of the squad volunteered.

"Oh?" Lt. Vance was standing beside Delgado now. "Is that true, PFC Graham?"

"Not quite, sir." Graham was not trying to sound modest. There was no emotion whatsoever in his voice.

"Looks to me like you fellas oughta take five and smoke 'em if you got 'em." Delgado gently took the man's arm and pointed to a cluster of soldiers waiting along the riverbank.

Vance turned and yelled at one of the troopers manning a defensive position nearby. "Got those PRC-25's working yet?"

He was answered with a thumbs-up gesture.

"Okay! Then take one of 'em along with four men and an MG team and *di-di-mau* down the road there until you come to a deuce-and-a-half. Verify casualties and secure the area, then report back on the commo."

"Right!" came the terse reply this time, and the man jumped from behind a pile of logs and went from foxhole to foxhole, taking one man from each.

Delgado watched them trot past, rifles at a casual but ready port-arms. Except for the last man. He carried his M-16 by the carrying handle, like a suitcase, and fixed an ear-to-ear insane grin on Vance as he danced past.

Delgado laughed quietly. "That's one *dinky-dau* dude."

"Definitely," agreed Orson, who wasn't even paying attention.

Vance handed Graham a sheet of olive drab colored paper from his field notebook. "Write down exactly what happened, before you forget any of it," he directed without a trace of compassion in his tone. "And when we get back to the company area, I'm gonna have you write it again." He paused to let that sink in. "Okay, Graham?"

"Yeah, sure, Lieutenant. No sweat. Ain't none of us gonna juice it up for the armchair commandos at Division Headquarters. Nobody here's buckin' for medals or—"

"I am!" Orson interrupted, expanding his chest importantly. "I think I deserve a Congressional Medal of Honor, personally. But I'll let you be the judge of that after you read *Corporal* Graham's report."

"Corporal?" Doc Delgado cocked an eyebrow at the trooper.

"Don't you gents believe in rewarding displays of great heroism and courage with—" Orson began. But he was beginning to sound drunk on adrenaline, and Graham clamped a filthy, ash-smeared hand over his mouth. The others helped Graham lead the protesting private away.

"Quite a card," Delgado decided, watching the group walk down toward the riverbank, away from where the lieutenant told them to write their report.

Vance marched off in the opposite direction without saying another word.

When dawn broke heavy and humid across the swamps, Sgt. Brock gently shook Treat Brody awake. After chasing the sampan from the main river channel into this narrow tributary and encountering the heavy automatic weapons fire in the dark, the three Americans had unanimously decided to remain concealed in the dense riverbank foliage until sunlight.

The Whoremonger was already awake, and had been

listening to a distant parrot's odd mating song for several minutes now, so he was not startled when Brock touched him. Treat woke the third soldier sleeping in the sampan.

After giving everyone a few extra minutes to make sure they were alert and prepared for the worst, Brock silently pushed the wooden craft away from the bank, out into the main channel. As if trained to work as a team, the three soldiers then began paddling against the current, upstream.

Brody quickly pointed to a mismatched layer of vines only fifty yards from where they had spent the night, and dropping quietly over the side of the sampan, Sgt. Brock quietly swam over to the heavily camouflaged sampan.

He spent only a moment scanning the area, then quickly returned to his own vessel, which Treat kept against the bank a few meters downstream, just out of sight. He'd been schooled in the secrets of jungle survival long ago and, like Sgt. Brock, knew that a single leaf turned upside-down during a camouflaging detail could ruin the whole project.

"We leave the river here," Sgt. Brock whispered. "Camou' the boat right there," he pointed to a nook in the riverbank, "and pull ourselves up those vines onto land. Then sweep the area toward the north."

Treat Brody glanced over at the rising sun to get his bearings, then nodded.

"What about—" the third soldier started to ask, but Brock allowed no unnecessary noise. He waved the man silent, eyes burning into him. Brody noticed his nametag read NAVOX.

"First person to locate tracks, respond with a mynah-bird call, or some other off-the-wall bird whistle. Any problem with that? Can you both pull it off without acting like dodos?"

Brody found himself growing relieved Brock wasn't doing his Le Loi imitation. He produced a semi-convincing parrot screech, and Navox followed with an

217

almost hypnotic chorus of jungle bird chatter that rose and fell on the musical scale. Sgt. Brock had to wave him silent again, but this time it was with a tight, amused grin.

As it turned out, all the ornithological expertise was unnecessary. Tracks were found directly in front of the spot where they pulled themselves up a tangle of vines onto the soft earth bank.

Sgt. Brock withdrew a pad and scribbled down a few words, then passed it to Brody.

Two women and two men. Belongs to our target.

Nodding in agreement, Brody flashed the pad in Navox's direction without surrendering it, then pulled a pen from his own pocket and quickly wrote a reply beneath the eight words.

At least Blondie's still on her feet.

Brody dropped to one knee and ran his finger along the inner arch of the print. About a size seven, he decided. Longer than any of the four Vietnamese escorting her.

His grin fading slightly in thought, Sgt. Brock nodded, then motioned for them to start following the tracks. He would take the lead. Brock was puzzled about the fifth set of footprints. He'd only observed one woman and two males escorting LaVey. Perhaps the fourth Cong had been lying low in the sampan. Before moving on, he checked all five sets closer, and his frown deepened: only the Caucasian's held traces of blood.

Navox waited until the tall NCO started down the trail and was several meters up ahead before nodding to Brody and following him in a low crouch.

The Whoremonger, squatting Vietnamese-style between huge, man-sized ferns, waited until the corporal was nearly out of sight down a bend in the narrow, overgrown trail before rising to take up the end of the three-man patrol. He rubbed the collection of gunship crashsite amulets hanging from his dogtags chain for luck, then started after Navox.

Trinh Thi Kim finished the banana, then tossed the sticky peel onto Chrissy LaVey. Kim had been staring with unmasked contempt at the white-haired woman during their entire ten-minute break. The Australian entertainer was careful to avoid meeting her hate-filled glare, and concentrated on staring into the jungle instead, or just closing her eyes tightly.

Even now, with the banana peel sliding down the side of her hair onto a cheek, LaVey maintained control. Eyes shut, she pretended nothing had happened. With her wrists bound behind her back, there was little she could do anyway. An empty ammunition bandolier had been wrapped around her lower face several times and tied in a knot at the base of her skull, covering her mouth. It was probably best, she decided. They would no doubt shoot her here and now if she was able to speak her mind. Yes, if she could talk, she'd definitely lose her cool and verbally rip into the Asian woman reclining on her haunches a few feet away.

She listened to the laughter from the two men urinating into the stream behind her, and tried to ignore them as the banana peel rolled off her cheek onto the ground. In her mind, she saw them glancing back over their shoulders, watching their female leader harassing the captive, and wondering when she would allow them a few private little moments of interrogation. They were two Vietnamese who definitely knew how to taunt and tease. That thought truly worried Chrissy LaVey. So far, they had not really abused her. But once this fiery woman guerrilla made good her escape from the dragnet of helicopters and PBR patrols, would she execute her—or worse: hand her over to the two goons on the riverbank for their own personal pleasure and entertainment?

LaVey knew they would be moving again soon. Two hours had passed since they left the sampan before dawn and started off through the man-high reeds and warm, ankle-deep water. Every half hour they took a break. Not so much for rest, LaVey knew, but so that the woman in charge could listen to the jungle behind them, listen to the sounds following them, and determine which were natural, and which might be man-made.

One, then two minutes passed. When the Vietnamese woman did not direct another silent insult at Chrissy, and they still had not resumed their trek through the insect-infested marsh, LaVey chanced a glance at her.

Kim was examining the canister again. She had tried all manner and methods of prying and forcing the seams and seals, short of shooting the stubborn thing. But the CIA drop tube refused to open and surrender its contents.

They had never taught her about anything like this at the indoctrination and training classes, Kim mused as she held the silver, twelve-inch-long container in front of her eyes, closely inspecting the dual seals in search of an answer to their secrets. It was approximately five inches in diameter, and appeared to open not unlike a jetfighter cockpit. How it opened was beyond her comprehension, though. At least for now. Even her two male counterparts, who were always invaluable when it came to fixing jeep engines or scaling palm trees for coconuts and pineapples, were at a loss to explain the tube's mechanics.

Frowning as the cylinder defeated her attempts to violate it again, Kim glanced at the Rolex she'd taken off a dead Green Beret the week before, and motioned LaVey onto her feet. With her chin, Kim pointed down the trail. LaVey would be leading the way again. She did not realize it was because, though Kim was familiar with this stretch of the Mekong, the young VC guerrilla hadn't been down this specific trail in over a year, and had no way of knowing whether or not local cadre-cell insurgents had planted any boobytraps lately.

A second female moved down the narrow, winding trail, directly behind Kim. To LaVey she seemed about ten years older, but Kim was still definitely in charge. The second woman showed signs of having once been extremely pretty, but fighting in the wilderness all these years had taken a toll on her appearance. She reminded Chrissy of herself: still reflecting a past beauty whenever she smiled over some unexpected surprise or remark, but unable to hide the stress lines the rest of the time. More than once, she purposefully tried to trip LaVey near bends in the trail overlooking the river far below. The two Vietnamese females had argued twice already about her. How she was slowing them up, or something along those lines. The older one wanted to get rid of the white-haired woman. Kim did not.

Not yet, anyway.

When they stopped to rest again, thirty minutes later, Kim removed the bandolier from around LaVey's mouth. As if she'd planned it that way, they stopped beneath another banana grove. But this time Kim did not throw the small Indochinese variety at her.

Slowly, she peeled the fruit, then allowed Chrissy to bite off a piece at the end. "The old woman," Kim said, using her chin again to indicate the only other female on the small team, "she wants me to kill you."

Chrissy's eyes flashed over at the older woman, and the look of concern brought a chuckle to Kim's lips. "Nebbah mind." The grin quickly left her features. "She speaks no English. Very little, anyway."

"And are you going to kill me?" LaVey asked matter-of-factly.

Kim stopped peeling another banana and glanced up at her, both surprised and intrigued.

"You said what?" She'd obviously heard the question, but wanted to hear LaVey's voice again.

"I said—"

"You are not American." Kim's eyes dropped to LaVey's ample bosom, then glanced away, into the trees, and she resumed peeling the banana.

"No. I am Australian."

"Austral—Austral—" Kim attempted to pronounce the word, but with considerable difficulty.

One of the men dropped into a squat beside Chrissy. "Aussie," he muttered with obvious distaste.

"Ohhh," Kim replied knowingly. "Aussie. Ahhh."

"Yes, Aussie." The slightest trace of pride showed through Chrissy's dust-coated features. She directed a glare at the man staring at her cleavage, but he didn't seem to notice. Or didn't care.

"Aussies fight in war, too," Kim decided. "They fight on wrong side—with Saigon government. They are lackey of the Thieu regime."

"So I die anyway." LaVey's resigned tone held little hope in it.

"Maybe." Kim began sounding cryptic. "Maybe not. Old woman there say you too much trouble. I say maybe you make good hostage."

"Me?" LaVey responded with a skeptical titter.

Kim's eyes narrowed. She moved closer to LaVey, and for a moment, Chrissy thought she was going to be slapped. But Kim restrained herself. With her fingertips, she tapped the rigid outlines of the blond woman's nipples. "You are white woman with white hair." Anger raged in Kim's dark, sloe eyes as she remembered someone or someplace from her past. "With big *breasts!*" she imitated a swooning sailor. "Bookoo GI pay lotta *P* for body like yours. U.S. government pay. Black-market boss pay. Cholon slavetraders pay. Kim only have to choose which one. And in meantime, can keep my men happy tonight." She indicated the two filthy Viet Cong drooling over LaVey's attributes nearby.

Listening closely to everything Kim said, one of the men was nodding wildly in agreement now. "They need fat, white woman keep them warm tonight," Kim continued. "Consider it your contribution to the revolution."

It was a taunt designed to get her a black eye, not the satisfaction of knowing and proving this Vietnamese tart wrong. LaVey remained quiet. She would let Kim do all the talking.

"For right now," Kim said, "I let you live. Do not worry. Maybe you live long time." She motioned for them all to return to the trail.

The older woman laughed at her words, and LaVey wondered if perhaps she didn't understand everything that had been said so far.

"And maybe you die before we reach tonight's camp," Kim added.

CHAPTER 24

Brody's mistake had been in paying more attention to Sgt. Brock than to the jungle itself. Because he was watching the NCO's every move, expecting perhaps something out of the ordinary to transpire as they patrolled deeper and deeper into the swamps, Treat did not notice the signs.

Signs that others had passed by this same way. And recently. Mud was still rising at the core of a few footprints. Swamp water trickled down into the heel and instep impressions. A snapped reed was still struggling in total and unnoticed futility to repair itself along the tears—something only a true jungle expert would catch. Something Brody should have spotted. Luckily, Sgt. Brock did.

The instant his gunhand came up to wave the two men behind him into unmoving crouches, they were hit along one side by the ambush. The captured American claymore decapitated Navox as he dropped to one knee in the middle, a dozen paces behind Brock.

Before he proned out in the ankle-deep water, Brody watched the rolling blast flatten all the elephant grass around and throw Sgt. Brock to the side, off the trail. Even before his M-16 was completely soaked, Brody was rolling from the trail too, away from the automatic weapons fire that now raked back and forth where the three Americans had just been standing.

From the clatter of discharges, Brody estimated that they'd encountered only a small force—a half dozen rifles at most. Probably the same group they were originally tracking, though he had seen no faces. And now the hunters had become the hunted.

Brody wanted to kick himself. How could he have been so careless? But then too, Sgt. Brock barely had time to issue a warning. These Cong were good. No doubt it was because they were led by the woman. Vietnamese women approached their duties as guerrilla warriors with a passion. And he couldn't help but feel he'd encountered this one before. Somewhere. Up north, perhaps. Plei Me, or the Ia Drang Valley. Maybe that VC snakenest, Binh Dinh Province. Toy with gut feelings and your guilty conscience later, he growled to himself.

True to his training, Treat rolled first one way, then another, before rising to get his bearings, just in case an enemy rifleman had him in his sights and was preparing to shoot. Then the cavalryman rolled a third direction, rose to his knees, decided the reeds weren't high enough, and dropped to his elbows again—just as a burst of AK rounds stitched across the water in front of his face.

He low-crawled in the direction he'd last seen Sgt. Brock flying from the trail, and listened intently to the din of rifle cracks, hoping to hear that distinctive M-16 pop.

AK-47s delivered a sharp crack that corkscrewed into his ears and would deliver a headache in five minutes, but he could listen to the dull, smothered pop of 5.56 cartridges exploding all day long.

Sgt. Brock was nowhere to be seen up ahead. Nowhere to be seen, or heard! Brody's speed increased as he slid through the muck and brown water, trying to find the NCO in the mistlike blanket of gunsmoke drifting over the swamp.

225

"Brock!" he finally yelled, as more rounds splashed water to his left. They obviously knew every move he was making, so silence was no longer mandatory. "Sgt. Brock!" he called again, but still without luck.

The roar of rushing water reached Brody's ears, and he realized he was moving toward another tributary, one larger than the stream or canal where they'd camouflaged their sampan. The noise was coming from below somewhere. He raised his head in the reeds high enough for the first time to realize that he was no longer in the heart of the marsh, but on a gently sloping hill. The ground was suddenly soggy beneath his palms. Whoever was shooting at him was looking down at his position from above. And their shots were getting closer.

"Sgt. Brock!" Treat Brody called again, but there was still no answer from the missing NCO. A string of bullets slammed into the moist earth all around, closing in on the lone cavalryman, and Brody rolled with all his might, forgetting about his rifle yet somehow managing to hold on to it as he moved down through the wet elephant grass.

Suddenly he realized he was at the edge of a low cliff. Below, ten or fifteen feet, was a branch of the Mekong. He didn't feel like jumping that far, but he'd run out of reeds and was exposed now as he rolled to a stop in the open. He did not want to jump, but he had little choice. From the corner of one eye, Brody saw her, standing far above, on the hillside, her face obscured by the rifle propped against her shoulder: a woman.

A sharp discharge split the muggy air, and he felt himself flying back, out into space, down toward the river.

Brody watched the tracer fly a few inches over his face.

Before he splashed into the river, Treat watched the man who had thrown him out of the bullet's path, Sgt. Brock, leap off the low cliff after him, grinning wildly and curling his tall frame up into a cannonball.

226

The Snakeman considered it a one-in-a-million sighting. That he should spot Treat Brody flying backward through the air off a cliff and down into the river, especially after they'd been cruising above the entire tributary without success for over an hour, was an unusual stroke of luck. He thanked Buddha or whoever else might be in charge upstairs, then went to work.

Gabriel was piloting *Pegasus*, and he responded accordingly. It was obvious Brody and another soldier were attempting to elude a hostile enemy force. Tracers sailing out over the cliff's edge to disappear in the tree line on the other side of the river, were testimony to that much. So Gabe The Gunslinger banked hard to the right, swinging directly over the estimated Viet Cong position, and Snakeman went to work.

For nearly thirty seconds, Fletch poured an unceasing hail of M-60 rounds down into the forest of man-high reeds where he'd spotted the initial muzzle flashes erupting.

"Anything?" Gabe clicked in.

The barrel of his hatch gun glowing now, Fletcher eased off on the trigger and leaned out over the weapon into space. He scanned the maze of trails and interlocking canals through his black visor for a moment. The ground tracers had stopped. He could observe no movement. Disappointed, he clicked in and muttered over the intercom, "Negatron, bossman. Charlie, or whoever it fucking was, vanished on the haze—as usual."

As soon as the doorgunner answered in the negative, *Pegasus* banked hard in the opposite direction, dipped with the air currents, swerved low between two solitary palm trees in a casual evasive maneuver, then flared into a hover directly over the river but several hundred yards downstream from where they'd first seen Brody and his companion.

Gabriel had calculated accurately. The two soldiers' heads bobbed about in the rapids directly beneath the ship now.

"Droppin' the ladder on 'em," Fletcher announced routinely. He left his post, withdrew a rolled-up rope ladder from a special compartment in the cabin, and rushed to the opposite hatch. "Heads up, you cocksuckers!" he warned with a dry chuckle, then tossed the device down through space.

Pegasus was hovering approximately thirty meters above the river, and as the other doorgunner directed a steady stream of cover fire along the bank from which Brock and Brody had jumped, the two soldiers swam to the rope and began clamoring up it frantically.

Water streaming down through his hair onto his face, Brody greeted Fletcher with slapped fists as he was pulled aboard. "Damn good to see ya, Snakeman!" Brody yelled, the adrenaline surging through his system. "It's a fuckin' miracle you clowns showed up when you did! I was truly gettin' tired o' swimmin'."

"The Void got careless today, Whoremonger!" Fletcher yelled back over the beating rotorblades. "Screwed herself and let you two skates slip through her clutches."

Fletcher's enthusiasm drained like a waterbucket suddenly filled with bulletholes when he saw Sgt. Brock racing up the ropeladder next. "Well, if it ain't His Majesty Le-Loi," he muttered under his breath in mixed awe and skepticism. Fletcher was about to make one of his cute remarks about the NCO's mystical powers apparently failing him this mission, but Brock's warm smile silenced him.

"You did fine, son." He placed a broad hand on Elliott's shoulder, and the Snakeman felt a chill swirl down through his entire body at the electricity-filled sound of Brock's voice. "I called for *Peg*, and you courageous men brought her to me."

"Wha'?" the other gunny asked softly, in the mood to argue.

228

Brock ignored him. "It was no miracle," he said, and Fletcher and Treat Brody both locked eyes, wondering how he could have heard their conversation while still struggling from the raging river onto the ropeladder. "I simply *willed* Gabriel to this spot, and you found us. I will not forget the deed you performed today." And then he rushed over to the ammo supply lockers and dropped into a contemplative crouch before them, eyes fixed on the pile of empty brass between the doorgunner's boots.

Fletcher and Brody both watched Sgt. Brock slowly close his eyes as Gabriel swiftly ascended, heading back to the CP. Brock closed his eyes as if on the verge of going into one of his trances again. Snakeman and The Whoremonger locked eyes again, then broke contact as Elliott returned to his hatch-60 in silence.

CHAPTER 25

One week later

Lt. Vance stood at his riverbank command post, waiting for a radio response from Col. Buchanan. The Colonel was floating about, high overhead somewhere, in his C&C chopper, detached from it all.

Buchanan had not seemed particularly interested in the downed Loach affair. It was a C.I.A. matter to him, Vance was sure—something better left to The Agency to handle. Buchanan was working on important plans vital to a First Cav victory over the riverine Cong forces in the Mekong Delta. After all, that was one of the main reasons they had been called down into the area, to help the PBR patrols rid the area of the annoying sampan insurgency clogging the canals and waterways. Operation Coronado would soon be in full swing.

Vance's team had camped at the crash site for over a week now, however. After the initial sampan chase, it had been two days before the C.I.A. commandos limped back in, their bullet-riddled rubber boat under their arms.

Vance had asked for volunteers to help the Agency

men complete a thorough search of the Loach, and when a second drop tube was located and there seemed to be no other sensitive materials aboard, the cavalrymen blew the wreckage out of the trees. It flew with a screeching gasp through the dense canopy at the rain forest's edge, and plummeted with a protesting roar down into the river, where it promptly sank to the bottom. It had been such a mangled mess, the Agency opted to destroy the craft on-scene rather than waste further time and effort trying to retrieve what remained for rear-echelon salvage repairs.

Col. Buchanan had then ordered them to remain in the area. Numerous enemy troop movements and sampan activity had been detected nearby. Friendly reinforcements were already enroute from Mytho, he assured Vance. Charlie either wanted that Loach bad, or was simply massing in an attempt to annihilate the sudden American presence in their territory. Either way, the First Cav would stay and fight.

Vance watched a freshly painted light observation helicopter land along the riverbank less than an hour after the second canister was found. Rotors still turning at near full pitch and its pilot making no attempt to dismount, the Loach sat on the edge of the cliff in wary defiance until one of the commandos, still clad in his black waterproof coveralls, finally rushed over and handed the droptube up through the Plexiglass hatch.

Vance watched as the tiny craft ascended almost straight up while the commando, head bowed low now and forearm shielding his face, was still within reach of the landing skids. When the Loach was just a black speck at the base of the storm clouds, Vance walked over to the agent.

"I don't suppose there's any way of finding out what was so important about that cargo, is there? Just between you and me, of course."

The agent shrugged, his eyes still following the Loach, and he replied, "Beats me, skipper. Same ol' shit. Probably aerial photos of enemy troop movements along the Ho Chi Minh Trail or some such crap. If I had the need-to-know, you can bet your butt this spook would be behind a desk up in Saigon flirtin' with the indigenous secretarial pool and not down here in the boonies swimmin' in a piss-green river!"

"Oh, I see," Vance said tentatively. They watched four Hueys float in off the dark horizon and land in a large, flat LZ the cavalrymen had spent the last forty-eight hours clearing.

"Shee-it." The commando shook his head at all the noise, until it passed.

"Same with the other?" Vance asked.

"The other canister?"

"Right."

"Probably. Who knows? I told 'em long ago they oughta just invest in some kinda hotshot radio relay for transferance of sensitive information, but you think the powers-that-be would listen to a bottom-echelon low-life like me? Ha!" His hands flew up in resignation. "No fuckin' way, Lou." And the commando walked away without another word.

The contents must be critically sensitive, Vance decided. He was well aware the Agency and certain segments of the War Room at Puzzle Palace already had access to the type of equipment the commando described. They were used routinely, on a day-to-day basis. But Loaches were still utilized for data relays that were too important to risk airwave interception by the North Vietnamese.

That meant the drop tube must have contained one hell of a message, Vance decided silently. And now it was in the hands of some long-haired commsymp Sergeants Zack and Brock had allowed to escape.

He watched another gaggle of helicopters approaching in the distance. We've lost more important things to the communists over the years, Vance shook his head from side to side. What's one more canister of coded crap, anyway?

The lieutenant stared at the two dozen helicopters

232

parked along the riverbank beneath their canopy of camouflaged netting. From a couple dozen men at the height of the initial skirmish, they'd gone to over two hundred troopers, and some captains from Delta and Bravo companies already had them spread out in a semicircle away from the river, forming a defensive perimeter to protect the ships and the men camping between them.

On the other side of the river, two entire platoons manned LPs extending far into the rain forest, in an attempt at preventing the VC or NVA from moving in to mount any surprise nighttime mortar attacks on the camp.

Within a few days, the task force would be up to maximum strength. Reinforcements were still arriving every other hour from Saigon, Mytho, and the Central Highlands. Vance laughed to himself. They'd not heard a shot fired in anger since the skirmish that preceded the female Cong's escape. Poor choice of words, he decided. But the Americans were massing. Soon Buchanan and the General would be ready to mount the big mission—a search-and-destroy operation the likes of which few veteran commies in the Delta had ever experienced.

Since the rescue of Treat Brody and Sgt. Brock, they had already taken two smaller sweeps through the area, searching for Chrissy LaVey and the C.I.A. canister, but without success. The female Cong and her gang had disappeared into the endless sea of shoulder-high elephant grass.

Unbeknownst to Buchanan, Vance had positioned several ambush teams throughout the area, on the outskirts of the initial search grid Brody had earlier designated on his map. Operation Coronado's main purpose was to decimate and, if possible, permanently eliminate the area riverine network of sampan transports. Vance doubted the latter would ever be accomplished, but he would definitely use the first premise to authorize implementation of his own plan to capture the woman guerrilla and her band of hotshot renegades, as well as the rescue and return of the Aussie dancer and the drop tube.

"Well, whatta ya know." Vance rested his hands on his hips when he recognized one of the bright, eager faces climbing down from an arriving slick. "Private Nelson. It's about time you showed up, troop." He walked over to the helicopter and returned Nelson's salute with a casual motion that spoke tomes about his irritation.

"I was . . . uh . . ." Nelson stammered, but a tall, stocky shadow appeared out of the treeline behind him.

"I had PFC Nelson on a shit detail back at Cho Gao, sir." Nelson's head whirled around. It was Leo Zack.

"Oh?" Lt. Vance sounded skeptical.

"Right, sir. Then the storm rolled in, and we had that mess with them finding a body and all."

"I heard something about it." Vance rubbed his chin. He could care less about the dead NCO back at Cho Gao, however. The man long had had a bad rep with command staff as a lazy REMF padding his upcoming pension with illegal blackmarket transactions and suspected "misappropriation of government property," so Vance lost no sleep over the sergeant's untimely demise.

"The Duty Officer had me round up some o' the troops for a security detail," Zack stretched the truth slightly, "until the MPs could arrive from Mytho. PFC Nelson was one of the first men I spotted. And, as you know," a sly grin cracked the sergeant's dark features, "he's very competent."

Vance replied with a disappointed frown. "Very well, Sergeant," he said. "Take Nelson here and whatever amount of twinks you need off those ships prangin' in now. Take 'em over to relieve the men guarding the access roadway there."

"Right, Lieutenant!" Relieved to have an assignment that would take both him and Nelson away from the officer, Zack saluted sharply, waited for Vance to return his usual casual half-salute, then led the private away.

When they were out of earshot, Nelson asked him, "Have you heard anything about—"

Zack silenced him with a hard glare. His voice lowered considerably from the tone he'd used with Vance, Zack practically whispered. "Forget what happened back at the villa," he warned for both their benefit. "It's taken care of."

"Taken care of?" Nelson flashed back briefly to that rainy night the week before, when he had been on the losing end of a fistfight with Sgt. Franklin Parker. After Zack came to his rescue and they dug the grave, Leo had pulled something from a thigh pocket and draped it over the dead man's face before throwing the first shovelful of dirt down into the hole. Initially, Nelson had just assumed it was an army-issue hankerchef. He hadn't even really seen the object, but what else could it be?

"It was a VC flag," Zack seemed to read his thoughts. "I took it off one o' them base camps up in Binh Dinh last month. I overheard one of the investigators talking about it. I think they're gonna close the case as Cong-related."

Nelson sighed. "That's a break. Whoever heard of Charlie goin' to the trouble of buryin' one of his victims?"

"Unless he was on an intelligence recon and hoping to leave no evidence of his visit behind afterwards."

"And we hope that's the angle CID's gonna go with."

"Right. If they don't—"

"Then we're up shit creek without a paddle."

"Well, I don't think it would mean stockade city, but things could get tense around here."

"Ain't that the ever-lovin' truth."

"Especially if they connect the name Parker with . . ." Zack went silent suddenly. The less Nelson knew about the past incidents, the better.

"What?" Nelson grabbed Zack's wrist gently, as if

touch would elicit the rest of the riddle.

"Forget it," the big NCO muttered, irritation coloring his tone. "Don' mean nothin', Nasty Nel. Come on, let's round up some pogues and get on with the job."

"Okay, Sarge!" Nelson smiled, a sudden elation filling him with energy. He loved it when Leo The Lionhearted called him Nasty Nel instead of shithead.

An hour later, after Nelson realized he'd been assigned to Sgt. Brock's decimated squad, the Private First Class finally began feeling at ease again. Which was due, in large part, to the presence of Brody The Whoremonger.

Nelson had never expressed his feeling verbally to Treat, but the recently busted buck sergeant was his hero. Nelson had always felt safe and in secure hands when Trick-or-Treat—as only the double vets referred to Brody—was leading the Lurp patrol or setting up the night defensive positions. He even felt motivated to volunteer for the more dangerous assignments when he knew Brody would be in charge. The man did not mess around. Cong died when The Whoremonger went hunting, and the body count for friendlies stayed low.

Sgt. Brock, on the other hand, worried Nelson. He never had put any stock into all that *dinky-dau* Le Loi shit. Had Treat Brody's face not been present among all the newbies guarding the access road, Nelson would have seriously considered requesting that Zack assign him to one of the jungle LPs on the other side of the river. The mortality rate risk over there probably rose one or two hundred percent, he was sure, but anything was better than having to follow the orders of an off-his-rocker NCO who thought he was a reincarnated 500-year-old Annamese warrior.

Nelson found Sgt. Brock easier to get along with than he had originally predicted, however. Upon realizing the two Echo Company troopers were old friends, he

236

granted Treat's request they be allowed to man the same position.

Brody had just finished recounting his soggy riverine adventure, and Nelson was considering mentioning the dead NCO back at the villa in Cho Gao, when they were alerted to a noise approaching from far off down the road.

One of the newbies on the other side of the roadway cupped an open palm to his ear. "An engine?"

"Sounds like it." Brody dropped down behind their five layers of sandbags anyway. "A jeep. American, not Arvin."

"Still needs a tune-up," Nelson commented.

"Whoever took a chance at drivin' all the way out here instead of hoppin' a ride aboard one of the slicks has gotta be fuckin' *dinky-dau*," Brody decided as the army jeep appeared around a bend in the roadway two hundred yards away.

"To the max," Nelson added. He glanced over his shoulder at the sun. It was changing from bright yellow to dull orange and seemed to be flattening along the bottom slightly as it rode the western horizon. Long, thin wisps of cloud drifted in front of it, making Nelson wish he'd brought along his pocket camera. But it was back at Cho Gao with his other garrison gear. The sun would set within the hour. Whoever was making the trip apparently planned to spend the night with them. The vehicle was not a heavily armed gunjeep; it was not one of the half-crazy, half-courageous Infantry MP patrols.

Brody finally recognized the driver. "Motherfuckin' Farney."

"What a goofy fuck." Nelson lowered his M-16 and began shaking his head.

"Evenin', ladies!" The company clerk skidded up sideways, a little too dramatically for Brody's tastes. Billowing dust rolled in behind him, coating many of the cavalrymen with a fine layer of the local black dirt. Farney reached into the back seat and pulled a duffelbag up off the floorboards. "Mail call!"

"It's 'bout goddamned time," one of the pogues complained. "I haven't received anything since arriving in-country." He leaned into the jeep to help Farney, and the clerk stopped him with a hostile glare.

"And you still haven't." His cheeks warped in mock insult. "Nothing for the newbies yet. I recognized every name comin' in"—Farney glanced at the man's nametag and frowned at the complex Polish spelling—"and yours wasn't one of 'em, Alphabet."

Sgt. Brock diffused the potential confrontation by saying, "Take it all up to the lieutenant's CP. Vance can distribute it later. We have to keep this roadway open and—"

"Yeah, yeah." Farney smiled as he reached into the top part of the duffelbag. "Spare me the brilliant military and strategically tactical bullshit, okay, Sgt. Le-fucking-Loi?" He had noticed two of the men moving toward the jeep, and recognized them from their initial in-processing day. New men. Orson and Graham.

"Listen-up, slick," Brock began. But an unintimidated Farney waved him silent.

"I take it back. There *is* something here for a twink or two." He pulled a packet from the top of the bag, several smaller envelopes held together with a thick, o.d. green rubberband. "Private-with-no-time-in-grade Shannon Orson," he read the label taped to the rubberband. "Christ, must be three dozen here." He handed the bundle to Orson, who flipped through the addresses without removing the rubberband.

"Fucking liberal lunatics." Orson tossed the bundle over his back without opening even one of the letters.

"Hey!" Farney erupted in mock protest. "Good men risked their lives to make sure the mail made its way to you, chump! What gives?"

A corporal who'd been in-country six months and had yet to receive any mail rushed over to the roadside gulley and retrieved the packet. "I need the readin' material." He glanced back at Orson. "If you don' mind, troop!"

"No sweat," Orson replied with disgust. "They're all from the same place—my old lady's peacenik group. They're gettin' together now and sendin' me junk mail en masse, tryin' to convert ol' Orgasm to pacifism or something. Mother-to-son and Friend-of-Mother-to-son propaganda or some such shit. It's enough to make a genuine volunteer vomit."

" 'Some such shit,' " the soldier mimicked Orson with a little laugh as he walked back to his position down the road.

"Need some 'readin' material'?" Farney called over to the man before he got very far. "Got a whole shitload o' junk mail nobody back at Cho Gao wanted to claim." And he reached down into the duffelbag, rummaged around, and came up with a handful of stateside newspapers, rolled up and sealed in brown paper.

"That's 'cause nobody's back at Cho Gao." Brody laughed without feeling. "They're all here!"

"Check this crap out." One of the other soldiers already had several newspapers unraveled. A grainy, front-page photo on one suburban Denver tabloid showed what appeared to be four American GIs holding down a Vietnamese woman while a fifth stood between her outstretched legs, his back to the photographer as, it appeared, he was unfastening the belt holding up his trousers. The photographer had chosen an angle that would leave the female victim's crotch hidden by the soldier preparing to rape her. In the background, a gaggle of helicopters was ascending beyond a high treeline.

"Hey, that looks like one of our gunships." Sgt. Brock's forefinger rubbed against a Cobra hovering just outside the formation of Hueys.

"Who gives a shit about the choppers," Brody muttered. "Who's gettin' their rocks off at *our* expense?" He was concerned with the GIs in the picture.

"Really," one of the newbies responded, though he was not quite sure what Corporal Brody was referring

239

to.

"I don't recognize *any* o' those dudes," Sgt. Brock decided after squinting for several seconds.

"Me neither," agreed Treat Brody. But the picture's quality wasn't that good in the first place. It could have been men from any squad in the entire First Air Cavalry Division. Or it could have been grunts from another unit, with Airmobile craft in the background by coincidence. "Maybe they put two negatives together."

"Hell, this piece o' shit coulda been taken back in Alabama, for Christ's sake," Brock decided. "Just 'cause her face is Asian, don' mean she's Vietnamese."

"Right," one of the newbies volunteered his two-cents' worth.

"But the palm trees."

"She's probably some bargirl from back in The World, earnin' some *P* on the side."

"Yeah."

"Looks to me like she's enjoyin' it."

"Trickin' in Tennessee or somethin' for the National Guard troops."

"But the palm trees, guys."

"Fuck the damn palm trees, twink. Who the hell asked for your no-account opinion, anyway?"

"Well, fuck me till it hurts," the private imitated Treat Brody, and everyone laughed.

The conversation went on that way for quite some time until Farney said, "Listen to this shit." He read from the editor's bold-print byline appearing above the main article that accompanied the photographs. " 'The Thornton *Theseus* has recently received documents and photos from an anonymous source in South Vietnam detailing war atrocities being committed by American forces attached to Operation Coronado—' "

Brody shook his head in resignation. "That's us."

" '—In the Mekong Delta. Though the accuracy of the allegations, made by one who we believe to be a member of the armed forces serving with the unit involved, has not been verified, we at the *Theseus* have

240

no reason to doubt the content of the following article, and we invite the anonymous contributor to keep us posted on developments in that faroff example of the United States' latest military adventure.' "

"Fuck."

"Goddamned left-wing, bleeding-heart news media."

"Never fucking fails."

"I'd just like to get my hands on the smuck-suck that sent this crap to 'em in the first place," Brody said.

"The asshole definitely needs an attitude adjustment." Sgt. Brock spat at the earth between his jungle boots. Nelson smiled inwardly, wondering if Master Le Loi would have reacted that way 500 years ago.

"What he really needs is an enema with an M-16 muzzle." Brody was still shaking his head as Graham rubbed elbows for a better look at the article.

"Maybe the guy's just tellin' it like he sees it," the disgruntled draftee said softly.

"Whose fuckin' side you on, anyway?" One of the newbies pushed Graham slightly, and the former pacifist's fists came up.

"Up your ass, jerk," Graham snapped, and Orson thought he saw a rekindling of the fire he'd noticed in the soldier's eyes after Graham killed the enemy machinegunner.

"Hey, I was just kiddin'." The accuser's hands rose in meek surrender. "Don't get so fried under the collar, okay?"

Brody snatched up the newspaper, ignoring all the protests. "I don't think anyone should be readin' this commie propaganda until we take a good look at it," he told Sgt. Brock.

"Good idea," the tall sergeant said, turning to leave. He didn't seem interested in being the one to review, edit, or censor the document, however. That time-consuming task was obviously being left to The Whoremonger. The story was a good five tabloid pages long, with additional photographs on the inside.

Treat rolled the newspaper up and started off toward the CP. He would check on the defensive positions first—make sure none of the men needed anything.

Before he was very far from Farney's jeep, he glanced back over a shoulder and focused on one of the pogues. Graham seemed just a little bit too happy and amused by the newspaper article. Brody made a mental note to keep an eye on the man.

"What was all the commotion about down there?" Another newbie's words intruded into Treat Brody's thoughts a few minutes later, after he'd checked three of the roadside foxholes.

"Aw, nothin'," Brody muttered. "Company clerk deliverin' the mail is all. Some of the guys bitchin' 'cause Orgasm's hoggin' all the perfumed correspondence again."

"That guy sure gets a lot o' mail from the ladies."

"Yeah. So it seems." Brody wasn't in the mood to expound on the women being mostly peace activists and war protestors who mailed the poor kid four- and five-page long lectures about the "evils" of volunteering for Vietnam. And he didn't mention the newspaper article. "Anything you guys need here? Got enough ammo? Canteens topped off?"

"No sweat, sarge." The pogue's foxhole partner, a soldier leaning back against sandbags and reading a Doc Savage novel, spoke without looking up from his paperback. The rim of his helmet rode the tip of his nose, shielding his eyes from Treat, and The Whoremonger decided the man looked like all the confident, combat-hardened GIs taking advantage of a rare break between battles that he'd seen in almost every war movie ever made. The thing that made Brody smile was that the man knew it too.

"Cut the 'sarge,'" Brody corrected him. "They kicked my butt and made me a corporal again."

"For leavin' *Peg* to chase down that commie bitch back up at the Brass Monkey coupla weeks ago?"

"Rodg." His smile faded with reflection. "But you can call me Whoremonger. Most everyone else around here does."

"You'll always be 'Sarge' to me, Sarge." The machine gunner was a corporal too, and he spoke with an odd twist of mutual respect, so Brody did not challenge him as the GI turned a page and went back to his 1930's-vintage adventure.

"Say, can I ask you something about one o' the dudes back down there by the jeep, the one wearin' the E-5 stripes?" the younger cavalryman spoke up quickly.

"Sure. Brock?"

"That's what I was gonna ask ya. His name's Brock, huh?"

"Yeah. You know the guy?"

"Yeah, from Orange County High. It's gotta be ol' Badass Brock."

"'Badass Brock'?" A slight grin crept across Brody's hardened features again.

"Nickname didn't really apply," the soldier revealed. Brody glanced down at his nametag: CONNORS. "Tall and stocky, but really a nice guy. Never threw his weight around that I can remember. Didn't even go out for the football team, though I'm sure he coulda made captain, easy."

"Maybe he's queer." Brody was not serious.

"Ha!" Connors laughed but abruptly dipped his shoulders as if afraid the NCO down the road might notice and just *know* they were talking about him. "Fags are for fraggin'."

"Yeah. I hear where you're comin' from, friend."

Connors glanced over at his trench partner, but the corporal was still turning pages of his adventure novel, ignoring their idle chatter. "Ol' Brock did have sort of a reputation as kind of the school weirdo. I'm kinda surprised, in fact, that he not only made it into the U.S. Army, but Uncle Sammy let him climb the ladder to

NCO status."

" 'School weirdo'?"

"Yeah. And I'll tell you why. It happened in study hall. Ol' Brock suddenly had this seizure or something."

"You mean like an epileptic seizure?"

"No, man. No, not an epileptic seizure. He didn't fall down on the floor or nothin' like that. Ol' Brock, he suddenly lets out this squeal to get everyone's attention, and sits up ramrod straight in his chair. I mean, I was sittin' right beside the dude, and my hair stood up just from the look on the guy's face."

Brody watched Connors carefully as he wiped his forehead with the back of his hand, as if the memory was still bone chilling. He did not think the soldier was making this story up as he went along. "What kind of look?" he asked.

"A strange look, my man. I mean, it was ever-lovin' mindfuck to the max, you know? His eyes are bulgin' out and the veins along his neck are bulgin' out too, and he's clutchin' the edges of his desk, chest expanding like a balloon that's gonna burst, and . . ."

"And?" Brody dropped into an Asian-style squat, intrigued by the story now.

"Then Brock himself *speaks*." Connors said the word "speaks" as if to announce some important, long-awaited event was about to take place.

"Brock 'speaks'?" Treat Brody was tiring of the theatrics, but decided to give the man a few more minutes.

"He opened his mouth, and the guy was speaking in another voice, man. Ol' Brock, he curls his lips back like a dog, bares his teeth, and says something like, 'Burn in hell with me, you virgin-hustling whore!' And ol' Brock—" Connors chuckled slightly here. "Ol' Brock, his neck arches to the right suddenly, head tilting nearly upside-down, and he's saying all this to Miss Pritchard, the old bag study hall teacher.

"So anyway, ol' Brock, he gets this big, shit-eatin'

ear-to-ear grin on his face when he sees Old Lady Pritchard back away, clutching at her bosom, and he adds, 'That's right, woman, I'm talking about *you*!' and his right hand flies up, and he's pointin' at her and saying 'You seduce little boys on their way home from school and take them into the cellar and . . .'"

Connors fell silent. He obviously didn't want to repeat all the words of the story.

"Hhmmm." Brody rocked on his heels slightly, pondering what the private had just told him. "He didn't claim to be 'Master Le Loi,' did he?"

Connors looked up at him. "Le *who*?"

"Forget it. Is that it, troop?" Brody asked.

"Oh, anyways, ol' Brock, he starts chantin' in a foreign language, and his eyes roll up into their sockets, leaving only the whites."

"And the guys in white suits didn't come and take him away in a straitjacket?" Brody challenged.

Connors' expression softened in thought as he contemplated Treat's question. "You know, that was what was so funny about the whole thing. After Brock accused Old Lady Pritchard of liking baby dicks," Connors chuckled nervously, "he kinda snapped out of it all."

"Snapped out of it?"

"Yeah. Shook his head like he'd just been woke up from a Numba Ten bookoo-bad dream, and said, 'What's going on?' and everyone just kinda backed off."

"But—"

"Nobody ever said another word about the incident. Now I know what you're thinking, but believe me: everyone just kinda clammed up about the whole thing. Everyone who was there, anyway."

Treat Brody glanced down the roadway as he rose to leave Connors' foxhole. It was getting dark now, but he could clearly see the outline of a man's face fifty yards away in the tree line. It was Brock.

Brock was staring at him and Connors and the corporal reading a Doc Savage novel, and that realization sent a shiver through Treat Brody's body that would not go away for several hours afterward.

CHAPTER 26

Australian USO entertainer Chrissy LaVey was not very optimistic about her present situation.

Naked except for her sheer, nearly see-thru bra and panties—"Silky Saigon Specials," a famous American comedian had once called them—and flat on her back, her wrists and ankles were tied to stakes in the floor of an underground tunnel.

That an underground tunnel should exist anywhere in this godforsaken stretch of soggy, waterlogged land known as the Mekong Delta was a shock to LaVey. But the earthen floor was indeed dry, and spiderwebs lined the tunnel's hidden entrance. The wooden wall and ceiling support beams looked old, old enough to be from the days of French colonialism in Indochina.

Now and then she could hear the slapping of helicopter rotorblades against the land overhead, so they must not be that far beneath the surface. LaVey could not remember climbing or being carried down into the tunnel. She simply awoke here, limbs restrained, left eye swollen shut.

She kept her eyes closed, fighting back the groans rumbling in her throat as she attempted to make it appear she was still unconscious. The Vietnamese women had paid her little attention, but one of the men

247

kept returning to her side. He would drop into a squat next to her arm, run his fingertips along the inner swell of her breasts without actually fondling her, then scamper off into the shadows whenever Kim reached over to slap him on the top of the head in unspoken reprimand. LaVey wondered if the man might not be slightly retarded, or possibly mentally disabled.

The beautiful singer did not ponder the subject for long. A huge, furry centipede was crawling along her exposed thigh, and her attention shifted to the prickly sensation nearing her groin.

Trinh Thi Kim extended a slender, firmly muscled leg and knocked the centipede away with the edge of her foot, watching the white woman's face carefully the entire time. The Australian's emotionless expression did not seem to change, however. No sign of relief, no sudden softening of the lines at the edges of her eyes.

The guerrilla who was paying an inordinate amount of attention to LaVey scurried over, snatched up the angry centipede by its antennae before it could sting him, and tossed it into the cooking pot.

Kim listened to the critter's legs sizzle as they melted away in the *nuoc-mam* fish sauce. She frowned as her eyes dropped along the white woman's shapely curves. LaVey was becoming more trouble than she was worth.

Kim regretted having struck the Australian with her AK. She shouldn't have kicked her, either. Such conduct was against the rules a true revolutionary lived by. The thought forced a stifled laugh from her: What rules? she asked herself. The North Vietnamese were notorious for abusing enemy prisoners taken along the Ho Chi Minh Trail, up through Laos and back to Hanoi. The Viet Cong were worse. And why shouldn't they be? She nodded in self-forgiveness. *After what we've gone through* . . . Trinh Thi Kim thought of the American called Patterson, and how she had used a heavy hammer to nail the VC flag patch to his back. Up north. Long ago. In the Ia Drang.

They were AWOL now, technically, Kim and her

248

ragtag band of anti-foreigner, pro-reunification insurgents. Absent Without Leave from their assigned area of operations. But so many communists *and* nationalists had perished recently that no one would probably even notice. They had died in large part due to the arrival in South Vietnam of a fierce fighting force the likes of which Ho Chi Minh's cronies had never seen before: the First Air Cavalry Division. With their terrifying helicopter gunships and airmobile battle concept, this new breed of troopers provided not only a challenge but a renewal of that old adrenaline surge Kim feared had abandoned her these last few years, since the Saigon assignments. She felt compelled to follow the fleet of Hueys wherever they went. Until her sapper attacks blew the last one up on the ground, or her snipers knocked the final bird from the sky.

It had been simple enough to learn where the Cav was going after Binh Dinh. One only had to climb a tamarind at the edge of the perimeter for a treetop seat during one of Bull Buchanan's numerous pep talks. After every operation, and before all upcoming missions, the colonel always mentioned the challenges that awaited them at their next destination. And those destinations rarely remained a secret. When it came to their sudden move south, beyond Saigon, into the Delta, there was no tight lid of security clamped on the Division's activities.

Vendors who'd camped out on the city's edge for days beforehand met the arriving Americans in Mytho with an endless procession of rice cakes, baggies filled with steaming sugarcane cubes or ice coffee, and baskets full of long, slender French breadrolls, filled with hot butter. After S-2 ensured the bread was not also laced with slivers of glass, the men were allowed to patronize whatever vendors caught their fancy, so long as they remained alert. As soon as the mission shifted into operational mode, the grunts would be out in the swamps, humping through waist-deep rice paddies and shoulder-high elephant grass, in pursuit of Charlie.

249

Buchanan saw no harm in allowing them to "let their hair down" in the meantime.

Trinh Thi Kim stared at LaVey, wondering what she should do. Should she cut the white woman's throat, and leave her in this hellhole when they decided to move on? Should she let Dung, the imbecile from Ia Drang, rape her, then release her? Let her try and find her way back to friendly forces, past the panthers and boobytraps and swamp snakes?

Another wave of gunships roared past overhead. The earthen wall trembled against her back. Kim was not even sure what her next move would be. That they were traveling in the same area where the Loach happened to crash was a break she had not anticipated, but the Delta was not the Highlands, or even Binh Dinh Province. She found it more difficult to negotiate the terrain while stalking or eluding the enemy. She was not comfortable fighting the riverine war. She missed the high, mist-enshrouded valleys, the endless rain forests. Here, there were only intermittent snatches of jungle, it seemed, at least along this stretch of the Mekong River. They had been lucky to stumble across the old Viet Minh hideout, too, after the fleet of gunships swept in to saturate the area with machine-gun bullets, after the soldier Brody escaped her ambush.

Treat Brody. In the darkness of the underground tank, Kim saw his face, grinning that same Whoremonger grin of his, and she wondered if he remembered her at all. She smiled back at the vision floating in front of her eyes. And it vanished, because, hard as it was for Kim to admit to herself, she realized they were not smiling about the same things.

Treat Brody expected to see more Agency commandos in black jumpsuits deplane when the wasplike Loach flared into camp the next morning at sunrise. But only one man climbed down from the chopper, and he was not from the Central Intelligence Agency at all.

Brody read CID in the grim-looking warrant officer's features—Criminal Investigations Division—the United States Army's olive drab detectives, though the CID was separate from, and independent of, the Military Police Corps.

He watched the short, stocky soldier greet Vance with a crisp salute, and Brody swallowed. The lieutenant had turned, and was glancing over a shoulder in Treat's direction.

"Brody!" Vance was waving him over now. "Corporal Brody. *If* you don't mind.

"This is Mister Dennison, Brody."

Before he realized it, Treat was standing in front of the CID agent.

Dennison appeared to be in his mid-thirties. He was short but stocky, with brown, close-cropped hair that stood up off his scalp, reminding Brody of a dog's fur bristling just before the animal attacked. There was nothing hostile-looking about Dennison's face, however. Clean-shaven and round. Brody wondered if the lopsided grin was of the perpetual persuasion.

"How ya doin', troop?" Dennison's hand reached out and his smile faded as his eyes locked with Brody's. The handshake was firm, the expression suddenly businesslike, the eyes piercing but without the hint of hostility. This was a man on a mission of truth, Treat decided, and he obviously took his job seriously.

"Fine, Mister Dennison," Brody responded. Warrant Officers were always called "mister" instead of "sir."

"Mister Dennison's here investigating the Larson matter," Vance explained. The lieutenant wore a blank face when he spoke. "He wanted to have a few words with you, since you and . . . The Professor were so tight." And then Vance was off on another one of his countless errands.

Brody found his throat going dry again. He was aware that Dennison was closely watching his face, gauging his expression. He turned and stared at the

251

Loach as it lifted off, belly strobe fading in the night sky until it was just another star twinkling against the tropical vastness of the galaxies out there.

"Quite a sight, isn't it?" Dennison walked over to a nearby pile of sandbags and set the briefcase he was holding down without opening it.

"I'm not sure I quite—"

"The stars, Corporal. The stars. There's nowhere in the world they shine quite so brilliantly as down here in the tropics."

"Oh?" Brody's surprise did not come across as genuine. Perhaps it was because he'd heard that some-where before. "Yeah, they're really bright in The Nam. Kinda strange, when you think about it all. The stars, and the forest and all that natural beauty kinda crap."

"How so?" Dennison sat on top of his briefcase. He looked like a man who had all night to listen.

Brody was immediately aware of what the CID agent was up to. Dennison could care less what the corporal's feelings on the local wilderness or the uncaring planets above might be. He was feeling Brody out, deciding how to approach the enlisted man for information.

And Treat was not offended. The guy had a job to do, he decided. Just like everyone else in The Nam. "Well," he started to explain, hoping he would not sound off-base, "with all the killin' and dyin' that goes on around here."

Dennison glanced away, down the road, at all the young, teenaged faces staring off into the pitch-black unknown beyond their perimeter. "Yes?"

"The trees can still be so green in the morning, when the sun first rises. Or right after a rainstorm. Yeah, right after a monsoon downpour, everything kind of sparkles with life. It's no longer a dirty war, but an okay place to be. I love it here on days like that."

"I know. I understand." The CID agent sounded more like a chaplain called in to console a shell-shocked casualty than an investigator looking for leads on dope smuggling.

252

"So, anyway." Brody slung his M-16 over his back upside-down and folded his arms across his chest. "What exactly can I do for you? Last I heard, The Professor was still on the MIA roster, presumed dead."

Dennison laughed openly. "Come on, Corporal Brody," he said. "If anything, he's a POW on his way to the Hanoi Hilton. But the Department of the Army's got a gut feeling ol' Shawn Larson bugged out and went over the hill."

Brody looked taken aback. "*Our* Shawn Larson?" His eyes grew large. "Surely you jest, Mister Dennison. The Professor was kinda weird, and truly anti-war, anti-social, and just about anti-everything, but he's no deserter."

"They tell me he wrote several suicide notes."

Brody's laugh was sincere this time. "As in more than one?" He feigned disbelief. "Hell, The Professor kept one long-running, ongoing suicide *book*, sir. It became sort of his trademark. Whenever we mustered for a mission and Larson was late, or didn't show up at all, Leo'd send me or Two-Step or Corky back to the hellhole—that's the bunker we constructed up in Ia Drang—'cause that was where you could always find him. Too busy to fight the war and risk gettin' killed in the gunships, because he had his suicide note to finish."

"That was one of the things we never recovered. His journal, or whatever you want to call it. Some of your superiors thought you might have it stashed away somewhere, corporal. As a momento of your friendship or something."

Brody's hands rose defensively. "No, not me, bossman. The Prof kept his notebook in his rucksack. Either it burned with him in the chopper crash, or his NVA captors are tryin' to decipher it at this very moment." Brody snickered. "Fuckin' dinks probably think it's big-time code or something, and not a suicide note at all."

"I see. So you two were not really that close after all."

Brody's face became sad, and he glanced down at his boots. "The Professor made it a point to stay away from everyone, Mister Dennison. You know the routine: don't get too close to the other guys, so if 'n when they get blown away by Charlie it won't hurt as much."

Dennison's head dropped too. He nodded, but didn't say anything.

"So why is CID in on Larson's disappearance, anyway?" Treat asked. "Since when does Uncle Sammy send his crime detectives in on a missing-in-action romeo-foxtrot?"

Dennison fixed an accusing stare on The Whoremonger. "I think you know, Corporal."

Brody locked eyes with the agent for a moment, realized defiance would get him nowhere and wasn't worth his energy anyway, and dropped his gaze, nodding in the affirmative. "Dope, right?"

"Right. Bookoo bong-loads of it. High-grade stuff."

"That's what was in all those duffelbags he kept shipping back to The World, huh?" The sadness returned to Brody's grim features.

"You knew?"

The doorgunner was no fool. He wasn't leaving Cho Gao in handcuffs on a conspiracy charge. "No," he responded quickly. "I don't think anybody *knew*. Not for sure. But all the guys suspected."

"Oh?"

"We asked him about the duffelbags once. Broken Arrow claimed he was shippin' LBFM's stateside so he could open a whorehouse when he got back, but—"

"LBFM's?"

"Little brown fucking machines."

"Oh."

"Larson kept a whole harem at a secret place in An Khe, though I never actually saw any of the women myself. Everybody talked about it though, and The Stork—"

"Warrant Officer Hal Krutch?"

"I see you recognize the nickname."

254

"Great slick pilot. Med-evaced my worthless young ass outta Gia Dinh one night back in '64."

"Yeah?" A hint of excitement sparkled in Brody's eyes. "The Stork was in The Nam way back in '64?"

"Yep. That was back when I was a Saigon Commando. Me and my partner drove smack dab into an ambush on the northeast side of Saigontown."

"Yeah, I heard them Charlie Congs in Sin City are vicious little bastards."

Dennison laughed as they both watched a Phantom jet make a low pass on the far side of the river, then ascend toward the stars without dropping any ordnance.

"Yep. Owe what's become of my life to The Stork. Sounds kinda funny, don't it: The Stork. Shee-it."

"He's dead, you know."

Dennison shook his head slowly. "Yeah. Came across his name in the *Stars & Stripes* KIA roster one morning. Really blew me away. The fucker saved my life. He shoulda packed it in when his Tour-365 was up, but he stayed on. Like you. And me."

"Well, I think he was finally ready to go back, this time." Brody sighed, but he didn't elaborate. "So why don't you go home? Back to The World. Why press your luck, Mister Dennison?"

"Me? This is home, buddy. The Nam. Home sweet home. Sounds stupid, I know. But CID work has become my career. I'm really into it, but I'd go insane workin' bullshit larceny cases up the *ying-yang* stateside. No, I'll take Saigon, or Mytho, or Danang any day. The Nam's all I care for, anymore. It's all I've got left." He opened the briefcase and pulled out a thin manila folder.

Brody changed the subject as Dennison working by flarelight, shuffled through pieces of paper. "I hope you're not going to take a written statement from me."

The CID agent pulled a photocopy of a mugshot from the file. "We'll see, we'll see," he said cryptically. "Know this man?" He handed the xerox to Treat.

It was Sgt. Brock.

Brody swallowed hard. He heard the noise his Adam's apple made as it moved along the dry throat, but he didn't think Dennison could see his discomfort in the dark. "Not sure," he replied. "What's he done?"

Dennison glanced around to make sure no other soldiers were within earshot. "We believe he might have been Larson's contact—his middle man, in the dope-smuggling racket."

"This guy?" His lower jaw dropped in surprise. "Looks like a square."

"Name's Brock. An E-5. Kind of a loony-tunes from what I've heard, but a good all-around NCO nonetheless when it comes to war zones. Worthless stateside, though."

"Looks familiar, but . . ."

Dennison already knew Brock was a squad leader with Echo Company now—Lt. Vance had told him. But he was still toying with this doorgunner's ethics, attempting to determine where and how his loyalties stood. That would establish the method and line of questioning with which Dennison would proceed.

"Take your time. Look it over carefully, and—"

A bright white flash of light tore the sheet of paper from the CID agent's fingers as he was handing it to Brody. At first, the doorgunner thought of Brock. In his mind, he saw an incensed and betrayed Sgt. Brock hurling a lightningbolt at The Whoremonger. But then he heard the rattle of distant discharges and realized the glowing flash had been a tracer.

The shots were being fired from an AK-47. Both men dropped prone at the edge of the roadway. "You got a weapon?" Brody shouted as a clamor of sporadic shooting erupted along the western perimeter.

"Just the .45 on my hip." Dennison was breathing hard. Dirt was in his eyes, and the leg with the bullet fragment souvenirs from Gia Dinh '64 was starting to act up. "And twenty-one rounds in three clips," he added as an afterthought.

"Plus one in the chamber?" Brody's face pressed

against the earth as another strip of rounds stitched across their position from the tree line two hundred yards away.

"Right." Dennison had his service weapon out now. Both soldiers scanned the distant trees. White muzzle flashes erupted here and there. Brody brought his riflebutt to his shoulder and began returning fire on semi-automatic. Dennison was aiming at the tree line, but, well aware he was out of maximum effective pistol range, never pulled the trigger.

"Don't this beat all," Dennison muttered. "Caught in the middle of a genuine out-in-the-sticks boonie-rat firefight, and I don't even have a rifle!"

"Kinda gets the ol' juices goin', doesn't it?" Brody grinned as, ears ringing slightly now, he switched to AUTO and directed a five-round burst at one of the muzzle flashes. Both men watched as the enemy rifleman's tracers flew skyward in a harmless arc as he was knocked backward, off his feet.

"Just wish I had an M-16," Dennison complained.

"Stick around," Brody muttered. "I'm sure there'll be a coupla extras lyin' around before this abortion is over."

CHAPTER 27

Trinh Thi Kim moved quickly from tree to tree in the pitch-black darkness, hoping to make it look like there were at least a half dozen VC firing at the Americans. Dung's brother lay dead, and the other two—Dung himself, and Nguyet—had remained back at the underground tank guarding the Aussie woman. Kim was on her own now.

Besides the Chinese-made Kalashnikov in her hands, two more rifles were slung over Kim's shoulders: a Soviet SKS, and a captured M-16. Her initial plan had involved switching weapons as she moved from tree to tree, but the pace had grown too frantic, she was far too excited now. Kim found herself barely able to eject empty magazines and slam home fresh clips.

Lead splinters had punctured several inches of her right thigh, but the wounds were small, the bleeding minimal. She pulled the last banana mag from the pouch on her web belt, shoved it into the rifle's feeder well, then dropped back.

Kim was about to make herself scarce—disappear into the jungle and sprint back underground before the Americans recovered, left their fighting holes, and came gunning for her. But the branches overhead were suddenly slapping down in her face wildly. The air seemed to be splitting apart and rushing back together, then she felt the pressure beating at the unyielding earth. As the downblast pressed her hair against her face and eyes, Kim stared up at the gunship hovering a few meters above the treetops. The rotorwash was intense, but she still managed to bring the AK to her shoulder.

After the spotlights swept through the trees on either side of her, Kim sighted in on the ship's belly mural. The painting depicted a black cat with its back arching before a dull orange moon. Kim aimed at the full moon and unleashed an entire magazine of bullets on rock-and-roll.

Screaming like a metallic predator in pain, the helicopter began ascending swiftly after several of the rounds punched up through its fiberglass and magnesium floorboards. Its turbines kicked in with a whining roar that hurt the ears, but the gunship, suddenly powerless, began dropping back toward earth.

Kim zigzagged back through the trees as the Huey slammed into the treetops, its rotorblades still twirling with frantic swishes as the engine rattled to a stop. Men aboard the craft screamed their lives into the night as the gunship exploded and fireballs rose up through the branches.

After the chopper crashed to a grinding halt on its side, a soldier stumbled from the Huey's mangled cabin. His upper torso was on fire, his face in flames and unrecognizable as he staggered across the fuel-slick earth.

Hesitating, she aimed at the man's chest as he stumbled about in slow-motion circles. But before the AK discharged, the burning GI was snatched from Kim's sight by several soldiers who knocked him to the ground with a crossfire of flying tackles.

She paused to watch them trying to smother the flames with their flak jackets. Then Kim turned and disappeared into the rain forest.

CID Agent Dennison rode escort with Treat Brody on the body-bag slick back to Cho Gao the following morning. Six men had died aboard the exploding gunship. Col. Buchanan wanted the bodies choppered north to Saigon and on their way back to The World ASAP. He preferred not to have any bad omens lying around, spoiling Operation Coronado's upcoming sweep of the Tang Hoa area.

"Can I buy you a beer over at the club?" Dennison asked Brody, after they'd helped deliver the corpses to the Officer in Charge of the Dead.

"Which club?" The Whoremonger threw a suspicious grimace in Dennison's direction.

He smiled. "The officer's club. In Mytho. You make quite a picture in your blood-caked fatigues. Oughta draw a few stares from the old farts assigned to—"

"No shit. I don't think the lifers'd much appreciate a gore-spattered enlisted man tracking up their nice teakwood tiles."

"You'll be my guest." Dennison brushed the dried mud from his own uniform. "I don't look much better," he admitted. "They'll have to throw us both out if anyone has any objections. Hell, most of 'em will fight over buying a round o' drinks, and try to milk you for all the information they can get about this Operation Coronado clusterfuck."

"You think so?"

"I know so, slick. You'll enjoy yourself. Besides, I've got more questions to ask, and we need some atmosphere—some time 'way from the war-type atmosphere, if ya catch my drift."

Mild enthusiasm leaked into Brody's tone. "Just point me in the direction of the nearest unclaimed jeep."

"Rank has it privileges: *you* drive."

Four hours and three six-packs later, Dennison had revealed several other choice tidbits about his investigation. Sgt. Brock figured into it more than Treat had anticipated.

Brock, it seemed, first had come to the attention of the Criminal Investigations Division five years ago, shortly after enlisting in the Service. "Brock was experimenting with acid for a while," Dennison told him. "Had a bad trip about two years ago. It took an entire squad of MPs to subdue his bad ass. The story goes, he snapped a set of handcuffs in half, and the Mike Papas broke three or four nightsticks over his noggin before they could get wrist and ankle shackles on him."

"And Uncle Sammy didn't boot his ass out of the military with a bad-conduct discharge for something like that?" Brody couldn't believe what he was hearing.

Dennison sighed. "It was the same old story. They gave him two options."

"The stockade, or—"

The CID agent nodded. "The Nam."

"So that was the reason we witnessed the double-autopsies," Brody surmised.

"Righto, partner."

Brody stared down into his glass, trying to forget what he'd seen back in the field hospital at Cho Gao. Bodies blown to bits on the battlefield was one thing, but watching a MAST surgeon cut the corpse's chest open down the middle, then sift through the dead man's insides using plastic gloves was a little beyond Treat's idea of fun on a Saturday morning.

Most of the decreased were from Sgt. Brock's squad again. There was no doubt in anyone's mind that they'd died at the hands of the enemy, but Dennison suspected that, somehow, Brock was using the dead bodies to ship dope back to the states. Dennison's theory was that an associate stationed in CONUS would intercept the body before it was released to next-of-kin. He believed the hash and heroin was hidden inside the corpses' ribcage. The scheme had already been tried and detected before.

"Has Sgt. Brock solicited you for any donations?"

the agent asked Brody, after Treat was beginning to feel a slight buzz from the Budweiser; it took The Whoremonger a good six or seven cans before alcohol could take him higher than when he was drunk on adrenaline.

The doorgunner did not respond immediately.

"Or have you ever overheard him soliciting any of the other men for money?" Dennison added.

"Soliciting?"

"For this Le Loi character you were telling me about. Money to support, to help finance his 'mission.'"

"Hell, Sgt. Brock don't need no *P* to do that, Mister Dennison. He and his followers just find a place to gather where they won't be bothered, and he kicks back, relaxes, and gets right into the ol' reincarnated warrior routine."

"And you don't count yourself among his followers?" Dennison challenged with a wink.

"Not any longer, I don't." Brody decided for himself, then and there. "No, I used to, I'll admit it. But not anymore."

"So you're sure about the contributions bit."

"Never heard any of that kind of talk, Mister Dennison." Brody kept a straight face as they locked eyes again.

A tall, slender Vietnamese woman caught Dennison's attention. Wearing a sky-blue *ao dai* over billowing black silk pantaloons, she carried a tray with drinks past their table. Dennison winked when she glanced their way, but the cocktail waitress blushed, stared in the opposite direction, and increased her pace. "Not bad," he mentioned, for Brody's benefit.

"I'm trying to quit," was the dry response.

"Sex in general, or just Vietnamese women?" Dennison was joking, but his new friend's tone was deadpan.

"You can't live with 'em . . ."

". . . And you can't live without 'em." The CID agent poured another can's worth into the large plastic glass and downed half of it in one long swallow.

"It's just that . . . well, you can't just . . . I mean, it

seems you can't just get laid in this goddamned country anymore, you know? There's no slam, bam, thank you ma'am. All these Viet chicks wanna dance on your head and do a job on your mind, you *bic*?"

"Yeah, I think I *bic*, bud. Sounds to me like you just been meetin' the wrong chicks at the wrong places. You let 'em get into your blood too easy. What ya gotta do is—"

"I don't like goin' to whorehouses to get my rocks off," Brody interrupted.

"I don't know a whole lot of other ways to get your knob sucked if you don't want complications. Less'n you like seducin' nightclub bargirls for quickies or even an all-nighter now and then. Not that you're gonna find any nightclub within a twenty-mile radius of here. But that isn't what I was going to say anyway, Treat."

"It wasn't?"

"Why do they call you The Whoremonger, anyway?" Dennison asked.

"Who told you anyone calls me that?"

"Come on." Dennison glanced at his wristwatch. "We've been in here all day, and it'll be curfew in a coupla more hours. I ain't got all night, chump."

He was smiling when Brody glanced up. "You mean we've gotta catch a slick back out to the river tonight?"

"Naw, I cleared it with Vance. You and I can go whorin' around tonight if we want, but somehow you didn't strike me as bein' that kinda guy. And me, I'm married."

"To a local, I'll bet."

"Guilty as charged: Mytho born and raised."

"Is she good-lookin'?" Brody felt the instant idiot for asking.

Pride etched in the wrinkles along his cheeks, Dennison produced a wallet photo. "And *that's* after three baby-sans, boy!"

Brody whistled softly. "Mighty nice, Mister."

"Call me Dave. 'Mister Dennison' takes half an hour to say, and besides, there's no one around here who

263

gives a water buffalo fart about rank."

Brody studied the photo closely. The woman appeared to be in her late twenties, at most. She wore the traditional *ao dai* gown. A frail-looking hand held a straw conical hat atop her head at a crooked angle, like the picture was taken just as a gust of wind tried to steal the hat. She had the usual long black hair, but there was something in this woman's expression Brody had never seen before. Something in her eyes. There was something about her high cheekbones, too. Something that spoke royalty to Treat Brody. The straw hat was obviously meant to add color to the shot. This was no peasant girl. "Mytho born and raised?" He sounded almost skeptical. "She looks like one of those high-class princesses from the Imperial City of—"

"Hue?"

"Right." Brody carefully closed the wallet, noticing the edge of a gold CID badge sparkle under its black felt flap as he did so. He handed it back to Dennison.

"Yah, we've heard that before from people. Actually, Thuy's parents are from Thanh Lam, a village just a couple klicks south of Hue, on Highway One. We don't admit to it much, though. People in Saigon and the Delta can be funny about things like that. They can really distrust northerners, and insult 'em or make fun of them."

"They consider Hue *north*?"

"You'd be surprised. Many do. After the real northerners were given the option to move into South Vietnam in '54, Thuy's folks decided to move even farther south than the Imperial City. Her father says the American presence here means nothing. 'The communists will conquer the south someday,' he says all the time, 'and I want to have as much warning as possible when Ho Chi Minh starts marching down Thunder Road.'"

"So how did you know about my nickname?" The Whoremonger changed the subject again.

"Oh." Dennison leaned back in his chair and stretched his arms out. "You'd be surprised how many little tidbits of information everyone's file holds."

Brody's eyes widened slightly. "You've got a file on me?"

Dennison responded with a don't-get-excited shrug. "Sure. Didn't you know every platoon commander fills out a special report each time one of his men kills another man, be that other man enemy or otherwise?"

"'Enemy or otherwise'?"

"We don't want to get into technicalities, do we?"

"I thought we were just going to get drunk."

"Exactly." Dennison leaned back in his chair again and glanced over a shoulder. "Hey, *Co Dep*, young thing!" He called to the waitress with a raised voice that remained in the polite range. "Another round on Big D."

It was a different woman this time. "Okay, Davey-boy." She giggled and scurried off through the maze of tables.

"What did she call you?" Brody asked quickly. "'Davey-boy'?"

"Don' mean nothin', pal. You hang around this dive long enough, they all start callin' you by your first name."

"I wonder if she's got a sister half as cute." Brody hadn't missed the sparkling jewels on her left hand.

"Hell, she's available, kid. Wedding rings don't mean nothin' in this joint. They all wear 'em to keep the old MACV farts from tryin' to hustle 'em twelve hours a day."

Brody didn't care how his next remark made him sound. "Naw, forget it. I was just makin' small talk, Dave. Like I said, I'm gonna lay off gettin' romantically involved with indigenous types for a while. Until I get my head back together again."

"Some little lady of the evening did quite a number on the ol' Whoremonger, eh?" Dennison's loud laugh was a cruel and merciless one.

"It was mindfuck to the max," Brody admitted. Koy's face flickered in the liquid gold at the bottom of his glass, like a weak battery-operated flashlight in an underground VC tunnel. He watched it go out, and, for a moment, smelled death on the air.

"Wanna talk about it?"

"Naw." The waitress had arrived with two more cans of Budweiser, and Brody began chugging until it bubbled out over the edges of his mouth. Finally, he set the can down. "Maybe some other time."

"Just let me know." Dennison handed Brody an army-issue business card. "It's got my telephone listed down there in the corner. I wrote my home number on the back, in case you ever want to . . . talk."

"Thanks, Dave." He slipped the card into a breast pocket. "But don't go feelin' sorry for The Whoremonger. He's a tough old fuck." Treat spoke in the third person. "He's gotten over worse in the past. He'll survive this. Let's change the subject again, okay?"

"Okay." Dennison clasped his hands on top of the table in front of him, sliding the empty beer cans out of the way. "Let's talk business."

"Were you aware Sgt. Brock's men have all designated him the beneficiary on their GI life insurance policies?"

CHAPTER 28

"How long can you cover for me?"

Zack stared down at Nelson and shook his head from side to side. "I can't cover for you at all, slick! You tryin' to get Leo in the lockup?"

"Come on, Sarge." Nelson pulled a duffelbag full of empty brass cartridges from *Pegasus*'s hatch and lifted it onto a shoulder. "Can't you cut me a little slack?"

"Eat it like a man, junior."

"But it's been nearly two weeks. I really gotta see Anna."

"You mean your ding-dong's gotta ring her chimes, that's what the hell you mean, troop!"

"Yeah, well, something like that. Come on, how long can you cover for me?"

Zack dropped into a squat. Moonlight reflected off the layer of sweat covering his shaved crown. "Listen up, slick!" He grabbed the front of Nelson's shirt and pulled him closer as he whispered. The empty cartridges inside the duffel clinked about accusingly. "The less attention you bring to us from the Brass, the better our chances are of beatin' this rap, understand?"

"Zack!" The private didn't want to hear any of that. "Ain't no one gonna know. Ain't no one gonna miss Nasty Nel for just a couple hours, okay? Come on, Leo, whatta ya say?"

"I oughta kick your worthless white butt," the big NCO threatened good-naturedly. "Let me tell you one thing, though: if the tower scrambles us for a Brass Monkey, or Charlie hits down at the river, your ass is grass and—"

"You're the lawnmower." Nelson had already turned to walk away.

"And don't you forget it!" Zack called after him.

Warrant Officer Gabriel climbed down from the cockpit door and sauntered up to Leo, straightening out his gig line and customized web belt buckle in a manner that made it look like half his chopper-jockstrap was stuck in the crack of his haunches. "What was that all about?" He motioned toward the enlisted man carrying the heavy duffel of M-60 brass over to the armory.

They watched Nelson dump the bag in front of Specialist Farney—who doubled as armorer on weekends because the real armorer was doubling as CQ— then walk off toward the meat market at the front gate.

"Aw, nothin', Mister Gabe," Leo The Lionhearted responded with a sarcastic frown below icy black eyes as he dropped down from the cabin hatch. "Just another swingin' dick lookin' for someplace to stick it."

"Ahhh-so!" Cliff Gabriel saluted the departing Nelson, then wrapped an arm around Zack's shoulder and aimed him in the direction of the meat market. "Kids, these days. A shack-up job?"

Zack shook his head in mock sorrow. "I think so."

"Hhmph." Gabe The Gunslinger imitated the taller NCO. "Kids, these days," he repeated. "They got no fucking respect for tradition."

"Roger that."

"Now let's get on down to the cage and haggle with the hens over the price of blowjobs."

"I missed you. I really missed you so very much!"

Nelson held Anna tight as she kissed him repeatedly about the throat and chin. "I missed you too, honey. I dreamed about you while I was aboard *Pegasus*. While I was *riding* her! Can you believe that?"

Anna rose up on her tiptoes and kissed him hard across the lips. "I thought you would never come back," she said, after they broke for air.

"What?" He brushed the tears from her cheek.

"I was afraid you would not return to me."

Nelson was in no mood for downer scenes. "Hey, baby. Yours truly rides into battle with Brock & Brody Inc. They both got the magic, honey; they're Echo Company's charms! Nothin' could happen to your Nasty Nel while those two got him under their wings. So just mellow out, relax, and—"

"I was not worried about the Viet Cong." Anna stared up into his eyes long and hard, without blinking. "I was not worried about the North Vietnamese communists."

"Oh?"

"I was worried you found another woman. A girl somewhere else. That you were bored with Anna already."

Nelson's laugh silenced her. He moved toward the kitchen area of Anna's small cubicle. "Honey-san, the only woman youz gots to worry about is Lady Death, 'cause when *Peg* and I go out at night to light up the town, the bad bitch hides! She hides from us, Anna."

"*Peg*?" Anna asked. She had listened to him talk enough before about his friends and his love for gunship duty that she was not worried about this Lady Death nonsense. Vietnamese custom was similar: brag about fearing nothing, including death, and perhaps she would pass over you, snatching away someone else instead.

Nelson glanced over a shoulder and saw the look of concern on her face. "Our chopper, honey," he said. "*Pegasus*. She's our helicopter. She takes us to the open-air market where we sell off our cherries so the Void won't claim its due." He spoke matter-of-factly, using a tone that inferred she should have known all that already.

Anna was not wearing the relieved face he had expected to see. She stood there frozen, head tilted to one side. Finally, she said, "You have not seen your woman in nearly fourteen days, and all you can think about is food?"

He did not slow in his preparations. "Noodles, my dear. Noodles aren't food, they're special." He bent over and picked his ruck off the floor, set it on the narrow wooden table. "Noodles and something even more special."

Anna started over toward Nelson as he rummaged about in the pack. "No!" His hand shot out in mock warning. "Stay over there, woman! It's a surprise."

"But—"

"Don't give Nasty Nel no lip, or you're gonna find your sweet little tight ass plantin' rice up in—"

"Don't talk to Anna like that!" She rushed up and began slapping him playfully. Hands protecting his face, Nelson backed away. After Anna maneuvered him away from the kitchen, she rushed back over to the ruck.

Inside, she found a carton wrapped up in plastic. "Just like last time." The disappointment was heavy in her voice as Anna referred to Nasty Nel's pubic-hair collection.

He assumed a stern tone. "It's not what you think, young lady."

"Oh? And how do you know what I think?"

"Huh?" Nelson grabbed the package from Anna. Fists flying—and not as playfully as before—she fought for it. But keeping the small box over his head, out of reach, Nelson began unwrapping it.

"What?" She stared at the contents after he laid the carton down on the table and opened its lid.

"'What?'" he mimicked her. "Don't you recognize an oyster when you see one, Anna honey-lover girl?" He gently took her hand and rubbed it against his

270

crotch. "They're supposed to be good for, uh, romantic-type activity."

"So I have heard." She did not sound as excited as he had hoped, but Nelson did not let it affect him. He resumed toying with the kitchen utensils, and opened the small icebox he'd purchased from the PX in Mytho before his latest jaunt down to the river with the boys. Nelson slid the oysters into a large bowl, then poured a trayful of ice over them.

"Nelson sure he knows what he's doing?" Anna's fingers grabbed flesh slightly above his beltline and began twisting, but Nelson didn't flinch.

"Now all we've gots to do," he said, "is boil the ol' noodles, and we're all set. Too bad you don't have a balcony. Now *that* would add some romance to all this and—"

"We," Anna corrected him.

"Huh?"

"Too bad *we* don't have balcony. This your home, too."

Nelson glanced around critically. "Uh, I'm not sure ol' Nasty Nel's quite ready yet to call this place home."

"You like sleeping in rain forest better?"

Somehow she did not seem as insulted as he had expected.

"Well, no, of course not, but . . ."

Her smile brightened, and she rose up on her tiptoes again. "Then you should rent apartment for Anna—for *us*. In the city. In Mytho."

"Mytho? Won't that be expensive, honey-san?"

"Would you stop calling me honey-san!" she suddenly snapped, slugging him in the arm. "It sounds *stupido*!"

Nelson began laughing. Had there actually been a trace of Italian accent in her remark? "Okay, okay." He filled the soup pan with water and placed it on the hotplate.

"Not expensive." Her smile returned tentatively. "I check already."

"You checked already? Without asking the bossman's permission, little lady?" Nelson's eyes grew big and bold.

Anna knew he was just kidding. She grabbed the small Thai-style broom leaning in a corner and threatened him with it. "And don't call me 'little lady' again. Anna is my name."

That shocked Nelson. That she would say something like that really surprised him, but he didn't let it show outwardly. Not a single twitch revealed his growing discord. "Okay . . . shorty," he said simply.

Laughing, he let her chase him around the tiny room for a few moments. Then he tackled her, and they rolled onto the sleeping mat. "I really did miss you, Anna," he said.

"Your water is boiling," she replied with a straight face, eyes daring him to make the next move. "And it seems that is not all that grows hot in Anna's house tonight."

Nelson's hands went to work, unbuttoning her blouse. "Two weeks is a long time to be away from you. This shouldn't take long." He grinned. Nelson had no shame, and less pride.

"You would subject your future wife to a quickie?" her eyes seemed to sparkle in gentle, trusting submission, though.

Nelson ignored the verbal bail. "I'm sure there's enough water in the pot to last until I'm through."

As if on cue, there came several knocks at the door. Nelson could vaguely hear the restrained chatter of several women standing outside. "We're not throwing a party tonight, are we, dear?" His eyes bulged slightly as they bore into hers.

Giggling, Anna rolled him off and raced to the door, rebuttoning her blouse as she skipped across the room. When she reached it, she paused a moment to allow Nelson to get to his own feet, then drew the door back.

Smiling and waving and jabbering in rapid-fire Vietnamese, seven or eight women all competing to carry a small platter marched into the room. After they set it down on the kitchen table, some of the women curtsied or bowed. Nelson thought he recognized several of the faces from the night of the fist fight. And then they were gone, fast as they appeared. The last one out the doorway, an old mama-san in her eighties, stopped to pinch Nelson approvingly on the cheek, and then she took her black, betel-nut smile and disappeared with the rest.

In somewhat of a daze from the sudden flurry of activity, Nelson began sniffing at the air. "Well, whatever they brought in, it certainly smells good," he said. "Seafood?"

"Yes." Anna rolled back the tinfoil to reveal a small mountain of white clams. "Should go very good with your oysters." Steam rose from the glistening, ivorylike pile. She tried to pick up one of the inch-wide steamed clams, but it was still too hot.

"Special occasion?" Nelson was by her side now, gently kissing her neck.

"Maybe," she said. "I tell you later."

He began nibbling on her ear and whispering, in crude Vietnamese, that he found her scent irresistible.

She shoved him away. "Do not try and sweet-talk Anna!"

Movement in his peripheral vision returned Nelson's attention to the platter on the table. "What the heck?"

As if by magic, many of the clams were opening. "Isn't it pretty?" Anna sounded like an innocent schoolgirl as he draped an arm over her shoulder and they watched several clams tumble down from the pile as the ones underneath began opening too.

"I've never seen anything like it."

"My friends, they boil for us just now, maybe five minutes ago. *Xin-loi* for the clams—it kill them. They die, shells open up. Okay," she announced in an authoritative, wife-to-husband tone, "you sit down. Enjoy." She slid one of the two folding PX chairs Nelson had brought down from Mytho out from the table, then went about brewing the Viet coffee and stirring the ice-cube-covered oysters.

"I'm not sure what . . . I'm not sure how I—"

Anna quickly balanced the coffeegrain flasks atop two tall, brightly decorated glasses, and sat down beside him. She placed a paper plate in front of Nelson and, using chopsticks, selected several of the larger oysters for him.

"Screw the oysters. They're old hat." He laughed, pointing at the pile of steaming white clamshells. "I'm in the mood for something new, so tell me what to do."

Anna laughed and elbowed him lightly.

"Is simple," she said, taking a long, intricately carved bamboo sliver from a canister holding ivory and wooden chopsticks. "Pick a clam, and use toothpick to pluck out the meat."

"Oh." Nelson allowed her to prepare the first few for him. Anna removed the dime-sized morsel of meat and slid it onto his tongue, like mother to baby.

"Uhmmmm." He licked his lips. "Very tasty. Yes, excellent. But they go so fast, they're so small!"

"We have many, many left," she reminded him, waving her chopsticks at the huge pile. "You wait and see. We will be lucky to *fini* all of it!"

An hour later, when they were reclining in their chairs, leaning against each other, content and overfed, Nelson glanced at the blue porcelain bowl sitting between their two glasses of Viet coffee. "We didn't even touch the oysters," he remarked without complaint.

"I'm sorry." Anna stared at the dark brown drops of coffee falling from the brewing flasks down into their glasses. She sat up suddenly. "*Ca-phe* Numba *Three* ready now," she announced. "Energy for you, my lover-man, or you go to sleep fo' sure!" Anna patted his somewhat bloated belly affectionately.

She removed the aluminum flasks containing the coffee grounds, and handed Nelson his third glass of the strong brew. "Drink," she told him, "but be careful. Still bookoo hot, okay?"

"Okay." He blew a kiss to her, too lazy to rise further from the chair.

"And I show you something." She picked up one of the empty clamshells and sat it on the table directly in front of them. It was not the largest from the plate of empty shells, but by far the most beautiful, with sharp, natural whirls along the edges.

Anna reached over to her box of sewing instruments and withdrew the new pair of scissors Nelson had also found at the PX. "Vietnamese custom." She nodded solemnly, taking a small sample of hair from the top of his head and snipping it away before he could summon the energy to protest.

Anna carefully placed the thick, blond strands into the bottom half of the clamshell, then cut a half inch of her own jet-black hair from the bangs above her eyes, and placed them on top of Nelson's contribution. He did not notice it, but the clam Anna had picked also happened to be one of the last to be removed from the hot water at the bottom of the platter. It was still warm, the hinges soft as at the moment of the mollusk's demise.

Taking Nelson's fingers, she picked up the shell and closed both halves. With her own fingertips on top of his, she held it shut while she explained the custom. "Vietnamese lovers believe when they seal small piece of hair like this, they remain in love forever. Or until clamshell open," she said, suddenly removing his hand. The clamshell appeared tightly shut, but Anna kept her own fingertips around it awhile longer as added insurance. "Very seldom have the clamshells ever opened. *I* have never known anyone to whom it has happened."

"That's a very nice custom." Nelson nodded, eyes darting to the oysters. He was feeling hungry again already.

"It is better than your custom of keeping hair from other women in bottles," she said with distaste, elbowing him again.

"I thought we agreed not to discuss my little collection anymore, Anna."

"Do you love me, Nelson?" she asked without warning.

"I thought we would wait a year before we used that word." His head bobbed about from side to side on his shoulders, taunting her.

Anna drew a dainty fist back playfully, but restrained herself at the last moment. "Do you care for me?" she asked instead. "Do you care for Anna more than anyone on this earth—except your parents, of course. I wish your family and your parents the best of health and happiness, always, Nelson."

He drew his face close to hers, until they were nearly nose to nose. "To tell you the truth, honey-san, I care for you more than my parents or anyone else on this earth."

"Don't say that." She glanced away disapprovingly, but Anna's heart was racing with happiness now.

"But it's true."

Anna released the clamshell. It was tightly shut now. She felt confident a grenade blast would not even be able to open it, though such a thought irritated her. In Vietnam, words were power. Vietnamese did not speak of bad things happening lest they occur shortly thereafter. Thoughts were not as powerful, but nearly so, and Anna could be very superstitious about such things. She placed the bright white shell in the palm of his hand. "I want you to keep this with you," she told him, "for good luck."

"Oh? Wouldn't it be safer here? Here, in our . . . *home*."

She shook her head.

"Very well." He sighed, feigning resignation. "I already wear this." He lifted the modest gold necklace from inside his shirt. A brass amulet of the Buddha, favored by Arvin soldiers, hung from it, encased in a protective layer of plastic. "And this." His hand rose, and a twenty-two-karat gold ring on the left wedding finger gleamed beneath the wall lantern. The ring held a dime-sized, smoothly rounded crystal that threw shards of purple and crimson light back at the lantern. It was not a band of marriage, but symbolized another Asian tradition: if smaller slivers of multi-colored crystal began to grow within the stone, immense good luck would befall the wearer.

Anna pressed the clamshell into his palm. "Please keep it with you, anyway." Her eyes pleaded, and Nelson felt touched. "Wherever you go, all the time. It will remind you of me . . . of us."

"You're not going to cry, are you?" He smiled down at her, after placing the shell in his shirt pocket, buttoning the flap securely, and pulling her close.

"I feel like crying," she admitted. "But they would be tears of happiness."

Nelson kissed the silklike strands of hair along her forehead and slowly rocked her back and forth in his arms for a long time.

A thought trickled back to gnaw at him, and Nelson asked, "You said this was a special occasion, Anna, that you would tell me something later."

She opened her eyes and stared at the pile of opened clams drying beneath the slowly twirling ceiling fan Nelson had installed only the day before he last left her for that jungle bitch the gunship troopers branded Void Vicious. "Nebbah mind," she said gently, in a dreamy voice. "It can wait. Was not important."

The uneasy feeling in the pit of Nelson's stomach would not go away, however. "No," he said, "go ahead and tell me now. Otherwise, you might forget."

A barely audible titter escaped the woman in his arms. She seemed to curl up slightly, almost into the fetal position, trying to hide from him without leaving his arms. "No," she whispered, "Anna will not forget."

Nelson waited until he sensed Anna was near dozing off, and then he slowly slid his hand up under her blouse until the fingers cupped the firm underslope of a breast. He could feel the pace of her heartbeat quicken, though Anna did not move.

Moving his thumb and forefinger up, he rubbed the nipple gently until it grew taut, popping erect. "Tell me, Anna."

Grimacing, she opened her eyes and stared up into his own.

Nelson thought he spotted something new in Anna. Her face seemed to shine.

Slowly, she took hold of his hand and moved it down between the slopes of her breasts, lower and lower.

Nelson's mischievous grin made its first appearance since they had dined. "Now you're talking," he said.

But their hands stopped at her stomach, falling no farther.

Anna placed both her tiny palms flat against the rough knuckles of his gunhand and pressed gently until his skin grew warm from the touch of her own flesh. "I am going to have your child," she announced proudly.

CHAPTER 29

Nelson leaned into the hatch-60, gritting his teeth. But each time he unleashed a burst of rounds, the red tracers floated down into the treetops harmlessly, several dozen meters behind the targets of opportunity.

Gabriel clicked into the intercom with a half-concerned, half-teasing tone. "Having a problem at the back of the bus?"

Nelson did not respond. He tried to concentrate on his aim—on the mental coordination necessary to estimate the gunship's speed, the distance from ship to ground, and the number of meters he would have to lead the flow of bullets in order to allow for the drop factor. He tried his best to bring it all together. But all he could see were the tears in Anna's eyes after he exploded back in Cho-Gao.

"Meltdown!" someone was yelling into his disturbed thoughts. "Nelson! You're into a meltdown, goddamnit!" Snakeman Fletcher had clicked in to warn him, then abandoned his own M-60 and rushed over to bang him upside the headset when he was ignored. Nelson glanced down at the barrel of his doorgun. It was glowing blood red, bullets were flying down toward earth nonstop, yet striking nothing but treetops—and he wasn't even aware his finger had the trigger locked back.

"What's the problem back there, ladies?" Gabe's peter pilot clicked in after Nelson shook the fog from his head, switched barrels, and Fletcher returned to his side of the Huey.

"Nothin', champ!" Elliott shook his head from side to side as *Pegasus* banked hard to the left, circling around, back to the point of contact. "Nelson's just pussy-whipped. He's got clit juice in his eyes or something. I'll straighten him out. Don't sweat it."

"Snakeman knows best," The Gunslinger clicked in.

Thanks, Cliff, Fletcher nodded mentally as the helicopter rose several hundred feet up over the treetops, then suddenly dived down toward the snakelike river meandering far below.

They had been hovering with five other gunships over the main channel of the Mekong, providing cover fire for several PBRs inspecting a string of suspected VC sampans, when the radio call for help broke through static on the VHF band. A platoon-sized patrol sweeping the riverbanks in search of the Australian hostage and CIA drop tube had encountered heavy enemy resistance less than two miles away.

When they arrived on-station, the gunship crews found a heavily fortified Viet Cong wharf crawling with black pajama-clad guerrillas. The Americans had stumbled across a secret way station in the vast communist supply network honeycombing the Delta.

A half dozen heavily armed choppers can inflict considerable damage to even a battalion-sized contingent of the enemy, however. For Fletcher, it was like waiting his turn at a shooting gallery. *Pegasus* was third ship in line, and the Hueys before her would swoop low past the riverbank encampment, one at a time, doorgunners decimating the unorganized, half-asleep guerrillas the Lurp patrol had located at pre-dawn. Fletcher would stomp up and down, groaning and grunting his near-religious routine of jungle war chants and rainforest battle cries, hanging onto the M-60's pistolgrip as he did his little dance of death, waiting his turn.

Nelson, on the other hand, couldn't seem to get into the swing of things. And he'd waited so long to get back behind a hatch-60 after nearly a month working ground patrols and perimeter or LP duty, guarding the gunships when they weren't airmobile.

Snakeman Fletcher wasn't really worried about the kid—more irritated than anything. He'd worked with men before who were suffering from women problems. The Snake could smell pussy and its love potion all over Nasty Nel. It only meant more confirmed kills for Fletcher's Hog Heaven honor roll. Gabriel had already made allowances for the private's obvious no-money-no-honey hangover, adjusting his approaches so that Snakeman's hatch always faced the enemy.

Nelson felt terrible inside now. Not only was he traveling a guilt trip on Anna's account, but his inability to separate his love life from the mission was making everything harder on his team members. The fact that Nelson was well aware Snakeman was happy to do all the killing, and Gunslinger Gabriel enjoyed the challenge of adjusting his wrong-way maneuvers in and out of the other gunships, honing his pilot's skills, didn't serve to lessen Nelson's inner conflicts. *I'm sorry, guys!* he mumbled mentally, stumbling slightly on the pile of empty brass accumulating beneath his boots. *I'm okay now. Nasty Nel's back in the saddle!*

But Gabriel kept him pointed out over the wide Mekong, and there was nothing to shoot at. He watched Anna's face drift from cloud to cloud, following *Pegasus* over the unforgiving Void.

When she told him she was with child, Nelson had exploded. He jumped up out of his chair, nearly dropping her from his lap, onto the floor. Anna stumbled backward, into a corner, where she cowered, fearful he might become violent toward the news.

"You do not want me to bear your son?" Anna had said, the tears flowing freely now.

"I'm a soldier, goddamnit! How am I ever going to

afford raising a family? How would I ever find time to bring up babies? If the Army wanted me to have a kid, it would have motherfucking issued me one!"

They had argued about how it could have happened—Nelson accusing her of being stupid and naive, Anna reminding him she had offered her virginity in return for his love, and knew nothing about the consequences. Finding blame with himself suddenly for not thinking about birth control options beforehand, for leaving that up to the woman, Nelson fell silent. He began pacing the room which had seemed to become smaller and smaller with each breath he took.

She stood up and pointed a finger at him accusingly. "Then I was right!"

"Right about what, for Christ's sake?"

"Anna is only a short-time girl for Nelson. Soon, after you tire of Anna, you leave her for someone else. For skinny city girl who does not grow fat with child!"

"Stop talking like you're not standing right here in front of me. It pisses me off when you do that!"

"Anna has become nothing but a whore girl. Your son will be born of a whore!" And she threw his jungle boots at him. "Get *out!*" she screamed.

Nelson had slammed the door behind him when he left.

"Get your shit together!" He heard Gabriel's voice, a jumble of electronic echoes because *Pegasus* was suddenly descending so swiftly. "Lima Zulu in dirty-sex, and she's hot as a whore's hole on Saturday night!"

Nelson's eyeballs rolled up into their sockets, mentally reprimanding himself for all his recent poor judgment calls. Here he was dropping into Void Vicious, probably never to survive, and he'd left Anna during a fight, tears streaking her beautiful face, without even saying goodbye. Or apologizing. For he had been truly sorry from the first moment of the outburst. But Nelson was also young and stubborn and suffering from a gunny's macho, confirmed-bachelor pride, and that had locked his lips tight as a chastity belt.

Treetops rose above the silver blur of rotorblade tips. He tightened his hand around the M-60's pistol grip, preparing to unload on wild-eyed, Asian faces. But as soon as *Pegasus* pranged to a stop on the carpet of rotting, spider-infested logs, all he saw were gunpowder-smeared Americans.

Experience told him casualties would then be rushed toward the chopper for immediate extraction, but only two GIs started for the gunship, one limping with a bloody leg wound as he kept an arm around another soldier's shoulder.

The bodies of nearly a hundred Viet Cong littered the riverbank wharf and MG emplacements positioned along the tree line. "You gunnies did a Numba One job on Charlie!" The man with lead in his thigh climbed aboard, slid on his buttocks across the floor of the cabin away from the vulnerable hatch, then pulled an empty ammo bandolier from his ruck and began wrapping it around the dressing a combat medic had already applied.

"Yeah?" Snakeman was all smiles, basking in the rare recognition.

"*Ching-ching*, GI! You practically did our job for us! I haven't seen shooting like that since I went to a Wild West Show at one o' them movie studios in Hollyweird!"

"Far out!" Fletcher kissed his own knuckles as Nelson watched with a slight, preoccupied grin. It seemed the rest of the grunts were remaining on the ground.

"Are you up back there?" Gabriel called over his shoulder without clicking in.

"We're up!" Fletcher replied, teeth bared like a hungry wolf as he leered at the wounded man, then the collage of multi-hued, mist-enshrouded greens extending outside the hatch for as far as the eye could see.

Pegasus ascended suddenly, and as she rose above the treetops, Fletcher, held aboard by the monkeystraps connected to his webbelt, leaned out through the hatch

283

into space and, using both hands, directed an obscene gesture down at Void Vicious and the bodies she had claimed this day.

"Ain't this a crock?" Orson was sifting through the latest issue of the Thorton, Colorado, *Theseus*. "The traitor son-of-a-bitch who's makin' the First Air Cav look like a bunch of warmongering baby-killers and civilian-abusers has written another expose on Operation Coronado."

PFC Graham glanced over at the full page of amateurish back-and-white photos accompanying the article and shook his head wearily. "That's what we're supposedly fighting for over here, isn't it?" He glanced at the shattered crystal on his wristwatch.

"Oh, yeah?"

"We're here in glorious Southeast Asia to preserve the right to free speech and keep the commies from paddlin' to Santa Monica beach, among other things, right?" Graham spoke without serious conviction.

"Well, I guess so, but 'free speech' only applies to factual articles that come at least somewhat close to representing the truth, don't it?"

"Is the article really so far from the truth, Orson?" Graham rubbed at his blood-soaked knee.

"Oh, come on, Shannon."

"Don't call me that." Graham paused to take in a deep breath. "You take, for instance, that after-action sweep following the firefight down at the river this morning. Through that village coupla klicks away."

"More like coupla hundred yards away." Orson didn't feel it was anywhere close to two kilometers from the battle site.

"Well, we had no right to go bustin' into those people's homes like that and—"

"I don't exactly call thatched huts with gunnysack covers

284

for doors someone's home," Orson interrupted him.

"Sure they are. This isn't the States, okay? Sure, we could make a show of force by surrounding the place if we suspected it contained VC sympathizers, and that maybe they were harboring some of the Cong that ran from the fight afterwards. But you don't force yourself on the people like that, invading their privacy and—"

"Oh! We interrupted their morning entertainment, did we? I didn't hear *Lassie* comin' from no TV sets. Shit, Shannon, half the people were out ankle-deep in rice paddy mud anyway. Whatta ya wanna do, announce over a bullhorn you're going to conduct a hut-to-hut search and give 'em time to climb down through the trapdoors half of 'em had hidden under those cooking barrels. Did you forget about all the weapons we confiscated, all the rifles we found hidden in the rice pile? An AK-47 is a communist-bloc firearm, Graham-Cracker. It wasn't manufactured by Mattel like our M-16s. Shit, I'm almost beginnin' to think maybe *you* had something to do with these commsymp, left-wing newspaper reports."

"*I* didn't write that goddamned crap!" Graham's voice rose threateningly. "And if I ever hear you say something like that again to anyone, even as a joke, I'll—"

"Okay, okay." Orson's open hands came up. "I said I was almost beginning to think bad things about ya, Graham-Cracker. I didn't say I *suspected* anything yet.

"So how would you justify the bit about the baby-killing?" Orson continued.

Graham glanced about the aid-station waiting room. A dozen other soldiers with minor wounds sat on wooden medical supply crates that were currently doubling as stools. "That one." He pointed at a soldier sitting by himself in a corner near the huge underground bunker's entrance.

"Sgt. Brody?" Orson's eyebrows rose slightly.

"*Corporal* Brody, jizz-breath. I heard from a grunt who heard it from another grunt who heard it from one of the doorgunners."

"Oh, real reliable info we're talkin' 'bout here." Orson folded his arms across his chest with the flare of a true skeptic and leaned back against the paneled wall.

"Brody went apeshit a couple weeks before we arrived in-country. Blew away a Viet mother who was in the criminally negligent act"—his tone turned sarcastic—"of suckling her infant daughter. Now does that come under the heading of baby-killing, or do sunflowers grow near a latrine?"

Orson frowned. He'd heard a considerably different version. But before he could say anything in The Whoremonger's defense, a young Vietnamese nurse wearing a nametag that read HIEU entered through two swinging doors behind the sandbagged desk at the front of the room. "Private First Class Graham!" she called.

"You just keep an eye on that Brody character," he whispered into Orson's ear before getting up. When Nurse Hieu saw the blood-soaked trousers, she rushed over to help. "It's okay, ma'am." He smiled, mild but manageable pain creasing his features. "It's just a flesh wound."

"Heroes are prohibited here." She clamped a small but surprisingly strong hand onto his shoulders, forcing Graham back down onto the crate. Over her shoulder, she called for a corpsman to bring a wheelchair.

After they left, Orson handed the stateside tabloid to a squadmate seated beside him, and muttered, "We better start keeping a closer eye on ol' Graham-Cracker." The fellow grunt responded with a nod that said "Articles like this only make our reputation meaner. Impresses the broads, for when you get back to The World."

Orson bent low to check the dressing on his own minor calf wound, then glanced back at Brody again. He sat up instantly for a better look.

An American nurse had entered the brightly lit bunker from the stairwell, and she was holding a small, dark-complected child in her arms as she spoke to Treat

Brody. Blond, slim, classy, she could be *the* Nurse Lisa Maddox all the chopper pilots lusted after. They seemed to be having a one-sided conversation; Maddox was doing all the talking.

Orson moved closer to the trio, hoping to eavesdrop.

"She's doing fine, Corporal Brody." Maddox gently rocked the little girl in her arms. The child's eyes were open, but she stared out across the room, at the far wall, ignoring the voices as she rested her head against Lisa's breast.

A thick body-bandage covered the girl's chest and stomach. "Would you like to hold her, Treat?" Maddox dropped to one knee beside the veteran doorgunner—the man who had chased down this child's mother, shot her repeatedly, then nearly died himself when the woman detonated a stick grenade as her last act of defiance. "I seem to recall you telling me some time back that you wanted to help this child, Treat, that you were considering adopting her. I'm not holding you to any remarks you might have made while emotionally distraught, of course. But just hold this little child, Treat. She will warm your heart. I think holding her for a moment or two will help you heal inside."

Brody, who'd been staring straight ahead, turned to face Maddox. He was confused. Bewildered, and searching for answers. All he wanted now was to be left alone.

"Here." Maddox nudged his shoulder, using the little girl's bare feet. Brody rocked slightly from side to side, but did not respond. "Take her," she whispered. "As a favor to me."

The bunker's ceiling rumbled slightly as several low-flying jets passed overhead. In the muggy distance, explosions rumbled. They were coming from the direction of the riverfront, and the lieutenant wondered if Brody was thinking about his buddies fighting down at the Mekong, or the dead woman whose child she now held to her heart.

"I'm sorry, Nurse Maddox," he said softly.

Forgetting the tiny bits of shrapnel imbedded in his lower back, Brody walked away without another word, and started up the stairs, into the bright shafts of sunlight lancing down from outside.

CHAPTER 30

Trinh Thi Kim was breathing so hard, she feared some of the Americans might hear her. Spine arched uncomfortably as she leaned back against a wide tree trunk, she watched her breasts swell and dip as her lungs heaved. The rain forest's humidity was oppressive, and she could not seem to get enough air. Mosquitoes buzzed in front of her face; she tried to ignore them. AK-47 held at port arms across her chest, she waited, eyes wide as they darted back and forth.

Several U.S. cavalrymen rushed past, the closest only a score of feet away. But none noticed her frozen in the jungle shadows.

This was the last time, she told herself as gunship rotors beat at the dry, sticky air blanketing the intertwined branches overhead. Never again would she take such a chance, jeopardizing the mission.

Kim thought she had come to know the area well enough. She was only scouting the terrain at pre-dawn, searching for a new and safer hideout for their female prisoner. When the five white faces, blackened by charcoal and greasepaint, popped out of the reeds in front of her, she nearly died from shock. An American recon patrol was also checking the riverbanks along the waterways.

Instinctively, her rifle had come up. It was switched to FULL AUTO but jammed after two rounds burped forth with dull, dreamlike reports. One of the soldiers fell with a leg wound, and Kim dropped backward over several logs—bruising her back—and was able to elude the Lurps by zigzagging through the elephant grass, heading back in the same direction from which she had originally come.

A panther, angry with all the commotion, lunged at her from the edge of the trail, miraculously missed, and was trampled by two of the Americans, who began pummeling the animal with their fists until several shots finally rang out and the huge brown cat lay dead.

By then, Kim had diverted from her intended path, hoping to circle around all the activity and drop down underground before the GIs could catch up with her.

That was when she stumbled into the pitch-black, heavily camouflaged encampment of combined VC and North Vietnamese troops hidden beneath dense canopy along a bend in the river.

The alert sentries did not ask for any passwords, they simply commenced shooting. And right then half the Americans were rushing up behind her.

Kim dropped to the earth and rolled through the elephant grass nonstop for nearly a minute as the communists engaged the Americans. A crescendo of exploding rifle rounds rose on both sides. Then, except for sporadic shooting here and there, nothing. Only an odd, haunting quiet.

The dull *whump!* of mortars began then, as she knew it would. Kim rose to her feet and ran fast, sensing she was headed in the right direction until she reached the low hills overlooking the river.

It was flowing the wrong way!

Which actually meant, of course, that Kim had her bearings confused. They were actually reversed, which was unusual for her. The fatigue was beginning to show, Kim decided. She faced two options now: find a hiding place in the immediate area until things cooled down, or try to make her way surreptitiously back through both forces to her unit. It would be unwise to try and join forces with the local insurgents or NVA Army at this time. They would be too charged up to deal with new faces, especially a woman's. And lying dog where she now hid would only end with her imminent death. The Americans would surely sweep the entire area several times at daybreak, and recently they had been using bloodhounds to track down tunnel Cong. She wouldn't stand a chance, and she knew it.

So Trinh Thi Kim moved through the trees, silent and elusive, like a rain forest ghost. The battle raged on all around her for several tense minutes, and helicopter gunships descending to the GIs' aid from across the river didn't help matters much. But she would make it. Kim could feel it in her gut as more soldiers rushed past, oblivious to her presence in the shadows.

A snake began curling around her bare ankle. But just as abruptly its scaly coils reversed direction, and the reptile slithered off across the rotting jungle carpet.

The snake had been a two-step bamboo krait viper, the most deadly serpent in Vietnam. The creature had been a sign. Buddha did not want her to die this day. She had yet to reach her destiny.

She hurried off through the dense tree trunks, no longer afraid.

Lt. Vance had a suspicious smile on his lips as he walked away from Company Clerk Farney's jeep. After airmobile reinforcements helped clean up the rat's nest of communists upstream from battalion CP, and the enemy body count had been radioed in to the MACV Annex at Disneyland East in Saigon, the specialist had arrived with his biweekly duffelbag full of mail.

Jacob Vance was smiling because, for once, he had received something at mail call other than junk mail from the American Legion and VFW. His smile was not a suspicious one because he sensed anything dangerous in the packet—like the pizza pan of human feces he'd received from an anti-war group at the University of

Berkeley the week before, sprinkled with pepper, wrapped in plastic, and carefully sealed, of course, to fool the watchdogs at APO.

No, his suspicions were aroused because of the typewritten return address on the five-by-seven padded envelope:

MAJOR GENERAL VICTOR S. VANCE III
N.S.C.
THE PENTAGON
WASHINGTON D.C.

Lt. Vance chuckled uneasily. Thank God he wasn't born No. 4, he comforted himself. Victor S. Vance The Fourth was an older brother, serving in Turkey—a light Colonel now, if memory served him right. The two brothers were not close. They wrote now and then, out of professional and family courtesy, but the letters seemed to come more and more infrequently.

The General never wrote.

Unless, of course, he wanted something. Vance began ripping open the packet, cursing under his breath as he pricked himself with a staple.

By the time he had the envelope open, the lieutenant had found a peaceful, secluded tree under which he could read in the shade. He wiped the latest wave of unceasing sweat from his forehead.

A small training manual, less than fifty pages, was the first item to drop from the packet. It had the General's name as author on it. Victor S. Vance III's name was larger than the manual's title, in fact:

JUNGLE ESCAPE & EVASION TACTICS FOR
USE BY PERSONNEL ASSIGNED TO R.V.N.

Vance laughed openly. What did his father know about surviving in R.V.N., the Republic of Viet Nam? Vance shook his head, amused. The General had spent the last ten years at the Pentagon.

Vance glanced at the return address again. Now he was assigned to something called the NSC. Some new-

292

fangled hush-hush spooky-tunes outfit, no doubt, he decided.

"Oh, well," he said, slipping the cigarette-pack-sized manual into a thigh pocket, "it's the thought that counts."

Vance was somewhat disappointed to find there were no photos enclosed—even if just another 8×10 black-and-white glossy of the General in his Class-A's with an autograph on it, like the one he'd received at his graduation from West Point.

He unfolded the PX stationary, laughed again, saying out loud, "A big-shot general, but still using olive drab stationary with little soldiers striking courageous poses in the corner, eh, pop?" But then the smile faded. The letter was only two paragraphs long. After over a year without hearing from him, and now all he rated was two lousy paragraphs.

Dear Jacob,

I hope this finds you in good health, son. I would apologize for not writing sooner—I'm awfully proud of your role there in South Vietnam—but you know ole Vic: not much good at writing letters. How 'bout if I send you an autographed copy of my military memoirs when it comes out? (That was a lame attempt at humor, Jake.)

Actually, the reason I'm writing is that, as usual, I need another favor from you, son. Do you remember General Nelson, from the good old days before you left for West Point? I believe he was a Full Bird Colonel back then. Well, anyway, he has a son only a few years younger than you. I believe he took the enlisted man's route. Should be a PFC, according to the records check I had Sally conduct, with a first name of Neil. He's assigned to the First Air Cav there, with your battalion and company—Echo of the 7th. Do an old man a favor, would you, Jake? Keep an eye out for the kid. He's Mike Nelson's one and only son, and you know how that goes. He asked me to check with you, and it's the first time I ever recall Mike asking for anything.

Don't bring nothin' back an old soldier's mug o' army-issue brew can't cure.

V.S. Vance III

Shaking his head with disbelief, Vance wadded up the letter and threw it back over a shoulder. "V.S. Vance the third?" he asked himself aloud. "Whoever heard of a father signing a letter to his son 'V.S. Vance the third'?" Just once, he would like to have received one signed simply "Dad."

"Aw, fuck it." He stood, walked over and retrieved the crumpled paper. Wouldn't do to have Charlie wander through here and find it, he rationalized, slipping the letter into the thigh pocket with the training manual. If they knew the officer son of a bigwig back-in-The-World general was leading a platoon through the Cho Gao sticks, they might make a concentrated effort at capturing him for the certain media attention that would follow. As a hostage, he might make quite a bargaining chip as far as the rest of the Brass was concerned. But Jacob Vance was confident his father would never cooperate with communist terrorists.

"What the hell," he muttered, jogging in place for a moment to get his blood flowing again. Then he started back toward the straight line of parked helicopter gunships. Where he knew he'd find Nelson, brooding by himself inside one of the ships.

He'd been meaning to talk to the private anyway. Nelson had been acting depressed lately, and his attitude was rubbing off on the rest of the crew. Even Snakeman Fletcher was grumbling about all the riverine escort duty as of late, and Fletch rarely complained about anything, so long as the Brass left him to his hatch-60 with an endless belt of machine-gun ammo.

At first he feared perhaps the young soldier was

reacting to the earlier razzings Vance had given him about the pubic-hair collection. But then he heard the flightline talk about which men were having pussy problems, and he realized Nelson's low morale was not due entirely to the lieutenant's earlier overzealous attempts at keeping his people shipshape.

Nelson was not reclining anywhere inside *Pegasus*'s cabin, which was where Vance could usually find him—cleaning his hatch MG, or M-16, or polishing his boots, repairing his gear. There was some activity a few ships down, though. Several of the men were gathered around a blond-haired soldier, so the lieutenant headed that direction, his mood brightening. He would show the letter to Nelson; let him know that his father cared about him. That both their fathers cared.

Vance began whistling a pleasant Vietnamese tune that was forever played on the ARVN-AM band. He didn't know the title, or what 99 percent of the words meant, but he truly enjoyed the music, and often found it returning to him when he was happy.

He didn't want to ask one of the housegirls what the words meant—being a language specialist, he should already know. But this was an odd dialect, and he feared they might reveal it was a sad song about war and lost love. The Saigonese dwelled on that quite a bit, it seemed. He found he could not blame them.

The first enlisted man to spot him approaching whispered something harshly to the others, and there seemed to be a slight shuffling of items between the troops gathered around the Huey hatch.

"How's it hangin', fellas?" He tried to remain bright and cheerful while still shouldering his way into the middle of the group.

PFC Nelson was at the center. He tried to slip something into his rucksack without Vance seeing it. The lieutenant made no immediate attempt to confiscate the item. He glanced around, recognizing several faces. "Aren't you men the group Captain Montoya gave a night's pass to?" Several laughs and head nods answered his question. "Just now draggin' your limp dicks in, eh?"

Snakeman Fletcher was closest to Vance. "You're thinkin' we're smokin' some dope back here, aren't you, sir? Well, it ain't that way, it ain't that way at all."

Em-Ho Lee stepped forward, an ear-to-ear grin intact below the narrowed, Japanese-American eyes. "Nelson here was kind enough to do us all a favor, Lieutenant. That's all." He rubbed at his crotch without realizing it.

Vance folded his arms across his chest. "Why don't you let me see what's in the ruck, Private Nelson."

Shrugging, Nelson's shoulders drooped slightly in self-pity. "If you insist, sir."

"I insist."

Nelson pulled out a brand-new egg carton filled with recently acquired clear plastic vials. "I didn't steal 'em from the aid station, sir, if that's what you're thinking."

Vance recognized the vials' contents immediately: strands of pubic hair, also recently acquired, it appeared. He threw up his hands in resignation and turned to leave, saying, "I don't wanna know, Nelson. I don't fucking wanna know."

"Nurse Maddox gave 'em to me, sir," Nelson said in his own self-defense.

" 'Cause he's so handsome." Fletcher's remark came across soaked in sarcasm.

"He's just doin' us all a favor, Lieutenant!" Em-Ho Lee said. "The Snake suggested we start keeping souvenirs of our expeditions to the ville—like Nasty Nel used to do back stateside."

"Nelson agreed to be the curator of our pubic-hair museum, sir!" Snakeman called out. Vance, still waving his hands, walked away.

Snakeman snickered. "His face was o.d. green."

Doc Delgado laughed openly. "I think the guy's gonna be sick."

CHAPTER 31

"Orson's my name."

"Yeah, yeah, I know." Farney handed Private Orson another bundle of letters instead of shaking his hand. "Don't you think I recognize you by now? Christ."

"You called?" Snakeman Fletcher stepped forward, hand raised to further announce his presence.

Farney continued speaking without acknowledging the doorgunner. "You receive more mail than the entire Echo Company combined!"

Orson tossed the bundle of letters back over a shoulder without even glancing at the return addresses this time.

"Jesus H!" Fletcher was busy going through the pile of rolled up, hometown newspapers. "Fifth in the series!"

"Sounds like he found the latest issue of the Thornton *Theseus*," Corky Cordova muttered to Doc Delgado.

"Lemme see that!" Nelson snatched the paper away. The photo on the front page was a blow-up of something a First Cav trooper had drawn onto his helmet's camou-cover. The stencil was a frontal-view likeness of a woman lying on her back with her legs spread, knees bent so that the entire image seemed an optical illusion, appearing more like jumpwings or pilot's wings than anything obscene. The GI had scrawled "*BUSH*PILOT'S WINGS" beneath the odd design, and the newspaper's editor had captioned the photo: "Air Cavalrymen earn this unauthorized 'merit badge' to wear on their jungle fatigues only after they have participated in a minimum of one dozen gang rapes of defenseless Vietnamese women."

"What a motherfuckin' ever-lovin' crock o' unadulterated bullshit!" Nelson tore the paper to shreds.

"Hey! I was readin' that, doofus!" Fletcher protested.

"If I ever find out who the low-life scumbag is who's writin' this bullshit series for this commsymp gossip rag, I'm gonna—"

"Okay, okay!" The Snakeman wrapped an arm around Nelson's shoulder. "We get your drift, hero."

Cordova elbowed Delgado quietly. "Nasty Nel sounds like he's been hittin' the *ba-muoi-ba*."

"Yep," the medic agreed with Corky's diagnosis.

"The guy doesn't seem so off-base." Graham emerged from the semicircle of GIs after Farney completed the mail call. He was referring to the series author. "I mean, if you really sit down and look at the whole thing—"

"Who the hell is this guy?" Nelson erupted, completely forgetting about the night he escorted Graham and Orson along the perimeter, the same night he had first met Anna. "Where you comin' from, boy?"

"He sounds like a goddamned communist sympathizer to me, Nasty Nel," an anonymous hero in the back of the semicircle called out. Several other men razzed Nelson on. With all the dead bodies they'd seen lately, it had still been quite some time since anyone watched a good-old honest, red-blooded, back-on-the-farm fistfight.

"I'll bet you *are* a goddamned communist, pro-Soviet, un-American asshole, aren't you, Graham-

Cracker?" Nelson locked eyes with him. "And I'll bet you're not only a goddamned communist, pro-Soviet, un-American, egg-suckin' dog, I'll bet you're the son of a bitch who's been writin' these articles!"

"This string of articles seems like a bunch of lies, but what about double-vets snapping whores' necks when they shot their wad? It's the same fucking thing."

"They're VC whores!" another faceless voice called out. "That's different!"

"Rape is rape," Graham maintained.

"Worthless bleeding-heart liberal," someone muttered as the group began breaking up.

"And what about your crazy Hog Heaven club? Or the Dirty Thirty fraternity I keep hearing about? Isn't it all insane? I mean, is any of it that much different from what's in the stories?"

"I *knew* you were the one!" Nelson's fist flew out, knocking Graham off his feet. "I knew you're the one's been writin' the shit. You're a traitor, Graham-Cracker! A motherfucking traitor to the First Air Cav!" Nelson kicked dirt in his face.

Graham wiped the blood from his nose. "I did not write anything," he maintained, rising to his feet.

Nelson charged, head lowered, bull-like. He slammed into Graham's chest, and they both rolled to the ground, kicking and punching at each other.

The men began cheering. But less than a minute after the fight started, jeeps skidded up from opposite directions. Vance and Zack were in one, Farney in the other.

"Break it up! Break it up!" Zack waded in and pulled the two combatants apart. As if shaken from a drunken binge, several of the higher-ranking enlisted men suddenly rushed forward to help restrain both soldiers. "You clowns forget who you're supposed to be fighting here in The Veeyet-Nam! His name's Charlie! Not Graham!" He stared at Nelson, then turned to face Graham. "Not Nelson!"

"Everyone back to your ships!" Vance announced without dismounting from his jeep. He looked very bored with the whole incident.

"Now, has either of you two ladies got a problem with that?" Zack was still yelling at the two wrestlers.

"Lieutenant, if I may!" Farney stood up behind his jeep's windshield, looking like he wanted to make an announcement before all the men dispersed.

Vance shrugged. "Be my guest." He pulled the escape and evasion manual from his thigh pocket and began thumbing through it.

"Listen up!" Farney yelled, cupping his hands over his mouth like a bullhorn. Some of the men stopped to listen. Most kept walking. "Cho Gao's on red alert! No one's to attempt to hitch a slick back there for any reasons except official duty, and you better be in the company of a crew chief, is that clear?" As if to accent his point, a series of dull explosions rumbled in the direction of the village.

"Everyone back to their birds!" Zack directed. "I got a gut feelin' Arvin's gonna be callin' for gunship support before the night's over!"

After the men began clearing out, Farney called down to Nelson. He was not smiling. "Hey, loverboy! Just thought you should know: the QCs have rounded up all the housegirls back at the main camp—the women from the villa included!"

"Anna too?" Nelson massaged a swollen eye that was rapidly turning black and blue.

"Suppose so, slick. I wasn't matchin' faces with tealoks. Vietnamese MPs rounded up all the women at the villa to put 'em in a detention camp somewhere. Has somethin' to do with that dead NCO from Headquarters they found in a shallow grave coupla weeks back."

"Yeah, thanks!" Nelson turned to Vance. "I just gotta check on Anna, Lieutenant!" he pleaded. "Just this once. Can you cut me some slack, sir?"

"Out of the question, Private." Vance motioned for Zack to get back in the jeep. "Cho Gao's on red alert, didn't you hear? You're a soldier, not a fucking big brother. You've got duties right here. That woman is not even your wife, and in the green machine, girly-friends don't count."

CHAPTER 32

Nelson stared down over the barrel of his hatch-60, watching the treetops rush past below in a green blur. Now and then the roof of a thatched hut came into view, only to vanish beneath breaks in the multi-hued canopy. Smoke trails on the jungle's edge rose over the marsh-like terrain from several evening cooking fires, turning the twilight from its natural purple to a ghostly gray. The rooftops appeared below more frequently now, and then the jagged strips of jungle and vast rice paddy terraces gave way to long lines of ramshackle housing. Cho Gao came into view, and Nelson felt a strange inner bond tugging at him when he saw the parked formations of Huey gunships.

Cho Gao had become all-important. Apologizing to Anna was Nelson's top priority now. He would take her in his arms, and before he released her, she would know. Anna would know Nelson was her man, the father of their child.

One week had passed since the village militia and First Cav compound went on red alert. Fierce fighting had erupted inside Cho Gao that first evening, after a VC death squad was intercepted attempting to kidnap a provincial chief visiting his daughter. Outnumbered by the ARVC forces four to one, Charlie had pulled back, and the next six nights rockets and mortars were fired into town from the surrounding jungle instead.

Whether coincidence or not, NVA forces hit Operation Coronado's riverside CP the same night, and only now had the pitched battle, with all its splintered and shifting skirmishes, ended. High casualties on both sides were in ghastly evidence.

Nelson was working a gunny slot with Snakeman, escorting bodies of the American KIA's back to Cho Gao for further processing north and, finally, back to The World.

As soon as *Pegasus* touched down, Fletcher and Gabriel both told him to go ahead and split; they didn't want his long, sad-dog face ruining their long-awaited binge at the club. Nelson ran to the CP, where he found Farney sitting outside in his jeep, boots resting on the steering wheel as he wrote on a clipboard.

"Can you give me a lift down into the ville?" he asked the company clerk. "I need a ride real bad, pal!"

Farney did not look up from his clipboard, but continued scribbling at a *Stars & Stripes* crossword puzzle. "Surely you jest, troop."

Nelson flew forward and grabbed the man by his shirtfront. "I need a ride real bad, *pal!*"

Farney's eyes grew large. "Nelson! Didn't recognize you, bud! Sorry."

"Then you'll take me down into—"

"No can do, GI." He raised his hands helplessly. The clipboard clattered across the jeep's sandbagged floorboards. "Whole town's still on red alert." He pointed in the direction of Cho Gao, a couple miles off. The horizon was aglow with flickering crimson. "Those ain't cooking fires, friend. Those is houses burnin' to the ground."

Nelson jumped into the front passenger seat. "Maybe we can get an MP escort."

"The Mike Papas were the ones who ordered us to stay inside the compound unless we were airmobile."

"But—"

"But you wanna pussyfoot on down to that civilian detention center on the north side o' town, right? Ol' Nelson's just addicted to ass—am I on target?"

"I've gotta see her, Farney!"

"Tomorrow, kid." The clerk reached for his clipboard and resumed writing.

"Tomorrow?"

"Be here at zero seven hundred. That's after the sun comes up, for you lifer-types. In the morning, I can risk a balls-to-the-wind run into town. But if you're gonna get all romantic and stinky-fingered, I can't guarantee waiting around for ya."

"That's fine! Zero seven hundred?"

"Right. Meantime, go catch some Z's, kid. You look like shit."

"Oh yeah, right." Nelson knew there would be no way he could sleep tonight, but neither could he attempt to get past the gate guards. Even if he succeeded, he might never be able to locate the detention center on foot. Only Farney seemed to know where it was located. And the first *canh-sat* he approached for directions would probably throw him in the can for curfew violation, if he wasn't shot outright.

Push-ups.

Nelson would go back to his old hooch and do 500 push-ups. That should get the adrenaline out of his system. Perhaps then he could fall asleep.

"And Nelson?" Farney's words intruded into his thoughts.

"Yeah?"

"Don't sweat it so much, man. No disrespect intended, but a hole is a hole. There's a million more of 'em out there, just waitin' to latch onto ya. Besides, she's behind bars, kid, remember? She ain't goin' nowhere. She'll still be there in the morning."

"I swear to ya, Nelson: this was where it was at."

Farney rested his elbows on the jeep's steering wheel, slack-jawed.

"You better not be fucking with me, asshole."

"I'm serious as a heart attack, kid! This is where—"

"I'll fucking kill you if you're fuckin' with me, Farney."

Eyes growing large in an attempt to convey his sincerity, the clerk rested a hand on Nelson's wrist. "I'm tellin' you, bud, this is where it used to be. I don't dick around 'bout shit like this. What I said last night, that was a casual crock o' crap, man. I was just tryin' to help you out, just tryin' to give you another outlook toward the situation."

"I really love her, do you hear what I'm saying? I love that woman with every ounce of feeling inside me. I can't even put it into words. I . . . ."

The words were leaving Nelson's lips like bullets from a hatch-60 on rapidfire. He couldn't control what he was saying.

"I'm sorry, man. I'm really fucking sorry." Farney's tone was unusually sad.

"She was going to have my child."

"Shit, that's really a bummer, man." Farney struck the steering wheel with his fist. Twice. The entire vehicle shuddered from the impacts. "Life sucks, man; it really motherfucking sucks, you know? You didn't deserve this."

The warm, muggy breeze shifted, and smoke drifting out from the bottom of the crater consumed them for a moment, then rose to the east, into the rising sun. Nelson breathed in the smoke, wondering if he was breathing in Anna. Or what was left of her and his unborn baby.

The half-block parcel of land on which the detention center once stood was now a smoldering crater, filled with rubble and scattered pools of blood. Bodies, all burned beyond recognition, littered the crater's edge.

"Your business here, please?"

A Vietnamese national policeman was suddenly

standing on Nelson's side of the jeep, submachine gun hanging from a shoulder sling against his hip at a businesslike angle. Nelson remained stone-faced and silent, staring out at the different wisps of silver smoke rising like bewildered ghosts, their souls scattered on the wind before they could reach the sky.

"This used to be the detention center, right?" Farney asked. "The civilian detention center?" Farney just wanted to make 100 percent sure they were at the right place.

"Yes." The *canh-sat* nodded somberly. "Bookoo prisoner *fini*." His gunhand came up, waving over his head as he rambled off something in Vietnamese. Nelson was sure it was some religious mumbo-jumbo about death by fire and how Buddha turned his uncaring back in disgust on those who died that way.

"Was it a rocket?" Farney asked.

"Yes, yes." The *canh-sat* nodded eagerly. "VC rocket! VC rocket kill bookoo VC!" He started laughing. "Everyone die!"

Farney kicked the engine over and shifted the jeep into reverse, wanting to leave before Nelson disarmed the policeman and killed him with his own weapon. But the PFC seemed oddly silent and unmoving. The veins along his temple were twitching, but he seemed oblivious to everything the officer had said.

"Let's get out of here," he finally told the company clerk. But by then the jeep's wheels were already rolling. Back toward camp. Back to battle.

Nelson unbuttoned the flap over his breastpocket and reached inside as Farney swerved in and out of the rough-'n-puff security checkpoints without slowing. The young doorgunner pulled a small white clamshell out, stared at it for a few seconds, then kissed it lightly.

Farney glanced over, wondering what Nelson was holding and thinking it looked like the kind of good-luck kiss gamblers gave the ivory before throwing dice.

Eyes tightly shut now, and tears streaming down his face, Nelson tossed the sealed clamshell out over the windshield, ahead of their jeep.

Farney was not sure if it was the speed of their vehicle or the wind direction, or the diminishing momentum of the clamshell, but a heartbeat after Nelson threw the memento of lost love out of his life, the breeze seemed to latch onto it and fling it back at him.

The clamshell bounced off Nelson's forehead. Farney listened to it roll about on the jeep's floorboards before coming to rest between his passenger's blood-stained jungle boots.

Chrissy LaVey chose her words carefully. "I came here to Vietnam only because there is nothing left for me back in Australia."

"No family?" Kim sounded skeptical. "No man?" Her tone grew cruel.

LaVey hesitated, then decided she had nothing to lose by telling the truth. Today was the day. She could sense it. This woman squatting before her was just toying with her. Today they would kill her. The walls of the underground hiding place creaked and groaned as bombs rumbled on the surface less than a mile away. Few sampans could be found on the river anymore. The word was out: PBR patrols were stopping and searching anything that floated. The Americans had stopped their recon patrols and were calling in artillery to destroy the last enemy strongholds.

"No man, recently," LaVey admitted.

Kim laughed. "A pretty lady like you?" She lifted her chin in obvious disgust. "Ha! I do not believe it."

"The only men in my life were my brothers," LaVey said, amending her life history and family background slightly to suit the moment. "They both died here, in this land. In your country: Vietnam."

"Hhmph." Kim did not seem overly impressed, but she did not laugh, either.

"They fought and died for the wrong side. The

Aussies fight on the wrong side!" Nguyet hissed from a dark corner of the bunker where she sat cleaning her AK.

"Be silent," Kim muttered. She turned to face LaVey again. "We are leaving tonight," she announced.

"It is dangerous up there." LaVey spoke as if she was preparing to say farewell to a sister who had remained distant all these years.

"Yes," Kim admitted. "I do not expect to see tomorrow's sunrise." She lowered her voice with a smile, but still spoke loud enough for Nguyet to hear. The only man left was curled up against one wall, sleeping; it was all he seemed to do anymore since his brother's death a few nights before. "But the GIs' jets will soon bring in napalm. I have seen it happen before: their final bye-bye to Charlie, as they call us. Down here, we would be incinerated."

Chrissy shuddered despite the heat.

"I am sorry your brothers died here," Kim said. "They died for nothing. They died in vain."

LaVey paused before responding. She thought back to all the letters she had exchanged with her brother. "He wrote many times telling me he truly believed in what Australia and the United States and all the other allies were doing here," she said finally. "That they were sincerely trying to protect South Vietnam from communist aggression. He loved it here. He was going to marry a Vietnamese woman. He extended an extra six months for an assignment in the rear, away from all the killing, so he could be closer to her."

"A Vietnamese woman?" Kim searched LaVey's face for some sign of jealously, but she found only love and compassion.

"A rocket fell on their apartment house two weeks after the extension went into effect." A solitary tear inched its way down Chrissy's cheek. "My brother died instantly, they tell me. His girlfriend—they hadn't married yet—she lost both legs and an arm. Now she lives in a home with other civilian amputees. I visited her once. Only once. It was a terrible place. I still send her money now and then, when I can spare it."

"You will not be going with us tonight." Kim rose to her feet and began changing from a tattered smock into her fighting outfit: black calico trousers and tiger-striped shirt.

LaVey watched her slowly fold the smock up into a tiny ball and slip it into her backpack beside a rolled-up mosquito net. "I know," she said. "Today you shoot me."

Kim laughed, but she sounded sad and defeated. "No," she told LaVey. "I cannot spare the bullet, my Aussie friend."

Visions of the two women strangling her with a strand of concertina wire or running a bayonet through her heart flashed through LaVey's head.

"I am going to release you." Kim slipped the ARVN-pattern blouse down over her head, then pulled a long, gleaming commando knife from the sheath strapped to her calf. She dropped into a squat beside LaVey again and began cutting her bonds.

"You are going to release me?" LaVey sounded neither surprised or elated, just tired.

"Under one condition. You shall wait down here for one hour after we leave. Then you will walk toward the American camp. I cannot guarantee a tiger will not eat you or an elephant will not smash you flat or a Phantom jet will not mistake you for a good nationalist and drop a napalm bomb on your head. But I will point you in the right direction, and then you are on your own."

"I will be able to take care of myself."

Kim nodded at the respectful tone. "I'm sure you will. When you reach the American camp, I want you to tell them that you were treated humanely by the Viet Cong."

LaVey did not flash back to the beating or harassment. She simply nodded, the opportunity for freedom suddenly releasing adrenaline and new hope into her system.

"I want you to tell them about me. About how I protected you from the jungle for so many days; about how I found compassion in my heart, and finally released you."

"But I do not even know your entire name."

"The soldiers fighting here in the Delta are the same soldiers we harassed up north, in the Ia Drang; in Binh Dinh Province, also. Go to them. Find a soldier named Patterson. Tell him about me. About how I did not kill you when I could have."

"He knows you? This Patterson will remember you?"

"How could he forget the Vietnamese woman who nailed a VC flag to his back?" Kim laughed, and though her eyes seemed to sparkle for a moment with the memory, it was still a sad, lonely laugh.

Five hours later, after the sun had set and twilight engulfed her homeland of sorrows and pain, Trinh Thi Kim woke the man lying against the wall. She spoke to him in rapid Vietnamese for a few seconds, but he only sat there dazed, uncomprehending. Finally, after Nguyet appeared ready too, he rose and donned his sapper's coveralls.

The man seemed to have lost all interest in LaVey. He slid the straps of his ruck over sunken shoulders, grabbed his rifle and ammo belt, and started climbing the ladder that led up to the surface.

My brother was wrong, Chrissy thought, as she watched the man move ever so slowly. These people do care about life. They do have strong family relationships.

"I wish you a long and happy life." Kim nodded as she started up the ladder behind him. "Your brothers died so you could live."

Before LaVey could say anything, Kim was gone.

Nguyet started up the ladder. Her lips were curled back in a silent snarl as she locked eyes with Chrissy, but she said nothing. When she reached the top, a muffled exchange of words reached LaVey's ears below—something about the lantern. Kim had told her to leave it on, in case they had to return to the underground sanctuary. But Nguyet had turned it off anyway, in open defiance of Kim's orders, and Kim had noticed. The two argued for a moment, but then Nguyet started back down the ladder.

And LaVey realized the woman had extinguished the lantern for just that purpose, knowing she would be ordered back down into the tank: it would give her a reason to be alone with Chrissy, if for only a few minutes.

The instant her sandals touched the floor of the tank, Nguyet rushed over to LaVey, striking her in the chin with a riflebutt.

LaVey was not an experienced fighter. She was not quick enough to fend off the blow. A little cry escaped her, but it was not loud enough to travel up the ladder ahead of the angry Nguyet.

Pain lanced down the entire length of her body, then seemed to ricochet back up into her brain. She felt suddenly helpless—as if she were floating in a void.

CHAPTER 33

Kim stared at the ancient, bleached-white skeletons hanging over branches and dangling from vines, and all the childhood fears rushed through her body.

She had heard about this place. The Viet Cong avoided it. Even the more professional NVA Regular forces gave Soc Sai a wide berth.

Soc Sai was actually the name of a small hamlet one kilometer to the south, but this vast network of treehouselike defensive positions built into the middle layer of the jungle's triple canopy ceiling went by the same title. Many Vietnamese moved from the village to Mytho or Cho Gao so as not to be associated with the eerie battleground.

Operation Coronado had reached Soc Sai an hour after Kim and her two comrades left their underground lair. Artillery pounded outlying positions in a five-hundred-meter circle around the area. PBR gunboats cruised the larger streams and canals running mazelike beneath Soc Sai. Their undermanned crews were supplemented by teams of cavalrymen, reassigned off the gunships that had been destroyed on the ground during last week's sapper attacks on Cho Gao.

The Americans did not think they would find much resistance at Soc Sai. They were well aware how much the Vietnamese, both VC and anti-communists, avoided the area like the plague. So they decided to use the area as one of their stepping-stone base camps as the Division moved west through the Mekong Delta. It would probably be the safest place around, a quiet eye of the storm where the men could relax between musters—so long as they were not afraid of ghosts.

Kim scurried about from tree to tree, fifty feet off the ground, checking all the old bamboo bridges and rope ladders that ran like a complex latticework of protective nets beneath the fortified canopy positions. She was checking the branch-to-branch routes in all four directions, deciding which would make the best avenue of escape if and when the Americans detected their presence.

Kim's sixth sense made her freeze at the instant she was about to jump down from one branch's planks to another. She had just passed over a small group of Americans, eating their C-rations and talking boisterously as if they feared no evil beneath the dense canopy of tangled vines and branches, for they were the meanest, baddest dudes in Soc Sai. That was some fifty or sixty yards back. Now, she looked down, and saw a soldier with blond hair sitting on a tree trunk, all by himself.

Kim tilted her head to one side slightly. She had never seen a man contemplating his rifle muzzle in quite the same way before.

PFC Nelson was not AWOL yet.

He wandered away from Brody's squad when they began breaking out the C-rations, and now he was totally alone. Alone with his thoughts and guilt and pain. He was not AWOL yet, but he was not going back, either.

313

How had Anna come to mean so much to him? He had only known her for a few weeks, a couple of months. Perhaps it was the child. Talk of unborn babies and sons-to-be could alter an otherwise sane man's judgment.

He did not feel he could go on. The guilt pressed down on him every moment he was awake, like a weight heavy as all the world's woes. At night, it was worse. In his nightmares, he watched the burning flesh peel away from Anna's face.

He tried talking to Zack, looking for some words of wisdom that would help him get his head back together. But the NCO seemed preoccupied about something too, and wasn't his usual talkative self. He was suffering his own brand of guilt, over the fistfight in Cho Gao and the dead black man who had been washed from his shallow grave by rain and storm.

It had been the same way with Brody. He was all caught up with this Am-I-Brock-or-am-I-Le-Loi-today shit, and Nelson was fast losing respect for the veteran doorgunner. Yet who was he to make decisions about anybody or anything?

Explosions rumbled in the distance, and he thought about Graham, and the broken nose he had given the man. He wished that he could postpone this; that he could walk back over to the group of cavalrymen and say he was sorry; that they were all in this mess together, and they had to lock arms and cooperate if they were to survive their Tour 365.

But PFC Nelson would not be completing his twelve-month guaranteed tour of duty in-country. In The Nam. RVN.

He switched his rifle's fire selector to AUTO. "Full automatic," he muttered, shaking his head for the last time. "Better to go out in a rock-and-roll blaze than like a flare on the breeze." He placed the M-16's cold, steel muzzle into his mouth and began thinking of Anna, trying to picture her face . . . how she would appear in heaven, but the image would not come.

314

Nelson reached down to push in the trigger. A sharp pain suddenly slammed across the back of his neck.

"Kim, hurry!" Nguyet called out in Vietnamese. "We must go! Before it is too late!"

The jungle's triple canopy was in flames. Col. Buchanan had ordered his men to resume search-and-destroy tactics after Nelson's mutilated body was found. When Lt. Vance radioed to Buchanan's C&C Loach that the VC had stuffed Nelson's severed penis into his mouth and hung the decapitated head from a branch directly over the main trail through Soc Sai, The Bull ordered a napalm strike.

He wanted Nelson's recovered body airlifted out. And then he wanted Soc Sai burned to the ground.

PFC Nelson's ears dangling from the dogtags chain around her neck, Kim fired an entire magazine of shells into the CIA canister, deciding to destroy it, if nothing else, once and for all.

Surprisingly, it popped open. Puffs of smoke from the tracers rose from the rolled-up papers inside.

Kim glanced up, but Nguyet and her brother were already gone. She pulled the blackened and bullet-riddled papers from the drop tube, and stared in disbelief at them for several moments. Then, with a disgusted sneer, she tossed the drop tube aside.

Kim listened to it clatter down through the branches. She glanced back over a shoulder one last time at the flames consuming the eerie architectural wonder that had been Soc Sai, then she fled with the others.

At least it had not been a total loss; a total disaster. She had a souvenir to show her friends back in Pleiku, if she survived long enough to make it that far north: a matched set of American ears, and the soldier's dogtags, as well.

CID Agent Dave Dennison patted Treat Brody on the

helmet, and The Whoremonger fired. The Light Anti-tank Weapon soared with a grinding blast down the trail, impacting against the tree truck directly over the NVA machine-gun nest. LAW shoulder-launched rockets only require one operator, but Dennison had patted Brody for luck, and it worked: shrapnel raining down on the North Vietnamese killed all but one of the communists.

"Now *that's* the way to shoot!" Dennison cheered him on, but it was their last LAW, and one determined rifleman remained in the reinforced bunker fifty yards away.

Brody did not seem happy with the accomplishment. "Cheer up, Treat!" Dennison said, as cavalrymen behind them unleashed a din of discharges, attempting to finish off the NVA Regular. "It's not all that bad!"

"I just can't seem to get back in the swing of things," Brody admitted. "What with Nelson's death, and Brock being . . . well, you know . . ."

"A fake."

"Yeah, well, not really a fake."

"A psycho."

The two men shared an intimate half foot of cover behind a fallen log. No one else could hear what they were saying as the tracers streaked overhead, criss-crossing in both directions. "I can't believe we're talking so calmly while a goddamned firefight's raging all around us like this!" Brody suddenly yelled, rising to one knee to fire.

"Because we both been in this business too long!" Dennison pulled him back down just as a burst from the enemy RPD slammed into the earth on the other side of their log. They were showered with dirt clods and lead splinters.

Before Brody could agree, a huge man raced past, screaming at the top of his lungs, and firing his M-16 from the hip.

Sgt. Brock.

"I told you the motherfucker was crazy!" Dennison

316

was almost laughing.

It was not Le Loi's lucky day.

A long, sustained burst of automatic weapons fire struck the big NCO in the chest. He staggered backward, but his shoulders leaned forward like he was trying to fall face first to the ground, trying to die. But the bullets kept Brock on his feet, punching him back several steps, until he tripped over a log and fell backward, down off the side of the trail, out of sight.

"What a crazy fuck," Brody muttered, glancing around. No one was going to be heroic and sprint to their doom down the trail to check on Brock.

"No shit," Dennison said.

Two large shadows suddenly passed slowly above the cavalrymen.

Pegasus hovered above a break in the triple canopy, off to one side, while Warlokk's Cobra darted about, in and out of the treetops, peppering the NVA position with unceasing mini-gun fire.

Five minutes later, it was all over. The NVA machine-gun nest had fallen silent. "MOVE!" Vance yelled. The nearby stretch of rain forest was on fire. The flames would be reaching this latest jungle battlefield shortly.

"Come on." Dennison motioned for Brody to join him. They zigzagged down the trail, and were the first to reach the Air Cav's most recent hero.

Dennison dropped to one knee beside the unmoving NCO. Brody slammed his bayonet into the soft earth, and leaned against the rifle's buttplate.

Sgt. Brock was dead. No doubt about it. Dead as they come. He was face down in the rotting jungle floor.

Dennison never saw the tripwire.

The anti-personnel mine popped up from the spider-infested carpet of rotting leaves and dead snakeskin, detonating three feet off the ground.

Brody was several yards behind him, and only sus-

317

tained a small shrapnel wound.

The explosion tore Dennison's legs off and ripped the side of his face away. Somehow he was still alive; still able to scream. His pain echoed through the trees for several minutes until Doc Delgado arrived with morphine.

Pegasus appeared overhead shortly thereafter, and as Delgado hurried to stabilize Dennison before med-evac transport, the painkiller took effect, and his head finally dropped back against the moist dirt, no longer trying desperately to see what had happened to his legs.

He recognized Brody. No one else. As the life drained from his eyes, and Doc Delgado suddenly leaned back, giving up, Dennison clamped a hand on the back of Brody's neck, pulling him down until they were nose to nose."Zack," he muttered, blood bubbling up along the edges of his shredded, toothless mouth.

"No, Dave, it's me—Brody."

"Tell Zack . . ." Dennison whispered as his chest began seizing up, heart racing out of control as his lifeblood emptied out onto the ground.

"Zack? Yeah! Zack's downstream, runnin' a patrol along the south grids, lookin' for that Aussie broad."

Dennison's grip tightened. "Tell Zack that I know . . ." Dennison began choking on his own blood. Delgado tried to intervene, tried to roll him onto his side, but the CID agent would not be budged. "Tell Zack . . . I served in Korea . . . I know all about Parker . . . . Tell him he's safe."

"It's a lost cause," Doc Delgado mumbled to the men crowded behind them, "but let's get him aboard the Dustoff!"

Warrant Officer Dave Dennison was dead before they lifted him out of the crushed tiger lilies and flattened mushrooms and began rushing him toward the gunship with a winged horse painted across the bottom of her snout.

Chrissy LaVey's eyes popped open. She was in

318

strange surroundings. She felt like the legendary genie trapped in its bottle. Nothing looked or smelled familiar. *Why have I not awakened in my hotel room in Saigon?* she asked herself, puzzled.

And then Chrissy remembered. Her head whirled to both sides, but she was alone in the underground lair.

At least she was alive.

Somehow, instinctively perhaps, the rest of her body remained frozen. And then she realized why: Nguyet had removed her bra, and taped a grenade between her breasts. She knew nothing about the explosive's operation, so she remained still, assessing her situation.

Two long lines of fishing wire ran from the grenade's pin. The opposite end of one rose to the nearest wall, where it was taped to a wood support beam. The second looped up, out of sight, along the dark makeshift access ladder. She assumed it was connected to the trapdoor.

"That bitch," she said out loud. She knew that if the pin came out of the grenade, it would explode.

Nguyet had carefully strung her up so that she would die in one of two ways: being blown to bits because she rolled over while unconscious, causing the pin to be plucked out. Or being blown to bits when the Americans finally found her and they pulled up the trapdoor.

Chrissy knew nothing about the grenade's handle. Staring down at the object nestled in her cleavage, it suddenly seemed so much more complex an item than the bombs in the movies. But she was smart enough to realize the wires played an important part here.

If she just pulled the wires down, being careful to maintain the same amount of stress on the sections tied to the grenade, then she could wait patiently for someone to find her, and *they* could decide what to do next.

The earth rumbled, and LaVey remembered how critical the situation was becoming topside. She would not be able to wait at all. There would be no time.

That was when the trapdoor began squealing. Metal ground against metal.

Then she heard the voices. And dogs barking. The

319

Americans had found her. "Wait!" she screamed, loud as she could. But then her eyes watched the string grow taut as a flashlight beam lanced down into the dark tank.

LaVey rolled over, onto her stomach as the pin was pulled from the grenade.

Visions of all the brave soldiers who had saved their friends and died in the process by diving onto an enemy grenade flashed through her head as she held her hands against her ears.

LaVey began laughing. The grenade had failed to detonate.

And she was lying there on the floor, half naked, holding her ears in preparation for the big bang that hadn't come.

"Miss LaVey! Is that you?" Sgt. Leo Zack climbed down into the tank slowly, his flashlight beam playing about, scanning the walls and corners before he lowered his guard.

"I'm boobytrapped!" she screamed.

"Everybody out!" Zack motioned the rest of the men back up the ladder. "We've got fire in the hole!"

LaVey stopped laughing as she heard the American's boots hit the dirt a few feet away from her.

"Now, stay very still, ma'am," Leo said, trying to keep his eyes off Chrissy's shapely body." It's a grenade, right?"

LaVey nodded slowly. "The wires pulled the pin when the trapdoor opened. Please help me . . . I don't want to die." She was crying now.

Leo stretched out on his stomach, face to face with Chrissy. "'Scuse my hand, ma'am, but I have to find the pin before this thing blows." Working his hand between her breasts slowly, he felt for the pin, hoping LaVey could keep enough pressure on the handle to prevent the grenade from exploding.

"Got it! Hold steady . . . steady . . . there!" Leo said as he pulled his hand from between the soft breasts and sat up. "It's safe to move now, Miss LaVey."

320

Forgetting her nakedness, Chrissy jumped up and hugged Leo tightly, kissing him on the neck.

"Hey, Sarge! Ain't no time for romance. Chopper's waitin'," one of the men called down, smirking.

"Wipe that shit-eatin' smile off your face, soldier, or I'll kick your newbie ass!" Leo shouted up to the men. "And get down here to help this lady—now!"

Snakeman Fletcher had no idea where all the Cong had been hiding, but they were coming out of the woodwork now. A dozen rounds had stitched across *Peg*'s tailboom after the gunship landed to extract what remained of Zack's squad. The Americans had grouped along a bend in the river where Air Force sniffer dogs had located the underground lair, and the VC began firing as soon as the men began boarding the craft. Fletcher felt the Cong were being driven from the jungle by the fire and just happened to have their escape route blocked by the appearance of slicks at the LZ. Either way, they now had their hands full.

Warlokk and the other Cobra jock were darting about in their usual prize-winning style, decimating the enemy soldiers by the scores, and Fletcher leaned into his hatch-60, raking the tree line with unceasing streams of smoking tracerfire.

He had not planned it, but Snakeman suddenly found himself aiming at Graham's back. The soldier was a good thirty yards away, and had just sprinted from behind a fallen log to a ravine affording greater cover.

Fletcher was more upset about the anti–First Cav newspaper articles of late than even Nelson was, and he too felt Graham was the scab behind the notorious series.

The tensions of the last three weeks suddenly pressed down on Fletcher like a giant, invisible weight. The fighting. Nelson. The bogus articles. For just an instant, mentally, he snapped.

But when Snakeman jerked in the trigger, his hog-60 misfired for the first time since he could remember. "Damn!" He slammed the feeding tray with his fist, flipped up the cover, and yanked the bent link free. He forced a fresh belt into the weapon, banged the lid shut again, and started to pull back on the cooking handle when he realized that, except for the wild flapping of helicopter rotors, the battlefield had gone quiet. Many of the men were leaving their places of concealment and rushing up toward the treeline.

The VC had disengaged, falling back into the bamboo without dragging off their dead. Some of the Americans grouped together and ran off into the trees, chasing blood trails, but within half a hour they all returned empty-handed.

The Cong had vanished like rain-forest ghosts.

"We're gonna keep *Peg* wound up, Snakeman, but why don't ya go down there and find out what the score is," Gabriel clicked in.

Removing his headset and black visor, Fletcher nodded. He removed the M-16 slung upside-down across his back, and hopped down to the ground.

"Oh, man," someone was saying. Broken Arrow and Em-Ho and several of the men were clustered around a body. "Oh, man!"

"Break up the circle-jerk!" Fletcher yelled, shoving Graham roughly aside first. "One Charlie with a single stick grenade'd take all you gutless wonders out!" But Snakeman was frozen to the spot, too, by what he saw.

Orson lay dead in the razor-sharp reeds, a VC bullethole in his forehead. Blood trickled like a leaky faucet from the gaping exit wound in the back of his skull.

"I can't fucking believe it," Em-Ho was saying.

Fletcher dropped to one knee to examine the objects that were causing so much concern and commotion among the men.

Lying halfway out of Orson's rucksack were several

rolls of film and an uncompleted draft of submission No. 7 in the Thornton *Theseus* series of anti-war articles condemning the First Air Cavalry Division.

CHAPTER 34

One week later

Treat Brody checked the address in the little book, glanced up at the faded number on the apartment building wall, then back down at the address book. No matter how many times he had come here over the last seven days, he was never quite sure he was at the right place. The dwellings in this neighborhood along Mytho's southside riverfront all looked alike to him: two-storied stucco villas with French-style red tile roofs. But yes, this had to be it. Brody slipped Dennison's addressbook back into his pocket, careful not to drop the little girl. She clung to his neck, playing quietly with an earlobe and running her fingers repeatedly, almost trancelike, through his hair.

Swallowing his apprehension, he started the climb up the stairs to the second-floor veranda flat.

Before the corpsmen took Dennison's body away the week before, Brody had searched his pockets and removed some personal belongings. Among them, the address book.

The entries had been cryptic in some sections of the book he would not have expected otherwise from a dedicated CID agent. It took Brody nearly twelve hours that first day to find his wife's apartment. And break the news to her. She took it like a true trooper's wife; he heard her sobs only after the door closed behind him.

Thuy was very receptive to the idea of raising little Anna—that was the name he chose for her—in honor of Nelson and his woman. Thuy had a warm and caring heart. She was unable to turn away the orphan, regardless of the financial problems she expected to encounter now that her man was dead. He told her he would help in any way he could.

"I know you'll do well, honey." Treat kissed little Anna on the cheek when they reached the second floor, as if preparing to send her on stage for a pre-school beauty contest audition. As usual, the child remained silent. He was confident that, someday, Thuy would be able to get her to talk. He had returned to Thuy's home every day for the past week after helping her bury Dennison. Dave had willed that his remains be buried in The Nam. Slowly, she too would get over her grief.

Now was the moment of truth. Would the child be accepted into such a close-knit family so soon after tragedy had struck them? Brody prayed to Buddha or whoever else might be listening that such be the case.

And then he knocked at Thuy's door.

When Dennison's wife opened it, she didn't even seem to notice Brody, but swept little Anna from his arms amid a chorus of curious, birdlike chatter from her three daughters.

Brody knew from that moment that he had done the right thing. He watched Thuy carry little Anna into the cavernous living room and set her in front of the small black-and-white TV set. Thuy's oldest daughter rushed into the kitchen, out of sight, and reappeared with a birthday cake. On it, three candles glowed.

Smiling, Brody felt suddenly out of place. He wondered how they knew whether or not it was little Anna's birthday. Perhaps it was just another Vietnamese custom Brody had yet to learn about. It didn't really matter. Little Anna had a good home now. She would not become just another war waif, abandoned on the streets of Mytho.

Brody's smile deepened, and he felt his eyes growing moist. One could barely see the bandages beneath little Anna's white cotton dress.

"And where do you think you're going, Corporal Brody?"

Treat halted halfway down the stairs. He thought he recognized that voice—it was an American woman's. But what would she be doing here?

"Lisa!" he called out, turning back to find the army nurse leaning out through the doorway. Today she was wearing civilian clothes: a pretty, pink pantsuit. Her blond hair was piled up on top of her head. She seemed so out of place in Vietnam. Brody quickly corrected himself. "Lieutenant Maddox! What are you doing here?"

"'Lisa' will do fine," she said.

But of course, why *wouldn't* she be here? Maddox had nursed little Anna back to health, had convinced Treat he could find a good home for her and that, failing such a project, he could sacrifice some of his romantic reputation and make the child his own step-daughter.

Brody had spent many nights thinking about it. But in the end, he told himself The Whoremonger was not ready to be a father. Not even a play father.

Nelson's smiling, always-scheming face flashed in front of his eyes, and Brody felt his lower lip start to tremble. It had been a long time since he cried in front of anyone. He hoped he would not break down now, in front of Lisa.

"Get yo' behind in here, slick!" The lieutenant used her most commanding, military voice, and Brody felt the uneasiness leave his heart.

Grinning now, he climbed back to the top of the stairs and quickened his pace toward the doorway. Maddox winked. "Thuy has someone special she wants you to meet."

Inside the doorway, Thuy was indeed waiting to present someone for Treat Brody's inspection. He en-

326

tered to find Dennison's wife with her arm around one of the most beautiful women Brody had ever seen in his life. She had piercing black eyes that seemed to search his soul when Brody walked into the room. Long dark hair fanned across graceful-looking shoulders. She shifted her stance nervously, and he noticed the form-clinging blue and white *ao dai* for the first time. She was a goddess from the Imperial City of Hue, it seemed, come to save Brody The Whoremonger from himself.

"Treat, I would like you to meet my younger sister, Tuyen."

Their eyes locked for a moment, and then Tuyen, the perfect lady, allowed her gaze to drop submissively to the floor.

Brody felt his heart race.

Lt. Vance stared down at the thick packet of letters Farney had handed him. "What do you want me to do with these?" he asked the company clerk.

"They're from those peaceniks who keep sending hate mail to Orson."

"Don't they know he's dead? You should just stamp 'Return To Sender/Deceased' on 'em, or something." Vance complained.

"That's what I had planned to do, sir." Farney was already walking back to the CP, obviously too busy to argue. "The colonel told me to tell you to personally answer every one of those jerks and inform them Private Orson was killed in action, 'fighting honorably in the service of his country to help halt communist aggression in Southeast Asia, et cetera.'"

"Et cetera? Jesus." Vance stared down at the bundle. "There must be fifty letters here." He glanced up, noticed that Farney had disappeared down inside the command bunker, and threw the bundle back over his shoulder.

"Mornin', sir." Two privates walked by, their finger-tips glued to the rims of their caps.

Jesus, Vance muttered to himself, and saluted. He was never going to get anything done in the middle of camp here. He slipped the letter he'd been working on back inside its envelope, and tried to decide where he could go so as not to be bothered.

The main gate.

Most of his men avoided the main gate because there were MPs there, so he walked the fifty or so yards past the meat market, with its assortment of prostitutes, camp followers, and indigenous employees waiting to be signed on post, and returned the young military policeman's crisp salute.

Vance eyed a stool sitting on the sidewalk outside the static post. "Mind if I have a seat?" he asked infor-mally.

Swallowing nervously, the MP nodded, wondering what the lieutenant was really doing here. But a convoy pulled up to the gate, and the PFC became busy checking manifests and trip tickets.

Vance thought about Orson again. He had often wondered why the kid wrote all those scathing newspa-per articles about the Division. The only theory he could come up with was that it was Orson's way of getting back at his peace-activist mother.

Shrugging, Vance made a mental note to stop ponder-ing Orson's motivations and get back to the letter he was working on now. The one informing his father about Nelson.

Vance watched the long lines of refugees walking along the highway in front of the camp. The VC sent another wave of rockets into Cho Gao, and thousands more civilians were dazed and homeless. He stared at their gaunt, blackened faces and torn clothes, and shook his head slightly in sorrow and helplessness.

Vance was not sure what he wanted to tell his father. Something about Nelson's loyalty and devotion to the Service, surely. But there was something more—something about the whole affair he found dreadful and disheartening; something he had to ask the General for advice on. He just could not put his finger on it.

Suddenly, Vance turned his head, to find a Vietnamese woman standing next to him. Her long, black hair was disheveled, askew with twigs and pieces of dry leaves. Her face was streaked with dried tears and ash. She had a filthy, haggard look in her bloodshot eyes, and a razor-thin scar on her chin. The woman looked like she had just traveled to hell and back without a ticket.

"Good morning, sir," she said politely, almost meekly. "My name is Anna."

Vance's breathing stopped, and his eyes, twitching with a nauseating mixture of fatigue and shock now, inspected her frail body from head to toe. She seemed to be wrapped in one long, tattered, black rag. She had blood-soaked bandages on one arm. He could see that her belly was beginning to show the first signs that she was pregnant.

"Could you please tell me where to find PFC Nelson?" The woman lifted a hand limply to display a thin gold engagement ring on her wedding finger. "We are to be married soon," she said in her soft, singsong voice. "Nelson wants to have bookoo baby-sans." She rubbed her belly ever so slightly, but with great pride and affection for her unborn son sparkling faintly in her dark sloe eyes. "And if you will tell me where I can find him, I might even name one after you."

Vance could see the mild gleam of insanity in her eyes, too. The gleam of insanity and relief at having survived Cho Gao and the rocket attacks and another year of her country at war, at having finally made it back through God-knows-what to her man. The dream of a lifetime was finally at her fingertips.

"Nelson loves Anna very much," she said, "and promised to take her to the stateside."

"He good American."

EPILOGUE

Launched September 15, 1966, Operation Coronado V involved "riverine" search and destroy missions along the Mekong Delta region of South Vietnam, primarily in intercepting and engaging enemy sampans and other river craft. American troops took increasingly to PBR patrol boats in their efforts to bring the war to Charlie on his own turf.

Trapping numerous Viet Cong guerrillas from the 514th Local Force Battalion in the Cam Son area of Dinh Tuong Province, U.S. Forces executed a three-pronged series of "scooping-up" ambushes which, after forty-eight hours of nonstop fighting in several instances, and numerous follow-up skirmishes throughout the fall months of the Year of the Horse, brought the communist body count into four figures. The original Coronado V battle itself saw 213 VC killed. American and ARVN units sustained 16 KIA's and 146 men wounded in action.

GLOSSARY

AA   Antiaircraft weapon
AC   Aircraft Commander
Acting Jack   Acting NCO
AIT   Advanced Individual Training
AK-47   Automatic rifle used by VC/NVA
Animal   See *Monster*
AO   Area of Operations
Ao Dai   Traditional Vietnamese gown
APH-5   Helmet worn by gunship pilots
APO   Army Post Office
Arc-Light   B-52 bombing mission
ArCOM   Army Commendation Medal
Article-15   Disciplinary action
Ash-'n'-Trash   Relay flight

Bad Paper   Dishonorable discharge
Ba Muoi Ba   Vietnamese beer
Banana Clip   Ammo magazine holding 30 bullets
Bao Chi   Press or news media
Basic   Boot camp
BCT   Basic Combat Training (Boot)
Bic   Vietnamese for "Understand?"
Big-20   Army career of 20 years
Bird   Helicopter

BLA   Black Liberation Army

Bloods   Black soldiers

Blues   An airmobile company

Body Count   Number of enemy KIA

Bookoo   Vietnamese for "many" (actually bastardization of French *beaucoup*)

Bought the Farm   Died and life insurance policy paid for the mortgage

Brass Monkey   Interagency radio call for help

Brew   Usually coffee, but sometimes beer

Bring Smoke   To shoot someone

Broken-Down   Disassembled

Buddha Zone   Death

Bush ('Bush)   Ambush

Butter Bar   2nd Lieutenant

CA   Combat Assault

Cam Ong   Viet for "Thank you"

Cartridge   Shell casing for bullet

C&C   Command & Control chopper

Chao   Vietnamese greeting

Charlie   Viet Cong (from military phonetic: Victor Charlie)

Charlie Tango   Control Tower

Cherry   New man in unit

Cherry Boy   Virgin

Chicken Plate   Pilot's chest/groin armor

Chi-Com   Chinese Communist

Chieu Hoi   Program where communists can surrender and become scouts

Choi-oi   Viet exclamation

CIB   Combat Infantry Badge

CID   Criminal Investigation Division

Clip   Ammo magazine

CMOH   Congressional Medal of Honor

CO   Commanding Officer

Cobra   helicopter gunship used for combat assaults/escorts only

Cockbang   Bangkok, Thailand

Conex   Shipping container (metal)
Coz   Short for Cozmoline
CP   Command Post
CSM   Command Sergeant Major
Cunt Cap   Green narrow cap worn with khakis

Dash-13   Helicopter maintenance report
Dau   Viet for pain
Deadlined   Down for repairs
Dep   Viet for beautiful
DEROS   Date of Estimated Return from Overseas
Deuce-and-a-Half   2½-ton truck
DFC   Distinguished Flying Cross
DI   Drill Instructor (Sgt.)
Di Di   Viet for "Leave or go!"
Dink   Derogatory term for Vietnamese national
Dinky Dau   Viet for "crazy"
Disneyland East   MACV complex including annex
DMZ   Demilitarized Zone
Dogtags   Small aluminum tag worn by soldiers with
    name, serial number, religion, and blood type im-
    printed on it
DOOM Pussy   Danang Officers Open Mess
Door gunner   Soldier who mans M-60 machine gun
    mounted in side hatch of Huey gunship
Dung Lai   Viet for "Halt!"
Dustoff   Med-Evac chopper

Early Out   Unscheduled ETS
EM   Enlisted Man
ER   Emergency Room (hospital)
ETS   End Tour of (military) Service

Field Phone   Hand-generated portable phones used in
    bunkers
Fini   Viet for "Stop" or "The End"
First Louie   1st Lieutenant
First Team   Motto of 1st Air Cav
Flak Jacket   Body armor

FNG   Fucking new guy
FOB   Fly over board misson
Foxtrot   Vietnamese female
Foxtrot Tosser   Flame thrower
Frag   Fragmentation grenade
FTA   Fuck the Army

Gaggle   Loose flight of slicks
Get Some   Kill someone
GI   Government Issue, or, a soldier
Greenbacks   U.S. currency
Green Machine   U.S. Army
Gunship   Attack helicopter armed with machine guns
    and rockets
Gurney   Stretcher with wheels

Ham & Motherfuckers   C-rations serving of ham and
    lima beans
Herpetologist   One who studies reptiles and amphibians
HOG-60   M-60 machine gun
Hot LZ   Landing zone under hostile fire
Housegirl   Indigenous personnel hired to clean build-
    ings, wash laundry, etc.
Huey   Primary troop-carrying helicopter

IC   Installation Commander
IG   Inspector General
In-Country   Within Vietnam
Intel   Intelligence (military)
IP   That point in a mission where descent toward target
    begins

JAG   Judge Advocate General
Jane   Jane's Military Reference books
Jesus Nut   The bolt that holds rotor blade to helicopter
Jody   Any American girlfriends
Jolly Green   Chinook helicopter

KIA   Killed in Action

Kimchi　　Korean fish sauce salad
Klick　　Kilometer
KP　　Mess hall duty

Lai Day　　Viet for "come here"
LAW　　Light Anti-Tank Weapon
Lay Dog　　Lie low in jungle during recon patrol
LBFM　　Little Brown Fucking Machine
LBJ　　Long Binh Jail(main stockade)
Leg　　Infantryman not airborne qualified
Lifeline　　Straps holding gunny aboard chopper while he
　　fires M-60 out the hatch
Lifer　　Career solider
Links　　Metal strip holding ammo belt together
Loach　　Small spotter/scout chopper
LP　　Listening Post
LRRP　　Long-Range Recon Patrol
LSA　　Gun oil
Lurp　　One who participates in LRRPs
LZ　　Landing Zone

M-14　　American carbine
M-16　　Primary U.S. Automatic Rifle
M-26　　Fragmentation grenade
M-60　　Primary U.S. Machine gun
M-79　　Grenade launcher (rifle)
MACV　　Military Assistance Command, Vietnam
Magazine　　Metal container that feeds bullets into
　　weapon. Holds 20 or 30 rounds per unit
Mag Pouch　　Magazine holder worn on web belt
MAST　　Mobile Army Surgical Team
Med-Evac　　Medical Evacuation Chopper
Mess Hall　　GI cafeteria
MG　　Machine gun
MI　　Military Intelligence
MIA　　Missing in Action
Mike-Mike　　Millimeters
Mike Papas　　Military Policemen
Mister Zippo　　Flame-thrower operator

335

Miao   Central Highlands witch doctor

Monkeyhouse   Stockade or jail

Monkeystrap   See *Lifeline*

Monster   12-21 claymore antipersonnel mines jury-rigged to detonate simultaneously

Montagnarde   Hill tribe people of Central Highlands, RVN

MPC   Money Payment Certificates (scrip) issued to GIs in RVN in lieu of greenbacks

Muster   A quick assemblage of soldiers with little or no warning

My   Viet for "American"

Net   Radio net

NETT   New Equipment Training Team

Newby   New GI in-country

Numba One   Something very good

Numba Ten   Something very bad

Nuoc Nam   Viet fish sauce

NVA   North Vietnamese Army

OD   Olive Drab

OR   Operating Room (Hospital)

P   Piasters

PA   Public Address system

PCS   Permanent Change of (Duty) Station (transfer out of RVN)

Peter Pilot   Copilot in training

PF   Popular Forces (Vietnamese)

PFC   Private First Class

Phantom   Jet fighter plane

Phu   Vietnamese noodle soup

Piaster   Vietnamese currency

PJ   Photojournalist

Point   The most dangerous position on patrol. The point man walks ahead and to the side of the others, acting as a lookout

PRG   Provisional Revolutionary Govt. (the Commu-

nists)
Prang   Land a helicopter roughly
Prick-25   PR-25 field radio
Profile   Medical exemption
Psy-Ops   Psychological operation
PT   Physical Training
Puff   Heavily armed aircraft
Purple Heart   Medal given for wounds received in combat
Purple Vision   Night vision
Puzzle Heart   The MACV HQ building

Quad-50   Truck equipped with four 50-caliber MGs
QC   Vietnamese MP

Rat Fuck   Mission doomed from the start
Regular   An enlistee or full-time soldier as opposed to PFs and Reserves, NG, etc.
REMF   Rear Echelon Motherfucker
R&R   Rest and Relaxation
Re-Up   Re-enlist
Rikky-Tik   Quickly or fast
Rock 'n' Roll   Automatic fire
Roger   Affirmative
ROK   Republic of Korea
Rotor   Overhead helicopter blade
Round   Bullet
RPG   Rocket-propelled grenade
Ruck(sack)   GI's backpack
RVN   Republic of (South) Vietnam

Saigon   Capital of RVN
SAM   Surface-to-Air Missile
Sapper   Guerrilla terrorist equipped with satchel charge (explosives)
SAR   Downed-chopper rescue mission
Scramble   Alert reaction to call for help, CA or rescue operation.
Scrip   See *MPC*

7.62 M-60 ammunition

Sierra Echo Southeast (Northwest is November Whiskey, etc.)

Single-Digit Fidget A nervous single-digit midget

Single-Digit Midget One with fewer than ten days remaining in Vietnam

SKS Russian-made carbine

Slick Helicopter

Slicksleeve Private E-1

Slug Bullet

SNAFU Situation normal: all fucked up

Soggy Frog Green Beret laying dog

SOP Standard Operating Procedure (also known as Shit Output)

Spiderhole Tunnel entrance

Strac Sharp appearance

Steel Pot Helmet

Striker Montagnarde hamlet defender

Sub-Gunny Substitute door gunner

TDY Temporary Duty Assignment

Terr Terrorist

"33" Local Vietnamese beer

Thumper See *M-79*

Ti Ti Viet for little

Tour 365 The year-long tour of duty a GI spends in RVN

Tower Rat Tower guard

Tracer Chemically treated bullet that gives off a glow en route to its target

Triage That method in which medics determine which victims are most seriously hurt and therefore treated first

Trooper Soldier

201 File Personnel file

Two-Point-Five Gunship rockets

UCMJ Uniformed Code of Military Justice

Unass Leave seat quickly

VC   Viet Cong

Victor Charlie   VC

Viet Cong   South Vietnamese Communists

VNP   Vietnamese National Police

Void Vicious   Final approach to a Hot LZ; or the jungle
    when hostile

Warrant Officer   Pilots

Wasted   Killed

Web Belt   Utility belt GIs use to carry equipment,
    sidearms, etc.

Whiskey   Military phonetic for "West"

WIA   Wounded In Action

Wilco   Will comply

Willie Peter   White phosphorous

Wire   Perimeter (trip wire sets off booby trap)

The World   Any place outside Vietnam

Xin Loi   Viet for "sorry about that" or "good-bye"

XM-21   Gunship mini-gun

XO   Executive Officer

'Yarde   Montagnarde

ZIP   Derogatory term for Vietnamese National

Zulu   Military phonetic for the letter Z (LZ or Landing
    Zone might be referred to as a Lima Zulu)

Rock and roll with Brody and the men of First Air Cavalry on their toughest assignment yet: to kill two American soldiers spotted leading VC brigades against the Green Machine as the bloody guerrilla fight for control of the Dong Tre Hills explodes in . . .

CHOPPER 1 #5: RENEGADE MIAs

THE AUTHOR served with the United States Army in Southeast Asia for three years, where he received the Bronze Star Medal. His unit was awarded the Vietnamese Cross of Gallantry. He has written eighteen other adventure novels on the Vietnam War under several pseudonyms, and alternates between homes in the Orient and Little Saigon, USA.